CHANGE OF DAYS

by
Ian Hawley

Same Horizons
New Illusions.

Cover Illustration by
James Chadderton

Edited by
Henry Ker

Published by Squeeze Marketing Ltd

Ian Hawley

First published in the UK in 2013 by Squeeze Marketing Ltd
13 Stonepail Road
Gatley, Cheadle, Cheshire SK8 4EZ

Copyright © Ian Hawley, 2013
The right of Ian Hawley to be identified as the author of this
work has been asserted by him.
ISBN 9781 906671 082

A CIP catalogue record for this book is available from the British Library.

Front cover art and illustration © James Chadderton, 2013

Printed and bound in the UK

FORWARD

I have tried to make this book as accurate as possible, and there are so many people who have assisted me in its writing in an attempt to make it as realistic and scientifically plausible as possible.

I was inspired after researching the Mayan "end of the world" theory, and hearing a talk about the 5th and final age of man. The statement alone made me wonder, if man wasn't the dominant species anymore, what would be?

I studied the myths and legends of our past, and there I finally found the answers that I was looking for. Many cultures talked about mythical creatures that used to scare the people and steal the children. In fact, our fairy stories are just a development of those early ideas and fears: don't go into the dark forest as there are things in there that will get you; watch out for the monster under the bed; and many, many more.

Surprisingly, these old, isolated cultures from around the world talked about the same creatures of legend, the same monsters that hunted man in a distant time. If they existed, what happened to them and what was holding them back from returning? When the solution came Change of Days came into being.

I am not saying the story is going to happen, or that the world has not gone through changes before like this but, when you examine the data, they don't say it has either. James Chadderton created the artwork around Change of Days and he has set the scene perfectly.

I hope you enjoy reading this, but do make sure you check under your bed - you never know what might be there waiting.

Ian Hawley

Ian Hawley

Dedicated to Marion.

Change of Days

The old storyteller tried to keep the stories alive in our minds. He tried to warn us as we sat and listened to the crazy old man tell his tales. He spoke about the creatures that crept into our home at night and stole our babies, and warned us not to go into the deep forests for fear of the creatures that lived there.

We called him old and stupid for making up stories. We laughed at the absurdity of his tales and chastised him for trying to scare the children, telling him he should know better, that there is nothing hiding in the shadows.

We told him that we didn't need him anymore. We have big movie theatres now to tell us stories, and slick computer games that we can play with. The world has moved on, and no-one believes in the bogeyman anymore.

He just nodded politely and thanked us for hearing his stories. He had listened to our observations, but, he would continue to tell his stories. He had wanted to warn us and keep the children safe.

When we'd gone he would close his door and drop the bar in place. He checked under his bed before he went to sleep and slept with the light on. For he knew, as did the other story tellers around the world, that not all are stories made up, not all stories are untrue.

Where will you be when the change of days comes?

● ● ● ● ● ● ● ● ●

Ian Hawley

CHANGE OF DAYS

by

Ian Hawley

BOOK ONE:
Same Horizons,
New Illusions.

● ● ● ● ● ● ● ●

The drive to the airport wasn't that far, but the snow had caused problems on the roads and it would be slow going before he'd reach the motorway. He reversed carefully from the drive and gave one last look at his home before pulling away.

First thing he'd do, after parking at the airport, was to buy a strong coffee - he would need something to keep him awake until he got onto the plane. Although it was only a short trip, he'd been advised to pack for cold weather, something he'd never had to do before in India. Snow had been coming down hard almost everywhere, forcing him to take more luggage than normal, but at least it should be a quick fix and he hoped that, within a few days, he would be back to his family before Christmas.

As he drove he went through the check list in his head one more time:

Work clothes? Check.

Boots and shoes? Check.

Laptop? Check.

Book for the flight? Check.

Mobile phone? Damn, had he left it on the sideboard? He remembered bringing it down after charging it but did he pick it up? He didn't really have time to turn round now and catch his plane, but he'd promised to call his beloved Julia and she would be upset if he didn't. He could see his jacket under his briefcase on the passenger seat and he reached across to grab it. Top inside pocket, he thought as he lent over, but it slipped from the seat into the foot well as he moved and he had to lunge to grab it. Pulling it back onto the seat he reached inside and felt around the pockets. A wave of relief washed over him as his hand closed around both his wallet and phone and he pulled both out.

He smiled, at the same moment as he kissed his phone, something smashed into his windscreen and rolled over his roof. Grabbing the wheel, he slammed his brakes down hard. The ice on the roads gave him little to no traction and he felt the rear end slide out behind him. A fence appeared out of the darkness and he smashed through it. He tried to pull to the left to gain control but his air bags deployed as he collided with a tractor.

When he opened his eyes, the airbag had deflated and he was resting forward on the steering wheel. He touched the side of his head and felt the sharp pain of an open cut and he sat looking at his bloody fingers for a moment before his memory jumped back into place.

"Oh no!" he moaned to himself. "What did I hit?"
He pushed his door open and fell out onto the frozen field, scrambling against the car as he pulled himself up and staggered to the boot. Shoving his luggage aside, he rummaged for his torch. His left eye was starting to close over by the time he finally found it.

He staggered back towards the road, slipping on the uneven ground once or twice before he reached the remains of the gate he had driven through. The cold wind whipped cruelly at his face as he turned onto the road. He could just make out the shape of something lying in the verge at the side of the road.

It looked too big to be a rabbit, but as there were no deer in the area that he knew of, he wondered what he could have hit. The closer he got to it, the more child-sized the shape became, and he moaned to himself. What is a kid doing out on a night like this? It's almost two in the morning, why would they be out in this? He slowed down as he approached, hoping that whoever it was, wasn't dead. He knelt down by the body just as the moon shifted behind the cloud and the road went dark.

"Damn it!" he cursed as he shook the torch, trying to get it to come on before remembering that he had bought some new batteries for it last week, but left them in the glove box. With no other option he stood and ran back to his car but lost his footing on the icy road as he returned and landed hard on his back, knocking the wind from his lungs. His head span as he gasped for air. The pain in his side felt like a broken rib at least, and he groaned as he forced himself back onto his feet.

Finally reaching the body he stood silently over it, almost afraid of what he would see when he turned the light on, not believing what he had actually done. His hands shook uncontrollably as he aimed the torch towards the body, and it took him a moment for his mind tried to take into account what he was seeing in its light. `I couldn't have hit them that hard could I?` His mind screamed at him.

The body seemed out of proportion, all twisted and thin. He reached out and carefully rolled it over. He tried to focus, trying to make the image before him make sense, but his one good eye continued to tear up as the cold air hit it.

I couldn't have caused all this damage could I? Why is it almost naked? He questioned himself as he stepped back, still dazed from the crash as a twig snapped loudly in the darkness behind him and he dropped the torch. It flashed once as it hit the ground and went out.

"Hello!" he called. "Hello, can you... can you call the police?" his head ached as he turned to see the shapes that appeared behind him. "There's been an accident." he tried to explain. "It just stepped out in front of me. I didn't mean to..." his voice was silenced before it had a chance to explain any further.

When dawn finally came, fresh snow had settled over the pool of his frozen blood and a howling wind blew the snow across the road and field, burying Joshua's car as it soaked into the soft leather of his seats through his open door before pooling around his phone. He wouldn't be missed for three days, and after that there wouldn't be anyone to look for him anyway.

Frank grunted as he pulled the manhole cover free, before dropping it with a clank onto the road. He blew onto his hands to try and keep some sense of warmth in them while he waited for his partner Graham to arrive. It was too cold to be doing this really, but the overtime was too damn tempting, especially for Christmas.

It was only supposed to be a five minute job, but health and bloody safety said he couldn't do it alone, so now, he stood freezing to death by the side of the road while he waited for someone else to turn up to hold his light.

He pulled a cigarette from his pocket and tried to light it with shaking hands, cursing each time he failed. Eventually, he managed to get one going and he drew deeply on it, letting the warmth of the smoke burn his lungs as he waited for any signs of his partner. He threw the stub of the cigarette into the snow before climbing back into his van. His flask of coffee had gone cold an hour before, and he rummaged through the glove box for anything to eat.

"Come on," he shouted as he slammed the glove box, empty of anything to eat or drink, shut. As he turned to open the door, pressed against the glass was a disfigured face and he yelled in fright.

"Did I scare ya Frank?"

"You idiot!" He kicked out against the door as Graham stood back. "You're stupid you are, you almost gave me a heart attack."

"Sorry, Frank." He pushed his bottom lip out as he tried to look sorry, but failed. "I just couldn't resist. Your face was so funny though."

"Yeah, very funny." He climbed out of the van and feigned a kick at his partner before they walked to the manhole. "What took you so long anyway?"

"You have seen the weather ain't ya?" He looked up at the sky and held his hands out to catch the snow. "And I had to clear L47 through to 54 before I could come to you."

"Well." He nodded. "At least you're here now. You going down first or you want me to?"

"Na, I'll go first." He slid his feet over the edge and started to climb down the ladder. "We don't want your old legs to get cramp on the way down do we?"

Frank kicked snow at his disappearing head and he waited for Graham's signal before he lowered his tool belts down. He could see

5

the helmet lamp bobbing as it descended, finally stopping thirty feet below. The light turned a few times as he looked down the tunnels before it vanished.

"Graham!" Frank shouted. "Graham! Come on, it's freezing up here, it's not time to joke around."

He was getting angry now, Graham was a nice enough chap in general, but he could be a pain in the neck when he wanted to be. Now, as he stood in the cold trying to finish the overtime so he could get home, he didn't find it funny.

"Graham!" he shouted again. "I'm freezing my knackers off up here. Graham!" Nothing returned but his echo and with a growl of disgust he started to lower the packs down the manhole. "I don't have time for this," he muttered to himself as he palmed the rope down the hole. "I could have gone off and done the job on my own, but that's not how it's done."

He felt the rope slacken off so he secured it to a post before he started to climb down, grumbling at each step.

"It's against health and safety this is," he moaned. "You're not supposed to wander alone down here anymore. Graham!" he shouted his name again.

Flakes of snow continued to fall on him as he carefully moved down the ladder. "Graham!" he called as he reached the bottom, he was just about to let go of the rungs when his feet slipped from under him. Water must have run down from the road above and frozen into a sheet of ice, and he was just thankful he'd not let go of the ladder.

He pressed down and felt the earth squelch under his boot. Maybe not frozen then, he thought, but slippery all the same. He reached down and grabbed his pack before shining his light down the tunnel in the direction Graham had gone. He'd only walked two paces before he stopped, the ground before him was covered in mud.

"Graham!" he shouted into the darkness. This was a sealed tunnel so there shouldn't be any mud down here unless there was a break in the pipe.

"Where are you, you ugly mug?" He steadied himself against

6

the wall and felt the thick sticky mud on his hands. "Oh, crap," he complained as he wiped them on his overalls. He checked it wasn't anything foul, as a sewer systems ran close by, but it smelt metallic, so he held his hand up into the light from his helmet to take a closer look.

What he'd first thought to be mud was a deep red colour and he fell backwards into the shaft as his mind registered what he was looking at. "What the hell." He turned onto his knees, crawling quickly back to the shaft as he felt something warm under his hands and he looked down into the remains of Graham.

He grabbed for the rungs as sounds started to emanate from further down the tunnel and he quickly pulled himself up the ladder, tears running down his face as he started to ascend.

"Sweet Jesus save me," he prayed as he climbed, not daring to look back down the shaft in case he saw something coming behind him, each step felt like an age but he finally reached the top and rolled out onto the road above, forcing the cover back over the manhole before he staggered back to his van.

"Base, Base you there?" he called into his radio. "For God's sake is anyone there?"

The thought that he had almost gone down there on his own was firmly at the front of his mind and he reached shakily inside his overall and pulled a cigarette out.

"Base, this is Frank, you there Joan?" What a time to take a toilet break. "Joan?" he screamed into the mike. A movement in the corner of his eye made him stop, his cigarette hanging loosely from his open mouth as he turned to look out of the side window. He sobbed as he saw something looking into the cab, its large eyes staring unblinkingly at him.

He quickly locked the doors before trying to pull his keys from his pocket; the face at the window just continued to watch him. Sobbing to himself uncontrollably now he tried to push the key into the ignition. A long drawn out hiss from behind him was the last thing he heard.

Philip smiled to himself as he walked on the warm sandy beach, the clear blue waves washed gently over his feet cooling his toes for a moment against the heat of the day before the wave ebbed back into the ocean once more.

He didn't know the beach, nor did he care to, though he felt he recognised it as a memory from long ago, but the day seemed too beautiful for questions and it was certainly too warm to worry himself over small details.

The Sun shone down on him as he meandered along. His footsteps lasting only as long as the next wave took to wash them away. He felt content, being totally alone now, he was finally able to be himself. He shared this little piece of paradise with no one, and he was glad of it. The world was such a busy place nowadays, and he felt that any time he could get to himself was worth it.

A pain in his ribs woke him from his pleasurable wanderings and he slowly opened his eyes. He wanted to fall back asleep, to return to his dream, but he couldn't relax. Each breath seemed to cause more pain. Why do I hurt? He thought to himself as he tried to wade through the murky memories of the previous night. Why am I in pain? What the hell did I do? He closed his eyes as he tried to recall the events of the previous night.

He could remember leaving work, so that at least was a start, but everything else seemed distant and blurry. He couldn't recall if he had even come home first or gone straight out. The alarm clock sprang to life besides him and he automatically grabbed out to muffle it. The damage to his ribs sent shooting pains into his chest as he twisted towards it and he moaned as he switched it off.

Despite the pain he finally managed to edge himself into a sitting position and switch the alarm off before he slid his feet out of the covers and down to the floor below. Something cold and sticky touched the ball of his bare foot and he quickly pulled it back under the covers. Holding his side, he slowly moved to look over the side of the bed, a little fearful of what he might see.

An almost empty pizza box lay on the floor below him, and he spotted the cause of his distress. A single slice of pizza with a toe mark deeply embedded in its cheesy crust sat in its centre. He rose carefully, trying to stop the pain in his side from getting worse and pushed the pizza box under the bed before staggering into the bathroom.

The room span as he switched the light on. The taste of acid in his mouth gave him just enough warning to get to the toilet and he threw up into the blue water. He felt his testicles rise as he heaved heavily again, and he groaned loudly. The pain in his ribs screamed out for him to stop as he felt another coming.

"Oh, God!" he moaned pathetically, feeling the hot bile run out of his nose as he cried to himself in pity. Finally free from the toilet, he forced his mouth under the bathroom tap and let the cold water swill in his mouth before spitting it out.

He dressed slowly to avoid falling over. He slid his legs one by one into his suit trousers before he realised they were on back to front, forcing him to start again. Finally dressed, he opened his curtains and looked out. He could just see the promise of dawn on the horizon as the snow continued to fall in thick unending clumps outside.

He greased his black hair back into some resemblance of style in front of the mirror in the hall. He still looked tired, but at least with his suit on, he didn't look quite as ill as he had when he'd woken up. He slammed his door behind him and slowly walked down the steps into the backyard of the restaurant next door, keeping a tight hold onto the rails so as not to slip, before making his way to the rear gate and alley beyond.

The snow was beginning to be a problem for everyone now, it wasn't that Manchester had never had snow, but in the last few years it had been getting deeper and deeper. He moved to pull the gate open, when a seagull suddenly screeched with rage at being disturbed from its breakfast in the bins, and beat its wings hard as it rose into the cold frigid air.

Philip stood with his back pressed flat against the wall. He stood silently for a moment, holding his hand to his chest as he waited for the terror to subside. It was too early in the day to be given a shock like that, and in his fragile condition he fought to control the urge to vomit. With his heart still pumping heavily in his ears, and with the end of his tongue numb from the shock, he pushed himself away from the wall and left the yard. He carefully followed the back alley until he finally reached the main road.

As he turned the corner he could see his bus pulling up at its stop, and with only a few people waiting he realised he'd have to run. His ribs ached as he half slipped, half skipped to the stop, waving his arm out so the bus wouldn't leave without him.

He dropped his fare thankfully into the tray and took his ticket. He only needed to travel a handful of stops, but with the snow falling so heavily, he didn't want to walk. He remained standing at the front, holding onto the rails as the bus pulled slowly away.

The bus smelt warm and stuffy. No one had opened any windows, and the air was thick with the smell of damp clothes, perfume, stale smoke and sweat. The people on the bus were the usual crowd, the same faces that didn't smile, or talk. Everyone looked so miserable, locked in their own private bubbles of existence, and no one had time for anyone else.

Finally off the bus, he smiled to himself as he walked the last stretch to work. When he thought about it, his life was so much better than others. Because his needs were lower, he was easier to please. He didn't have a wife, or a girlfriend to stress over, and he didn't smoke or drive a car. When he got home, his work was over and his time started. He could sit naked in his chair and watch TV for all life cared. Not that he did, he mused, but he could if he wanted to, and that was the point. He controlled his own path.

Sometimes when he got lonely he'd go to the pub, he came and went as he saw fit. Yes, he concluded. If I stop and sum up my life to date, apart from the pain in my ribs I'm happy. He was still smiling to himself when he pushed open the doors to his building and walked in. He stamped the snow from his feet on the large mat at the door before pressing the button for the lift.

It was one of these moments that years later he'd tried to remember. One of those easy days, when everything just seemed to happen, but in his memories, he was sure it looked better that it actually was.

The gull soared unhappily through the cold sky, the loss of its breakfast did nothing to improve its mood, and the thought of food sat heavily on its mind. Flying low over the streets in search of something to eat, it watched with hungry eyes as the city started to wake up below. It flew over the red tiled rooftops of closely packed terraces, watching as snowflakes that had banked up against a chimney pot slipped free, and dropped onto the footpath below.

As it banked away, it watched a man climb from the rear window of a house. He dropped something before him as he climbed free of the building, before grabbing it as he ran from the yard, but the bag glittered like metals and didn't seem to contain any food.

It had seen the human daily routines from its lofty vantage point for so many years now that unless there was the chance that food would be involved somewhere, it didn't care. It'd been too lazy and old to follow the flock, so it stayed close to the food, and to the relative warmth the city provided. It let the fitter generations fly south to produce tomorrows young, it would stay and grow fat on the wastes of man, and there was enough waste to keep it happy and fed forever.

Philip stopped working to listen to the news on his radio, it seemed the motorways had been closed again due to lack of grit, and a new strain of Swine Flu was making an appearance. The death toll from the weather was now over a hundred, and there seemed to be little hope of the snow stopping long enough for the emergency services to be of any help.

He swallowed two pain killers and swilled them down with his coffee before he continued on with his work. The pain in his ribs was making him angry, forcing him to gasp each time he moved and he wanted to get as much done as he could in the fifty precious minutes he had before the rest of the office arrived with their festive cheer.

Less than a week till Christmas, he thought, just six more days of happy looking people, with fake smiles and joy. For one small period a year people felt it necessary to be nice to each other. Life continued on as normal, it just went on behind a fake veil of joy and happiness.

He'd never really bothered about Christmas, his mother had been dead for some years now and as the only child of a fatherless family, he had no siblings to visit and no one to share his time with.

That first Christmas had been the hardest. After spending what little money they'd had in savings on the funeral costs, he'd then been told to vacate the council premises that he'd shared with his mother, so someone more deserving could move in. He spent that first Christmas alone, crying in a hostel.

No one back then had time to care about him, so he'd stopped caring as well. Now it was something he watched from a distance, something to be aware of, but not get involved in. Christmas, he'd decided years ago, was for other people, and they were welcome to it.

He remembered crying a lot at the beginning, he'd even contemplated suicide on those early dark lonely winter nights, but he'd realised that it wasn't Christmas that depressed him, nor was being alone, it was the people. He hated the way they acted, the false faces and mock smiles that they used at this time of year.

The morning dragged on, but at least the snow had finally slowed and by mid afternoon a clear sky promised a frost that night. For a short time the Sun shone and brightened the day, and the world felt right.

The gull took off into the clear blue sky, its stomach full of entrails and off cuts that it had stolen from the butchers shop bins. It settled on the ledge of an office block, fluffing its feathers to keep in the heat before settling down to watch the day pass by below.

The hustle and bustle was nothing more than movement to it, a potential food source and nothing more. There was so much waste in the city nowadays that it never had to look far for its dinner and it was growing fat and lazy because of it.

Any food that wasn't hidden from sight was fair game and it had stolen food from people's hands before today. It really liked the city, excess food was dropped to the floor for all and sundry to eat, and it had grown into a large and happy gull. Other gulls had learnt at their cost to keep away from it, although it was older, it was tougher than most, and the more food it ate the bigger and better it became.

As the Sun started to set against the horizon, it decided to find its supper before it was too dark to fly so it stretched his wings and launched itself from the ledge. It could see people moving below, it was aware of their existence of course, but only as we would be aware of the gulls.

An apple rolled from a table as a shopkeeper moved his goods back into his shop. A young girl dropped her chips on the floor as her friend pushed her against a boy, and they laughed before moving on. All easy pickings, but its mind was on meat and it could smell it in the wind. It screeched loudly at the thought of its supper before it banked in the frigid air and eagerly beat its wings towards it.

The setting Sun cast a warm glow over the building opposite and Philip smiled; it was a heart warming sight after the chill of the day. A group of teenagers ran laughing down the street below, one narrowly missing a man as he came out of a shop but they continued on without concern, as the man shouted after them. The world looked so much more interesting when you couldn't take part.

He wanted to finish work and escape from the tedium of the week, and his mind wandered towards the weekend. Maybe the cinema, he thought, they had to be showing something new, something with guns and explosions maybe. There was always Delamere Forest; a walk round the lake would be nice.

He could visualise the frozen lake and the frosted branches around it. The smell of ice as he walked around it with his Ipod on, his boots crunched on the crisp virgin snow that had settled around him. Someone called his name and he angrily dropped from his meanderings.

"What is it?" he snapped, realising too late that his review meeting with his manager hadn't finished yet.

"I said…" Mr Rushford repeated as he tapped his pen on the pad before him. "Do you have anything else to add to my suggestions, Mr Greenwood? Or should I just sack you now?" Mr Rushford stared at him, his fat little face flushing with anger as he spoke. "These review meetings are here to make sure that you can continue to do your job you know."

Philip cringed as he watched him wipe the spittle from the side of his mouth. He could see he was angry at being shouted at, but for the life of him, he couldn't remember what the monotonous old fool had been talking about? He racked his memory as he tried to grab the point at which he'd switched off.

"I'm sorry, Mr Rushford." Philip held his hands together under his chin while he desperately dug deeper into his memory, and then he smiled. He'd been drunk at the sound of his own voice as he'd talked about office changes and improvements.

"I just don't understand why we need to change the work we do already." His stomach started to settle as he felt the conversation coming back to him. "What I mean is that we don't miss anything, and everything is done on time, giving us enough time to double check the figures if required." Philip smiled as he picked up his pen and slid it into his pocket.

"That is what we're supposed to do after all, isn't it?" He

gestured to the reports and graphs on the table before him, "Surely, to make us rush would cause mistakes, and mistakes, as we know, cost money. We don't want to cause problems for you further up the ladder," he lied. He knew Mr Rushford hated the upper management, and he watched as a cold shiver appeared to run down his spine.

"My suggestion," he continued quickly, "Would be to stand our ground on any changes that are being pushed, and to sell ourselves for what we do. Explain to them how much money would be lost in interest payments alone if we got it wrong." He looked at Mr Rushford. "Surly that's what the management wants to see after all isn't it?" Philip held his breath as he waited to see if he would get away with it.

"Well." Mr Rushford coughed to clear his throat. "Yes. Yes Indeed. That's exactly right Philip." He patted his brow with his handkerchief. "Excellent. Yes, that's exactly what I was planning to do." He shuffled his paperwork on the desk. "Well done. Well done."

Philip could see he was trying to regain his composure as he shuffled his papers again, obviously not sure what had just happened, or how he'd lost control.

"Keep up the good work, Mr Greenwood. If you... If you work hard and keep focused, I can see good things for you in the company." He slid his pen back into his pocket. "If you should have any more ideas on how we can improve the department further. Just...erm... well." He paused for a moment as he thought. "My door is always open." He stood up, pausing before he left. "Excellent".

Philip sat silently watching Mr Rushford waddle back to his office before he stood and walked over to the window. A gull sat watching him from the ledge of the office block opposite. It was eating what looked like a popped red balloon; at least he hoped it was a balloon.

Suddenly it took flight, dropping from its position as though something had startled it, its wings quickly opened and it banked down the street as a flash rippled across the evening sky, turning the clouds from deep red to white as though a huge light bulb had been switched on and off quickly. The gull turned as it suddenly lost control of its orientation. It flew to the left and right before it flew straight towards Philip.

The window shook with the force of the impact and the lights in the office went out dropping him into an eerie darkness. A deep unnerving shiver ran up his spine as he staggered back into the table, and it took him a moment or two to realise it wasn't just the office that had lost its power, but the entirety of the area outside, and it took him a moment more to figure out that the gull had not been the cause.

His heart pounded in his chest and he fumbled in the darkness to the door. The main office wasn't much better. He could hear people calling, someone cried nearby and he made his way over to them.

"It's Philip. You okay?" he called into the darkness.

"I think I sprained my ankle."

He recognised Sandra's voice and slowly shuffled over to her.

"What the hell happened?" she whispered as his hand touched her shoulder. Every sound was magnified in the office since the air-conditioning had failed.

"No idea." He could just make out her shape in the darkness. "The power looks like it's out all over town, even the cars have stopped." He pulled her to her feet and rested her arm over his shoulder. "Is everyone else okay?" he shouted. A chorus of moans came back.

He sat Sandra down on a chair before starting to help the others. The Sun hadn't completely set, and by its light he could make out grey shapes against the darker background of the office walls. Suddenly the emergency lights flickered on and the fire alarm sprang into life.

"Everyone out!" he shouted as he helped Sandra to her feet.

The Saturday Sun rose on unusual quiet. No cars moved on the snow covered roads, and the shops remained dark. It was the lack of noise that the seagull noticed as it woke and it looked down on the city as it fluffed its wings to shake frost particles off from the previous night.

The world looked empty and it turned its head a few times as it tried to understand what was wrong, but there was only a peaceful silence so its thoughts moved on. If there was no direct danger then there were more important things to do. Stretching its wings it screeched to the silent world before launching itself into the cold air in search of breakfast.

Philip clicked the remote as he flicked from one channel to the next. He paused for a moment to watch, before moving on through the sport and finally clicking the TV off as he shuffled into the kitchen to make himself a coffee.

He enjoyed his weekends, no stress, no pressure- he could be himself. He shuffled back into the living room and settled once again into his old arm chair; he rubbed the sleep from his eyes and sipped his drink. After a few minutes of silence and with nothing better to do, he clicked the television back on.

The news came on and he watched as the two presenters chatted. The man wore a casual looking shirt and trousers, the woman, a low cut top and short skirt and he smiled that even the news had to glamorise itself nowadays just to make people watch, but he listened as the man started to talk about the power outage.

"We hand you over now to Nicky Edge, who is currently with Professor Jonathan Yates at Manchester University." He turned to look at the screen by his side. "Are you there Nicky?" The screen clicked to the image of a young fresh faced woman as she stood in the university entrance.

"Yes, I'm here." She smiled, trying to hide the fact she was shivering uncontrollably.

"I believe you have someone with you who can maybe explain what happened?"

"Indeed I do." The camera zoomed into her. "As I'm sure

everyone is aware, the majority of Europe suffered major power cuts yesterday, but this wasn't any normal power outage. I have here with me Professor Jonathan Yates." She smiled as a medium aged man stepped into the picture. "Who will hopefully be able to explain what happened. Professor Yates?" The man smiled nervously. He was the stereotypical image of a university professor, balding white hair and thick glasses, his tweed jacket collected snow on his shoulders.

"Er…" He looked nervously at the camera for a second before turning back to Nicky. "Yes, well, from, um, from the data we have been able to collect so far we can see that at approximately sixteen hundred hours yesterday, the Northern Hemisphere was hit by a plasma wave caused by a solar pulse." He looked very uneasy and he stumbled over a few words.

"A solar pulse?" Nicky asked.

"Yes," he nodded. "A wave of plasma that was ejected from the Sun." He paused as he thought. "How to explain better… oh yes. Think of the waves caused when a stone hits a body of water. Well, in this case, if you imagine the Sun is the stone. The magnetic winds that fire out can cause the Northern Lights and mildly effect electrical appliances and such like. They usually fire off at random angles, either missing us entirely or being defused by our own magnetic field." He paused to check that she had understood.

"Okay," she smiled reassuringly, "But surely these happen all the time?"

"Yes indeed they do, the Sun can eject large quantities of plasma when we have Sun spots. Most of them, as I said, travel off harmlessly into space and cause no concern to the earth at all, but what we experienced yesterday was different."

"I believe we have a presentation to explain this better?" Nicky nodded to someone off screen and an image of the Sun appeared.

"What you can see here," the professor's voice played over the image on the screen, "Is the Sun in its normal state. You can see the darker areas which are the Sun spots, areas of turbulence on the surface. These generally cause little to no damage to us at all."

Philip sipped his drink slowly as the image zoomed to show a flare magnificently erupt from the Sun's surface.

"But yesterday, this occurred." The image panned out, to show the entire Sun again. But this time, instead of a single flare erupting, the entire surface seemed to pulse at once. "This is known as a Halo." The camera cut back to the two stood next to each other. "Normal Coronal Ejections can take up to six days to get to us, giving us fair warning and time to prepare. However this was very quick, and we had less than two hours from flare to impact."

"So can we expect to see these happen again?"

"Will it happen again? I just can't tell you," he shrugged. "The solar cycle is peaking at the moment. We might see more, but I would hazard a guess that they will be a lot smaller than we experienced yesterday."

"Any advise to the people?"

"Not really. Just try to keep your cars parked in your garage if you have one. Store anything of electronic value in your microwave oddly enough as it will act as a deflector and shield them from the pulse, and remember to take the batteries out of everything you're not using."

"Well thank you, Professor." Nicky nodded and turned back to the camera. "Just remember to take the items out of the microwave before you use it." She smiled. "This is Nicky Edge handing back to the studio on a very cold and frosty Saturday morning."

"Well, thanks for that Nicky." The presenter smiled as the screen went blank. "So nothing to worry about, just keep some candles around just in case."

"She did look cold though didn't she," the female presenter observed.

"Yes, didn't she just," he laughed in reply. "Anyway, we hope to have the head of Manchester Fire and rescue in the studio a little later, but before then over to Graham for the weather." Philip swapped channels until he found one that wasn't talking about yesterday and settling back into his sofa.

● ● ● ● ● ● ● ●

Jane stopped setting the dinner table and looked out of the window as she heard Mike's car pull into the drive and she let out a sigh of relief. The roads looked terrible out there, and she hated the thought of his journey home. Every second she dreaded a phone call telling her something bad had happened.

"Kids, your dad's home," she shouted upstairs and seconds later the banging of feet on the stairs told her they'd heard. "Alex, slow down before you fall!" she barked. She watched as he almost fell, but managed to grab hold of the banister just in time. Finally reaching the bottom, he ran to open the door. His brother walked down the stairs a short moment later, and Jane smiled. Because John was almost two years older than his `little` brother, he liked to think he was more grown up, and that meant he should act a little more mature.

The past week with the children had been a trying one for her. They'd been hyperactive with the build up for Christmas, and with all the plans and preparation she needed to complete she'd been spread very thinly and she was looking forward to her rest tomorrow. She was convinced Mike thought that Christmas just magically happened on its own, that he really believed the magic Christmas fairy would arrive at the house and bring all the presents with it. Instead she had wrap and hide them all until Christmas Eve, and then she would cook the Turkey Dinner, peel the potatoes and everyone else would rest and relax and drink and be merry.

Every year, Jane would spend months searching the busy shops, looking for the toys that the TV had force fed her children. The toys that weren't even available until the start of December, and then there wasn't enough of them for everyone. All of this was oblivious to Alex as he stood waiting for his dad to get out of the car, and Mike waved as he saw him.

"Hiya, son," he shouted as he climbed out of the car, "Have you been good for your mum today?"

"I sure have, Dad," Alex grinned back. "I shovelled the snow from the drive for you. Look." Mike looked at the half hearted attempt to clear the drive, ending two foot from the door.

"Good job," he smiled. "Is that your snowman on the lawn?"

"Yeah," Alex nodded, "Me and John made it this afternoon, do you like him?"

"I do, just don't invite him in for dinner, he would leave wet patches on the carpet." He walked to the door as Alex laughed. "Alright, son, let me in will you."

Alex on cue sat on his foot and waited for him to half lift, half drag him into the house. Once finally inside, Alex ran happily back upstairs, leaving Mike to hang his coat in the hallway before kissing Jane on the forehead.

"It's almost Christmas," he sang and hugged her.

"Are you okay, dear?" His normal greeting consisted of a grunt and a sit down on the sofa in front of the TV.

"I've never felt better." He smiled as he kissed her again. "Did you sort out the thing for Alex? Only I was looking today at dinner and they where all out of stock."

"Yes," she smiled, "I got one so don't worry." Bless him, she thought, at least he's trying.

"He's going to be so excited. It's all he's been asking for." He picked at the food being prepared on the table.

"Tea will be ten minutes," she chastised, slapped his hand. "Why don't you go and get changed and relax a little?"

"Now that's a good idea." He walked to the fridge and grabbed a can of lager. "Is there anything good on telly tonight?"

"No." Jane didn't look up from the preparation. "Nothing special, I'm surprised they haven't put something on though, it's just repeats again." She bent to open the oven. "Oh! Deborah called before, she said she'd pop round later with Andrew to drop of the presents for the kids, so go and get changed, I don't want you to be rushing later."

"I will, I will. I promise." He smiled at her before sitting down next to John to watch Tom and Jerry.

Twenty minutes later the normal banter commenced over

dinner: "Don't eat too fast"; "Mind you don't drop it on the tablecloth"; "Now look what you've done"; "No you can't cover it in tomato sauce, it took me ages to cook that", and the obvious classic, "Eat it, it's good for you" all appeared, but finally, the plates sat empty and the kids departed to play, running full pelt up the stairs.

"Walk!" Mike shouted to them as they pounded up the stairs. "I tell you love, there's going to be an accident one of these days".

Suddenly Alex shouted something and foot steps hastily ran back downstairs.

"Slow down," Mike shouted angrily as they both charged into the room.

"Dad, Dad!" Alex shouted, obviously upset. "Someone's been in our room."

"The windows wide open," John continued, "And, and my toys are all over the floor." The look on his face said he wasn't joking and Mike was half way up the stairs by the time he had started to repeat to his mum what he had said.

Mike's heart pounded in his chest from adrenaline and fear as he entered the bedroom. Their bunk bed stood against the wall and the cold night air flooded in via the wide open window. Flakes of snow fluttered past the radiator before landing softly on the carpet. The nets blew out like ghostly fingers reaching to grab him as he pulled the window shut and pulling the curtains closed, locking the night outside.

The room was a mess, and although toys seemed to cover the floor, it didn't look as though anything was missing. He shook his head, it was more than likely the room had been a mess before, and they'd scared themselves into believing there was something wrong because the wind had blown in the way it had.

"Jane, it's alright," he shouted as he heard her come up the stairs behind him.

"What was it?" her head appeared round the door as she looked in.

"The room looks like normal, and there's nothing missing."

"No Mike," she shook her head, "I made sure they tidied in

here today, and it was tidy just before you got home, there's no way the kids made this mess." The look in her eyes was serious and he instinctively picked up John's cricket bat before walking back onto the landing.

He switched the light on in their room, the quilt lay in a pile on the floor and the wardrobe doors stood partially open. He absentmindedly dropped the quilt back onto the bed and closed the wardrobe. Whoever had broken in must have taken a quick look round and left again in a hurry.

"We've obviously nothing worth stealing, love." He laughed half heartedly as he turned off the light and turned back to the landing. The wardrobe door creaked softly in the darkness, and he was about to turn when he heard a muffled cry from the kid's room.

"Jane?" he called as he stepped onto the landing but stopped as a sharp pain shot up his back. It felt like hot coal had been pressed against his skin and he stood motionless for a second, before it started to spasm as though his disc had slipped again.

He grunted as a second, sharper pain dug deeply into his waist and he felt like he'd wet his pants. His knees gave out first and he dropped down, trying to grab the doorframe as he fell forward. He couldn't feel his legs, and the tears welled up behind his eyes as the pain intensified, and he coughed, spitting bright red blood onto the landing carpet.

With shaking hands he wiped his mouth in disbelief before trying to drag himself along. With great effort he grabbed the doorframe, and pulled himself slowly forward. He was going to shout to Jane for help when he spotted her. She was lying on her back in the middle of the floor.

There was something childlike sat on her chest and with tear filled eyes he watched as it stabbed something repeatedly into her chest, her body convulsed with each impact before she lay still.

He felt his body shaking in terror as it slowly looked at him before crawling from his wife's body. He wanted to sob, to scream out but the bubble in his throat made him gag as he tried to shout. His hair was pulled from behind, raising his head off the carpet and he felt something cold as it dragged slowly across his neck, and he dropped slowly out of the nightmare and into the cold embrace of death.

Alex had lain on the sofa watching the telly as John walked in carrying a plate of biscuits. Putting them on the table he went back for the milk he'd so carefully poured out for them both, as they waited for Mum and Dad to come back down the stairs.

As he walked in with the milk he spotted something reaching over the sofa towards his brother. It was hideously disfigured and it looked like something made from grey plaster. It stared at him with large unblinking eyes and opened its mouth to show misshapen teeth as it grinned at him.

More appeared behind it and the glasses slipped from his hands, spilling their contents over the floor. "Alex!" he hissed, "Come here now!"

"Mum's gonna shout at you John!" But he could see John wasn't looking at him, but behind him and he turned expecting to see his parents. Its hands were close, but as he screamed they pulled back, and he jumped from the sofa and ran to this brother before they backed their way into the kitchen.

John felt the backdoor handle press into his back and the fight or flight response told him to run. Turning quickly he pulled the door open and pushed Alex outside. The light from the kitchen stretched out over the snow of the back garden, and he sobbed as he stared into the faces of more of the creatures as they crawled unblinkingly towards the house from the darkness.

With no other place to go, they backed into the corner of the kitchen. Crouching down he held his brother close as they tried to squeeze themselves into as small a space as possible. As the kitchen door slowly closed he looked at his brother.

"I love you bro," was all John managed to say.

Philip kicked out reflexively as a large snowball hit the window and he knocked the thankfully empty cup from the table. He stormed angrily over and flung it open, ready to fire a torrent of abuse at whoever had thrown it. The second snowball narrowly missed him as it smacked against the window frame near his ear.

"Who the bloody hell threw that?" he shouted to the street below as he leaned out.

"You coming to the pub soft lad?" a voice shouted in reply as another snowball hit the window frame above his head, showering him with snow.

The snow had started to fall again in large chunks, and with so little traffic around at the moment, it sat almost two foot deep. It looked cold, but so was his flat, and it didn't take him long to make up his mind as he saw his friend shivering below.

"You sure it's open?"

"Of course I am. When have I ever been wrong?"

Philip smiled as he stepped out onto the road a couple of minutes later. Snow had a wonderful way of cleaning the streets, hiding the detritus of life under it and no cans or crisp wrappers could be seen. He shivered as they trudged their way through the snow, the cold seemingly able to find a way up into his spine despite his coat and jumper, though it didn't seem to affect Tom who walked on just the same, whistling as he went.

Philip liked Tom, he was a low-baggage sort of a guy, and that was why he liked him so much. If for whatever reason he didn't want to go out, Tom would just find someone else instead, there would be no hassle, no moaning from him, and when you did go out, he was just mad enough to make the night really interesting.

He'd met Tom at school almost fourteen years ago, and they'd been friends ever since. Like Philip, he was an only child and his father had left his mother for a younger woman. He didn't talk about his father at all anymore and Philip never asked.

Tom was a musician, not a very good one Philip always thought, well not in the classical sense anyway, but good enough to get work for a number of radio and TV stations. His jingles made sure he wasn't short of cash, and that gave him enough spare time to do what he wanted.

"How are your ribs?" Tom asked absentmindedly as they walked along.

"Right." Philip stopped in his tracks. "What happened to me? I knew it had something to do with you." And he punched Tom in the shoulder. "I can't remember Thursday night at all."

"You can't remember? Are you serious?" Tom laughed. "Oh that's just priceless, so you don't remember stealing the car?"

"Eh?"

"Or kissing that dancer?"

"No. No." He started to panic; he hated the thought that he'd done something stupid. "Aw, crap. I don't remember anything?"

"Good job you didn't do anything as lame as that then," Tom smirked as he pushed past him into *The Bricklayers Arms*.

"Same as usually lads?" the landlord smiled as they approached the bar, they nodded as they stamped the snow from their feet on the mat. The pub was almost empty, only the hardiest of drinkers seemed to have made it out.

"So what did I do?" Philip begged as the barman pulled two pints of beer for them and set them on the bar, Tom handed over the money and handed Philip the first pint.

"I didn't know if you'd make it in tonight lads." The barman smiled. "And the weather report says its going to get colder before it starts to warm up again."

"I didn't plan on doing much this weekend except drink beer anyway." Tom smiled before following Philip to a vacant table in a quieter quarter of the bar.

"So, what's up with you then? You have a face like a smacked arse." Tom sipped at his beer. "You're not getting enough sex, that's your problem, actually, you ain't getting any. I was with this girl last night that could bend over backwards and..."

"What did I do?" Philip cut him short. "Don't mess around

Tom, I need to know. You know I hate it when I can't remember."

"Honestly?"

"Yes," he snapped.

"Promise not to get angry!"

Philip moaned; the phrase 'Promise not to get angry' meant that Tom had done something to cause it. As kids it had been the main excuse when some hair brained plan went wrong, Samantha Cartwright had finished with him because of a 'Promise not to get angry moment', and he slowly lifted his head and looked at Tom.

"What did you do?"

"Promise first."

"Fine." He raised his hand in resignation. He had to know what he had done and Tom knew he could get off the hook for it by making him promise. "I promise not to get angry"

"Good." Tom finished his beer. "Well you get the next round in first while I pop for a leak," and he was gone before Philip could object.

When Philip returned with the fresh pints Tom wasn't alone. A group of girls sat with him, and he recognised a few from his work. Tom waved across to him and held up three fingers and Philip nodded before turning back to the bar.

"Another three of the same please." He put the pints down on the counter to wait for the extras.

"It might be a good night for you after all," Tom whispered in his ear as he stood at the bar. "These girls don't want to be single for Christmas. Christmas sex is the best, when it's cold outside but your nice and warm in bed with you face between their..."

"Carry these will you," Philip stopped him as he handed him the glasses. "And tell me why my ribs ache," he called as an after thought, but Tom had gone. Damn it, he cursed himself, there'd be no chance of finding out tonight now, he'd have to get him later, and so with a sigh he picked up the last two pints and followed after him.

I guess Tom might be right, he thought as he approached the table. Jen was with them, and he had a soft spot for her. She smiled as he came over and he slid into the booth next to her. The juke box played Christmas songs and the volume of conversation increased as the pub grew busier. It seemed as though everyone wanted to be out, despite the snow outside, and the conversation inevitably worked its way towards the power cuts or the weather.

"It's the end of the world," one of Jen's friends proclaimed. "A friend of mine knows a guy, whose cousin saw the face of Jesus in a mirror when the power failed."

"Really?" Tom smirked, "What did he look like?"

"He didn't say," she shrugged, not realising he was making fun of her. "But I've heard it from others too, so it must be true. Did you hear about that poor family that got attacked by those animals?"

"Are you okay?" Jen asked as she put her hand on Philip's leg. "You seem very quiet."

"Sorry." He smiled, feeling the warmth of her hand on his thigh. "There's just so much going on my mind keeps on wandering. I've still got so much to do before Christmas." It was nice to talk directly to someone, and he was quite happy to leave the rest of them talking between each other.

"I love getting presents," she announced. "It's the best part of Christmas for me, running down stairs to see all of them." Philip nodded though he didn't really know the feeling, he'd been lucky to get any presents at all.

By ten o'clock, the rest of the group had followed Tom into town, leaving Philip alone with Jen. He'd certainly drunk enough to ensure a hangover in the morning, but for the moment, the alcohol numbed his senses enough to release his usual tensions and throw caution to the wind and he was actually enjoying himself.

They talked about everything, how she was on her own this Christmas for the first time, how she hated work, what music she liked through to which shops she wanted her presents from. Philip listened, smiling when he needed to, but generally he just watched her lips moving.

The music went out at the same time as the lights and everything fell into a deadly silence. Jen's hand grip his leg in the darkness, a little higher than he'd expected and it clenched again as the landlord shouted.

"Everyone remain where they are please." A few giggles, and the smashing of a glass showed that not everyone had chosen to listen to him. Philip squeezed Jen's hand tightly as he tried to re-assure her that everything would be okay, when suddenly, the music started to play again and the lights flickered back on.

People cheered and laughed at the absurdity of the situation and the fear it provoked, no one seemed to like being in the dark. Jen finished her drink and carefully placed it on the table with the others. She seemed to be deep in thought, before she looked at Philip with a twinkle in her eye.

"How close is your place then?"

Philip slowly opened the box of pain killers and dropped two tablets into each glass, carefully stirred them as he tried his hardest not to catch the side of the glass with the spoon. His stomach told him not to drink anything, but he knew from experience that the magical elixir before him was exactly what he needed to cure his hangover.

Jen looked like she was dead when he returned, and she blinked slowly before struggling to sit up and take the drink from him, her bloodshot eyes looked as bad as his.

He carefully picked his way around the clothes that covered the floor as he moved to his side of the bed and drank deeply before lying down again. His stomach rolled and churned as he rested back into his pillow, and he smiled as he watched Jen wipe the glass before taking a sip.

"What?" she smiled embarrassed at the attention. "Stop it will you, you're making me blush."

"Sorry." He smirked at her as his eyes wandered over her nakedness. "You just look cute in your birthday suit."

She lay back down and rested her head on his chest and he hugged her, sharing their warmth as she ran her hand down his stomach. Her breathing slowed as she fell asleep again, and a contented smile crossed his face.

It was some hours later when they woke again, the Sun shone weakly through the curtains as he ran his fingers lightly through her hair, and she sighed softly in her sleep. He desperately needed the toilet, so with great care he rolled her to the side before slipping out of bed.

"Morning." She stretched as she saw him returning, the quilt just covering her breasts as she moved.

"Hi."

"Do you fancy any breakfast?" His stomach grumbled uncontrollably as he spoke.

"Oh, God yeah," she smiled weakly, "I'm starving, do you have croissants?"

"I'll check." He nodded with a smile as he walked back into the kitchen. Croissants, he mumbled to himself as he opened the cupboards one by one in the vain hope of finding something to eat, but he was out of everything, even coffee.

"Jen, I've nothing in that's worth eating," he shouted. "If you can give me ten minutes I'll walk to McDonald's and grab something, they should be open. What do you fancy?"

"Oh. McDonalds?" she called from the bedroom. "Well, I guess. If there's nothing else, what do they do for breakfast?"

"Er..." he was amazed she didn't know, maybe it was something she'd just never got round to having. "Bacon Muffins, Pancakes and that sort of stuff."

"Pancakes then, oh and if they do coffee can I have mine black?"

The streets were deserted. More snow had fallen during the night and banked up against the shop windows in the high street, making walking on the pavement difficult. Fortunately though, because he lived on a main road, a snowplough had miraculously made it through. So he walked on the road, just hoping McDonalds would be open when he got there.

He stopped at the first wrecked car he found. It had been pushed onto the curb obviously, to keep the roads clear and its metal carcase was still warm from the fire that had engulfed it. The snow had melted on the pavement around it, and judging by the number plate it was a new car, less than a year old, though now it was just scrap metal and melted plastic. He just hoped no one had been hurt.

Fifteen minutes later he was back with the food, fortunately some shops had managed to open, even if it was with a skeleton staff, and he stamped life back into his feet before walking back into the living room.

"Your crappy old TV won't come on," she pouted as she took her drink from him "It looks like it's had it. I can't believe this is even a digital set."

"I bet it's the fuse that's all." He'd had this problem before. "If you give me a moment, I'll change it."

"But it's so old. Is this only one you have?"

"What the TV? Yeah, why would I have more than one?"

"I just figured everyone did," Jen shrugged. "I have three, and this sofa is a little old as well. She seemed to be trying to find fault in almost everything he had and he didn't like it. This was his home, and he didn't like the idea of people telling him it was wrong, even if they were cute. She didn't even seem to see that what she was saying was wrong.

Once he'd changed the fuse the TV flickered into life and he sat down next to her on the sofa while he finished his breakfast. He felt very self conscious of the mess his flat was in, and wondering what she would pick on next. He scanned the room, looking at his wobbly book shelf, or the almost dead potted plants by the window. He felt Jen tense next to him, a gasp coming from her mouth.

"What's wrong with my flat now?" he blurted out, realising that she was watching the news report on the television and he quickly stopped to watch, hoping she hadn't heard him.

A news reporter stood with her back to a scene of devastation, burning debris and pieces of metal jutted from the ground at strange angles as fire crew sprayed the whole scene in thick white foam. The reporter was physically distraught by the carnage behind her and her voice broke as she spoke.

"I don't know if you can make out the scene behind me," she shouted above the noise of the still burning fires. "But the fire crews are still trying to gain control." An explosion made her duck and the camera crackled with the shock wave. "Official reports," she continued once the roar had passed, "blame the solar flare for the crash of the Flight 787 which lost control shortly after take off."

More fire engines were appearing on the scene as the flames continued to rise behind her.

"So far, there's been no sign of any survivors, and until the fires are brought under control there will be little chance of recovering the black box, though officials don't believe it will shed any further light on these terrible incidents." The camera panned across the scene of the crash.

"I don't know if you can make out the remains of the apartment block behind me, but of the hundred and forty people believed to be inside, none have so far been rescued," she coughed as more smoke passed in front of her, "and with so many fires still burning, the hope of finding…" a large flash filled the screen and the image changed to static before it dropped back to the studio, the news presenter shuffled his paperwork as he listened to his ear piece.

"Well, it looks like we've lost the transmission there, Susanna." He smiled. "But we'll try to get back to Jo as soon as we can. Please do remember that this is but one of the twenty-seven reported crash sites across America and Europe, and though the scene in New York is grim, there's still a good chance of finding survivors at the others." The screen changed to a list of flights and emergency contact numbers. "If you need any information on any of the incidents, then please contact the numbers shown on screen."

Jen reached over and held Philip's hand. He could feel her

shaking against him as they both sat silently watching the news unfold before them. The screen changed back to the studio where the two newsreaders continued the news.

"Thanks, Charlie," Susanna took over, "The terrible destructive power of the Sun hit home to most of America and Europe yesterday, and we have reports of problems from as far away as Poznan in Poland. So far, the reported death toll across the globe has been estimated at up to 450,000, with many more potentially trapped under rubble. We have no response from Downing Street in regards to the crashes, and the question on everyone's lips now is, can we expect more?" she held her hand to her ear as a message was relayed to her, covering her mouth as the information settled in.

"We've..." her voice broke as she tried to speak, tears running down her face for a moment before the camera cut across to her partner who looked almost as shaken as she was. He coughed to clear his throat and continued for her.

"I'm sorry," he began, "We've just received news that there's been a fatal explosion at the crash site in New York, early reports have come in that the planes fuel tank ruptured and the following explosion not only claimed the lives of our film crew but a large portion of the fire fighters." The female presenter ran passed behind him, obviously distraught by the news, but he continued, "There's nothing more really to report, our thoughts and prayers go out to the many families who have lost loved ones today, once again here is the list of contact numbers." The screen flicked over once more, obviously used to let the new readers compose themselves before they continued.

"This is terrible, all those people dead." Jen started to cry and he could feel her sobs against his chest. He couldn't deal with crying, he'd used up all his own tears so long ago that he didn't know how to cry anymore, so he just sat with her in silence, holding her close to him. By the time he'd finished his breakfast the screen had come back on; both presenters had been replaced by a new news reader.

"Thanks for staying with us," he smiled weakly. "Before the break, we were on site covering the terrible tragedy of flight 1709, one of the many incidents that have affected so many people in the last 24 hours." The reporter shuffled the paper on his desk. "We now know that a vast area of the American continent has been left in the dark after thousands of relay stations were destroyed by the pulse. Emergency sessions have been called in parliament to discuss emergency protocols and security measures in the eventuality that Europe should follow the same fate as our American cousins. Please bear with me a moment," he nodded to the Camera and held his finger to his ear as another message came in.

"It appears that before we lost contact the White House had just declared a state of emergency in response to the disasters, all flights both in and out have been cancelled. There is a total ban on anything passing through their airspace until further notice. A state of Martial Law has been declared in all the areas that have lost power."

"Although Europe seems to have escaped the main force of the blast, the side effects have still been felt closer to home, with thousands of accidents on the motorways so please do avoid any travelling today, unless it's absolutely necessary, and we are advising people to unplug everything that isn't business critical."

They sat silently together as more reports came in. He sat holding her as the pictures flicked from one fire to another, from one ambulance rushing down the road towards the hospital, to the image of an oil tanker burning where it had run aground in a small coastal town after its automated navigation system fried in the storm. By twelve o'clock it was finally announced that Europe would follow America's example, and a state of Martial Law was being declared.

"So you have until sunset to get to where you need to be. The army is setting up centres for local support in your area." The newsman looked at his co-worker with obvious concern. "We will continue to broadcast further news as it arrives, but for the moment, we return you to your regular viewing." After a slight pause, a cartoon appeared on the screen and Philip clicked the television off.

Jenny sat crying next to him and he wondered why, it wasn't that he was heartless, but over the last few years, he'd seen so much horror and death at the movies or on TV that unless it was local and he actually knew the people involved, it seemed to pass over him. It was terrible that so many people had died, but life went on.

"I wish I'd gone home now," she whispered. "I should have gone home."

"I didn't think last night was that bad?"

"No, not you silly," she forced a smile between her tears. "Last night was great." She leant over and kissed his cheek. "It's my parents. I didn't want to go home because I wanted to teach them a lesson." He started to laugh but realised she was being serious.

"You see," she continued. "Daddy didn't get me what I wanted for my Birthday last year," she pouted, "and it annoyed me so much, I decided to stay away for Christmas to teach him a lesson."

"What did you ask for?" he was almost afraid to ask but curiosity got the better of him. He didn't understand what went on in families. How they operated were a complete mystery to him.

"I only wanted a watch."

"And your parents wouldn't buy you one?" he almost felt sorry for her but there was a nagging feeling he didn't have the full picture.

"Daddy said that because of the recession he couldn't afford it," she pouted again as she spoke, actually looking upset. "It was such a nice little *Maurice Lacroix*, but Daddy said no." The Daddy comment worried him. Grown women didn't normally call their parents Mummy and Daddy, well, certainly not the sort of people he usually associated with. The way she pouted was also getting annoying, it was cute at first but she seemed to be using it as a weapon.

"So how much was it?"

"It was only seven hundred pounds," she said so matter of factually that he almost missed it. "I normally get more than that, but he said because they'd bought me the flat and everything, he had to say no. He's never said no before." The pout returned.

"I take it you're an only child?" more to confirm his suspicions than to ask the question.

"Oh, yes. Mummy said that she wouldn't have anymore, not

after what I did to her figure."

"Oh?" was all he could think of to say.

"I guess people do put on weight when they are pregnant." He tried to smile.

"I should really tell him to stop paying for my credit card but that would just be silly."

Philip looked at her. How many tantrums had she used to get her own way in the past and he found himself judging her. Her figure was amazing, and she obviously worked out, and after that thing she'd shown him last night, she worked out a lot, but it was strange how you never really know the people you work with. You knew them well enough to talk to, to know if they were married or had kids, but the real person remains hidden until you started to dig. At least the sex would be good, and he made a decision.

"Well, why don't you stay here for Christmas?" he blurted out.

"Seriously?" she paused as she looked round his flat, but smiled as she looked back to him. "Why not?" She nodded, "That would be fun, and I'm sure I could find something to keep us occupied. I'll need to get home though and get some more clothing and stuff." She paused as she thought to herself. "I'll make you a list of things you'll need to get me and we can meet back here later. We can have a turkey and roast potatoes and a champagne breakfast. It will be wonderful."

"Er…" He felt a sudden panic start to rise inside.

"Well that's settled then." She jumped up and ran into the bedroom to grab her things. She returned a few minutes later and sat on his lap, bending down as she slid her boots on. "Easy tiger, you can have me later." She smiled as she moved his hand from her leg. "For now you have a job to do." She leant over and handed him a list.

"You really need all of this?" he asked as he surveyed the epic novel before him.

"Well, we need to eat, and I don't eat just anything." She stood up, pulling her dress down. "I put down some air fresheners and such, some flowers would look nice in here too," she added absentmindedly. "Give me a few minutes and we can go. I should be able to get home and grab my things before you get back."

He looked at the list again as she walked back into the bedroom to grab the last of her stuff. This was going to cost him a small fortune, it contained everything from cleaning fluids, washing powder and spray polish to goose fat and a pound of fresh chestnuts for the stuffing. "You take your time," he called.

The supermarket was packed and he had to queue just to get inside. Food left the shelves in piles and the poor shelf stackers couldn't keep up with the demand, people grabbed full trays of beans or meats before they could be even unwrapped by the worker.

He stood to the side as a fight broke out between two middle-aged men over a tray of beans. As punches swung between both of them, two shop assistants ran over, pulling them apart before escorting both outside. Their trolleys quickly emptied by the people who stood nearby.

He shook his head as he looked again at the list in his hand before dropping it on the floor. She'd have to survive on what he could get, he thought. Someone barged heavily into his back, knocking him into the shelves before ruffling his hair, he was about to throw a punch of his own when a familiar voice laughed in his ear.

"Good morning," Tom laughed. "You end up having a good night last night?"

"Hey Tom." He nodded, "Yeah, it was a good night, but I'm starting to think I might have bitten off more than I can chew."

"Why's that? Could little Philip not perform?" he pushed out his bottom lip as he spoke.

"No you dick." Philip punched him. "It's not that. Trust me, the sex was great."

"So what's your issue? You had a good time; you finally got your end away, yeah? Mind you, she did look a little posh for you, but you don't have to see her again if you don't want to."

Philip looked down the aisle, avoiding eye contact.

"What's up, man? Listen, I didn't mean to wind you up, if she's finished with ya don't worry, plenty more women out there. Did she leave ya, she did, didn't she?"

"Not exactly no." He closed his eyes. "I sort of…well, I sort of asked her to stay with me over Christmas." He cringed, knowing he would get a slap and he wasn't wrong.

"What's the matter with you, have you forgotten the rules?" Tom grabbed his shoulder. "A girlfriend is for the night, not for Christmas. Have I taught you nothing young Jedi? The first girl that bends over for you and you invite her to live with you?"

"I didn't…" he tried to protest.

"Yes you did." He pressed his finger hard into his shoulder. "What are you going to do once Christmas is over? Did you think of that?"

"No," he mumbled as he looked down at his shoes.

"No, you didn't." Tom shook his head at him. "Next thing you know she'll be telling you the flat isn't big enough, or that you need to get rid of your porn collection."

"All right, I get the picture. She's great in bed, but there are too many family issues with her, she still calls her parents Mummy and Daddy for God's sake."

"Hey, hold on there." Tom held up his hand. "Kelly called me Big Daddy last night. There isn't anything wrong with that."

"No," Philip conceded. "For you, I guess its okay, but to call her actual parents that, and you should have seen the list she gave me of stuff to get."

"Where is it?"

"I binned it."

"Good. See, you aren't as stupid as you look sometimes." He waggled his finger at him. "Only sometimes though, so don't let it go to your head. So you're not getting it her?"

"Na, I'm just going to get some basics, B food group stuff. Beans, Bread and Beer."

"Yeah, that's what I was looking for, but I can't be arsed getting into that queue. Gonna leave it till later and grab whatever's left."

"Listen, I'll pop round tomorrow and hang out at your place in my underpants until she decides to go home."

"Thanks, Tom," he laughed. "You gotta get back for anything or do you have time for a beer?"

"Wish I could mate, I really do, but I can't," Tom smirked.

"What are you up to?"

"Well Kelly's still at mine isn't she, and I can't leave her for too long."

"Why?"

"Look," he looked round to make sure no one could hear, "She's a kinky little one alright, so... she's sort of tied up at the moment, and I don't want to leave her for too long."

"You're twisted, you are."

"Hey, don't knock it until you try it man," he replied defensively. "It was her call; she said she'd been a very bad girl. What's a man to do but help a lady out?" he shrugged his shoulders. "Anyway, I've got to get back to her before the batteries..." he stopped and changed the conversation. "Anyway, I'll see you tomorrow and scare her off for you."

"Alright, thanks," Philip called as he pushed his way out of the shop, but as Tom reached the entrance he turned and shouted as loud as he could over the noise of the shop. "I'll wear my leather crotchless ones for you then, honey." And with a wave he was gone. Two old ladies watched him with disgust, so he put his head down to avoid the glares, and started to collect the basics he felt they would need to last them, as he stretched for a can of spam and his ribs ached again.

"Damn it." He moaned to himself as he realised he'd forgotten to ask about his ribs. Well tomorrow would be different, he'd pin him down until he told him what happened. He queued for over an hour to buy his meagre supplies. All he needed now was to grab the beer and get home. Fortunately, the off licence was fairly quiet. With most people focusing on the food problem, the beer was left to the smart and fun free. Make hay while the Sun shines, Philip thought as he started for home, the plastic handles already starting to cut off the circulation to his fingers.

The walk back to his flat wasn't far, but he had to stop three times just to let the blood flow into his fingers. As he rounded the final corner, he felt his ears pop and he suddenly felt like throwing up. He watched in confused panic as his fingers involuntarily release their hold on his bags, dropping them to the footpath as his body started to jerk before his knees gave out.

As he sank to the floor he could see others nearby staggering or falling with him. A car burst into flames as it passed, the driver screaming as the flames engulfed him inside his metal coffin; the bonnet popped open as it exploded, smashing the windows of nearby shops and Philip's world went dark.

Marcus watched his squad as the truck bounced along the road, there had been little time to reflect on what was going on in the world, but their orders seemed clear. Establish the operations centre and await further orders.

"Bang goes our Christmas vacation guys." Marcus tried to look positive as he shouted above the rattling of the truck, "How far did we all get?"

"I got as far as Birmingham." John shrugged. "My parents are seriously gutted. I was on leave until after the New Year, all the family were expected. Still, I guess things could be worse, I could be Paddy." He kicked the boot of the younger sulking soldier who sat next to Marcus. He was the newest member to the squad and was still the target for ridicule from the rest.

Patrick was a likable lad, still in his early twenties, with the fresh face of innocence about him. His black hair and Northern Irish accent had caused the rest to affectionately refer to him simply as Paddy.

"Paddy's girlfriend hasn't seen him for over three months," John smirked, "And he goes and gets called back before he can even get his pants off."

Paddy held two fingers up to John. "It's just not fair," he shook his head. "I had one hell of a Christmas organised. I didn't expect to see the outside of her bedroom for days. I never even got to see her wearing the present I got her, red lacy job it was. I spent a small fortune on it. She's a real cracker she is."

"Easy to pull and she's got a plastic toy inside?" Marcus couldn't resist, as the unit erupted in laughter, even Paddy smirked. It was good to hear them laughing. This was going to be an unhappy deployment as it was, and he'd be stretched just to keep the peace within his own unit over the next hour or so, never mind the next week or two.

"So," he asked, "I take it your intentions were honourable, Young Patrick?"

"I only wanted sex, Boss." Paddy smiled. "There was nothing kinky like."

"I thought she was a good Catholic girl."

"Na," he grinned, "That's her older sister, trust me, she isn't that religious."

"So there's no calling out to God then when you're at it?" Kate cut in, "The rumours must be true." She held out her little finger and bent it over.

"Cheeky cow!" Paddy shouted.

"Enough!" Marcus gave her a look to keep quiet; he liked Kate but as the only female in the unit she felt she had to fight harder than the others just to keep level. As the youngest sister from a family of three brothers he could see she was ready to push him a little further, and Paddy was so frustrated she would find it easy to break him.

He shook his head in her direction. "Leave it," he mouthed. She nodded back, knowing enough to leave it at that. Kate was a good solid soldier, if a little too rough and ready.

"I'm re-applying for leave as soon as we finish here," John sensibly changed the topic. As one of the oldest in the unit, he usually had a more mature nature. "Do you think this is going to be a long haul, Boss?"

"I don't know." Marcus shrugged. "It depends on the Sun I

guess, but from what I can gather, I'd bet it's not going to be finished before Christmas." There was a collective moan from the others in the truck. "Sorry guys." He waved his hands to calm everyone down. "We'll do the best we can to keep it civil, and as soon as any Green Slime comes in, you'll be the first to be told, I promise. But until then we follow the mission as usual."

"Christmas stuck in temporary digs?" Pierce moaned. His strong Welsh accent sounding musical as he complained. "Marcus, that's just rubbish. No booze. No fun. No action."

"We'll do the best we can guys, but that's all I know, unless you can shed any more light on the situation, Ken?" he asked the man who sat silently in the shadows of the crates towards the rear of the truck. Everyone looked surprised that someone else was with them. Marcus and the team knew him only as Ken and though they had completed missions with him before, they had never learnt his surname.

"Nothing from here I am afraid." He shook his head. "Green Slime has gone quiet on all fronts. I'm just here to enjoy the ride." He was a quiet individual, very much a loner. Marcus guessed he was in his mid-thirties, though he knew that appearance didn't mean anything with this man. He'd met him in the Gulf, two years prior. The hostilities had dropped off enough for the units to be assigned some well needed rest.

Marcus has been sitting alone in the mess tent when he'd spotted them. They looked just like any other group of soldiers, just sitting together talking about home and general life things, so he'd approached and asked if he could join them. They'd been welcoming enough, and they talked together about placements and missions.

He got to know Ken better over the next few days and he started to regularly sit with the group for meals, swapping stories about home, or the war, but the more he got to know them, the more he realised they weren't regulars. Their missions sounded more dangerous and deeper into enemy territory than he was used to, and when he finally asked their unit ID, he wasn't really surprised to hear they were SAS*.

They'd invited him to watch a beach assault training exercise they had planned for the following morning, and, a few hours later, he found himself sat on the cliffs, watching it via night scopes.

He didn't sit with them the following day. He felt now like he was only playing at being a soldier, but he'd developed a deep respect for Ken and he was pleased to have him onboard, even though he scared the crap out of him.

"Oh well," he laughed. "I'm sure Santa will know where to deliver the coal for you lot," he tried to lighten the mood a little but Paddy still looked depressed.

"We've been bad then have we?" Pierce joined in.

"You think Santa's coming down your chimney, Kate?" a voice called from the dark, filling the lorry with laughter.

"If I'm lucky," she smirked in reply. Marcus started to reply when the van shuddered to a halt as a sickening feeling washed over him, his muscles jumped as though an electric shock had shot through them, and the truck fell silent. He shook his head as he tried to clear the grogginess from his mind and stop himself from throwing up, and the others didn't look any better.

"Everyone okay back there?" the driver called as he slid the cabin window open.

"Yeah," he shouted as he squeezed his eyes closed. "Fine, I think."

"That was a bloody strong one. Thank god we insulated the canopy of the trucks eh?"

"Anything we can do to help?"

"Nope," the driver replied. "You all stay put and we'll be on our way again as soon as we swap the battery over."

"Rodger that," Marcus acknowledged.

"Anyone want a cigarette?" John offered his packet around as they waited for the driver to finish.

The snow fell on Philip's face in large soft clumps, slowly

coaxing him from his dreams. He moaned painfully as he moved, his forehead throbbed from the impact with the pavement and his limbs ached and he felt like he'd wet himself. He felt his stomach churn and he opened his eyes as he threw up into the gutter.

He felt like he'd been badly beaten by a very large baseball bat, and every muscle ached as he tried to push himself to his knees. He tried to focus, trying to make sense of the jumble of images that flashed in his mind. He tried to focus on his shopping, and slowly but surely the pavement came into view as he wiped the tears from his eyes with the back of his sleeve and looked around.

Other people close by started to move, some sat crying together where they had fallen, others stared blankly at the floor. He slowly started to pick up his shopping, putting the tins back into the bags as best he could despite his dizziness. As he turned to pick up his beer he noticed something. The snow had banked up against a woman, and it wasn't until one of her shoes slipped from her foot that he realised what he was looking at.

She must have been walking only a few feet behind him, but, as she'd passed out, she'd fallen through the window of a shop, a shard of glass slicing cruelly into her neck mingling her blood with the snow. He turned quickly away, throwing up once more into the gutter. In the distance a horn cut into the silence as army trucks rumbled into view. Ten trucks in total passed him, the last one, stopped a short distance down the street and as the tail gate dropped free, soldiers jumped out to help. One made his way over to Philip.

"Are you okay, sir?" he asked.

"Yeah," Philip nodded, "Yeah, I think so." He pointed to the prone body behind him. "I don't think she is alive."

"You leave her to us, sir." He looked into his eyes to make sure he was listening. "Can you make your way home or do you need help?"

"What? No." He still felt confused, but his memory was slowly coming back. "Sorry, yes, yes," he repeated. "I don't live far. I can make it."

"Well get yourself home and stay inside, sir." The soldier patted him on the shoulder. "We need to get everyone off the streets."

"Oh no," he whined. "I have someone coming to see me later."

"Not any more you don't" he stated flatly. "Unless they're with you in the next ten minutes, you're not going to see them tonight." The soldier turned away to check on the woman and Philip realised the conversation was over; there would be no discussion, no chance to beg or plead. So with nothing else to do, he set off down the street, dragging his feet through the snow as he walked in the vain hope that Jen would be able to follow them.

He kept his eyes firmly on the ground as he walked; there was no need to see what was going on around him. He could hear the people crying and calling for help, but all he wanted to do was get home, get back to the flat and close the door on the day.

The snow was falling in large flakes again as he mercifully kicked his door shut and he dropped the food bags in the kitchen before stumbling to his chair, dropping the booze by the side.

With a deep sigh he reached into the first bag and pulled out a bottle of vodka. Twisting the lid off, he held it to his lips, letting the cold liquid numb his body and mind from what was going on. Sometimes blacking out was a good option.

Ashfaq lay on his bed and he wasn't feeling very happy. It was Saturday night, but with the curfew in place it wasn't possible to meet up with his friends as normal and he hadn't been this bored for years. *'Have car, will travel.'* had been his motto since he'd passed his test. He didn't like to be stationary for too long; he had people to see, places to go, there were deals to be made and money to earn but instead he was stuck at home.

He wasn't a Gangster, though he liked to think of himself that way sometimes, he was more of a man of opportunity, a Middle Eastern Robin Hood. Normal life was for normal people. For him it would be nice cars and tropical holidays and being stuck inside was only going to slow him down.

He could hear his family downstairs, they sounded like they were having fun, but it wasn't for him. He was too old for board games. He'd tried to read, but a small draft from the window made his candle dance and flicker, casting odd shapes round the room.

He realised that there was only so much he could do without electricity. He could survive without the internet or TV, but without his mobile phone he was lost. Resigned to the fact there was little to do in his room he picked up the candle and opened his door. This wasn't going to be easy, he thought as he walked down the stairs. He'd faced bigger and meaner people in his life, he'd been in fights, but to spend the evening with his family was going to be tough.

It was a little after four by the time Marcus arrived at their temporary barracks. A local primary school had been taken over for the purpose and their four trucks pulled into the small car park before the order to disembark was called.

"Alright people," Marcus barked as he grouped his squad up in the main hall. "It looks like we've pulled the short straw, so we're on first patrol tonight with Corporal Williams's group." Everyone seemed to deflate a little. Normal protocol should have been to settle in a little before going out on patrol, but with the power out, time was of the essence.

"At least you're not filling the sandbags, or rolling the barb wire in the snow, so don't start crying about it, we know what we have to do." A chorus of grunts followed. "Now gather round for orders and routes." They bunched round a map of the area that had been pined to a stand. "Remember, because the power is out we don't have any radio contact, so two shamoolie's are going to be issued to each group leader. Red to call for support, the green flare to confirm your attendance and stop anyone else coming."

"Sure we need the flares, Boss? We should be able to handle any local looters on our own. We are armed after all." Patrick patted his SA80 rifle.

"I know, Paddy, but the Rodney's have insisted. It's most probably something to do with Health and Safety."

They all groaned. Health and Safety had become a big issue, and they felt sure that soon enough, they would take the guns off them because they could hurt someone.

He continued to mark out the routes each unit would take, ensuring they crossed paths every hour until 2 AM, when they would swap with the reserves group. "Then it's back here for hot chocolate and a sing song before I tuck you up in bed," he concluded with a smile.

"What are we carrying?" Kate called out from the back

"We've been told to only take the basics. One clip of ammo and some basic walking rations. Oh yes!" He held up a black torch. "I almost forgot; take spare batteries for the torches. If we do have another burst, you'll need to replace the batteries of anything that was running at the time. If you run out of batteries, then we have these wonderful high quality wind-up torches."

"You kidding, ain't you, Boss?" Pierce stood and caught the one Marcus tossed to him.

"I wish I was." He picked up another from the box. "This," he held it high enough for all to see, "is the best you've got until you can get back here for fresh batteries. We don't have that many, so use them carefully. It should be a clear night, so visibility should be good enough for eyes alone, but if you see anything use the torches." He looked around the team. "This is just a basic home security deployment, nothing to worry about, get what rest you can, it's going to be a cold night. Dismissed."

Ashfaq pushed open the living room door and walked in. He could see his father reading as he sat in the main chair. "Asalaaam-u-alaikum, Abu." He nodded to his father.

"Oh, so you've finally come to join us have you?" his father replied. "It's nice to see that we're still an option in your life, even if it is only because your car isn't working." He shook his head and went back to reading the paper.

He'd known it wasn't going to be an easy night. He knew he had neglected his family a little over the last few months, with work being what it was, he ended up with precious little time for himself, but he knew he should have put some aside for his family.

"Asalaaam-u-alaikum, Abujee." He sat next to his grandfather.

"Wa'alaikum asalaam," his grandfather smiled, "How are you?"

"Cold."

"Everyone's cold. Put another jumper on and stop complaining." His grandfather smiled. "So how many weeks has it been since we've seen you at the weekend, other than for food?"

Ashfaq shrugged. He thought a lot of his grandfather; he was a calm man, with a deep intelligence behind his eyes that said he didn't miss a thing. He warmed his fingers over the candles on the table.

"I understand you know." His grandfather smiled as he spoke, "Life's different from when I was a young man mind you, we didn't have all the mod cons you have today, our family was all we had."

"He should be married now," his father interjected. "Starting a family, giving us grandchildren."

Ash sighed and closed his eyes as he tried to calm himself down, this was the reason he'd tried to keep to himself. The fact that he had a good job, and kept himself out of trouble just wasn't enough for his father, and every time they talked, it eventually ended up with marriage and children.

"Leave him be," his grandfather defended. "He'll marry when he is ready. I remember you not wanting to get married so early, all the arguments and the sulking we got from you." He winked at Ash as his father grunted and pulled the paper back up.

Someone knocked at the back door and he stood and walked into the kitchen, pleased to be able to get away from his father. His mother stood at the door, talking to their neighbour when he entered and she stood holding a hot pan of soup.

"It's funny…" his neighbour smiled. "It was John that wanted that wood burning fire instead of the normal fire, but I guess it's a good idea now. Mind you, I won't admit that to him." She nodded towards her house as she said him, "But you're all welcome to come over if you get too cold."

"Thank you very much, Barbara, this is very kind of you." His mother put the hot pan on the kitchen work surface.

"Oh its no problem at all, I'll pop round later with some hot water for you before bed, just knock if you need anything in the mean time. See you later."

He could smell the soup as it wafted from the pot and he salivated at the thought of something warm in his stomach. "Is there anything I can do to help Ma?" he asked eagerly to speed up the process.

"It's freezing in here," Paddy moaned as he trudged into the classroom that would be their sleeping quarters for the mission, dragging his kitbag behind him. "And it smells of cabbages."

"Calm down, Paddy, will you, we're still setting up. Give me a hand setting the room up for the cots," said Kate.

"I don't do the cold," he muttered as he dropped his pack and started to move the chairs out of the way. "I need the Sun and the warmth I do, I get colds easy. I can't be doing with this ice and snow crap."

She watched him as he threw the chairs into a pile in the corner, he'd been depressed all day, and she could see the anger welling up inside him.

"Where the hell is the heating?" Paddy shouted to no one in particular.

"Calm down." She wanted to punch him. Everyone felt the

cold, and his complaining was starting to make her angry.

A soldier walked in carrying a small stove heater that he placed on the floor before opening the window to push the plastic chimney out, much to the disgust of Paddy.

"Just hurry up," he barked. "You're letting the cold in."

"Hold on, buddy, the generators have fused. You're lucky to have the heater."

"I don't care, just get a move on with it then and stop talking."

"Oh don't you worry yourself." He turned away as he pushed the chimney stack into the rear of the stove. "I know you *ARAB's* need your heat."

"What did you say?" Paddy exploded, jumping up as he approached the new comer, his chest all fluffed up for a fight. "Listen you *STAB*," Paddy spat. "Get your arse out of here before I stick my gun so far up it, next time you fart you'll blow your head off." He stood with his shoulders pulled back like an angry pigeon. His unimpressive five foot six stature had given him a chip on his shoulder that often got them into trouble.

"Enough!" Marcus bellowed from the doorway. "If you've that much energy Paddy you can get yourself outside and help fill the sandbags, and you!" he turned to the soldier who had the misfortune to have been smiling. "Get out of here and get that generator working. Now!"

Kate liked Marcus, he was a good solid leader, and he wasn't afraid to bark you down when he needed to. The look on his face said, don't push me, and she almost felt sorry for the soldier as he rushed to the door.

"Yes sir." He saluted. "Sorry sir."

Paddy stared at the soldier as he left before punching a desk, his face red with anger as he clenched and unclenched his fists.

"What's wrong with you?" Marcus barked as he twisted him physically round to face him, but he just kept on staring at his feet.

"Sorry, Boss," he eventually mumbled, still not lifting his head, he looked like he was crying, but she couldn't be sure from this angle.

"No one wants to be here, Paddy, but you need to make the best of a bad situation. Are you hearing me?"

Paddy finally looked up as he gained control of his anger. "I know." He saluted. "Sorry, Marcus."

"That's better, now get some rest." Marcus nodded to Kate as he left, shutting the door behind him.

She watched Paddy for a few moments as he stood there fidgeting, she could tell there was something deeper behind the outburst, but couldn't put her finger on what might have caused it. He started to talk as she unfolded the first sleeping cot.

"I was gonna propose," his voice was quiet and broken, "I got the ring and everything, it was supposed to be the best Christmas ever." She hated the way people had to unload their problems, a need to tell someone whatever was on their mind. She didn't normally get involved in personal issues unless she was making fun of them, but for some reason, Paddy wanted to open up to her. Why me, she thought to herself.

"Listen," she tried to sound supportive, "If the Green Slime's right, this isn't going to be a long assignment. The power should be back on in a few days and you can get back to her, nothings wasted."

"I guess you're right." He nodded. "I just set myself up for it, you know I wanted to do it right, to do it proper so it lasted, I even spoke to her father a few weeks ago, actually asked for his permission."

"You never asked me you sod." Kate threw a sock at him in mock anger. "But If you want to get married, I guess I can spare ten minutes," she continued. "Nine minutes for the service, forty seconds to get undressed and twenty seconds to consummate it."

"No offence, Kate, but I wanted to marry a lady." Paddy ducked as the other sock sailed towards him.

"Don't make me shoot you." She stood up, relieved to see the humour appearing back on his face, and in a rare show of compassion, she put her arm around his shoulder. "Are you gonna be okay?" she asked with honest concern.

"Yeah," he nodded. "Thanks, Kate. I guess you're right. This shouldn't be a long deployment. Don't tell the others though," he whispered as the rest of the squad entered.

"Sure thing." She patted him on the shoulder and moved back to the cot.

"What have we disturbed here?" Pierce nudged John.

"Must be lovers," he smirked. "Paddy and Kate sitting in a tree…" he sang.

"Just shut up and unpack," she laughed.

"Are you bunking in with us then, Kate?" John asked raising his eyebrows.

"Well there's no way I'm getting undressed in this cold, so don't get excited."

"No worries there, Kate," John smirked. "Pierce here has started to develop a nice pair of boobs on his own."

"You cheeky sod." Pierce smacked him with his pack.

"It's your move." Ashfaq nodded to his brother, satisfied that his piece was protected. His brother scratched his forehead as he thought. It wasn't really much of a match, he'd been playing chess for years, but his brother was only just learning, so every now and then, he'd let a piece fall to him.

Checkmate could be in five moves, but he played another piece instead, anything to pass the time. The conversation drifted in from the other room and he stopped to listen. His father was obviously moaning about him again to anyone who would listen.

He'd tried to explain that the world was different from the way it was for his father, and that marriage in Pakistan was more about building bonds between your neighbour or business partner than love. It wasn't that he was totally against arranged marriages either, they worked for some people, some of his closest friends had recently got married and they seemed to be happy.

He had tried. He'd met with the girls his parents had arranged, but he wanted to marry someone who liked the same things he liked. He'd come into the back room to get away from his father and his constant bickering. It would have been so much easier if he could have gone out instead.

"Are they at it again, Abujee?" he asked his grandfather as he walked in.

"Indeed they are my boy, indeed they are."

He coughed at his brother and nodded towards the door and he obediently stood up and left the room. His grandfather closed the door behind him before returning to the table and sitting down.

"Whose move is it?" he asked as he looked over the chessboard.

"I guess it's yours now."

"This is a bit of a messy board," he observed absentmindedly as he looked it over.

"Why do they always push me to get married?" Ash asked.

"Before I answer, tell me this." His grandfather smiled. "Why do you play chess with your brother when you know you could beat him easily?"

"I play so he can learn."

"Is that the only reason?"

"I suppose..." He paused as he thought about it. "I play because the more he learns the better he'll be."

"You play with him because you're bored," his grandfather stated. "It's nothing about teaching him. You're bored, plain and simple." He moved a piece. "And so is your father. He misses children round the house. You're all getting older now. He wants to be a grandfather, and feel young again as he plays with his grandchildren."

Ash sat silently staring at the board. It was true that his father had started to push him to get married only a few years ago, just after his brother had turned thirteen.

"So my father wants grandkids?" He looked at his grandfather.

"Yes," he smiled in reply. "Oh, don't get me wrong. He wants to see you grow up into a fine man and father too, but he misses the sounds of laughter in the house. So do I." He rubbed his chin. "All we have now is loud music and mobile phones." He lent forward and ruffled his hair. "So don't be too hard on him. He has your best interests at heart."

Kate finished rebuilding her rifle, and slid the magazine home with a satisfying click.

"Are you finally done?" Pierce called from his cot, bored from watching her getting ready. "It's true, women are always last."

"We might be last, but we're worth waiting for." She smiled as she stood up, hefting her pack over her shoulder. "How many magazines you planning to take?" she asked.

"Marcus said one should be okay. Why? Are you taking more?"

"Hell yeah, I like to be prepared. It might be more weight, but I feel better about it. Remember Basra?"

"You won't let me forget that, will you?" he laughed.

"And I never will. If you can carry it, take it, that's my motto." She picked up the remaining magazines from her cot and slipped them into her webbing.

"Fine." Pierce dropped more of his clips into his backpack and slipped it over his shoulders.

"What else you got in there?" Kate called as she walked towards the door.

"Food, dear Kate, I get hungry when I walk."

"Alright then," Marcus called impatiently as they enter the hall. "Everyone's finally here I see. A few things before we start. The dinner hall has been dedicated as an infirmary."

Kate absentmindedly looked round the group as he talked. It was the usual pre-operation briefing, something most of them had heard a hundred times before.

Paddy sat on the stage with his helmet on his knees, and he brushed his hands through his tangled black hair as he listened to Marcus. He was still too young to have the full experience of the others, but he was a pro compared to the two recruits they'd been assigned.

Brian and Mike stood sharp and ready, listening to every word Marcus said like good little puppies, even their uniforms looked shiny and new.

Glen hung around at the rear, he was an experienced medic and a good man in a fight and she'd worked with him on many patrols. His square chin and rough demeanour were a total contrast to his bedside manner and skill.

"Alright then," Marcus was still talking as she drifted back into listening. "The power remains out, so it's going to be a dark and cold out there, but that's nothing we didn't expect. Just try to keep the shamoolie's and glow sticks to minimal use... oh and do try to keep together." He looked at the new guys. "I don't want to have to search for anyone who can't follow the route, and just for you, because I saw the look in your face, a shamoolie is a flare."

"Two units of four: Kate, Paddy, Glen and Brian are team one; myself, John, Pierce and Mike are team two. You all have your patrol zones and try to detain rather than kill. If you run into any problems, fire the red flare. We have eyes on the roof able to offer extra support from base if required. Our patrols will cross every hour. Keep safe." He nodded. "Let's move."

Ash slammed his door and sat down on his bed. His father had ignored him when he'd tried to talk to him and just grunted from behind his newspaper, not even looking at him as he'd tried to explain.

At the end of the day there was only such much he was prepared to try, so he had left him to his paper and come back to his room to read. He picked up the Qur'an. but decided he wasn't in the right frame of mind, so he pulled his car magazines from his shelf instead. Maybe he'd have better luck talking later on.

The cold hit them as soon as they left the school. He'd thought it was cold inside, but now realised how very wrong he'd been. With a nod to Kate, Marcus pulled his scarf up over his nose and led his patrol on. It surprised him how quiet everything was. The snow muffled almost everything and his boots sounded unnaturally loud as he walked.

Candles burnt in windows as they passed, and if it wasn't for the burnt out cars, it might have been a festive scene. They walked in silence for some time, just taking in the majesty of the snow filled world around them. He smiled as he realised that anyone outside would leave an easy trail to follow, maybe this wouldn't be so bad after all.

The first hour passed quickly and it wasn't long before he spotted Kate and her group ahead. They'd stopped on the corner, taking an impromptu break as they waited for him to join them. Glen and Paddy stood to the side, smoking like chimneys, dancing on their feet to try to keep their blood moving.

"There's nothing to report so far." Kate shivered as she spoke. "Other than the feckin cold."

"Same here," he nodded. "All's quiet on the western front then." A door opened behind them and they turned, a little old lady waved to them from her doorway.

"Can I help you?" Marcus called as he forced the gate open against the snow and made his way up her path. "You're not supposed to be outside, love."

"Oh, I know that, dear." She smiled as he approached, "I just wondered if you'd like a cup of tea dear." Her voice was quiet, with a slight Scottish accent.

"That would be very kind of you," Kate called before Marcus could decline the offer. She walked up behind him and he turned to look at her. "It would be very rude not to accept, Marcus," she explained with a smirk.

Despite the three pairs of socks he was wearing he could feel the cold, and the thought of a cup of tea made his mouth salivate, so he nodded his agreement to Kate. "That would be very kind of you, thank you."

"Can I offer a hand?" Kate stepped past him.

"A lady soldier?" the old lady smiled. "Now I didn't expect that. I would be grateful of the help dear, if you don't mind." She took Kate's hand and led her back into the house. "I'm a little bored to be honest," she continued. "I can only do so much knitting by candlelight before my eyes start to go."

"Take five guys." He turned to the rest of the squad. "Try to keep the noise down though." He felt conscious that every sound they made echoed off the snow, though most people had closed their windows to keep what heat they could inside, he didn't want any complaints about their noise.

Ten minutes later they gave their thanks to Ethel, and continued on with their patrol. Kate had promised to knock on her door as they passed, just to check on her and make sure she was okay.

They'd passed each other twice before the snow finally stopped. They'd been offered sandwiches and hot chocolate from the odd house they passed, but most people had stayed silently inside.

"Twelve o'clock and all is well," Mike whispered.

"It's not that well," Pierce called back as they walked on. "I can't feel my privates."

Ashfaq didn't feel the talk had gone as well as he'd hoped, and he wished he'd not tried again now. He knew he shouldn't have been pulled into the argument, but his father just knew how to wind him up.

He'd tried to understand, tried to explain that he understood, but his father hadn't stopped shouting long enough for him to get a word in edgeways. He'd ended up storming out of the room, slamming the door behind him, which in hindsight wasn't the best course of action to take either, but he'd been so angry he just needed to get out.

So now, he sat alone in the living room. He read the Qur'an as he calmed himself down, searching for what insight it could offer. He felt ashamed at allowing himself to get angry, even Abujee had left the room when they started to shout again.

His father was sitting alone in the front room and he knew he should go and talk to him, but he feared the outcome. They were both still angry with each other, both too hot headed. He had his head in the present; his father was in the past. He calmed himself once more, breathing slowly before he carefully turned the page and continued to read.

Marcus could feel the frost cutting into his feet and he stamped his boots on the ground to dislodge the snow before trying to wriggle life back into his toes. Their shift would be over soon, a chance to get some warmth back before they settled down for some well earned sleep. The night had been quiet as expected, and the only enemy they faced so far was boredom.

They were about ten minutes from the rendezvous point when a rumbling sound reverberated in the air causing them all to stop. He could hear what sounded like a heavy lorry racing towards them and Marcus signalled to his squad to hold.

"Where is that coming from?" It was defiantly the sound of a truck, a sixteen wheeler he thought, maybe more. The houses started to shake in the distance, and their windows rattled before he realised it wasn't a truck but an earthquake.

Dislodged snow fell from the streetlight as the quake passed them by, its direction no longer in question, it had come from near the centre of the city.

"What you want to do, Boss?" Pierce shouted as he cocked his weapon.

"Nothing we can do, just stay ready and keep the people

inside." He knew the order was the right one, but something huge must have made that shockwave, and not having radio contact to find out made him nervous. "Let's move on."

The silence that followed the shockwave settled over the streets, and every footstep sounded louder than before but it wasn't long before they heard the first faint pop of a flare.

"Over there," John pointed down the street. In the distance a red flare slowly floated to the ground, he waited for a green confirmation flare, but nothing happened.

"Give me a leg up," Marcus shouted as he ran for a telegraph pole, "I need to gain height". As he reached the top rung a second red flare rose into the sky before him. "I can see two reds so far," he called down. "They're approximately two miles away."

He held his breath as he waited for a green to show support, but another flare went up like a firework into the sky, and another red shamoolie fell slowly to the earth, then another. He held on, watching as the skyline lit up with red flares, more and more and they seemed to be coming slowly closer.

"What the ..?." he hissed under his breathe. In the five minutes he'd been watching, over thirty flares had gone up in the distance, all of them red. Gunfire could now be heard. Sporadic bursts of automatic fire before they fell suddenly silent again. He quickly climbed down.

He checked his ammo. "Something's terribly wrong out there, and it's coming our way." The next flare was close, so close it had to be from Kate's team, and Marcus didn't hesitate to take action. They moved quickly through the empty streets, and caught sight of Kate's unit before the flare had time to land and they ran up behind them.

A small shadow detached itself from a garden further up the street and Kate fired without hesitation, lifting the shape clean off its feet, spinning it backwards into the snow.

"She's shot a kid," Pierce shouted in disbelief and Kate span round, rifle raised and ready, before relaxing as she recognised them.

"Get Paddy, we'll cover you." She pointed down the street. A shape could be seen lying in the gutter and Marcus signalled for Mike and John to go forward as he pulled Kate to the side.

"What the hell is going on?" he demanded. "All I can see are red flares." Kate looked flustered which wasn't a normal thing for her. He'd seen her in action many times in Basra and even during some of the more serious encounters, she hadn't looked like this.

"Kate!" he shouted, snapping her out of her thoughts. "Report?"

"We..." she stammered. "We watched the first flares go up so we held here. Paddy saw a kid walking down the street so he ran to help him, but it wasn't a kid, it jumped at him, screeching and clawing. It stabbed him before he had a chance to raise his weapon." She looked down at the snow. "Then more came charging at us." She shook her head. "Whatever they are, they aren't kids, Marcus. They aren't kids."

John and Mike dragged Paddy back and lay him in the snow but there was no time to help him before the alarm was shouted.

"Here come some more!" someone shouted from the shadows. Shapes moved against the snow but they looked different from the things that had attacked, larger and slower.

"Hold you fire, Hold you fire," Pierce shouted waving his hand. "They're civilians." A group of twenty or so people ran silently into view, either too scared, or too cold to shout, some held children as they ran to escape the horrors behind them.

"John. Get one of these doors open," he pointed to the houses at their side. "Get these people off the streets."

"Which one?"

"Any one," he snapped angrily.

Nodding at his own stupidity, John ran down the closest driveway, banging hard on the door. No one answered so he pulled his sidearm and fired, shattering the glass inwards before reaching in and opening the door. He vanished inside and it was a tense few seconds before he re-appeared waving his hand.

"Get inside," Marcus shouted to the civilians, but they didn't move, unsure what to do as their fear took over and shut their brain down. So he grabbed the nearest one, dragging him to the driveway and almost threw him through the door. "Get inside now." He fired into the cold air and they jumped at the crack of the round but they started to move inside.

"Kate, you see anything."

"Not yet." She didn't turn round but kept her eyes focused on the end of the street.

"John, I need you to get the civilians inside, give us covering fire from the upstairs window. Glen, get Paddy in and see if you can help him. Pierce!"

"Yes, Boss," he shouted from across the street.

"Take Jason forward ten metres, if you see anything, hold them as long as you can then get back here. Mike, cover the rear, Twenty metres out." He watched as the flare slowly descended behind a house and Pierce signalled he was firing another. It arced into the night, flashing brightly before the chute deployed and it slowly came back to earth. Kate turned her back to the car, rested on her haunches, her forehead touching the barrel of her rifle as she cradled it before her.

Even though she was a professional soldier, sometimes the human inside climbed to the surface, and in a fire fight, there are lots of emotions to deal with. He was just about to say something when the crackle of gunfire brought them quickly back into a ready position.

"Here they come!" Pierce shouted as they ran into view, their boots churned the snow as they raced back to the cars. Marcus watched as Jason lost his footing, landing hard on his back, his gun sliding from his hands to the side of the road.

"Jason!" Marcus screamed in alarm, but Pierce was already too far ahead to go back, the only chance he had was if they could give him time to catch his breath. As the first thing came into range Kate dropped it, the round going clean through its torso, lifting it from its feet and throwing it lifeless to the snow. More appeared behind it and were cut down as quickly as the first. Jason rolled onto his side and was pushing himself to a standing position when almost a hundred streamed round the corner.

Marcus could do nothing but watch as they swarmed around

him, dragging him to the ground. Jason threw himself towards his weapon, but was swallowed by the sheer number of attackers and his scream filled the air. Marcus flipped to full automatic and fired until his clip ran dry.

When Ash opened his eyes his candle had gone out and he realised he'd must have fallen asleep. He shivered in the darkness and he wondered what had disturbed him. As he reached to light another candle he brushed the box with his fingers and knocked them over the arm of the sofa onto the floor.

He moaned to himself as he stood and pulled the sofa forward so he could find them. He knelt down and started to rub his hand over the carpet, trying to locate them in the darkness as the front door banged loudly and he jumped, banging his back on something in the darkness. He could hear his father shouting as he made his way to open it.

"Hello. Who's there?" he heard him shout angrily, and Ash stopped his searching to listen. It was probably the army doing a check up or something, he figured, he'd seen the patrols going past a few times during the night and felt pleased that his father was angry at someone else for a change.

A sound from the hallway made him stop and the floor shook as something heavy hit it and seconds later the backroom door clicked open. There was something stood in the doorway, he couldn't see it, but he could feel it. From his position behind the sofa he heard a hiss and he froze, every hair on his body stood on end until he heard the footsteps running upstairs. His heartbeat pounded heavily in his chest. He tried to remain quiet, to remain hidden from whatever was in the house.

They attacked in their hundreds and his rifle glowed red as the bullets tore into flesh and bone, all thoughts and worries gone from him now as the heat of the battle drew him on. "Ammo!" Marcus shouted "I need Ammo!"

"Here." Kate threw a magazine at him before continuing to fire. He reloaded and joined the fight once more, the snow before them melted as the hot blood of the dead flowed towards the gutters. A small group of the things skittered along the gardens to their left, trying to get around behind them, but Glen fired from the upstairs window across the street and cut them down. A heavy hand landed on his shoulder and he span round.

"Easy." Ken fired over him. "I need you to get everyone into the house. I'll lead them off and swing back to you when I can."

"There's too many of them," he objected.

"That's why you need to get inside; keep low and out of sight or your ammo will run out." He reloaded. "When the grenades go off, you move."

Marcus didn't see any point in arguing, the facts were clear enough. He knew if they stayed, they would eventually be overrun and everyone would die, so he signalled Ken's intentions to the rest.

"Good luck." Marcus grasped his hand for a second and silent words passed between them. Ken threw his empty machine gun to the side and pulled two grenades from his webbing, the pins arced into the air before he hurled the grenades towards the enemy. Marcus watched them bounce along the road before exploding in a shower of shrapnel and fire, decimating the ranks of creatures as they surged towards them.

Ash was gasping for breath; his asthma felt like someone was sitting on his chest, crushing him slowly. He'd heard the screams of his sister upstairs. The sobs of his family as they were dragged out into the darkness and their screams continued to echo round his head.

The house was silent now as though nothing had happened. A cold breeze blew in through the open door freezing him as he hid, but still he couldn't move, his body rooted to the spot with fear as tears ran down his face. He felt dizzy as the oxygen reduced in his lungs and he slowly passed into a fitful sleep, filled with shadows and death.

"Upstairs," Marcus commanded as the door banged open, bounced hard against the wall. "Move!" He slammed the door closed behind them and pressed his back against it, waiting for the thud as the creatures tried to follow them, but nothing came. Once they'd secured the landing he followed, shouting instructions as he ran.

"Kate, cover the front windows but keep low, no firing unless I give the order. Pierce, take the back. The rest of you find something to block the stairway with. Move." He knelt at the top of the stairs, aiming at the door, waiting for them to come.

He saw movement outside, dark shapes against the whiteness of the snow and he held his breathe, ready to kill anything that tried to enter, but they moved on. John appeared behind him dragging a wardrobe from one of the rooms and Mike helped him push it over the banister. It crashed onto the stairs below and slid down until it pressed against the door, jamming it in place.

"Good, keep it up." He patted them on the back. "I need this stairwell sealed. Nothing gets up here without us knowing about it, we're going to hold here for the night."

Glen shook his head as he entered. "I'm sorry Marcus. There was nothing I could do." He pulled a bed sheet over Paddy's face. "The wound was too deep, without surgery I…"

"You did what you could," Marcus stopped him; there was no need for blame.

"What's going on?" Glen asked the question on everyone's lips, and he wished he had a better answer.

"I don't know," he shrugged. "We lost Jason, damn things just swept over him like he wasn't there." He could feel the adrenaline surging in his body after the fight and he needed to use it before it was gone. "Check the rest of the civilians for wounds; make sure they're settled in." Glen nodded silently as he turned and left.

Kate sat looking out of the window; at least ten people huddled silently in the corner of the room behind her. "How much ammo you got?" Marcus whispered from the doorway.

"I've another five in there." She pointed to her backpack by the side of the car outside. "Three clips on me though." She pulled one free and tossed it over.

"Is there any movement out there?"

"Nothing but red flares." Kate stopped him as he turned to leave, "Check Pierce. He had more clips in his pack, food too."

"Thanks," he nodded.

"How's Paddy?" she asked. He just shook his head as he left, they didn't have time to mourn yet. No one did.

"Mike, take first watch here." He walked onto the landing, already planning the operation. "If anything moves down stairs, shoot first and ask questions later, if it's Ken he'll let you know before hand." He turned to Pierce, "Kate says you're packing extra ammo and food."

"Yeah," he nodded. "I've got maybe another six clips and a handful of iron rations."

"Share out the ammo as best you can, we're going to sit this one out until dawn."

Dawn finally came to the world and the gull sat in the guttering of an old warehouse where it had slept the night. It could smell fresh meat in the air, not the normal meat that it was used to, but sweeter meat, mixed with the smell of fire and fear.

Nothing felt right. The noise of the day was missing and the smells in the air had changed, there was a crisp fresh feeling to everything, as though the world was holding its breath, waiting to see what would happen next. But all that was lost on the gull, food was its first and only thought and it beat its powerful wings against the cold frigid air and rose slowly into the dawn sky.

Philip woke. His body felt sluggish and numb and his head felt like it had been beaten with a large bar, every movement caused pain to flash behind his eyeballs. He tried to stand but his legs gave way and he fell back to the chair, groaning loudly as he vomited noisily onto the floor.

He wiped his face with his hands, but they shook so much that he only managed to spread it further across his chin. He retched again, splashing more sick into the already steaming puddle on his carpet and he could feel more rising. He tried to swallow air to stop it, but failed.

The room stank, and the acrid smell turned his stomach. He didn't want to try to stand again just yet, but he needed water, something to wash the taste from his mouth. He compromised by sliding onto the floor, narrowly missing the still warm puddle of sick with his hands as he slowly crawled towards the kitchen.

He pulled himself up on the counter, reaching forward with shaking hands towards the sink, the tap and the water.

When he woke a thin trickle of bile dripped from the work surface onto the floor near his face. He groaned as he forced himself to his knees, feeling better now, he managed to stand and fill his glass with water.

As he dabbed a tissue at his bleeding nose, he tried to recall why he'd drunk so much. His mind wanted to flash back to Friday morning, but something wasn't right, there was a section of his memory that was missing. Suddenly the image of Jenny flashed before his eyes and he staggered to the bedroom, hoping to find her still in bed, but the room was empty.

Grabbing a can of Red Bull from his defunct fridge he drank deeply as he wandered back to the window, resting his hand on the frame as he pulled the curtain back and looked out. "No!" he cried as he staggered back, dropping into his chair. "No, that's not right." He felt the shock coming, the memories flooded back, but the image of the devastation outside would be etched into his memory for the rest of his life.

Marcus jumped as Kate shook him. He'd stayed on watch at the front window until the first signs of dawn, but now, with the adrenaline gone, he felt tired and lethargic.

"It's getting light," she smiled. "You told me to wake you."

"Thanks, Kate," he nodded. "Can you wake everyone; I want to get back to base to report in. See what Intel we have."

"What should we do with Paddy?"

"Nothing." He shook his head. "We'll have to leave him here for now; we can come back later and pick him up."

"Rodger that," was all she said before leaving him to wake up. He rubbed his eyes before pushing himself from the floor and looked out onto the streets below. Hell had certainly arrived in time for Christmas.

"Everyone's ready?" he called five minutes later. No one had really been able to sleep, and everyone seemed eager to get going. So with a nod he turned and grabbed his rifle before walking back onto the hallway.

"Glen, I need you to stay here and protect the civilians for the moment."

He started to object but Marcus raised his hand.

"If the way to the HQ is clear, I'll send someone back to lead you in. The civilians are our priority at the moment." He could see he wasn't happy but there was no way he wanted civilians coming back with him, not yet. "Everyone else is with me."

The streets were littered with bodies, the odd human lay amongst the others. Further down the street he could see the bulkier shape of Brian, a fine layer of snow mercifully covering his remains.

"Hold here." He stepped out onto the road, walking slowly over to the unmoving form of his comrade before kneeling besides him and brushed the snow from his face.

There wasn't much left to look at, Marcus had seen lots of wounds before, sucking chest wounds and shrapnel damage, but this was different, white bone protruded from the broken flesh of his face and his eyes were missing, torn roughly from their sockets.

Taking care not to disturb him any further, he reached under Brian's blood stained jacket and removed his tags. He could see a number of the creatures lying nearby, and as he grabbed Brian's rifle he walked over to the closest one. It lay on its back, thick dark blood clotted in the snow around it as its large black eyes stared unblinkingly towards the sky.

Brushing the snow from its face with his boot he pulling its mouth open, two rows of darkly stained teeth, sharp and cruel, filled its mouth and with a shudder he left it where it lay. Turning back to what remained of his squad he signalled to move on and ran to catch them up.

● ● ● ● ● ● ● ● ●

The gull searched for food as it flew slowly over the city. It could see people below, but they didn't move as much as they had before. Warm thermals carried the sweet smell of flesh up to it from the many fires below, everything felt new, different but also the same.

It landed on a silent street and it started to feast on the crisp flesh of a body, pulling the outer skin away before it feasted on the soft flesh below, gorging itself on the waste of society. The fingers twitching involuntarily as it pulled on dead tendons as it dug deeper into the carcass.

Philip opened the door slightly and nervously peered outside. The noon Sun had done little to raise the heat of the day much beyond freezing and he pulled his coat firmly round himself as he edged his way down the steps into the yard.

The silence was so un-natural he could feel it in his soul, and it filled him with fear. He was ready to jump at the slightest signs of danger and by the time he finally reached the street, his heart was racing. He'd glimpsed the carnage from his window, but the full reality was much worse, closer and so much more real than he could ever have imagined. He closed his eyes as he composed himself, drawing from inside what strength he could before finally stepping out onto the quiet street.

Tears ran down his face as he passed the body of a young woman. She lay prone on the road before him, her clothing soaked in blood from cruel cuts that ran deeply along her back. He couldn't understand how they'd happened during the power surge, or why no one had covered her, no paramedics had tended to her and no police could be seen. He had no set plan. No place to aim for, just anywhere other than here. There must be somewhere safe he thought, somewhere with all the people.

"Get away," Ash screamed as he charged and he hurled the stone at the bird. The gull screeched as it flapped its wings and flew out of sight. "Get away," he repeated, weaker this time, his voice sounding hoarse now with terror and exhaustion. He reached the body and rolled it over, feeling the relief as he realised it wasn't one of his family.

He wiped his hands absentmindedly on his coat before he walked on, moving from one body to the next as he continued to search fruitlessly for any signs of them. The image of the night before continued to jump unbidden back into his mind.

Why had he stayed hidden, why hadn't he tried to help, why had he let them go? He could still hear them screaming in his mind as they were dragged out into the night. He'd stayed behind the sofa all night, his urine being the only heat his body would supply. He'd hidden there for an hour after dawn before finally building the courage to crawl into the hallway, it was then he'd found his father.

"I will find them," he promised as he cradled his father's head in his lap, tears running freely down his face. "I will find them." He'd buried him in a shallow grave in the back garden, his hands cut and blistered from digging as he passed what prayer he could over him. He was unsure at first on what direction to take, so he scouted around for signs of movement, but the snow seemed to be trampled everywhere and there was no clear path to follow.

When he'd found his neighbours body he'd realised he must be on the right path. She'd been a nice lady, always looking out for people, ready to help if anyone ever needed anything. Now she lay in the snow with her throat ripped open, but he was numb to the dead by then.

The sight of so much blood seemed to have caused his brain to click off. Now his eyes felt just as dead as the people around him. His stomach rumbled loudly, and he realised how hungry he actually was and he didn't pause as he heaved the dustbin through the front glass window of a nearby shop.

The snow crunched under his boots as Marcus led the squad silently down the road and he could see he wasn't the only one trying to rationalise the previous night. In a combat situation, you have a clear cut reason, either to protect something there, or someone back home, or just the fact that what you were doing was the right thing to do.

But now the rules didn't seem to apply. The world that they knew had broken, and this battle was on home ground and the usual command structure was non-existent. With the power out, the enemy had certainly chosen the perfect time to attack and he realised he would have to be the strong one until they could figure out what to do next.

"Listen up," he called. "The school's half a mile away so keep sharp. I know it's been a tough night, but just remember it's not over yet, we can't afford to let our guard down."

As the school came into view it was obvious there was something wrong. Smoke billowed from the windows on one side and no one manned the gates. It didn't look good, and the thought of approaching head on made him apprehensive, so he signalled them to group for instructions.

"I need this entrance to be by the book." He looked at each of them as he spoke. "I want a room by room sweep, but don't be trigger happy. We don't know what's inside, it could be our guys and we don't have enough ammo for a sustained fight."

"Three might be more of those things in there," Kate stated as she cocked her weapon. "I owe them for Paddy."

"And Jason as well," Mike reminded her.

"We will have time for revenge once we've established ourselves. The battle isn't over yet and I can guess they are going to be back tonight. Let's get this over with and collect supplies from here. I don't want to lose anyone else today. So I want Kate and Pierce to cover the left, Mike and John the right, and I'll go down the middle. Now move."

The glass in the doors had been smashed and four of the creatures lay dead at the side, bullet holes covered the woodwork as Marcus pushed them open, wincing as it creaked loudly. No one talked; no one asked questions, the simple fact now was to survive. At his signal they moved silently inside.

Ash ate a sparse and cold breakfast as he huddled in the doorway of the shop. Although it was slightly warmer inside, it felt weird, dark and scary now that everything was off, so he'd filled a bag with biscuits, cakes and fruit, and got back out again as quickly as he could. It wasn't the healthiest meal he'd ever had, but at least it was something.

He started to weep again as thoughts of his family filled his mind. When he was home he'd liked to be alone, to stay in his room out of the way, but he'd always known they were close. Now he was totally alone and he didn't like it. He sniffed and wiped his nose on the back of his sleeve.

"Mum says that breaking stuff is bad." The small voice was so close to him that he jumped, dropping the snack onto this lap. No more than three feet away a small child stood in blue slippers and a fleecy dressing gown, he looked cold and wet and he shivered as he stood there watching him.

"Why are you sad?" The boy lent his head to one side and stared at him, Ash didn't know what to say and eventually, the child continued. "My name is Tommy, Tommy Houghton, I'm almost six years old," he said proudly. "Have you seen my mum?"

Ash stared at him; he'd wandered for hours and seen no other signs of life and suddenly a child had found him. There seemed to be no fear in Tommy's eyes, no panic at all at being alone and he continued to talk.

"Can I have some chocolate?" He peered into the shopping bag. "My mum says I shouldn't eat chocolate for breakfast but I'm hungry."

"Sure..." Ash handed him the bag. "We won't tell your mum though. Okay?" He smiled.

"Thanks." Tommy shivered. Ash sat looking at him, wondering what to do next. He seemed like a nice enough kid, and he couldn't leave him like this. Not cold and shivering on the streets.

"Tommy. Have you ever heard the sound of a window breaking?" he smiled.

Ten minutes later they were both sat on the curb again, but now Tommy wore clean warm winter clothes. Ash smiled as he watched him munch his way through his second packet of crisps. "Are you warmer now?"

Tommy nodded enthusiastically as he ate.

"Don't eat so fast, there's no rush." It was nice to have some company, to not be alone.

"Why did you look for your mum here?" It was possible he'd seen her. She could easily have been any one of the bodies he'd passed already, but it obviously wasn't worth saying that to him.

"Dunno really." He shook his head as he ate. "My dad put me to bed cause me mum works at night, but she's always home when I wake up. But this morning she never came to get me." He looked down at his feet as he talked, kicking the snow with the toe of his new boots. "I got out of bed and looked for her but she must have gone out, so I walked to my auntie's on the next street, but she wasn't in... Then I thought she might be shoppin', she likes shoppin' does my mum, my dad says it's her hobby," he explained. "But she wasn't here either, and then I met you." Tommy stopped talking long enough to take a drink from a carton of juice.

Ash was finding it hard to keep track of the conversation but found he was smiling for the first time that day, he was starting to like this little fellow and the more he spoke the more he settled on him.

"My auntie is very big," Tommy stated. "She says it's all water, but my mum says that after my uncle died she just eats to make herself happy... I have a goldfish."

He knew he needed to travel fast if he was to stand any chance of catching up with his family and Tommy would only slow him down. He sat watching him, realising that it would have been better if they'd never met, but he couldn't leave him, not now. "Come on Tommy," he smiled. "Let's look for you mum together should we?"

Philip didn't know what else to do, so he wandered aimlessly towards the centre of town. Someone would be in at the pub, he reasoned, he could have a beer and find out what had happened to everyone else. Maybe this was all some sort of nasty joke; maybe there were cameras watching him right now.

"Hello!" he shouted. "Anyone here?" His voice echoed off the damaged buildings and the silence that followed panicked him, the streets should be bustling with people but everyone had gone. What could have happened? Where are the police and the soldiers?

The pieces in his mind didn't fit, didn't match any known plan or understanding he had. People didn't just vanish, it just didn't happen. He stopped for a moment next to a smouldering car and as he warmed his hands, he spotted the shadow. It only moved a little, but it was enough to confirm it wasn't his imagination.

"Hey!" his voice squeaking with excitement as he shouted, "Hey, you. Where is everyone? What's happened?" The shadow detached itself from the doorway and moved slowly towards him; half staggering, half stumbled as it approached. Philip panicked, was it a zombie? Had they attacked like he'd seen in so many movies? It stopped as he backed away before it fell to its knees sobbing uncontrollably. He didn't know what to do, but he relaxed a little. To his knowledge zombies didn't cry.

"Hey it's okay." He lowered himself down beside him as he tried to reassure him. "It's okay."

"It's my fault," the man sobbed. "I did nothing, nothing." Philip took him by the arm and pulled him to his feet, walking slowly with him, he lead him back to the doorway from which he'd appeared. As he got closer he could make out more movement inside, and the faint smell of coffee emanated from within.

"Hello!" he called as he walked the man inside. "Hello?" As his eyes grew accustomed to the gloom he started to see more people, most sat silently with their backs against the walls, some slept and other held each other silently.

"Welcome," a voice boomed from the rear, and a cheerful looking man in an apron appeared. He was balding and slightly overweight but carried himself with a solid stride and despite the many bandages that covered his arms, blood showed through in places. "Where you from then, lad, is anyone else with you?" he looked behind Philip but stopped when he realised he was alone and just nodded.

"My name's Donald." He held his hand out and Philip shook it. "Welcome, come in, are you hurt?" He looked him up and down, the cleaver that hung by his belt jangled as he moved. "Do you want a drink? Sure you do," he answered his own question. "Come on; let me get you something to warm you up."

Philip followed him through into the back room where a worktop had been converted into a make shift kitchen area. Two kettles steamed away over a set of small camping stoves and Donald picked one up and poured some hot water into a cup.

"Get that down you." He smiled as he passed it over. "It's a beef Oxo, add some pepper if you want." The drink was warm and steamy, and Philip stood with it cupped in his hands for a moment as he let the feeling of warmth spread through his fingers.

"Sorry." He put the cup down. "My name's Philip, and no, I'm not injured; just surprised to see people again, and to be honest you caught me a little off guard."

"He can be like that sometimes," a woman commented from the other side of the table. "A little overpowering at times, but he grows on you." She smiled as she wiped her hands on a towel.

"Shush now, Mabel." Donald smiled. "Well, Philip, you're the first man we've have seen today who isn't injured one way or another at least." He tapped his head to indicate not all injuries where on the outside. "Have you seen anyone else?"

"No, I'm sorry, not one else, but I don't understand."

"Understand what?" He motioned for him to sit down. "You're not hurt is what I meant, most of the men can't seem to adjust to it you see, they look like they've switched off. Trauma can do that to people sometimes, the survivor's guilt."

"I didn't mean that either," Philip stopped him. "I don't understand what's happened, who attacked?"

"What? You mean you missed it all?" Donald sat up in his

chair.

"Hold on... You're saying that there's more going on that just the power cuts?"

"Where the hell were you last night?"

"I was..." Philip paused but he needed to admit the truth. "I was drunk alright; it looks like I slept through everything."

"Well then." Donald slammed the chipped cleaver into the wood at his side. "I think I need to bring you up to speed."

They advanced silently down the corridor, desperately trying to avoid the broken glass and bits of plaster that might give warning to anything inside. Marcus held his weapon ready for the first signs of danger, but they reached the first junction without incident.

Five of the creatures lay dead before them, dark blood created iced pools on the cold floor and its surface cracked as they advanced over it. They moved forward slowly, clearing each classroom as they passed it.

In the third classroom they found the aftermath of a fierce battle. At least ten of the creatures lay dead inside, a score of bullet holes had been ripped into the children's pictures that hung from the walls. Marcus moved over to the remains of a soldier at the back of the room. He was on his back, his face a mass of blood, flesh and bone, only just visible as a human now. His shirt had been torn open were something had feasted on him, throwing his entrails around the room.

Marcus knelt and removed his tags, patting his pockets for ammo and supplies before signalling the others to move on. Mike stood close behind him, looking over his shoulder, shaking. "I think I know him..." He shook his head. "I mean, I knew him. We played pool last week, this is messed up." He held his head in his hands as he crouched next to his dead friend. "This isn't real. It can't be..." he sobbed.

Marcus was surprised he'd got them this far before the first broke. Everyone was on edge, and it was taking all of his training to keep himself from cracking up with them. He couldn't afford to lose control now. "Come on, Glen," he whispered as he put his hand on his shoulder, "We need to move on." But he didn't move, he just stared at the body sobbing quietly.

"Get up you wimp," Kate hissed as she grabbed him. "We won't get out of this unless we stay sharp and stick together. I know this is new to you, it's new to all of us, but we need to get out of here. So stand up, get your weapon, and help us get this done." Glen sniffed loudly and wiped his face with his hand before he picked up his rifle. He nodded to Marcus before walking out into the hallway beyond.

"They don't have enough experience," Kate grunted as she turned to follow him. Marcus watched her go, he knew she could be hard when she needed to be, you had to be in the army, especially if you were a woman. But sometimes her failure to tolerate human behaviour was a little too cold. He'd known her the longest in the unit, and wouldn't want anyone else covering him in a fire fight, but sometimes he just wished she'd back down a little.

Philip sat open mouthed as Donald proceeded to recount the events of the previous night, how it had all started with a rumbling noise that had woken him in the early hours.

"It must have been maybe half an hour after when I first heard banging at my door. I thought it was the soldiers, so Bessie and I," he patted his cricket bat that sat beside his chair, "Went down to see what was going on. It was a good job she came with me I can tell you. No sooner had I opened the door before two of these..." he tried to think of a word to describe them, "Things tried to jump me, it was dark and I guess I was lucky to be faced with only the two of them." He pulled his shirt aside, showing a deep wound in his shoulder. "They managed to cut me before I finished them." He drank from his cup in silence as he thought about the previous night. "Anyway," he continued, "I heard my neighbours screaming, so I went in swinging. I didn't think," he shrugged. "I just acted. Managed to kill them, but not before they'd killed my friends." He stared into his cup. "I didn't see any soldiers, but I did hear gun fire in the distance for a while. There must have been thousands of them, they dragged the people off to god knows where. Set fire to what they didn't want."

"So where did these people come from?" Philip gestured around him.

"I saved who I could," Donald nodded. "I've no idea how many we killed, but it wasn't enough. These are all I managed to help, when the fires reached us, we ran and ended up here." The story seemed impossible to Philip, like something out of a horror movie, but he could see the people and the terror in their eyes was real enough. He noticed Donald watching him as he tried to take it all in and with a nod to himself, obviously deciding something he stood up.

"Come with me," he gestured. "I've got something you need to see."

"It looks like we've found the Alamo," Marcus announced as they neared the main hall. He could smell the stench of death in the air, and the signs of heavy battle were everywhere. Blast marks from grenades had buckled the floor and bullet holes seemed to cover almost every surface; parts of creatures could be seen scattered across the floor.

The doors to the hall had been ripped from their hinges and thrown to the side and he paused outside as he built up his courage to enter. The stench inside was unbelievable. Blood and guts covered the floors, and there were so many body parts it was impossible to see how many people had died in here. He covered his mouth as he gagged and he could hear the rest of the squad behind him having the same problems.

"There's no one alive in here, back out." He only just managed to give the order and it was all he could do to stop himself throwing up, even Kate looked pale as they retreated back into the hallway. They'd seen dead bodies before. Mass graves that had been the result of someone's sick mind in foreign countries but even those horrific scenes didn't come close to the hall.

"They killed them all," Pierce whispered. "Even the kids..." he sniffed. Everyone stood numbly together looking back at the hall when something clattered behind the coat racks. There was something alive back there amongst the lost and found. their training kicked in and the mission was back on.

He signalled for Kate and Pierce to go to the right and circle round, and for Mike to approach from the left with John. With everyone in position he nodded and they started to move in, kicking coats and bags aside as they searched. Kate kicked a pile of coats and something hissed angrily back. "Found it," she called; her weapon aimed at the bundle as he moved over and pulled the coats away.

"I didn't know what else to do with them," Donald explained as they stepped out into the alley behind the building. "But at least out here they're out of sight of the others." He pointed to a pallet stack and Philip slowly moved forward on his own and peaked round the bins.

"What the hell!" he exclaimed as he backed away, almost falling over. The thing that lay before him wasn't human, even in death it filled his soul with primordial fear.

"I killed it just before dawn," Donald stated. "It was hidden in the back when we arrived." Philip felt his heart pounding in his chest. It looked like something from a cheap horror movie, its thin arms and long fingers looked artificial, but its smooth head and unblinking black eyes seemed to stare hungrily into his soul.

"What are they?" he asked. "Aliens?"

"Don't know. I didn't see any spaceships, and they don't have laser guns so I guess not." Philip nervously edged closer towards it as

Donald continued. "If I was a religious man and believed in that sort of stuff, I'd say demons, but to be honest…" he shrugged. "I have no idea."

He reached out and touched it, its smooth grey skin was leather-like, it was naked but for a crude leather strap that held a knife against its chest and Philip turned to look at Donald.

"Don't look at me." He held his hands up defensively. "It didn't have any balls when I killed it."

"I don't know," Ash sighed for the fifth time. "Why did the duck cross the road?"

"Because it was the chicken's day off, of course…" Tommy laughed, proud that he'd managed to fool him again. Ash didn't really mind, he liked it when Tommy laughed, it stopped him feeling so lonely and moved his mind away from the death around them.

He'd done what he could to shield Tommy from the death. On some roads it had been almost impossible to walk down without having to step over a body, and he'd had to make him close his eyes, so each time Tommy laughed, he felt a little better inside.

"Where's your mummy?" Tommy asked as he sat on his shoulders.

"I think my mummy is with yours, Tommy, maybe they've gone shopping together." It seemed a good enough response for the moment, better than the alternative answer.

"I like you." Tommy leaned forward, looking down onto his face from above.

"I like you too," he smiled in reply. Tommy seemed happy with that, and sat back contently on his shoulders, his hands wrapped round his neck. "Let's keep looking okay?" They walked on in silence and a few moments later Tommy start to fall asleep. Ash smiled to himself as he listened to his breathing. Maybe being a dad wouldn't have been the worst thing in the world.

● ● ● ● ● ● ● ●

The creature hissed loudly as the bright light hit it, clawing backwards to try to get away as it dragged itself away and Marcus could see where a bullet had torn into its thigh.

"What are you?" he shouted at it. "Where have you come from?" The creature turned to look at him, its unblinking eyes stared at him and it hissed angrily. There seemed to be no communication option between them and there was only one option open.

"Do it," he said and Kate pulled the trigger, the single round tore into its forehead and killed it instantly. Kate holstered her weapon as she watched the still twitching body and Marcus realised that this was the moment to get back on track.

"Mike, John, continue the search, double check all these things are dead. Kate, Pierce, grab ammo and supplies, bring anything useful back here, I don't want to hang around any longer than we need to. The stench in here is terrible so let's move." They peeled away, leaving him alone with the dead.

Nothing felt right anymore, the world was breaking apart around him and Marcus felt lost and alone. It was easy being in charge when there was someone above you pointing you in the right direction, someone making the big decision, but right now, he had no contact with anyone above, and the buck stopped with him.

He forced the dead creature's mouth open with his knife; its mouth contained rows of sharp pointy teeth, maybe three layers deep. He reasoned its large lidless eyes gave it better vision in the dark, obviously why they'd attacked at night.

"Marcus," Mike called excitedly. "We've got survivors." Two soldiers followed John back into the room. "They heard Kate's gunshot and were coming our way when we ran into them." They were both wounded, the taller of the two started to salute.

"Take it easy, lads," Marcus stopped him. "We don't need to worry about that now, we just need to find out what has happened"

"My name's Nick," the taller soldier nodded. "This here is Peter."

"Good, welcome aboard." They both looked exhausted. "John, can you get some hot water on the boil, I think everyone could do with a break, I know I could use a coffee."

"I'm not going to argue with that one," John nodded.

"I didn't think you would." He forced a smile, trying to look relaxed. "Mike, can you find me a first aid kit and check these guys over?" With a nod he vanished. "Right, Guys." He led them to a set of chairs as far away from the hall as he could. "Sit down. Tell me what happened here."

"You're the only ones that made it back," Nick began. "Our CO sent out a five man patrol to find out what was going on. It must have been about 0330 hours when we lost the perimeter sentries. I've never seen anything like it, they almost overran us, but we managed force them back until we were able to pull back to the hall." He shook his head as he recalled the battle.

"We barricaded the doors as best we could but there were too many of them..." he fell silent for a moment as he thought. "We tried to defend the civilians, we really did, but three of us were ordered to establish a secondary fall back location. No one else came." He shrugged, "We managed to hold them off long enough for them to give up on us; I guess there were easier targets."

"Three?" he questioned.

"Stewart, sir. He didn't make it. He got wounded during the first retreat and just bled out before our eyes." Nick was obviously still traumatised by the previous night "There was nothing we could do."

"You did what you could," Marcus reassured him. "Get some rest while I figure out our next move." Whatever that's going to be, he thought.

Philip drained the last of his drink with shaking hands, he felt physically sick, and the mother of all hangovers had settled on him. His hands shook as he handed his cup back to Donald and he refilled it for him. He'd taken some painkillers but didn't feel any better for them. "So what's the plan? What do we do?" he asked.

"The only thing we can do, we need to get these people to safety somehow and wait for the authorities to come. It's as far as I can think at the moment, but to be honest they're poorly dressed for travel in the snow."

"You're thinking about going shopping then?" It wasn't really a question, more a statement of obvious fact, even Philip could see that they wouldn't last long out there. Slippers and dressing gowns didn't appear in any winter survival guide, but it was all they had time to grab.

"I'm in," he announced. "All the plans I had have gone and I've got nothing better to do today."

"Mabel," Donald shouted, with little to prepare the two could set of almost instantly. "We'll be back in about an hour, so put the kettle on."

"Will do, Donald, be careful out there." She waved as she refilled the pots.

The floor was soon covered with an assortment of supplies, and a pot of strong black coffee simmered on a small burner. Marcus could hear Brian talking as he checked over the supplies.

"We should stay here," he babbled to anyone who would listen. "The army know where we are, and we can defend it. We should stay, we should stay." He'd seen this before, the denial stage. Many a new recruit on the battlefield found they needed somewhere to hide when things got too rough, somewhere to dig in and wait it out. He was trying to figure out how to approach him when suddenly Kate's voice cut in.

"Will you just shut up?"

"Who do you think you are?" Brian started to rise, but Kate kicked him down.

"You idiot." She glared down at him. "Can't you see what happened when we tried to defend this place before? Wake up and smell the dead."

"Enough!" Marcus barked as he pushed Kate away. He thought she was going to fight back and there was a tense moment as they stared at each other before Marcus spoke again. "Cover the perimeter," he ordered "Now!"

She snatched up her rifle and stormed out, kicking the door as she went.

"Finish your drinks; load up with everything you can carry. Let's hope we meet more soldiers on our way back to barracks. Mike, get our new boys bandaged and ready to move. We leave in ten." Keep them disciplined, keep them busy, Marcus reminded himself. Don't let them think about what's going on. Take charge and lead them home, or what's left of home, he thought.

Philip felt the walk would have been pleasant but for all the death and destruction around him, the sounds matched something closer to the highlands of Scotland than a large bustling city. No cars drove down the snow covered streets, no buses pumped pollution into the air, and other than the birds and the odd animal which crossed their path nothing made a sound.

They passed an assortment of book shops, toy shops, off licences, cafes and arcades which were all useless for their needs, so they'd trudged on. Donald whistled cheerfully as he walked, breaking up the otherwise oppressive silence around them until he suddenly stopped and shivered.

"I feel like I'm being watched," he announced as he looked around. "There!" He pointed to the upstairs window of a house across the street, its curtains still moving. "Best check they're alright, they most probably don't know what's happened. Maybe they where drunk like you." He smiled.

They opened the gate and walked up the path, Philip pressed the doorbell and he waited a moment before he impatiently pressed it again, keeping his finger down hard on the button, but still no signs of movement could be seen or heard inside.

"Why are you ringing the doorbell?" Donald suddenly asked. "There's no power."

"Damn, forgot." Philip slapped his forehead, pressing the bell just seemed such a natural thing to do. "If someone's injured inside they may be unable to get to the door."

"Stand back," Donald said after another minute of waiting and he kicked the door, splintering the lock. "Hello!" he shouted as he entered. "We saw you from the street. You're not safe here...Hello!" Philip opened the living room door. Other than the burnt out TV in the corner, everything looked normal so he slowly pulled it closed. "Looks empty down here," he advised.

"You stay here for now." Donald stopped on the first step. "I don't want to scare them; they're going to be confused enough without two strangers barging in. See what you can find in the kitchen will you."

A quick check of the cupboards resulted in a haul of half a loaf of bread, some tinned potatoes and a jar of coffee. Certainly not the well stocked cupboards expected for Christmas, the highlight of the search was finding a can of coke in the fridge door.

"Come to Papa." He smiled as he opened it, resting back against the work top as he waited for Donald. Everything felt odd still, the fact that he was stood in a strangers house, sipping stolen coke made him feel like a burglar. Pots filled the sink, frozen bubbles from the washing up liquid covered the plates and crystallised over the cups.

He shivered and moved to close the back door to try to keep what little heat there was inside, it was like he'd walked into a freezer. Even the blood on the floor had frozen, allowing a thin layer of snow to cover it; someone could slip and hurt themselves.

The can dropped from his fingers as he ran for the stairs, taking them three at a time. Donald was in front of him, pushing the front bedroom door open. "Hello," he heard him call called as a creature jumped forward, pushing him backwards onto the carpet, sending his machete spinning from his hands.

Not knowing what else to do, Philip threw himself at it, smashed into it with all his weight. He lifted it clear of Donald's prone form and landed heavily in the darkness of the room beyond, his teeth jarred as his head collided with something in the darkness and it was a moment before he regained his coordination, and pulled his knife free from his belt.

He heard a hiss close by and he lashed out instinctively as his terror grew inside. He felt the blade make contact, more out of luck than skill, and there was a tearing sound followed by a thud as something hit the floor.

"Philip, are you there?" Donald called from the doorway, trying to see what was going on. Philip reached out and grabbed the curtain, snapping it free from the rails as he pulled himself up, and the light flooded in blinding him, and he waited for his eyes to re-adjust. All he could see was red, not the red of a decorated room, or the red of a carpet, but the bright red of fresh blood, and he realised it couldn't all be from the creature.

The remains of the elderly occupants lay together in their bed. The creatures must have got in last night, Philip realised, and killed them as they slept. He looked at the dead creature on the floor, this one being caught in the house as the Sun rose, trapping it inside.

"Let's get out of here," Donald suggested as he offered him his hand before pulling him to his feet, and Philip was eager to agree.

Marcus stood at the school gates and watched as the unit walked, or hobbled past. They'd bandaged Peter's leg as best they could, but fresh blood continued to seep through the wound. Everyone looked stressed, and he was conscious of the fact their future was unsure, and he could feel the burden of command on his shoulders.

He'd liked being in command normally, when there was a structure above him that he could rely on, but now, with the future uncertain, he could feel the panic starting to grow. Just keep them busy, he reminded himself over and over; just keep them busy until you can find someone in charge. They at least had enough weapons and ammo now to support a small country, and they had stashed the rest for later.

"It's an early Christmas present." John smiled as he patted the sniper rifle he'd acquired, Pierce had grabbed a `Minimi` general purpose machine gun, and was weighed down by the ammo cartridges it needed. Kate was the last one out, and Marcus stopped her, letting the others move on a little before he said anything.

"I don't appreciate your attitude, Kate," he hissed angrily at her. "And I don't want to see any more of it. I value your opinion, you know I do, and I'll ask for it when I need it, but I don't want you to be second guessing everything I do, or go off half cocked when the pressure gets bad." He stared into her eyes. "This isn't a normal operation anymore, and we need to give everyone a little slack." He stared at her. "Do we understand each other?"

She stared straight back at him, their friendship had seen them through a number of situations before and he wondered how much longer it would last.

"I understand," Kate conceded as she turned and walked after the rest of the group. He stood looking back at the school for a moment, hoping that this was the right move to make. He knew exactly what they would face if they stayed here, but feared what would happen now they left its secure walls behind.

The crisp snow lay undisturbed, but for the path his men had made. Blood from Peter's leg had left small red droplets on the snow, and for a moment he stood looking at them. How festive, he thought, like small Christmas baubles, he smiled at the absurdity of the thought before stamping it into the snow as he ran to catch up with the others.

The gull circled the city. Most of the fires had died down now, and there were less thermal updrafts to assist it in its flight. Food was once more its primary objective as the cold made everything tougher and it burnt up more energy on everything it did; the best course of action was to gorge itself on as much meat as possible before it froze. It landed carefully on the roof of a car, before hopping down to the bonnet. The charred meat inside was still soft, and tore easily under its sharp powerful beak. After a moment of gorging itself, it heard something else landed heavily nearby and a bird hopped across the road towards it, before it gave a loud caw.

The gull wasn't concerned, it had dealt with this type of bird before, but a further sound came from overhead and another bird landed next to the first. The gull looked up from its feeding, it had been a while since anything had dared to challenge it, but these two wouldn't be a problem.

It screeched at the birds as a sign of aggression, unfolding its wings towards them. This was its food, and they should leave. They hopped back a little, but didn't fly away, and with a screech, it flapped its wings harder and jumped towards them, chasing them across the road and away from its lunch.

It turned back to the car and his food, eager to return to the rich fatty meat but stopped, at least thirty more birds sat watching it from the buildings around, thirty beaks ready to fight to remove the competition. In defiance the gull flapped its wings towards them in a last ditch effort, but there's a reason the word for a group of crows is a murder.

Ash's back ached and with every step his breath became more

and more laboured, he didn't know how long he'd been carrying Tommy for now, but he knew he needed somewhere to rest, somewhere to put him down. He guessed it must be around lunch time, give or take an hour, but the lack of any actual reference points made it difficult to be exact.

He smiled as he spotted a shape buried in snow that he recognised, the bus had obviously broken down during one of the power surges, its engine and cabin looked burnt out, and the windows on the lower deck had been smashed, but the upper deck looked complete and it offered a stopping point that he desperately needed.

He lowered Tommy down from his shoulders before boarding the bus. It was damp inside but it was better that the alternative, so he carefully climbed the stairs. It smelt terribly, but it was warmer up here and he carefully lowered Tommy onto a seat before slumping down opposite, he guessed he'd got at least thirty minutes before he'd wake again, certainly enough time to scout ahead.

He'd only been gone a few moments when he realised how much easier it was to travel when he was on his own. He could move faster, and he'd be able to eat as he walked rather than having to stop each time he needed energy and he found himself pondering whether he should return or just keep going.

Someone else would surely find him eventually, he reasoned. He was a tough little kid, and he'd found his way to Ash on his own hadn't he? Others must have survived out here, there just had to be more than the two of them alive in the city and the army must be around somewhere. The snow was falling in thick heavy lumps again, and the world felt smaller as the weather cocooned around him. He was almost passed the corner shop before he saw it, its light grey shadow against the thick cotton wool whiteness gave him just enough to aim for, and he pushed his way inside.

He didn't want to linger in the darkness of the shop for too long. Even though it was cold outside it felt safer to be out there than in here and he searched quickly and quietly and he was soon stood in the doorway looking out into the snow again.

He could hear the sound of something moving in the distance, quiet at first, then slowly getting louder as it approached, and he stepped from the doorway in the hope of seeing what it was, maybe he didn't need to worry about Tommy after all. Whatever it was certainly sounded close.

The windows exploded outward besides him, and masonry dropped from above, smashing down onto the pavement in front of him and he staggered back into the doorway as the quake moved past. It must have taken thirty seconds to finish and the rumbling of the earth was the only sound he could hear for some time.

He pulled himself to his feet as the sound receded into the distance, and he was brushing dust and snow from his trousers when he remembered Tommy. Fear welled up inside him as he ran back to the bus, the thoughts of what could have happened to him kept flashing in his head.

As he ran, he could feel his breath getting harsher, the cold air bit into his lungs and his asthma started to kick in. He didn't slow down despite the pain in his lungs, even when he slipped on the snow and fell, he pushed himself quickly back to his feet and forced himself to run on.

He turned the corner and gasped as he spotted the bus, it still stood where he had left it, but now its rear wheels hung freely over a deep fissure that had opened up in the tarmac behind it, and he carefully pulled the doors open and climbed inside.

"Tommy," he rasped, his voice now nothing more than a whisper. Grabbing the rails he pulled himself up the stairs, his chest ached and his heart felt like it was going to burst as he moved forward on unsteady legs. Tommy lay motionless on the seat, his arm hanging limply from the seat and he collapsed to his knees in front of him.

"Oh, no!" he gasped as he reached out with shaking hands, almost afraid to touch him. He was too emotional to accept what had happened. What had I been thinking, he cursed to himself, how could I have left him? "I'm sorry, Tommy," he whispered, tears running freely down his face as he carefully moved Tommy's hood back.

"Why are you sad? Did you forget my chocolate?" Tommy whispered. Ash gasped with joy as tears ran down his dirty, dust covered face and he sat on the floor as the exhaustion slowly took him over, and he felt himself falling as darkness engulfed him.

Philip walked along the beach, letting the cool waves lap against his sore feet and the Sun shone down on his face, caressing him as he meandered along, But something was wrong, it felt hotter than normal, almost painful on his face and he covered his eyes with his hands.

"You okay?" someone said and he jumped as someone shook him. Opening his eyes he looking round, trying to recall what had happened, and he stared at the face before him for a moment before his name came to his mind.

"Donald?" He twisted around, trying to see what was going on. "What happened?"

Donald motioned to the blaze behind them. "We're lucky, that's what. Felt like a large quake hit us. The house came down almost as soon as we left it." He motioned to the burning wreck next to them. "The car caught fire by the looks of it, bloody luck or we might have frozen to death, it kept us alive."

Philip shook the dream from his mind as he tried to piece together what had happened, the world seemed to be spinning before his eyes, he touched his forehead and blood came away on his fingers.

"It's just a graze by the looks of it," Donald confirmed as he held his head firmly in his hands and checked the wound. "But that was big; I've never felt a quake like that in the UK before." He pulled him carefully to his feet and they limped to the remains of the garden wall behind them. It was hard to recognise anything now, many buildings had cracked or fallen in on themselves, and it scared him that a few minutes earlier they had still been inside.

"Are you okay to get going?" Donald stood up. "We need to get this done."

"Shouldn't we get back to the others?" Philip asked.

"No." Donald shook his head. "If we go back now, we'll freeze tonight. We're here now, so let's grab what we can first." Philip nodded, he could see the logic in what Donald was saying so they set off once more, the snow continued to fall around them and the wind chill dropped everything by at least another ten degrees.

Fifteen minutes later they pushed a pair of shopping carts full of coats, boots and blankets back to the group. He still felt dizzy from the bang on his head, but it seemed to have stopped bleeding for now, at least. The quake damage became more and more obvious as they walked, sporadic fires had broken out in many houses again, and thick black smoke floated on the air.

Many of the taller buildings had collapsed in on themselves, or fallen across the road, forcing them to carry the trolleys at certain points just to keep on track, but finally they turned back into their street. There was little for them to recognise anymore, but two fires burnt brightly in oil drums as people feverishly tried to dig into the rubble that, until recently had been their shelter.

"Oh, bloody hell!" Donald cursed as he dropped the trolley and ran to help. "Did everyone get out?" he called, grabbing the first man he met, shaking him by the shoulders "Who was inside?" The man's face was covered in soot from the fires and his hands bled where he'd tried to tear the masonry aside, when he turned to look at Donald, his eyes held little hope for those inside.

"Mabel and Joe didn't make it out." The man shook his head. "The building just came down around us. Most of us came out when the first tremor happened, but Mabel went back in to get Joe." The man looked battered and bruised from digging.

"The roof gave way suddenly. We've tried to dig them out, honest we have, but we just can't get to them." He shook his head, his hair matted to the side of his head where the snow had melted. "We heard voices for a while." Donald stood motionless, staring at the rubble pile as the man continued, his hands dropped loosely to his side.

"We tried, we really tried, I'm sorry…" The end of his se[ntence]
into a sob as he turned to continue digging with the othe[r]

Donald rubbed his head as he looked at Philip, the[re seemed to]
be an argument going on in his head, once his struggle w~~as over some~~
choice had been made and he walked over to the man and stopped him
from digging.

"Listen up." His voice sounded strained and distant as he spoke.
"Whatever those things were that attacked last night, we can bet
they'll be back as soon as it gets dark. We can't do anymore here, not
now and we need to find somewhere safe to stay before night."

"What about Joe and Mabel!" the man shouted angrily. "They
may still be alive in there." He walked over to Donald. "We can't leave
them, Donald. You know you can't do this."

"I'm sorry." Donald turned to look at the rubble. "We just
don't have the time to dig them out."

Philip looked at the terrified faces before him. Children clung to
their parent's arms, women sat crying in the street as the men stopped
digging and slowly walked away. Donald started to flag, whatever his
struggle was he looked like he was losing.

"We have warm clothing," Philip shouted. "So if you need
a coat or some shoes come to me, the snow is thick out here but
Donald's right, we need to move before they come back, we have to
find somewhere to hide until dawn." Donald looked physically shaken,
tears ran down his cheeks but he managed to nod his thanks.

"We don't have many hours left before dark now," Philip
continued. "So everyone who isn't hurt needs to help those who are.
We're going towards the centre of town for now. We can hope to find
more people as we go; the army's got to be out there somewhere."

Philip didn't know how true his statement was, but not in the
way he had hoped.

Marcus cursed at their speed. Their problems really began

ien they found that Peter had been hiding the worst of his injuries and was in a worse shape than he'd let on. Kate found another knife wound in his side when he'd finally collapsed. Fortunately, it wasn't deep enough to be fatal, but deep enough to bring their march to a slow crawl.

In the hour they'd been walking they'd found a handful of sorry looking survivors, adding them to the group of civilians they'd defended the previous night, they had quite a crowd with them now, all walking slowly along. A few civilians they'd met had opted to stay behind, refusing to believe that anything was up other than the power problem, and no matter what they said they remained adamant. "Leave them," he'd ordered. "If they don't want to come, we can't force them."

Kate had settled into her soldier role again now and he watched her as she talked to the civilians, helping the weak or wounded as they walked.

"Boss!" she called as she ran to join him at the front. "It looks like we've a few cadets here, two of the young lads are from the ATC and they say they've done basic weapons training and I wanted to know if we could arm them? There are enough weapons to spare and we could certainly do with more people ready to fight before tonight?"

"Yes." He smiled. "That's a good idea. Just make sure you keep them to the middle of the group." She turned to leave but he stopped her. "Make sure they're on single shot, not full automatic." She smiled back at him, she seemed happier now than she had been for a while.

"No problem, Boss." She nodded.

"How's Peter holding up?"

"He's pretty tough for a STAB... Sorry. Old habits die hard," she said as she held her hand up with a smile. "The wound was deep and I'm surprised that he lasted this long before we spotted it, but he should do okay now, but I don't know how much longer he can keep going today."

"Okay, we'll find somewhere to stop in an hour, get his wound re-dressed while we get a brew on."

The tremor seemed to come out of nowhere and he staggered forward, Kate was knocked to the floor and everyone dived for cover as the buildings around them shook. With a mighty crack the earth opened before him, dropping away before his eyes. A chimney stack broke free from a house opposite, cracking and breaking the roof tiles as it fell inwards.

Eventually, as the dust settled, Marcus stood and climbed over the broken road. He could see the group pulling themselves to their feet, and he smiled as he heard Kate swearing from her prone position, her feet dangling precariously over the edge of the hole. Though there were a few minor bruises, there were fortunately no further injuries that would slow them down any further.

Taking advantage of their situation, he took stock of the group; he had eight soldiers in total, one of those a walking wounded, two cadets who looked young enough to be his kids if he'd had any, and a group of frightened civilians, including four pensioners. They need to find somewhere to bunker down for the night as there was no way they'd make it to headquarters at this pace, and they needed somewhere they could defend. Heat and food was going to be a real issue, especially with the elderly.

"Let's get moving," he ordered. "We don't have all day." A collection of moans and grumbles rose from the people but eventually they collected themselves together.

Thirty minutes later Pierce signalled for the column to stop and Marcus ran towards him to see what the issue was. As he ran, he realised he was hearing a sound, it was just on the edge of hearing, but got louder as he got closer to Pierce.

"It's White Christmas by Bing Crosby, Boss." Pierce pointed in the general direction he felt the sound was coming from. "Someone's playing Christmas songs."

The woman didn't move as Philip slowly approached her, she

just sat with her back against a lamppost and kept staring down the street towards them as the snow banked against her legs. It was only when he knelt beside her that he realised she was dead. He tried to close her eyes, but her eyelids were frozen in place.

"Come on lad." Donald stood over him. "There's nothing you can do for her now."

The first soldiers they found were dead, and by the looks of it they'd fought back as hard as they could, but just not hard enough. Their bodies lay in so many pieces, it was hard to tell where one ended and the next started.

"Are you doing okay?" Donald asked as they walked over to them.

"I don't know," he answered honestly. "I have no idea what I'm doing here."

"That's the right answer," Donald smiled. "If you hadn't been affected by all this," he gestured around him, "I'd be worried, it's only natural that this doesn't feel real."

Philip had watched Donald since they'd set out. He walked with a purpose that he found hard to match, and there was an air to the older man that simply said follow me, he always seemed to have a plan. "You seem okay though."

"Ha," Donald laughed. "The trick is to just keep going moving forward, don't allow yourself time to think, try not to dwell on anything for too long." He rolled the first soldier over and started to pat down his webbing, opening each pouch in turn and keeping anything that looked useful.

"Can you check him for weapons and ammo?" He nodded to a body a few feet away. "Try to imagine everything in black and white if you can, I read that somewhere once but it seems to work."

He reached gingerly towards the soldier, his head hung loosely from his neck with a look of terror etched on his face. His hands shook as he reached out and touched his cold skin, as he pulled at the webbing, he tore open a frozen wound in his chest.

"You need to watch out for that," Donald called. "Have you found anything?"

"Just a pistol and some ammo." He gagged at the smell; his hand covered his nose as he threw the pistol and a spare magazine he'd collected to Donald.

"Good," he nodded. "Let's move on and check the others."

Philip found it hard to recall the faces of the dead later, though at the time they stared at him as he robbed their cold corpses and he felt he would be stuck with them forever.

"Not a bad haul to start with," Donald nodded with satisfaction later. "We've got two pistols now at least and a couple of spare clips. The machine guns are empty though, obviously their primary weapons before they fell." He passed him a pistol. "You might as well keep hold one of these."

"But I've never used one," he objected. The idea of a gun wasn't something he had ever really thought about, but now, as it sat in his hands it felt heavy and dangerous.

"Look," Donald explained as he took the gun back. "The safety is here, just point the barrel at the target and pull the trigger." He handed it back. "Don't sweat it." Donald patted him on the back. "I'm with you."

Philip slipped the pistol into his belt. It felt cold and uncomfortable against his hips, and stuck into him as he walked, after a few steps he removed it and put it in his pocket.

"Alright everyone," he shouted to the waiting survivors, trying to sound more in control than he actually felt. "It's time to move on again, I'm afraid, do try to keep up this time, Mr Wilkinson."

Ashfaq looked at his father as the first light of dawn shone through the open door, bathing the hallway in a soft white light, highlighting the body as it lay motionless near the door.

"Dad?" he whispered as he approached, tears running freely

Ian Hawley

from his eyes. "Dad." He dropped to his knees, unable to move any closer, not wanting to see what they had done to him. "I'm sorry," he sobbed. "I'll find them dad, I promise I will. I'm sorry I let you down."

"Wake up," someone shouted. "Please wake up. Please." His toes felt cold and numb, his fingers too, he could feel himself being pulled, shaken. "Wake up!" He jumped and opened his eyes, scrambling backwards as he took stock of his surroundings. Tommy stood above him; tears running down his face, his eyes were red from crying.

"I couldn't wake you up," he sobbed. "I was alone and scared." Tommy threw himself onto him, hugging him tightly. He could feel the warmth of his cheek against his face and pulled him closer, slowly rocking him in his arms.

"It's okay Tommy," he gasped. "It's going be alright." His chest ached and his throat felt dry. "I'm not going anywhere without you. I won't let you down." He held Tommy's face in his hands as he looked into his eyes. "I promise. It's all going be okay." He felt the tears well in his own eyes; he knew he couldn't leave him, Tommy was family now, and he had to look after him.

It was almost half an hour later when the pair carefully climbed down the stairs but as they reached the last step, Ash stopped. There was a sound coming from the rear of the bus and a thin blood trail ran across the floor from a broken side window. Tommy tried to push past him to see, but he held him back.

"Keep back," he whispered. "I don't know what it is, but there's a lot of blood back there." He walked slowly towards it, and slowly a wing came into view, followed by the body and head of a seagull. It looked battered and bloody, its feathers had been pulled out in places and blood oozed from wounds on its head.

"It's a seagull, Tommy," he sighed in relief. "But it's been badly hurt; it looks like it's had a worse time than we've had." Tommy nervously peered round his waist.

"Aw, look at it, poor thing," he cooed. "My Mum says we should be nice to all of God's creatures, she says they have as much right to being here as we do, she says I can't kill ants and stuff so we gotta be nice."

"Okay, okay." It would be easier to just leave it, but he knew Tommy would be upset. "Why don't we give it something to keep it warm hey, like this?" He removed his scarf, and carefully dropped it over the gull, keeping his fingers away from its beak but it looked too tired to try to fight.

"Come on Tommy, let's leave it here. It will be okay on the bus, but we have got to move on. I bet its Mum is looking for it too." He pulled the doors open and the snow blew in. He stopped to wrap Tommy's scarf tight around his neck before they stepped out into the cold winter weather, the wind was strong and they both found it hard pressed to move forward.

"I'm cold," Tommy moaned. "I wanna go home." Ash looked down at him and realised he was crying. This little man had lost everything, and he hadn't complained once and Ash felt guilty for not realising, so he knelt down and unzipped his coat and wrapped Tommy inside before zipping it over him again.

"Thanks, Ash," he whispered to him as he hugged tightly round his neck. Although Ash felt warmer with him holding on, now with each step his breathing became more of a challenge; he managed to move maybe twenty steps each time before he needed to stop, and he knew his asthma was going to be a problem.

Ten minutes later and he could hardly lift his feet, he dragged them slowly through the snow as the remains of houses loomed to either side, with no cars or people to break the snow down it had settled in great piles against walls.

A dog barked excitedly from the doorway of a nearby house and it jumped through the snow towards them. Ash initially tried to shoo it away, but it looked safe enough, so he paid it little attention as it followed them down the road.

As he reached the junction he could see the outlines of a shopping centre in the distance, a grey box shape building against the whiteness of the world. It had been years since he'd last been here, something so local that he'd forgotten about it once he'd started driving and the world opened up to him, and suddenly he realised how much he really missed his car.

The dog continued to bark loudly as he walked, not aggressively but more in a friendly, excited way, as though it was hoping for food but it was enough to wake Tommy.

"What's that noise?" he asked from below the coat. He pushed his head out through the neck and looked down at the dog. "Cool." Tommy turned and looked him squarely in the face, not an inches from his chin. "Can we keep it?"

Ash looked down at him. Tommy's face was full of fun and excitement, and his eyes kept looking back to the dog and then back to Ash as he waited for an answer. He didn't know where they were going to sleep tonight, he didn't know what food he was going to eat or where he was going to get it from, and he didn't really think they would last much longer, so a dog wouldn't make much of a difference.

"Why not," he smiled.

"Thanks," Tommy beamed. "My Mum said I couldn't have a pet, said I was too..." he paused before trying to pronounce the word, "irisponsidle. So when we find her, you have to tell her he's yours."

"Not a problem," he smiled.

"Come on, Mutt," he called and the dog barked and jumped up around him before running off to urinate against the side of a car. He smiled as he watched the steam rise from the frozen tire. All of the cars he'd seen since they'd started out had been burnt out and destroyed, but as he reached the ramp to the car park, he started to wonder what cars had been left under the protection of its concrete shell.

He walked carefully up the ramp so as not to slip on the loose snow, skirting around a hole where a large piece for the floor had broken free. Everything was still and cold as he passed under the arch of the entrance, no lights shone inside and the snow cast an eerie glow over the dead vehicles. I hate the dark, he thought.

● ● ● ● ● ● ● ●

The pile of dead creatures was the first sign that Philip saw that said something was different here, almost ten of them lay stacked in a heap at the end of a road and Donald signalled to the group for quiet as they drew their weapons.

The road was filled with closely packed terraces, leading down to the bottom of a cul-de-sac. At the end, a crudely constructed barricade blocked the end of the street. They could see people working to sure-up the barricade and decided the best course of action would be to not sneak up on them. They both walked out in the middle of the road with his arms raised and a shout was heard from behind a barricade, more people started to appear before a cheer went up.

"They think we've come to save them lad, just keep smiling," Donald said in answer to his look. "Just keep walking and waving." Philip was amazed that the group had survived at all. The barricade had huge holes in it, easily large enough to let the creatures climb inside. He could make out tables and sofa's mingled in with anything else that came to hand and they both stopped as a man climbed down and walked over to greet them.

"Welcome." He shook their hands enthusiastically. "We'd started to believe were all that was left. My name's Ed. Edward Hiney." He gestured back to the barricade. "This is my family." A woman waved nervously back, her two children clamped firmly to her side. "The rest of our neighbours are back there too, can you believe the neighbourhood watch system actually worked." As he talked he kept on looking around, trying to see who else was with them.

"We realised something was going on when the shooting started," he continued. "Figured we didn't want to wait for the problem to get to us, so we started early and built up our defence, we've had problems with the yobs round here for years, stealing from the cars and such, so we'd all been sat ready just in case they turned up to cause damage with the power out, good job too, those things came screeching round the corner." He pointed to the bodies at the end of the road. "Sorry," he suddenly apologised. "Where are my manners, come in, how many other are with you, how many soldiers have you brought?"

"It's just us I'm afraid." Philip waved to the rest of the followers and they approached cautiously.

"Oh." Ed deflated a little. "Oh well, come in anyway." They all followed him as he climbed back over the defensive wall, Philip stopped at the top and stared at the little bit of civilisation they'd tried to create behind it. A long table had been set for dinner, even tablecloths had been laid out, and small plates contained an assortment of finger foods in the middle of the table. He could see around ten adults watching them as they entered most with cans of beer in their hands, their children hanging close by afraid of the strangers that had arrived.

"Have you seen or heard from the Army, or the police?" Ed was obviously eager to hear news that the cavalry was on its way.

"No." Philip shook his head. "Nothing alive anyway. Have you?"

"We can't get the radios to work. Nothing with batteries in will start. They could be out there for all we know but there's no way to get in touch with them."

"How many people are with you here?" Philip tried to count but presumed that not everyone was out.

"We had thirty seven before this all started." He sighed. "Mostly neighbours, but we have a few grandparents over for the Christmas period." He swallowed heavily as he tried to keep his emotions in check. "It should have been a time to celebrate, but I lost four good friends in the first two minutes last night. We lost another seven before dawn so there are only twenty six of us left now."

"You know it's not safe to stay here?" Donald interrupted. "You were lucky last night."

"Lucky?" Ed raised his voice angrily, "Lucky? We fought bloody hard, and it wasn't an easy night, good people died." Everyone had stopped to listen as Ed raised his voice; a few walked over, not sure what was going on. "Don't call us bloody Lucky."

"You're lucky you didn't all die last night, or worse." Donald faced up to Ed, his chest puffed out as he pointed his finger at him. "The only reason you're here now, is because there were easier pickings out there." Donald pointed back into the empty city they'd passed through. Ed turned his back on him, clenching his fist in anger and Donald was about to continue when Philip stopped him.

"Enough, both of you stop it!" He walked round to face them both. "I don't want to take anything away from what you've done here, Ed, but we've been out since dawn, and you're the first people we've seen alive. How long do you think you're going to last tonight when they come back in force, and they will come back. There's going to be less people here and more of them out there," he waved his hand outside the barricade. "You faced... what? A dozen last night, imagine a hundred, or a thousand." He turned to face the crowd that had developed close by, all eager for news.

"There just aren't enough of you to keep them at bay anymore, you have to see that. There aren't enough people even if we joined you, so we're moving on to find a safer place." He tried to make eye contact with as many as he could as he spoke. "Maybe the Army's still out there, maybe there are more survivors. I don't know for sure, but I do know you'll be overrun if you stay." A few of the women started to cry, the pressures of the previous night overwhelming them.

"We've all lost someone." He thought of Jenny. "Most have lost entire families. The last earthquake damaged the homes you're defending, and another tremor like the one before and you won't have anything left to fight for, and no where to run to."

"You expect to just walk in here and take over?" Ed muscled in. "Who the hell do you think you are? Why should we follow you? What gives you the right?" The torrent of questions came thick and fast, Ed's face was red with anger. "Do you think we can't do it without you?"

"You stupid..." Donald began, but Philip stopped him again.

"You're right. I don't know what's going on. I don't know what those things are, or why they attacked last night, and I don't care if you follow us or not… But anyone who wants to come with us can. It's your choice, you can stay and defend what's left of your homes, or you can come with us, it's your call. We may not do any better than you after tonight, but at least they're going to have to find us first."

Ed charged at Philip, but Donald grabbed him and pushed him backwards and he tripped against the kerb and fell onto his backside. No one moved, Ed scrambled to his feet and came at Philip again.

"I can't ask them to pack it all up and move." His face was inches away now. "This is the only thing I have left." Philip could see why Ed was angry, he was in charge here and suddenly someone else had turned up and tried to take it from him. "It's Christmas," he continued angrily, "It's supposed to be a time of joy and celebration, not a time for leaving your home and walking in the snow to God knows where." He turned to walk away but swung round again with his fists clenched.

"No! No! You're wrong, if we're going to die, then we're going to die here." His neighbours milled around nervously behind him, not sure who to listen to, torn between their loyalty to their leader, and their own self preservation. A young girl ran over to him, tears running freely from her eyes.

"Daddy, do we have to die?"

Marcus was surprised how far sound seemed to travel now the city was still and quiet. They had walked for ten minutes so far to the sounds of 'Slade' or 'Ertha Kitt' without finding the source, and then, all of a sudden, it was there in front of them.

Christmas lights glistened in the windows, and music belted forth into the street, children threw snowballs in the road, laughing and screaming. Scaffolding covered the whole house and chicken wire had been added to effectively cage everything inside, and as they approached, the door opened and a voice shouted out into the cold.

"Hurry up lads will ya, I don't want to let the heat out."

Ten minutes later Marcus was sat on an old tatty sofa with a mug of hot black coffee in his hands, the clock ticked gently on the wall and Christmas songs played around the house. For all intents and purposes, this was a normal house, on a normal day, in a normal world, and for neither love nor money could he figure why everything was still working.

The door opened and the owner walked in, a crude role up hanging from his lips; he was in his mid twenties, over weight with greasy hair. The red shorts and superman T-Shirt barely covered by the dressing gown and slippers did little to improve the image.

"Wanna mince pie, man?" he offered a plate across, his mouth full of food.

"No, no thanks." Marcus waved the plate away, he didn't trust the owner yet, he was obviously stoned and there were too many questions unanswered yet for him to let his guard down.

"You sure man?" he smiled. "They're good ones." He seemed to add this as a mark of approval.

"No," he declined firmly. "Thank you all the same. So tell me, er…"

"Jolly," he introduced himself, but Marcus wasn't sure if that was his name or his disposition. He certainly didn't seem to smile much.

"Okay then, Mr Jolly."

"Don't Mr me, man," he objected, obviously offended by the term. "It's just Jolly."

"Sorry," Marcus corrected himself. "Tell me, Jolly. Why do you still have electricity when everyone else doesn't?"

"Ah!" Jolly smiled as he tapped the side of his head. "That's the clever bit, that is." He swayed a little to the side as he checked to see who was listening before he continued. "It's the giant faraday cage outside the house." He waved his arms around him as he spoke. "I never trusted the government ya see, big brother watching what you do and that sort of thing, so I built protection." He took a deep pull from his role up before he continued, "And I've got two generators in the cellar that provide me with all the power I need, keeps me going. I got the idea from a movie, can't remember which one now, but it looked cool at the time." He smiled and pushed a whole mince pie into his mouth.   "You want more coffee?" Crumbs exploded from his mouth as he spoke.

"I'm okay thanks." Marcus covered his mug, partly to indicate he was alright, and partly to stop the crumbs entering. "I guess we are going to need to get moving again."

"Why leave, dude? It's turning dark already, and you need somewhere to stay. Stay here, there's space, and we can party." He nodded feverishly. "That's a steel reinforced door on the front and the windows all have solid shutters, the back garden has eight foot concrete and steel panels, topped with razor wire, and there's enough space in the house for everyone. Got it all done in case of a zombie invasion."

"Okay," Marcus nodded his agreement and thanks, common sense told him it was going to be safer here than outside, "We'll stay the night." He insisted the squad spent the rest of the day establishing an outer perimeter though. They set trip wires and claymores wherever they were needed, before finally settling the civilians down for the night in the cellar.

Marcus had to admit he was impressed with the Faraday cage idea, and Jolly was eager to show him round. He was starting to like Jolly, what you saw was what you got with him; he just wished he'd wash a little more.

"So the electric pulse gets discharged here," he indicated to a thick cable running into the ground, "So it bypasses the house. It's simple really, like a giant microwave." Fat ran down the side of Jolly's mouth as he bit into his second bacon sandwich, and he wiped it away with the sleeve of his dressing gown.

"So you live here alone?" Marcus asked as they entered the back door into the kitchen.

"Oh yeah, well sort of, I guess. My Mum went and kicked it around five years ago now, so it's been just me and the Gimp ever since."

"I'm sorry, the what?" he stopped, fearing he'd stumbled across something he really didn't want to know.

"The Gimp, oh, don't worry, it's his online gaming name, he gets owned when he plays see. He's my cousin, he's around here somewhere." He held his finger to his lips. "He's a bit of a stoner," he whispered as though it was a secret. "I've done okay for myself like," he continued at his normal volume. "Ma had a good number of insurance policies, and I made a killing on the internet, buying and selling star wars stuff." He almost smiled. "You wanna watch some porn?" he added as an afterthought.

"You did well there." Donald patted Ed on the back as they led the group forward.

"Really?" He shook his head, he felt angry inside, hollow. "I don't know. They had homes and food back there, now they're walking with us, and they've got neither. I just hope it was the right thing to do." He stopped walking and looked at Donald. "You do have an idea where we're going I take it?"

"That way," Donald pointed. "For the moment anyway, there has to be something better out there."

"So you don't have a plan at all?" Philip felt like a fool as he realised what he had done.

"What do you think?" Donald stared at him. "You think I went to bed last night and thought, I know, tomorrow, when the end of the world comes to an end, I'm going to do A, B and C?" Donald shook his head. "Wake up, Philip. Life doesn't work that way, but that doesn't mean there isn't a plan"

"So what's the plan?" he begged, hoping for some feeling of salvation. After the fight with Ed, he'd felt empty, watching all those people pack up, all those people lose hope.

"To live 'til tomorrow?" Donald smiled, slapping him on the back. "Look, it's simple," he explained. "We walk for another hour, we find somewhere to hide and post sentries and hopefully with all this fresh snow falling they won't find us." He waggled his finger at him as he thought of something else. "Talking about sentries, you need to get some of the younger lads to walk ahead of us."

"Why?"

"Well, we don't want to walk blindly into a problem, do we? Not with all these people with us." He continued to explain, "So we need a few lads to walk in front of us, maybe 100 metres or so to check out the area and warn us if there are problems."

"So, just ask them to walk ahead?" Philip thought it sounded easy enough.

"No," Donald corrected him. "Don't ask. Tell them. These people need to feel as though someone is in charge; it's the best way for them to continue to function. If they thought they had no direction, they would break and just stop here. Just giving the order makes it easier for them to accept." He looked around and pointed to a group of lads walking together. "They should do you. After that, start lightening the load, you need to get everyone to drop useless stuff, and believe me; they will have some stupid things with them. We need to travel light if we want to keep up this pace."

It surprised Philip what he found the survivors carrying, most of Donald's original group had nothing but the coats on their backs, but Ed's people seemed to have brought everything with them. He found laptops, briefcases and mobile phones and finally, after some considerable moaning, almost everything was reluctantly dropped at the roadside.

"Why should we drop our own things?" Ed argued with him when saw what he was doing. "You turn up, make us leave the safety of our homes to trek to God knows where, and now, you want us to throw away everything we have?" Philip could understand where he was coming from, but he could also see it was pointless to carry things that would never work again.

"I'll give you an option." He'd tried his best to sound calm and reasonable when he spoke to Ed, a contrast to Donald's approach.

"You can carry whatever you want, but, everyone's going to carry their own food, water, blankets, cooking utensils and fuel for the next couple of days. If you go hungry, you can eat your mobile phones or laptop, or..." he paused. "You can drop all the broken crap you're carrying and we'll all share the load. Tonight's going to be tough enough as it is; I can't see a laptop keeping you warm but it's totally up to you. I just can't be bothered arguing with you." He didn't look back as he walked away, but at the next stop he was pleased to see everything had gone.

"What's next, Boss?" the taller of the scouts called as the group approached them. The scouts had stopped at a junction in the road, and as they sat waiting for the rest to catch up they shared a cigarette between them.

"Good, okay. I need you to check at least 100 metres down each road. Make some noise and see if anyone's around, if you see anything dangerous, come straight back for support. I don't want any dead heroes." They all nodded that they had understood and moved on.

"Well done, lad." Donald smiled as they left. "Well done, indeed. We'll make a leader of you yet."

"Maybe." He watched them slowly vanish in the distance. "I'm just treating it like I'm in a movie at the moment. Everything's a little too surreal right now to take it all in." He pulled the pistol from his pocket and weighed it up in his hands. "When you think about it," he continued as he examined the weapon, "I woke up this morning with just a headache. Now I have all these people looking to me for the answers. Night's about an hour off, and we still need to get the supplies ready and find somewhere to stay."

"It's fun isn't it." Donald winked before turning back to the group.

"Philip!" the taller scout shouted as they re-appeared from the snow. "There are soldiers back there, well, what's left of them anyway." The lanky lad indicated behind them. "But we managed to collect some stuff, four pistols, two rifles and what looks like a machine gun, oh and a few grenades." He tipped out a sack he'd dragged back with him and an assortment of blood covered weapons fell out.

"Not bad." Donald nodded as he knelt down to examine them. "We've got two SA80 rifles and a Minimi machine gun. I don't suppose you found any ammo boxes for it?" he asked as he removed the magazine from the light machine gun.

"Na, sorry. We grabbed all we could find and came back."

"No worries. Would have been nice to have some ammo for these," he sighed. "Can you show me where the soldiers are? I'd like to check them over myself." Donald disappeared down the road with the scouts and Philip turned back to the group.

"Listen up everyone." He was surprised how quickly people stopped what they were doing to listen. "We need to get ready for tonight, so I need everyone to check the shops for supplies. Beans, tinned spaghetti, anything that's easy to cook and eat. You three," he pointed to a group, "I need you to get a couple of fires burning, find a few pans and let's boil up some of this snow, I'm sure we could all do with a drink to warm us up."

Donald looked surprised to see the volume of activity when he returned, and Philip casually walked over to him smiling as he sipped his coffee.

"Did you find anything of use?" he asked.

"No," Donald shook his head. "The poor lads look like they took a right beating, lots of those things dead around them." Philip could see the lads with Donald looked tired and worn. Seeing the dead bodies had obviously affected them considerably.

"Guys, you've done great today, so thank you." They smiled in response. "But I need to keep you for a little while longer. I need to find somewhere close by that's going to be a secure place to stay for the night. Do any of you know this area?" The tall ginger haired lad put his hand up.

"You're not in school, there's no need to put your hand up," Philip smiled.

"I lived round here a few years back." He pushed his fringe from the front of his face and left a dirt mark on his forehead. "There's a shopping centre not far away, I guess that would do."

"How far?"

"I'd guess twenty minutes walking, but if we take the bus we…" he paused for a moment as he thought about what he was saying. "That's if they were still running." He smiled, two of his teeth were missing and the grin was lopsided.

"Why don't you get yourselves a cuppa first?" Donald suggested.

"Na, we're good. Come on guys." He led the way, trotting off on the snow covered roads, his friends close behind. Philip suddenly felt dizzy as panic rose inside him. He'd managed to avoid thinking about what had happened almost all day, but now, as they got closer to finishing for the night, the panic was growing and he felt sick with it.

"Donald," his tone rose and his hands started to shake as he called him, "I don't get it, I just don't understand." He could feel tears welling up behind his eyes. He couldn't control it, like water from a burst dam his he could feel it as it rose inside him. Donald grabbed his shoulder and pulled him round the corner, pushed him not unkindly against the wall.

"Listen to me." Donald grabbed his shoulders and held him firm as he sobbed uncontrollably. "These people need you. They need a leader." He ignored Philip's crying. "And for my own reasons, I am not that man and Ed certainly isn't, so you are… It's not a debate, or an option, it's a fact. These people need someone to show them what to do." He let him go and he slid down the wall behind him.

"Something's gone wrong with the world. It's seriously messed up and I don't know any more than you, but I really don't believe we've any help on the way, there's no one coming to save us so we have to do what we can."

Philip felt like his head was about to explode. He always tried to avoid pressure, and it wasn't doing him any good now.

"Just pull yourself together ," Donald barked. "We've around an hour of daylight left if we're lucky, and we need to be secure before it gets much darker. Trust me, you're doing fine." He smiled reassuringly. "Really fine, just keep doing what you're doing, and we'll get by."

"But… I don't know what I am doing," he wailed. He didn't really know why he was crying, he just didn't seem to be able to stop. "I'm an accountant, Donald. I work with numbers. People are really dead!"

"I know." A sadness crossed Donald's face. "And there will be more if you don't get off your sorry arse. Today it's your turn to be the leader, these people trust you, you've been there for them so far, and they won't survive on their own, you know that. You've got the strength in you, this is just delayed shock, it will pass. Have some faith in yourself," he concluded, and with the conversation over, he was gone, leaving Philip alone.

He needed to find a way to wake himself up, he realised; maybe the vodka last night had been too strong; maybe he'd drunk too much. As he rested his head back against the wall, the pressure built behind his eyes and he questioned his sanity. Maybe he'd fallen and knocked himself out. Deep down, he knew it wasn't a dream, in his dreams blood would be redder and not as dark and dried as this.

He remembered reading once that the world consisted of three types of people, Sheep, Shepherd and Wolves. There are people to be led, people to lead and people to pray on the weak, and he found himself wondering which one he was. He pulled his pistol from his pocket. The closest he had ever got to a gun had been in the amusement arcades, so he held it out at arm's length and took aim down the site.

"Bang! Bang!" He laughed quietly to himself as he lowered it to his lap. "Bang, Bang…" he giggled as he remembered playing cowboys as a child, running around with cap guns, chasing off invisible enemies. He took aim again with the gun. A low wall across the road hid the enemy. "Bang!" he whispered, up in the trees, "Bang!" in the windows of the house across the street.

He squeezed the trigger, more out of memory of the simpler days as a child than anything else, and the window shattered as the recoil flipped the gun from his hand. He was up on his feet before he realised what he was doing and Donald and a few of the others appeared quickly round the corner.

"Sorry." He held his hands up laughing. "Everything's fine. My fault." He picked up the pistol and switched the safety. "I was just checking the weapon, didn't realise the safety was off," he explained as he smiled reassuringly, he could see Donald's face smirking at him as the others walked away.

"I thought you'd killed yourself," he scolded at first, and then a grin slowly creased across his face. "Did it feel good?"

"Oh, yeah!" Philip couldn't control his grin either. "It scared the hell out of me, but yeah, it felt really good. It felt real, if you know what I mean?"

"The first few times you fire are a rush, but after that, you start to figure how to aim. If we had more ammo I'd let you fire off a magazine or two, but for now we need to conserve what we have."

He looked at Donald as the snow continued to fall onto his broad shoulders. He looked older somehow than he had when they first met, more drained, and obviously, he was hiding something. There was a pain behind his eyes, and it was then that he realised he wasn't the only one having problems, but someone had to be the leader.

"Donald," he smiled. "I see what you mean about people needing someone to follow, I just don't get why it's me."

"You want the honest answer?" Donald looked him squarely in the eyes.

"Yeah, I think I do."

"It's because you don't have any emotional ties. You looked stronger than the others when I met you, less denial than the others and more common sense. Plus, you saved my life back there in that house and I won't forget that lightly. You showed concern and support when it was needed, but not looked for..." He looked up into the sky as he thought. "I didn't expect today to bring what it did, it just happened. If the building hadn't dropped this morning, we'd more than likely still be there." He fell silent and stared ahead of himself, sadness sweeping across his face.

"You okay?"

"Yeah," he nodded as he snapped out of his memories. "Yeah,

I'm fine, just thinking is all. Let's get these people inside."

Marcus closed the door and locked the cold outside. They'd done everything they could to secure the area. Sentries had been assigned, and the civilians were packed in for the night, the only thing left for him to do was to sit and wait, and hope to see the dawn.

Philip realised that all the things he'd hated about Christmas, all the things that he'd missed out on as a child now affected everyone, and he felt guilt inside, wondering if he had wished this upon them. It was strange. He missed the Christmas trees and the cheap foil decorations from the pub and he felt sad that he might never see them again.

He didn't really know how to talk to people, so he avoided them where he could. A woman walked passed at one point as he stood at the side of the road, her daughter holding onto her hand as they trudged onwards to God knows where. She'd even looked up and smiled at him even though they had nothing to be happy about. Just keep going he told himself, you'll wake up soon enough.

They walked on in total silence. Everyone seemed locked in their own thoughts as they made their way slowly forward, and it thankfully wasn't long before the advance team reappeared in the distance, and a distorted outline of a building appeared on the horizon.

"Boss, the centre is just ahead," the ginger haired lad reported. "You want us to go in and check it out?" He seemed to be actually enjoying the responsibility.

"Yes," Philip nodded. "Don't enter yet though, we don't know what's gone on inside there. Check out the perimeter first and look for a way in, we'll hold here until you confirm it's safe for us to come in."

With that he saluted and turned to walk away, but Philip stopped him.

"What's you're name by the way? I didn't get chance to ask before."

"It's Stephen, Boss."

"Well it's nice to meet you, Stephen." He shook his hand. "There's no need to call me Boss though, my name is Philip."

"We'll be back as soon as we can." He nodded with a smile before he ran to get the others.

"Alright everyone." He whistled loudly to catch their attention. "We stop here for ten minutes. Don't go inside unless someone has checked it out first." He turned and watched the lads vanish again in the distance.

"You're getting the feel of it now I see." Donald walked up behind him. "Are you feeling better about it?" Philip didn't turn around to look at Donald, but kept watching the shape of the building in the distance.

"A little, I guess." He paused and checked to see who was nearby; everyone seemed to be getting on with their own things, but he lent closer to him all the same. "To be honest, I'm scared

"Just remember, you're not alone." Donald stood next to him. "Just keep moving forward and never look back, and make sure that any choices you make are the best ones you can, and be confident even if you're not." Donald patted him on the shoulder before turning back to the group and Philip turned to watch him as he walked away. What's your story, Donald? He thought to himself, what drives you on.

Fifteen minutes later they followed Stephen as he led the way towards the shopping centre. The place was in a shambles, the quake had caused a large crack in the outside wall and most of the windows in the entrance had smashed, snow covered glass covering the floor.

"It's not good enough," Donald moaned as he entered. "Without a roof over our heads we're going to freeze, and we don't have enough people to cover all the entrances from attack."

"I see what you mean," Philip agreed as panic started to well in his stomach again. "But I don't know what other options we have.

Steve, where are the others?"

"Car park," he pointed. "It was the only place we could find to stop the snow getting us."

"Okay, show me the car park. Let's see if the roof on that is any better." A moment later they stood looking up at the multi-storey car park. Built above the shopping centre, it started thirty feet above the ground, and the four levels of parking spaces would give ample room for everyone to hide in. With only one entrance it looked as good a castle as they would find.

"This will have to do, get everyone inside." He tried to sound confident even though the panic building inside made him want to throw up.

The gull was in pain, it could feel where the other birds sharp beaks had tore into its flesh, and the weariness of battle made its muscles ache, but worse was the shame of running away. It had never run away from anything before, and no other gull had dared to challenge it in such a long time, but there had been just too many of them.

The darkness outside brought a chill wind, and it struggled to keep warm, maybe it was too old now, maybe it was just it time to give up and die, to sleep the long sleep. Death was so close, it would be easy to just accept it, to let sleep take it and never wake up again.

Something moved outside, footsteps scampered by and it backed himself further into the corner. Whatever they were stopped at the entrance and sniffed inside as though searching for something, before jumping off again and running to join the other sounds outside.

It should give up, life was too hard now. The easy pickings of yesterday had gone, and he had seen these new creatures up close, their cruel beaks were still fresh in its memory. It should give up, but something deep inside stopped it. It could sense a change in the air, maybe there was a promise of something worth waiting for.

Evening came quickly, and the night brought a biting wind that seemed to cut right through Philip's clothing, no matter how he tried to cover himself. Fortunately, the snow had stopped and the Moon shone down on the quiet city, casting an eldritch glow over the ruins of civilisation.

At ground level, the snow lay undisturbed and their footsteps had been mercifully covered by the last of the snow. People huddled together to keep warm, and the car park was a scary place to be at night. Philip shivered as he lay on the floor near the entrance, one arm retracted inside his coat as he tried to keep some warmth inside, his other hand held firmly onto his pistol which felt very cold and real in his hands. Donald sat a few yards away; his breath in the moonlight was the only thing that gave away his position.

It had been a frantic hour, but eventually the stairwells had been filled with rubble, and they'd blocked the entrance by pushing a couple of cars. A few large boards had been pressed up against the open slots of the parking bays on the second floor, giving some shelter to the old and young, and everyone eventually settled down as best they could.

"Remember everyone," Donald has said to all the guards before they settled down. "We don't know what tonight will bring, so I need everyone to keep alert, and keep your weapons ready."

"Can we have a fire?" someone shouted.

"No. Not a chance, not tonight." Donald shook his head. "It would just give away our position." The statement about the fires had caused a few raised voices from Ed's group, arguing that they had kept fires going last night, and they'd made it through.

"You lost a lot of good people because of them; we can't afford to lose anymore." He cast an eye over the group of complainers

"Tomorrow's another day, Donald," Ed scowled. "And a lot can happen between now and then," he sneered before leading his people away.

As Philip lay in the darkness he pondered on what Ed might do. He knew there was no love lost between him and Donald, but surely even he could see the logic in what was being asked for. The thought of Ed being in charge certainly worried him. Though he didn't want the leadership himself, he knew that Ed wouldn't be the right person either, and Donald wouldn't have it. He eventually fell into a fitful sleep, either due to the cold or fatigue but his head slowly nodded forward, and the blissful peace of night washed over him.

"Something's out there!" the whispers called to him, and it took precious seconds for his mind to wake up from its cold rest and open his eyes.

"Bottom of the ramp," someone hissed, he couldn't see who was talking, but the problem was clear enough. He pushed his arm out of his jacket and felt the pain as cramp pushed back, he could see Donald watching him from his position, and he put his finger to his lips before pointing towards the entrance.

He slowly released the safety and waited fearfully in the predawn light, trying his best to flex the blood back into his cold frozen fingers as sounds floated up to him from below. He could make out shuffling and grunting noises from outside, then something moved in the entrance.

It carefully climbed over the bonnet of one of the cars in the entrance before him, its thin arms reaching out in the darkness. He held his breath, not daring to make a sound, the gun in his hand suddenly feeling very heavy, very cumbersome, and his heart beat so fast he thought he'd have a heart attach.

It stood at the entrance peering into the darkness inside and he felt as though it was searching for him. The hairs on the back of his neck tingled, and it took all his effort to not just turn and run. After what felt like hours it finally turned to leave, jumping down to the join the others further back down the ramp, but it suddenly stopped, hissing loudly in the darkness as it span round to look back at their hiding place.

Have I made a noise? The thought flashed across his mind. Has it seen me? Others appeared next to the first and he tried to slide further back into the darkness as they started to climb inside. He could see them as they approached, scampering on all fours over the cars blocking the entrance, small and childlike in appearance. He could hear them rasping to each other, a hissing grunting language that was filled will malice and hate, and a shiver ran down his spine as they came closer.

Donald has warned them to wait for his signal should anything happen, and it took all his strength not to fire. Philip knew that at least five people lay hidden nearby, as ready and as nervous as he was. Each creature seemed to be sniffing the air, looking round furtively as they tried to locate something. Philip almost shouted out in anger as a scent in the air slowly reached him, how could someone have been so stupid? For years people had been warned that smoking could kill, and now it might have just condemned everyone to death.

"NOW!" Donald shouted in the darkness. He jumped, pulling back on the trigger and a shot rang out. At this range the creatures didn't stand a chance and within seconds they all lay dead.

"CEASE FIRE! Cease fire." Donald stood up and brushed the snow from his coat.

"Is everyone okay?" Philip called as he pushed himself to his feet; a chorus of yeses filled the air.

"We aren't out of the woods yet," Donald warned. "There may be more of them out there, and those gun shots will have travelled for miles. Get back to your positions and keep watch; dawn can't be far off now," he called as he stalked off up the ramp.

They all stood looking at the creatures' bodies, each one feeling wild and alive as the adrenaline of battle flowed through them, but now wasn't the time to celebrate, not yet.

"Back to positions," Philip ordered.

"I can see others out there, Boss!" someone called and Philip quickly ran back to the edge.

"Where?"

"There," Stephen shouted as he got closer. "See, they're running away."

"Bring them down," he shouted. "Don't let them escape." He took aim with his pistol and emptied his clip, the others opened up with him, and bullets fired wildly around the escaping creatures. One fell as a bullet tore into his back, but the other made it round the corner and was gone.

"Damn!" Philip shouted, holding his head in his hands.

"It's only one," someone called. "Not as though it can do much to us it is?"

"It won't be alone when it comes back later though, will it?" Philip snapped. "It knows where we are, and we can presume it will tell more." He knelt down in the darkness and felt the despair wash over him. They'd survived the night only to face an even bigger problem. A commotion rose behind him and he turned to see Donald drag a struggling man by his collar, and as they got close he slapped him to the floor.

Cigarettes hung from Ed's mouth and it looked like a whole packet had been stuffed in. Donald stalked over to one of the dead creatures and dragged it over to Ed's position, dropping it in front of him.

"See it!" he kicked the body. "You see this thing? You caused this, you stupid..." Donald roared with anger as he pointed his pistol at Ed's head. "If we'd lost any one of these lads tonight, I'd shoot you where you're lie."

"I, I didn't think alright," he shouted, still spitting tobacco from his mouth. "I'm sorry..." He stared at the creature before him, thick black blood oozed from the wounds in its chest. "I'm sorry." He sat staring at it for a moment in silence before turning to Philip.

"All I wanted was to be warm, at home. All I wanted was to feel normal again," he explained. "It felt like all this was a dream...you know... when I woke up, and....when I woke from my dream, just for a moment, everything felt normal, you know, like I was home again."

He turned to Donald before slowly looking round the group of men.

"I watched my friends die last night. I watched the world come crashing down around me, my kids crying with fear as they hid under their beds. I watched it all, and I just wanted everything to go back to normal." He gasped for air between sobs. "So when I wake up I, I have a fag don't I, I just didn't think, I'm sorry... I don't want to do this anymore! Let me go home, I just want to go home..." he sobbed uncontrollably.

Philip walked over and crouched next to him, putting his hand on his shoulder. "We all want to go home. No one wanted this to happen, but it has," he stated. "So now we have to make it through as best we can, for all we know, the Army's on the way and we just have to hold out a little longer." He looked out across the city.

"Look, it's almost dawn, nothing else is going to happen now, so let's get some fires going and get some breakfast on. They're going to know where we are now anyway. We may not be at home, but I bet we can still figure out between us how to make a bacon sandwich and a coffee. What do you say?"

Tears ran down Ed's face as he continued to pick tobacco from his mouth. "I kept on thinking that last night was the worst nightmare of my life. We were lucky yesterday, I see that now." He pressed his hands into his eyes, wiping away his tears.

"If we'd stayed at home, we'd have died, all of us. Even our children," he addressed everyone nearby. "I don't know what I can do to rectify tonight, but I have skills I can offer, if you will have me."

Philip pulled him to his feet. "Wipe your eyes before your family sees you. There's no need for you to feel any worse that you do already," he advised. "Donald, can you put him to work today?"

Donald stared at Ed, his fists clenched and unclenched.

"Donald!" he barked.

"Yeah, fine." Donald slowly blinked.

"Good, that's settled then. Now who can find us some bacon?"

"Boss, I swear it was gunfire," Nick reported. "A short burst at first, then more a few moments later. Came from that direction." He pointed north. "It was just before dawn."

"So there are others out there fighting." Marcus stood with him at the front gate. "Hopefully some of our units are still there."

"If anyone survived you mean."

"I'm sure there are other people still around." He ignored Nick's comment. "Where are you from, Nick? Are you a local lad?"

"Na," he shook his head. "Born in Blackpool, but my family moved to Chester when I was young."

"Chester's a nice place. I've been there a few times"

"Yeah. I guess," Nick nodded. "If it still is."

"Right, that's enough, you need to stop it!" Marcus snapped at him. "Enough of the doom and gloom okay. We don't know much yet; the attacks could be local only and reinforcements could be on the way, but until we know more, we keep positive and keep focused on the job at hand. You understand me soldier?"

"Yes, sir," he saluted. "I understand. Sorry."

"Don't apologise." He lent on the gate as they talked. "Everyone's feeling the stress at the moment, trust me on that, but we have civilians here, and we just need to keep them as positive as we can." Marcus smiled. "Go and get some breakfast, we'll need to set off again soon, but I'd like you to take Glen and see if you can hook up with whoever was shooting."

They walked back inside as Jolly pottered happily around in the kitchen as he tried to kill everyone with fat and greasy food. Marcus commandeered the front room and called a team meeting, so Nick could explain what had happened during the night.

"Good," Kate nodded. "That gives me time to re-dress Peter's wounds before we set off again, I don't want them to get infected."

"How is he?" Marcus smiled, Kate was tough, but when it came to Peter she seemed to turn into a little girl. She preferred to look after him herself despite Glen being the team medic.

"His wounds are getting better," she smiled. "Glen gave him some antibiotics, but more rest would do him good."

"Good. Keep an eye on him, but I want a full report on his

condition in two hours, if he isn't going to be fit to travel, he'll need to stay here with the civilians."

"I want no heroics," Marcus reminded them both as he walked them to the gate. "I want a quick recon only, nothing more. Our priorities are to get these people to safety, and that means aiming for the barracks. So one hour out and one back, remember there's no radio contact so you'll have no backup."

They saluted and he watched them until they were out of sight before re-entering the house where Jolly stood waiting for him.

"So..." Jolly waddled behind him as he entered, having to run every few steps to keep up. "Do you think your barracks are still in operation?" His Bermuda shorts and flip flops making him an odd sight and Marcus made a mental note to tell him about his odour later, someone had to.

"I can hope, but there are no guarantees. The way I figure it, everyone will try to get back there as a rendezvous point."

"Well, I've enough fuel to last at least a month here," he volunteered. "I can keep the people safe until you get there. It saves dragging them all that way with you, less to protect too."

"That's good of you, Jolly. I'll keep that in mind." He didn't want to admit that he was planning that anyway, it would be much easier if he felt it was his idea. "How do you feel?" he asked Peter as they entered the make shift surgery. Kate jumped and dropped the cloth she had been using to clean the wound with.

"I feel much better now, thank you, sir." He smiled as he lay on his back. "It hurts like hell to walk, but it's certainly getting better."

"Good. Get as much rest as you can. Kate, be ready to pull out when they get back."

Kate nodded reluctantly before Marcus turned and left them. Jolly continued to waddle behind him.

"You think there's something going on there?" Jolly whispered but Marcus ignored him. "So what's next?" he moved on. "What do we do now?"

"Well, for the moment we get ready. I'll take you up on your offer to leave the civilians here if you don't mind, and I'll leave Peter here as a guard, so at least you won't be undefended."

"Oh, trust me. We're anything but undefended. Gimp and I have fortified this place. It'd take an elephant to get in the front door, and I can electrify the back wall if I need to." Marcus had started to like Jolly. Okay, he was overweight, and had a slightly musty scent, but a decent guy none the less. Gimp on the other hand was something else entirely. He'd seen him around once or twice, a sullen lad with even worse hair than Jolly; he wouldn't speak to anyone directly, but just seemed to whisper to his cousin.

"Good," he smiled. "You're not worried about all this at all are you?"

"Not really," he replied matter of factually. "I saw this coming a few years ago."

"Eh?" Marcus stopped.

"Well, it amazes me that no one else did to be honest." They wandered back into the kitchen. "With all the solar flares on the increase it was bound to happen sooner or later." He grabbed a chocolate bar and dropped the wrapper on the table. "You see the Mayans got it right, we just screwed it up afterwards. I've been preparing for the end of the world for ages."

"What have the Mayans got to do with anything?"

"2012 and all that man." He looked excited as he spoke and Marcus wondered what he had started. "They reckoned the end of the world would be in the December of 2012, but that was only the start, you don't expect something like that to just happen in one day, it takes ages for it to build up, the race isn't over yet. Plus the old popes messed about with the years, so much in the past that we can't be sure if the year's right anyway."

"So all the suicides a few years ago, all the fear, was for nothing?"

"The world didn't end did it? Well, not then anyway." As he talked the chocolate moved round his mouth. "God man, I need a bong or something to talk to you about this." He looked around. "Gimp!" he shouted.

"No," Marcus stopped him. "I don't want it all, just enough."

"What do you know about solar maximums and minimums?"

"Er…"

"Okay. End of the world for dummies then," he smiled. "2012 was just the starting point of what we're seeing now, the Sun builds up enough power inside it before it pops. EMP city man."

"So what's the end?"

"Don't know that yet. But it's certainly gonna be one hell of a ride. They didn't reckon it was the end of the world, just the start of a new one."

"And the things that attacked, what are they suppose to be?"

"No idea there." He shook his head as he grabbed a packet of crisps. "I just prepared the house to protect what I had from the outside world, not from the underworld. If the web was still up, I'd search for you, but I can't." He shrugged. It was obvious to Marcus that the internet was Jolly's only form of communication to the outside world; when his power finally went out he'd go mad.

"You want a packet of crisps while we wait?" he offered.

So far Glen was enjoying the walk. The world was peaceful, and considering they'd only met the day before it surprised him on how many things they had in common, and as they passed Old Trafford their interested solidified.

"Crap team!" Nick stated.

"No argument from me," he agreed. "Who you support then?"

"Everton," he sang the team name with pride. "And you?"

"I'm a true blue my friend," Glen announced proudly. "I support a proper football team."

"I'm not going to comment," Nick smiled. "Mind you, I don't suppose there's much chance of them ever playing again, not now anyway." He kicked a brick across the road and it vanished into the snow. "But…" he nodded as he thought to himself, "there will always be football. Wherever a group of men collect, a ball shall be found."

"Words of wisdom, oh wise one," he laughed. "But I guess you're right. I bet cavemen kicked boulders around a million years ago." The streets had changed so much in the last few days, Glen found it was hard to position himself on any map. Old Trafford stood in the background, its steel girders bent in odd shapes where one wall had fallen away during the quakes.

"You know, I'm starting to think I could've been wrong about the direction; sounds seem to travel in strange ways when it's this quiet. I might've heard an echo after it bounced from a totally different direction, either way, I guess it's almost time to head back. Damn it," Nick cursed. "It's bloody snowing again. Join the Army, see the world." He laughed. "You know what's funny? I've been to the Middle East, Europe and Africa, and I end up stuck in Manchester in the snow."

"I was born in Blackpool, never been anywhere really," Nick shrugged. "Though a bit of summer would be good right about now, my feet are frozen."

"What's it like growing up in Blackpool? I've been drunk there more times than sober, but I've never really had the time to look around."

"As a kid it was all about cider under the pier. I didn't want to work on the fairgrounds, so as soon as I could, I left home and never really went back." His face looked sad. "I never really missed it until now, now that it's over."

They walked on a little in silence and he was just about to call a halt when a woman's voice shouted from across the road.

"Excuse me," a woman shouted. "You boys want a cuppa? A warm tea is just the thing for a cold day like this, or so my husband used to say," she trilled. "My John died eight years ago now, so just me and my cat Tiger, mind though, I haven't seen him for a day or so. Have you come to see the hole? I expect the council will have something to say when they try to repair it, it's a terrible mess. Listen to me talking on, I'll go and put the kettle on while you boys go ahead. Do you want coffee or tea when you get back?"

Philip looked out from the top floor of the car park, the smell of breakfast made his stomach grumble. He realised just how hungry he actually was, but he didn't feel like eating just yet, there was work to be done. He heard the slow methodical crunching of Donald in the snow behind him, he didn't turn round but continued to stare at the horizon as he spoke. "How many did we lose last night?"

"Seven in total." Donald walked up next to him and looked over the edge. "Four of them just didn't wake up; the cold must have got to them while they slept."

"And the others?" he asked.

"Suicides." Donald shook his head. "A father and his two kids jumped from the third floor."

Philip wasn't surprised, after everything that they'd been through it was obvious some would look to quit, getting out before something worse happened to them.

He'd seen so much death, so much blood over the last few days he'd almost got used to it, but some of the others found it harder; those who had lost more felt it worse. He heard someone laugh on the floor below; it was a strange sound, a sound that didn't fit anymore, yet it was something so simple, something that gave hope.

"It's surprising what a small amount of home comfort can bring. A cuppa tea and a slice of toast and people start to warm up." Donald rubbed his eyes, trying to wake himself up. "Why did you defend him?"

"Who?" Philip turned round to face him. "Ed?" He'd expected the question to come much sooner than this and he'd asked himself why he'd done it a few times now. Donald had supported him since they'd first met, whereas Ed had been cold and obnoxious from the start, but Philip felt he understood why now.

"Yeah," Donald confirmed. He brushed snow from the ledge as

he waited for the answer, watching it drift gently to the ground below.

"I suppose I understand that people make mistakes. That's just how life works. Ed's mistake was to have a fag when he woke up. Your mistake was making people feel terrified; they thought you were actually going to kill him. They thought you where going to kill him in cold blood, and after everything these people have been through, they couldn't see that."

He watched as the wind howled around them, picking up the fine snow and swirled it around the dead cars that littered the top floor. "You wanted me to take the lead so I did," he continued. "My choices, my responsibilities, and I'm not ready to give up on us just yet. So if that means I have to stop you killing someone, then that's what I need to do." They walked down the ramp into the relative shade of the level below. "You wanted me to do this remember, I didn't, but I can see now that someone had to."

"Philip," Donald stopped him before they walked any further. "Listen to me…" he could see he was obviously struggling with what he was about to say.

"These people aren't soldiers, they're not trained," Philip said before him.

"I know," he nodded. "I guess old habits die hard. It just surprised me how stupid people can be. I realise now that I went over the top a little?"

"A little?" he smiled as he replied. "I don't think anyone else noticed. Though some good may have come out of it, I think he's given up smoking."

Donald turned to leave but Philip stopped him. "Just give him a chance, okay, we all need a chance."

"Fair enough," Donald nodded.

"I need you to do something first though, we know at least one of them got away, so we can presume we've got more to come. I want you to see if you can get some boarding up before nightfall. Barricade the entrance a little better. See if Stephen can help, he should know what's round here that can be scavenged."

"I see what you're doing." Donald pointed at him mockingly. "Keep me busy, don't ask me when you should tell me." He smiled. "Sure thing, Boss. Leave that to me. What are you going to do?"

"I'm going to meet the people, see what we have to work with. They're all scared down there so we need to get a lot of them working to take their minds of things. I'll send people to you as soon as I can figure out what they can do."

Donald saluted and was gone, leaving him alone to wander the car park. He tried to speak to everyone, reassure them that everything was going to be okay, while finding out that they did, or what they could do to help. Each time he found someone with a skill that could be used he set them to work.

Philip stopped as he heard a noise from the back of the car park and he pulled his pistol slowly out as he approached. Suddenly, two new faces appeared from behind a car and they walked sheepishly towards him. The older Asian man looked to be around his age, black haired and unshaven; he was carrying a young boy of maybe six years old.

"Morning," the man shouted. "I didn't believe Tommy here when he said he could smell cooking, but now I see he was right. My name's Ashfaq. My friends call me Ash." They shook hands. "And this is Tommy."

● ● ● ● ● ● ● ● ●

Glen and Nick both stared at the woman as she stood at the gate to her garden; she wore a pink fluffy dressing gown that dropped down to her ankles and pink slippers. Curlers neatly lined in her hair and the cigarette that hung from her lips looked battered and bent.

"Er…" Glen looked to Nick for support, but he looked just as shocked. "Well then, tea for both of us please." He smiled, not knowing what else to say.

"I'll leave the door on the latch." She smiled before shuffled back up the steps to her house. "Just make sure you wipe your feet when you come in," she called before shutting the door.

"Well…" said Nick once she'd gone. "I didn't expect to see that."

Five minutes later their army boots stood neatly by the door. She'd insisted that they take them off so as not to dirty the carpet. So now they both sat on her floral patterned sofa, sipping cold tea from a pot as their feet froze.

"I take tablets to sleep you see, and didn't think anything of it really." She smoked heavily as she talked, and no sooner has she finished one before another was lit. "I like to keep to myself, if you know what I mean, not like some around here." She indicated out of the window. "It's not worth sticking your nose in where it don't belong, just gets you a load of trouble nowadays…" She shook her head in obvious disgust at something she'd thought before turning back to them. "As I was saying, I went to bed early as it was cold you see and I took my sleeping tablets, nothing wakes me once I 'ave 'em. My John…" she crossed herself, "God bless his soul, used to joke that the world could end and I wouldn't wake. They did help me mind you, he had a terrible snore, sounded like a chainsaw he did. I remember when we first met, he was much slimmer man then and…"

Glen was mesmerised. She didn't seem to stop to breathe and her train of thought was going all over the place.

"I'm sorry to interrupt," Glen stopped her. "But you said there was a hole".

"Oh yeah, love. You heard about that, did you? It's been a while since I had any young men come to visit, but yes, you must want to get back to the council and report it in, to get the repairs started. Where was I…?" She paused for a moment as she took a sip of her tea before sitting down next to Nick and patting his knee. He looked nervously across at Glen for support, but he just smiled and looked away.

"Well, I woke up in the morning, everything was quiet, and the snow wasn't falling so much, and I remembered I needed some things, tea bags, milk and such, I had a coupon for the tea bags…" she remembered with a smile. "So I got ready and went to the shops, only they weren't there anymore. I tried to call the police but the phone's not working, so I figured I would just wait. My daughters are due to visit tomorrow, she'll know what to do. She's a clever one is our Jane, works in HR or something, whatever that is. She's single." She gave Nick another look and smiled. "Are you single love?"

Philip felt his day ran smoothly for the most part, the food was plentiful, and Ed had created a small makeshift kitchen area where an industrious group of women kept tea and coffee on the boil all day. He had even managed to set up a children's area behind it, and filled it with an assortment of toys from the shops below.

"So you're an accountant then?" Ashfaq smirked. "You're not really what I thought one looked like, you seem a little more human and a little less geeky."

"If it makes you feel any better, I wasn't a very good one," he laughed. "But hey, it was a job, something to do while I figured out the rest of my life. So what did you do before all this?"

"I worked in contact centres; like you though, I did it just hoping inspiration would catch me. I had a few ideas for business but nothing really paid off." He waved over to Tommy as he played with the other children. "He's a good kid, kept me going yesterday." He smiled as he watched him play.

"We've checked but there's no sign of his mother here."

"I didn't think there would be," he shrugged. "You've come from the other side of town. I don't believe their dead though, not all of them."

"I've wonder about that myself. A few people have come out of houses when we passed them. Like me, they either missed the event, or didn't open their doors when the attack came, so there could be other groups of survivors out there. Maybe there are huge areas not touched by those things at all." They stopped near the kitchen. "Do you have any idea what they are?"

"A guess," Ashfaq nodded. "But it's only a theory."

"Let's hear it then, it can't be that bad."

"Can we get a drink first? I really could do with a brew."

Marion smiled as they walked over and happily poured them both a strong tea. She'd joined them yesterday on their journey, and her husband and son had jumped at the chance to help with the building of the defences.

She'd almost single-handedly pioneered the kitchen area, collecting pots and pans, and organising the collection of water and fuel to keep them going and they both thanked her before sitting down on a crude bench in the corner.

"There's a story in the Qur'an," Ash continued after he'd sipped at his sugary tea. "It the story about the Ya'jooj and Ma'jooj. They're evil creatures that are supposed to feed on mankind at the end of the world."

"So you think this is Armageddon then?" It sounded incredible, but the world had certainly gone to pot.

"I don't know what it is" He sipped his drink, shrugging his shoulders.

"I guess it's possible though. Armageddon..." He played with the word in his mouth, letting it flow over his lips. What would doomsday look like? What was in the Bible? Wasn't it something about fire and brimstone, seas of blood? He wished he'd paid more attention at school now. "So what are these creatures, these things that attacked?"

"Legend says that Alexander the Great trapped them underground, and they would escape at the end of the world." He fell silent for a moment before he started to recite something from memory, "The Ya'jooj and Ma'jooj will emerge and surge forth in anger, their numbers shall be so great that they will drink entire lakes in their passing. Or something like that," he finished.

"Well whatever those things are, they'd planned it well. They seemed to know when it was going to happen, and what to do when it did."

"I bet it's not over yet though. You've managed so far," he nodded approvingly as he looked around, "People are working to secure this place." He rubbed his hands together. "But I might be able to get a few of the cars working if you want," he smiled.

"You know about cars?"

"A little," he nodded.

"Well be my guest. It would make life a lot easier if we could get around quicker, especially with those things out there."

"She's mad," Nick stated as they finally walked in the direction Margaret had given towards the hole.

"She not mad, not in old people's standards anyway. My grandma was worse than that. Before the end she didn't know who my dad was. Margaret's just confused. She slept through everything, and has no one to talk to since." He stopped so suddenly that Nick almost walked into him. "Crap, where have all the houses gone."

They'd reached the corner of the road and the city changed before them. The houses seemed to run a quarter of the way down the street until a huge sink hole had opened up and swallowed the rest.

"What the hell!" Glen clicked his safety off as they slowly edged forward to look down into the hole.

Burst water mains mixed with raw sewage below, creating a stinking pool deep in its base. Human body parts lay everywhere, and blood mixed with the foul mud to form a thick pungent smelling concoction. Nothing moved below, and no birds flew over head; even the snow didn't seem to want to stick to the ground.

"This place is evil man. Let's get out of here." Nick shuddered.

"Right enough mate," he agreed. "Let's get back to Marcus. He's going to want to know about this." They backed away slowly, keeping their weapons aimed at the hole until they turned and ran.

"Best check on the mad one before we go," Glen shouted. "We can't leave her here."

"Does she have to come?"

"Yes she does. We can't leave her here, she's lucky to be still alive as it is."

"But she's mad…" Nick protested. "And she's going to slow us down."

"She might be able to tell us more when we get back to Marcus," he explained. "So you need to tell her it's a gas leak or something and she has to evacuate with us."

"Why me though?" Nick whined.

"That's easy," he grinned. "It's because she likes you."

Ten minutes later Margaret pulled a large suitcase behind her as she walked down the stairs, it banged loudly as it dropped down onto each step. "I didn't know what the weather's going to be like, so I packed a few skirts too." She smiled at Nick. "Don't go looking at my legs though." She brushed imaginary dust from his top, making Glen smile. "I haven't found Tiger yet though, we can't go without Tiger. He'll be lost without his Mummy to look after him".

"I'll send someone round for Tiger later," Glen lied.

"I suppose Tiger will be okay for a few hours without me," she reluctantly agreed. She dropped her suitcase by Glen's feet and took Nick's arm. He turned to smile at Glen, mouthing 'sorry', before turning back to talk to Margaret about her daughter, and with a sigh of resignation, Glen bent down to pick up the case. This wasn't going to be easy journey back.

Marcus had been worried about sending them out without backup or any way to contact them; it had been a risk and he felt better when Kate walked in with the news.

"They're back, Boss!" Kate smirked as she walked back into the kitchen.

"There'd better have a good reason for being over an hour

late." He followed her back to the street and watched as Glen opened the gate.

"Where's Nick?"

"He's behind me." Glen signalled over his shoulder as he dropped a suitcase to the floor.

"Is he injured?" He stepped past him and walked onto the footpath beyond.

"Not so much of an injury." Glen smirked, "More of a handicap." Marcus could just about see him in the distance; the snow fell in think clumps again now making him look disfigured as he walked slowly along. The closer he got, the odder he looked and it was only when he heard the voice cutting though the air that he could make out something resting on his back.

"Are we there yet? My legs are killing me. I need a brew. I can't last long without a cuppa, not at my age. My you've got a strong back, my Jane likes a man with a strong back. Hold on to me, I don't want to fall."

Philip walked around the car park, it was certainly starting to feel warmer with each board that went up against the outside, and although he felt sick to the stomach with worry, he made sure he put on a brave face whenever anyone was nearby.

The sound of banging and sawing could be heard from the lower levels as Donald set people to work. He tried to guess the time, but without the regular patterns around him it wasn't easy. He didn't want dusk creeping up on them before they were ready. With precious little ammo, he just hoped whatever Donald was planning would help them get through another night.

"Damn it," Marcus cursed as he slammed his hands on the table. "We can't just ignore it. Did you see any movement while you where there? Tell me you covered your tracks, nothing can follow you back here?" Glen looked quickly at Nick who just put his head down.

"Sorry Boss," he said. "Didn't even think to check, at least it's been snowing so we won't have left any real prints."

"That's not good enough." He felt the anger build up inside as he looked at Glen. "You should know better than that." He pointed angrily. "You might have compromised everything. Put everyone at risk." He stopped himself. Bracing both hands on the table, he breathed in and out slowly before looking up at both of his soldiers where they stood sheepishly before him.

"Marcus…" Nick said. "We're sorry."

"Well at least that takes one decision from me. We stay here for the night. We can't afford to leave everyone here without better protection, so no quick dash to HQ." He looked over the map. "We," he looked up at John who just nodded, "could do with checking out this hole. You guys ready for another walk?"

"Yes, sir," they both confirmed, eager to get away from Margaret and get back into Marcus's good books, so in less than ten minutes they were back on the road. With no distractions they made good time and arrived at the pit just over twenty minutes after setting off.

"Bloody hell, that's huge," John exclaimed as they reached their destination. "How wide is that do you reckon?"

"200 metres across maybe and it looks like it's going down 50 metres," Marcus guessed. From his vantage point he could just about see into the base of the crater, and an obvious entrance sat close to the opposite side near the bottom.

"Glen, take Nick and circle round to the other side, see if you can come at it from another angle. Make sure you keep low and out of sight, I don't want anything down there to know we're here. We'll scout right and meet you back here in ten minutes." They backed away and started to climb through the rubble of the houses that skirted the edge, climbing carefully so as not to dislodge anything.

"What's your thoughts, Boss?" John asked as they settled down in their new position.

"I really don't know." He pulled his field glasses from their pouch on his belt and looked down into the crater. Human bodies lay near the base where they slowly sank into the mud. He'd seen mass graves before, but this was different, those graves contained people who'd been shot, not devoured.

"You see anything moving?" John whispered nervously.

"Nothing," he shook his head, "but that doesn't mean anything. They could be watching us from the dark."

"It smells rank."

"A ruptured gas main maybe, either way we need to be careful." The others returned, and they all carefully scrambled into the remains of a house close to the edge. Marcus crouched looking out over the pit, not wanting to turn his back on it just in case anything should start to climb out.

"There are a couple of ramps running out on the other side, but this side looks heavier used, so I guess they must have gone back in that way."

"Right," Marcus confirmed, he didn't want to hang around any longer than they needed to, but he needed to know what they were up against. "Let's get back to Margaret's house and set up a low profile reconnaissance position so we can keep an eye on them."

It was an hour before dark now and the car park looked in the best shape it could. They'd managed to fix boards against most of the outer facing walls, and the lift shaft and stairways had been clogged with so much metal and rubble that nothing would come up that way.

"Make sure the handbrakes are off lads," Donald shouted as a group of men pushed the second car into position, petrol soaked rags stuffed into their fuel tanks. "Just in case we need to clear a path later," he smirked as Philip walked across. "Think of them as bombs on wheels."

"You're having fun," Philip smiled, Donald was visibly buzzing from the work they where doing.

"Just a little," he grinned, "it's been a while since I've had to think like this."

"Do you think we're ready?"

"I think we're as ready as we can be. Maybe nothing will happen..."

"You believe that?" Philip looked down the ramp to the snow below.

"No," Donald shook his head. "Not at all, they know we're here now and I bet they're not happy we killed their friends."

Philip wandered around the car park, checking the defences where he could; almost everyone had something to do, either strengthening the outer walls or making petrol bombs as they siphoned fuel from the now useless cars. Everyone seemed to be supporting each other, lending a hand where required and sharing water and food with strangers without a second thought.

"They're not strangers anymore," Donald smiled when he mentioned it over a bottle of water later. "They're all connected now. Survivors develop a bond with each other, that's why soldiers tend to only talk to other soldiers about their experiences."

"And if you weren't there."

"If you weren't there, you wouldn't understand."

"Like Saint Crispin's day, from Henry the Fifth," Philip suggested.

"Yeah," Donald smiled, "something like that. Survivors syndrome," he explained "and we need to use it before it goes."

It seemed logical enough to Philip; they were all equal now, all survivors. It didn't matter what you'd done before, the slate had now been wiped clean, and a unity started to build in everyone. People stopped and smiled as he passed them by and they seemed to have more faith in him that he did. He just hoped it wasn't unfounded.

● ● ● ● ● ● ● ●

Margaret's house smelt. The smell of cats and stale smoke fought for dominance against her perfume, making it almost impossible to relax, and everyone looked cold and on edge. But for the first time since the disaster Marcus felt like they were actually doing something positive.

Standard procedures had kicked in and each weapon have been striped and cleaned in preparation for the coming night. Packs had been re-packed and everyone sat with an air of anticipation as darkness finally started to fall.

"How many did you bring?" Marcus asked incredulously as John sorted his pack on the bed upstairs.

"Ten."

"Why the hell did you bring ten claymores with you?"

"I don't know," John shrugged. "I grabbed a load at the school; I guess I just forgot about them until now."

"That's Kate rubbing off on you, that is. That woman would bring a tank to a tea party," he laughed.

"I wish she would." He waggled his eyebrows. "Though I reckon she wants to rub off against someone else now."

"You're not jealous are you?"

"Me?" He looked up. "Na, not with Kate, don't get me wrong, she's a fine looking woman and all, but it would be like dating my sister, there's too much history." And he shuddered at the thought.

"You guys have been together for a while then I take it?" Nick sat by the window looking out onto the darkening street outside.

"Longer than I want to remember." Marcus ruffled John's hair as he stood to stretch his legs.

"Careful..." he objected as he brushed his hair back with his hands. "I need to look good for the ladies, you don't mess with my hair, Boss, and you know that."

"I wouldn't worry too much though, Nick." Marcus smiled ignoring John's complaints. "We'll grow on you soon enough."

"Like a fungus." John smiled as he started to clean his rifle. "Pretty soon you'll wish you'd never met us."

"Are you any good with that?" Nick pointed towards the rifle.

"Yeah, not bad I guess. I had a few weeks field training with one a few years back and got a taste for it." He held it up and reverently ran his hand down its side before looking through its sights. "I recon this baby must have been Ken's, but I guess he doesn't need it now."

"Hey," Marcus looked over. "Don't under estimate him. He could still be out there looking for it. If anyone could have got away, it's him." He'd forgotten about Ken after the first night, but he knew better than to count him out just yet.

"Don't worry." John nodded as he realised what he'd said. "I'll give it back if he asks for it." He walked over to Nick, handing it over and letting him feel its weight. "The AW50 Sniper rifle fires one of these with an accuracy of over 2000 meters." He handed over a large bullet. "Normally I wouldn't get to play with one of these, but I guess Santa's been good to me."

Nick put the rifle to his shoulder and aimed out of the window.

"What made you join up?" John asked him.

"I don't know really." He sighted out of the window as he thought. "I guess at the start it was for the women. I thought I'd look good in uniform." He smiled as he said it. "Then later, I got a taste for the action. My real life was boring, nothing new, you know what I mean? Wake up, go to work, come home, sleep and start again, no punctuation marks in your life, no breaks."

"Got more that you bargained for now though haven't you?" he smiled. "So what did you do when not playing at soldiers?"

"I'm a chef." He handed the rifle back. "I run my own place in Burnley, well, ran. I wasn't doing too badly for myself either; I had my regular customers that didn't die from food poisoning."

"A chef, that sounds posh."

"Well… I wouldn't call it posh exactly; it's more of a café, a good quality greasy spoon."

"Well now then, that's my sort of food," John smiled. "I can't be doing with all that posh crap. Sausage, egg and chips is all it takes to keep me happy, so what you making for tea?" Nick grabbed his pack and opened it, using his flashlight he rummaged round for the food packs.

"Well, we've got vegetable curry…" he continued to search, "And another vegetable curry." He rummaged round inside the pack. "Aw no, it's all vegetable curry."

"Who packed this?" John moaned

"Three guesses." Marcus walked over and pulled a pack at random from the pack, before reading it and dropping it back in.

"You let her choose our food, damn it, Boss!"

"I didn't let her." Marcus held his hand up. "She must have done it while we got ready."

"She pulled this crap last time, you remember?" John ripped open the pack and smelt inside. "I'm telling you, next time we go out, she's eating worm cakes."

They reluctantly ate their food in silence as they planned their revenge on Kate, and soon they started to settle down for the night. Nothing moved inside, and everyone sat covered in whatever they could find to keep warm, trying not to think about the empty silent world outside.

Marcus watched them from his position; the group's emotions had almost reached a critical mass, and he realised that only their operational training held them together, but they would have to find time to pay the piper eventually. Everyone worried about families or loved ones, friends and neighbours, who were alive, and who were dead.

He was lucky, he came from an army family, and being an only child seemed to have its advantages now. He'd spotted Nick worrying sometimes, on those odd moments when his mind wandered and he thought no one was watching. John and Glen were hardened soldiers, and could keep their emotions at bay longer, but Nick was TA; he hadn't seen real fighting before and most probably not killed before, and that was now pressing heavily on his shoulders.

He remembered his first fire fight, his first confirmed kill and how he felt inside. It didn't matter how much training you had, or how clean a kill it was, it still affected you, and he could see the man's face as he'd stood over him, his eyes staring into the clear sky.

It was a night not dissimilar to tonight, he recalled; a small pass in the highlands near the Afghanistan border where his patrol had followed tracks in the snow to a camp, very similar to their own tracks outside.

"Boss!" John whispered as he signalled down the street. No time now, he thought, all we can do is hope and pray they don't see them. No one breathed as a shape scampered passed outside, before more followed, many more. They scampered and ran out of the hole in their hundreds. Larger creatures trudged by, at least ten feet high and very muscular. For three minutes they watched the horde pass, their own tracks mercifully destroyed by the first of the creatures and he gave a silent prayer of thanks to whoever had been listening.

"They seemed to have a clear purpose in mind," John observed.

"I know," he nodded. "We need to find out where they're going. At least we should be able to track them in the snow."

"A blind man could follow them now." He looked over to Nick. He looked pale, and appeared to be sweating despite the cold, the image of so many of them had stirred up fears deep inside him and Marcus realised he needed to get him moving quickly, before the fear could take over.

"Let's go…"

Stephen was almost enjoying his shift on the car park roof. The stars shone in the unpolluted heavens above and the Milky Way curled its way slowly across to the horizon. A gentle frost settled on the snow below, only the odd cloud remained to spoil the otherwise beautiful vista.

"What was that?"

"What?" Stephen turned. "What did you see, Jack?" he asked nervously as he tried to peer into the darkness below, just in case he'd missed something, but Jack pointed towards the sky.

"It was up there." He tried to mark out its path. "Then it was gone, just sort of whooshed across, like a firework".

"That my friend," he smiled, "was a shooting star. I used to see loads of them when I went camping. You should make a wish," he suggested. "You never know, it might come true."

"Seriously?" he looked wide eyed at him. "They can grant wishes?"

"If you've been good," he smirked. He'd forgotten how gullible Jack could be. "Go on, we could do with all the good wishes we can get." They both stood in silence, staring up at the stars far above them until Jack finally got bored and wandered away, leaving him with his memories.

"Ste!" Jack called after a moment or two. "Ste, come here, there's something moving down there."

"Where?" He reached the side and looked over. "Where? I don't see anything."

"Over there," he pointed. "See that black area where there's no snow, it was just in front of there."

He squinted, trying to focus on whatever had startled him. The cold of the night had been pushed aside as the adrenaline set to work. "Oh no!" he whispered as a cloud that had blocked the moon moved on, and the light increased. "Go and get the others, quick."

It wasn't an absence of snow that Jack had seen; it was a mass of creatures. Black shapes in such numbers that the moon failed to penetrate further than their heads. If Jack had made any wishes they where forgotten as he ran, slipping down the ramp to raise the alarm.

"How many?" Philip stood with Donald and a few of the others as Jack arrived. No one felt like sleeping and everyone clamoured round to hear.

"Hard to tell," he shrugged. "There's maybe a couple of

hundred, maybe more."

Donald spat. "I didn't expect so many.." Philip looked at the listeners. A look of abject terror filled almost everyone's face and they milled aimlessly around, unsure on what to do, waiting for someone to speak, for someone to lead them.

Something stirred inside him and he felt angry as he looked at the frightened people, his people. It was his time to stand up and be counted. Everything slowed as his heat rate increased and strange calmness washed over him.

"Right then, this is it people." He straightened his back, standing proudly before them. "They think we're beaten…" He paused as he made eye contact with as many people as he could. "Well," he shouted, "they're wrong. You all know where to be, and what to do." He clenched his fists. "Let's burn these evil creatures back to hell."

A cheer went up, a false bravado from a scared people, but it seemed to work, and they started to move into action. Oil drums were set alight and weapons grabbed. By the time the adrenaline wears off, he thought, we'll be either victorious or dead.

"Okay." He pulled his pistol from his pocket. "Light the floor, let's see what we have to face." Two flaming bottles arced from gaps in the walls and he watched as they exploding into bright yellow flames onto the pavement below. A few strangled screams rose from the crackling fire as a few of the creatures burst into flames, and in the flaring light Philip looked down onto the attackers below and despair knotted his stomach.

"Mary mother of God," he whispered under his breath as he quickly crossed himself. His heart pumped heavily in his chest and a dizzy sensation washed over him as the mass of bodies moved away from the fire. Panic rose inside him, telling him to run and hide, to abandon the place and the people and hide under the covers until they'd gone. Be calm, be calm he chastised himself. Don't show fear, not now. He took a deep breath before turning back to everyone, trying to look as calm as possible despite his terror.

"This is it all right," he nodded. "I want the runners to get the next floors ready, get the children to safety at the back." Donald put his hand on his shoulder and they looked at each other, he nodded that he understood their chances as well as Philip did, but the same resolve was visible behind his eyes, they would not go down easy.

"Let's give them more fire lads," Donald barked. "Aim for the middle of them, burn as many as you can. Get ready to defend the entrance." Two barrels were kicked over and petrol gushed down the ramp. The liquid flowed towards a group of the creatures that already approached from below, their unblinking eyes full of hatred as they charged with their cruel knives drawn.

The fuel sloshed around their feet, washing the snow away as it ran on, pooling at the base. Donald waited for them to reach the half way mark before he gave the signal for the burning rag to be dropped onto it. With a roar the petrol ignited, engulfing the attacking creatures in hot burning death. A few started to run backwards, their bodies burning brightly in the darkness, but they fell before they reached the bottom. Thick smoke billowed upwards into the sky as they cooked, and Donald smiled as he watched them die.

"How many did you see out there?" Donald shouted to Philip above the roar of the flames.

"More than we can handle." The flames from the ramp cast a bright yellow glow over everyone near by. "We must have really hacked them off by being here still. If we can hold them off until dawn we might have a chance."

"Dawn? Are you kidding?" Donald shook his head. "At this rate, we won't hold them for more than an hour or two. You'd best set some more fires, get everyone armed and ready. Don't use the guns until we need to as once we run out of ammo, it's going to be hand to hand."

Kate watched the flashes from the upstairs window, and prayed everyone was okay. After the patrol had failed to return she'd ordered the house locked down, trusting her gut that they would be safe out there, but now, as the horizon flashed she started to worry.

It wasn't as though she could do anything. She knew that to try to find them now would be suicide, if it even was them fighting out there. So far there had been little sound that would tell her Marcus was in trouble, no sound of gun fire or grenades pointed to them being involved, so she closed the window and reluctantly went back to the patrol.

Another volley of petrol bombs landed on the road, but the creatures had learnt to keep their distance now, and only a few of the slower ones fell. Noises could be heard below as they tried to gain access via the lift shafts and stairwells, but they had been truly blocked and nothing would come up that way tonight.

Philip had positioned himself with the entrance group when the first of the giant monsters lumbered into view. It was a large, squat, heavy looking thing, hairless and slavering. It must have cleared twelve feet high when stretched, but it spent most of its time walking with a stoop, its muscular neck holding its small head steady as it lumbered forward. It roared at them as it reached the base of the ramp, sending a chill through the defenders that faced it. It held back cautiously as it waited for the petrol to burn down and as Philip watched, it started to go slowly out. It pounded the floor with its huge fists, showering pieces of concrete in all directions before it lowered its head and started towards them.

"We hold here…" Philip screamed as he stood in the doorway. "We stand and fight. If that thing gets inside, we're done for. Ready one of the cars." A blue Toyota was pushed to the edge of the ramp by the others and at his signal, the rag was lit and it was pushed out. A shower of sparks exploded from it as it hit the concrete sides, but it started to gain speed as it rolled towards the beast below.

He watched as the thing braced itself against the impact,

sliding slightly backwards as it caught the car. A moan rose from the defenders as it lifted it from the floor and held it above its head, roaring in defiance. It roared once more, just before the burning rag set the fuel tank alight, and in the darkness it exploded like a Sun. As the smoke and fire finally cleared, he could still see it stood defiantly before them, its huge feet planted firmly on the ramp and he could feel the panic building once more inside him.

A cold wind blew past them, clearing the last of the smoke from the remains of the creature, its upper body incinerated in the explosion and its feet staggered sideways before it fell over the edge, and this time, the roar rose from the car park. Even Philip allowed himself a small smile, though it quickly ended as he watched another creature approaching. "Get the second car ready..." he bellowed.

This new creature came quicker than the first, head down it charged up the ramp like a bull. He nodded and the car was set alight and pushed free, but once again the beast stopped it, throwing it quickly over the side where it exploded amongst a group of the smaller creatures, its fireball billowing up into the night sky.

With a roar of rage the creature continued; on all fours it attacked and the defenders started to back away. The world seemed to turn to treacle before Philip's eyes, his heart beat deafening in his ears. "Shoot it, open fire," he shouted as he snapped out of his terror. "Take it down! Kill it!" Every weapon they had opened up onto the beast and bullets ripped into its body, tearing open its flesh as they thudded deep into its torso. He watched as it fell to its knees, dark blood seeping from its wounds as it reached out to support itself and he stepped forward and finished it with a shot directly into its head.

Donald heard the gunfire from below and just hoped they had managed to hold the front gate. All his attention was on the group of creatures that had climbed up the back of the shopping centre and had managed to assault them from the rear.

They'd reached the roof before anyone had seen them, and with cruel blades they cut deep into anyone that got in their way. People fell screaming for mercy, men, women and children alike, and Donald had led a hastily created group at them. His cleaver swung steadily, tearing limbs from any that got near, and the floor was slick with blood as they pushed them, step by step, closer to the outer wall and the drop below.

Donald swung the cleaver deeply into the head of one that got too close and cursed as it stuck hard in the bone pulling it from his hands as it fell backwards into the darkness below. A second group of creatures charged, cutting him off from the other defenders. With nothing else to use, he grabbed the closest one with his bare hands, snapped its neck before using its carcass as a weapon, he swung it wildly by its ankle, knocking creatures aside as they got closer, but he knew he couldn't sustain this much longer.

Minor wounds on his arms and chest sapped at his strength, and he panted with exhaustion as they circled him, their unblinking eyes staring at him as they approached for the kill. "You want me?" he screamed in anger, too weak to do much more as he accepted his situation. "Come and get me."

A blade cut into his side and he managed to land a punch quickly into the creatures face, as he dropped to his knees he pulled the blade from his side and holding it close he waited for the end. Suddenly strong hands grabbed him and pulled him to his feet as Ed and his men fought their way through to him.

They dragged him to the safety of the floor below before turning to push the last of the attackers back over the edge, dropping them to the ground far below.

Donald could hear the thud of arrows as they hit into the outer woodwork, splintering the boards. He watched, unable to help, as one struck a man deep in his chest, knocking him backwards onto a loaded table as his lifeless fingers dropped the lit Molotov cocktail he'd held and the world went white.

The screams of the dying echoed through the car park as the table erupted, throwing fire over anyone who stood nearby. He grunted as he forced himself to stand, before staggering over to a woman who had been caught in the flames, trying uselessly to pat down the fire that burnt hotly against her legs.

Philip watched as the last of the larger creatures started up the ramp towards them. A large group of the smaller ones followed closely behind, driving it forward and it roared as they poked it, urging it on. Petrol fell from above, and the flames once more coursed down the ramp. The smaller ones either burst into flames or ran back to the relative safety below, but the flames missed the monster, and he ordered them to open fire again, but the little ammo they had wasn't enough to stop it, and the wounded creature kept coming.

One by one their guns clicked empty. There was no time to reload, even if they had more ammo, no time to do anything but fall back, to retreat further back into the car park and hope it couldn't get inside. With hands like spades it grabbed the sides of the entrance and roared at the scrambling mass of people as they fell away before it.

It tore a lump of concrete from the supporting beam above its head, showering sharp stones down onto them and Philip threw himself backwards, trying to avoid the shrapnel, but a piece glanced off the side of his head, and he felt himself trip over the feet of someone behind, before falling hard to the floor.

He watched in terror as it turned its yellow eyes on him. Saliva dripping from its open mouth as it reached down and grabbed his foot. He screamed as it squeezed hard on his ankle, effortlessly dragging him closer, despite his struggling. His back left the floor as it raised him closer to its face. A group of defenders tried to charge, but it swung out wildly towards them, lifting them from their feet as it tossed them like dolls against the outer walls.

He was so close now he could smell it. The thick putrid smell of rotting flesh on its breath made him gag. He kicked out wildly and connected with its chin, making it roar in anger more than in pain, and it banged him headfirst into the floor, dazing him before lifting him once more towards it mouth.

The world span and he could feel himself losing consciousness; he forced himself to twist, to look at his attacker one last time before the end, to face his death with what dignity he could muster. It looked back at him, those cold eyes viewing him without compassion. He felt like he was just meat to it, and just a mouthful at that.

Philip had never felt so small or as mortal as he did now. He tried to struggle, but his arms had stopped working, his vision started to blur. The last thing he saw before the world went black was the creature's head, as it exploded before him.

"Are you okay, Donald?" Ed ran over to help him with the woman, but the burns had been too bad for her to handle. "I'm sorry," was all he could say as he lowered her slowly to the group.

"Not your fault," Donald grunted between the pains. He closed her eyes with his hands before pulling himself shakily to his feet as Ed reached out to support him. He ached in so many places, and blood soaked into his shirt from his many wounds.

"You need to rest. You're bleeding badly." Ed looked concerned. "You need to sit down."

"I'll be okay." He walked forward on shaking legs, but accepted Ed's shoulder for support. "Thanks to you and yours anyway," Donald smiled.

"You would have done the same thing," Ed nodded in reply. After a few seconds he stopped and offered his hand. "Hi, my name is Ed."

"Hi, Ed," Donald smiled. "It's a pleasure to meet you. You ready to get dirty again?"

"I've nothing better to…" but he never finished his conversation as a large bang rang in the air from outside, and as they ran to the walls to see what was going on, machine gun fire erupted from the remains of the houses behind the enemy.

"Someone's out there," Donald shouted above the bedlam. "Let's give them a hand." Petrol bombs rained down into the mass of creatures below. The appearance of another enemy behind them had momentarily panicked the creatures, forcing them to back away from the gunfire, and the rear of the group was now well in range of the throwers.

Each bottle set fire to a dozens or more of them, spreading flames quickly through the ranks. Donald's joy was short lived though, as the fear of fire overrode their fear of bullets and they surged towards the gunmen once more.

They scrambled and crawled their way towards the remains of the houses and the mystery men inside. Donald could do nothing but watch as they got closer, fearing the worst for their would-be saviours when suddenly a set of explosions rocked the building as the front lines of the enemy seemed to evaporate into mist before his eyes.

"Claymore mines!" Donald screamed in excitement. "There've got claymores" He pressed his face into the gap in the walls to watch as a second wave crashed forward, and he giggled as they exploded as 700 steel balls tore into them from each mine and the rush stopped. Panic was setting in below and caught between one death or another, they started to kill each other in their attempts to escape.

"Pour it down on them," Ed shouted from the floor above. "Burn them all." The screams of the dying only invigorated the defenders more, and anything they could get their hands on fell like rain onto the enemy. Flash grenades exploded at the edges of the group, forcing them into a closely packed mass, and within five minutes the funeral pyre below was hundreds deep and the smell of roasted flesh filled the car park as Donald called a cease fire.

He walked onto the open platform of the first level and waved towards the buildings opposite and three soldiers stepped into view. The odd gunshot indicated a sole creature contact as they approached the walls.

"Welcome gentlemen," Donald shouted jubilantly as the people cheered behind him. "You lads are a sight for sore eyes I can tell you."

● ● ● ● ● ● ● ● ●

Donald sent a runner to the entrance to let them know allies were on their way in. The worst case now would be for some adrenaline filled guard to open fire on the new arrivals and a short time later they entered the car park. Seeing the soldiers gave hope to everyone in the centre; the army had finally arrived, everything would be better now, but Donald could see that this wasn't quite the case.

"My name's Marcus," the lead soldier introduced himself.

"It's good to see you guys I can tell you." One of the soldiers pulled out a first aid kit and started to deal with his wounds. "I'm good. Honestly," he objected. "There are people who need you more than I do." The medic stopped and looked to Marcus for direction, obviously concerned with the volume of wounds he had.

"I think he's tough enough to hang on, Glen," Marcus nodded. "Take the kit back to the entrance, there are people down there that need you more."

"Philip!" Donald slapped his head, realised that he hadn't come up with the soldiers and he grabbed Ed. "We need to get down there, now."

They ran to the entrance, slowing as they approached, as the scene unfolded before them. Bodies lay where they had fallen, their limbs bent and twisted in odd angles by the impact of the creature. The survivors sat together, sharing a cigarette in the early light of dawn, but he couldn't see Philip anywhere.

"Where is he? Where's Philip?" He grabbed the closest man, shaking him until he looked up.

"He was the last to move." The man shook his head. "He kept firing until the last moment, gave us a chance to escape."

"Where is he?" Donald insisted. The man pointed to the carcass near the door. The still steaming bulk of the creature blocked one side of the entrance, and as they approached an arm could be seen lying loosely from underneath.

"Philip!" he called. "Oh, I'm sorry..." He crouched and held his hand, feeling guilty for leaving him in such an open position, he moved to leave but the hand grabbed hold, not tightly, but enough to say he wasn't dead, not yet.

"Guys!" he screamed. "Give me a hand moving this thing, move it off him, he isn't dead." Everyone pitched in and they finally managed to create enough room to pull him free. Though he looked pale, he managed to weakly smile as he cleared the carcass and Glen moved in to help him. Ed pulled Donald back to give them space to work, and it was some time later that they were able to see him again.

"How is he?" Donald asked Glen when he finally finished bandaging Philip.

"He's lucky," Glen confirmed as he walked over, wiping his hands. "It looks like he got away with only a few broken ribs and a sprained ankle."

"How?" It didn't seem possible he'd got away so lightly. "He was right under that thing?"

"Trapped in its armpit," Glen nodded with a smirk. "Any further and he's have been crushed, like I said, he's lucky. You can come in and see him."

"I don't feel lucky," Philip moaned as Donald entered. He was covered in blood and bits of flesh from the creature but he looked a lot worse than he obviously was. "My ankle hurts like hell, and I stink something rotten."

Donald laughed, just pleased to hear his friend talking again. Though the battle had taken its toll on the defenders, it was a good outcome. They'd lost fewer than twenty people in total and though maybe twice that had been injured, they'd all lived to see the dawn.

"So what happened?" Philip tried to sit up but stopped as the pain shot up his leg and he lay back again. "I take it we won?"

"What's the last thing you remember?"

"I remember..." Philip stared at the ceiling. "That big thing grabbing me, picking me up and I thought I was going to die." He

153

turned to look at Donald. "But its head just exploded like magic. It dropped me and that's it."

"That was me," John nodded from the rear of the group, patting the rifle he rested in his arms.

"Okay," he nodded, finally starting to understand. "So when did the Army get here?"

"Maybe it's best if I fill you in," Marcus interrupted as he stood forward. "Captain Marcus Fletcher, sir." He saluted.

"Well you're a sight for sore eyes," Philip smiled. "I'm glad you're here, we thought we were on our own for a bit there." Philip could see Marcus's expression and it didn't look full of confidence. "How many of you are there?"

"Not many." He shook his head. "We're not part of an advance team or anything, and to be honest, I've had no contact with anyone else."

"I don't understand," Ed interrupted. "You're the Army!"

"What's left of it." Marcus shook his head. "Those things hit everywhere, and because of budget cuts, we were thin on the ground as it was, most of our lads are half way across the globe fighting." They fell silent as the thought of salvation evaporated before them, and it was a moment before anyone spoke.

"Okay," Philip sighed. "I guess things could have gone a lot worse for us. Let's not worry too much about how many of you there are, let's just organise what we have and get on with it."

As the day wore on, Philip watched the slow procession of people enter the car park. They'd moved the dead from the ramp and Donald stood at the top to welcome everyone inside, directing them towards him as he sat at a table with his ankle raised and a notebook in his hands.

He had already worked his way through everyone in the car park, and by listing them by name and skills he'd managed to create a number of work parties, defence, foragers and cooks. So now his plan was to assign the people that entered to a group to ensure everyone contributed, it was a simple idea, and one that kept everyone busy.

One of the last to enter was Jolly. Philip had already heard about him from Marcus and was pleased to finally meet the man in person; when he finally waddled over the top of the ramp, he was out of breath and he sat down unceremoniously next to Philip.

"So, Mr Jolly," Philip began. "What exactly do you do?"

"Well firstly," Jolly wiped his brow with his sleeve. Despite the cold outside he was visibly sweating, "It's just Jolly. No 'mister' or anything special." He talked in between taking great intakes of breath. "And I can make anything; my speciality is for things that go bang."

"Marcus has suggested I get you started on the top floor. They've created a number of huts up there for you, they're not perfect but they should do you until we can find somewhere better."

"Don't worry about me," he smiled. "Once the gang gets here with my stuff I'll be fine."

"How do you know how to make these things?" From what Marcus has told him, Jolly sounded like Q from James Bond.

"Well, I guess I got most of it from the internet," Jolly mused. "There's lots of online magazines and stuff that tell you how to do stuff, you know, how to make landmines from house hold stuff, totally illegal but it's so cool." Jolly looked excited as he talked, the top floor would certainly be the best place to put him.

"Okay," he nodded. "Well, you'd best go and get set up." Jolly nodded and shuffled away, a thin gangly lad that Marcus had called Gimp following at his heels, and he watched them until they vanished from sight.

● ● ● ● ● ● ● ● ●

He sat counting up the people on each list when a roar filled the car park. It wasn't the noise of a creature, but it was a noise he'd ever expected to hear again. People stopped working to listen, looking round as they tried to figure out what it was.

It was a sound they'd heard daily for all their lives, and the absence had been so shocking and sudden that they hadn't realised it wasn't there until now. He forced himself to his feet as an old blue Beatle drove down the ramp towards him. Its exhaust spluttering somewhat, but it held out until it drew level with him.

"What do you think of my ride?" Ash leant out of the window. A bandage covered a wound on his head from the night before, and Tommy sat next to him smiling excitedly. "It looks like the older the car is, the better they survived" he explained "I just replaced the battery acid and the spark plugs and here we are."

"I helped too, didn't I, Ash?" Tommy smiled at Philip.

"Yeah, mate. You sure did." He ruffled his hair. "So, you want a lift somewhere?"

The first day after the battle came to a close and Marcus posted his guards on the roof and set the remaining claymores around the perimeter, advising everyone to stay inside just in case. Philip was sitting with Ash and Ed when he finally arrived.

"You did well with the car today." He smiled at Ash. "How many more do you think you can get working?"

"I don't know." Ash shook his head. "Maybe another two or three. It depends on their condition and what I can scavenge." His face was covered in grease stains. "All the modern ones are fried, but I can salvage enough from them to at least get a few more started."

"If they can just about get us from A to B I'll be more than happy," Donald called as he walked over with a tray of hot drinks.

"Marion seems to be doing well in the kitchen considering we've double the number of people. I take it we have enough food for everyone?" Ed asked as he took his cup.

"We've more than enough for the moment," Donald nodded. "Thankfully, with it being almost Christmas everyone had stocked up. So almost every house we search has stuff in it we can use." He sat down next to Philip. "As long as we have fresh water we should be fine for months." Philip sipped his coffee as the general conversation rose. Quite why they were making all the decisions was beyond him, but no one had complained so far.

During the day, more and more people had turned to him for advise and a rumour was spreading that he'd single handilly fought the creature at the entrance to give the rest time to get away and he felt guilty for not stopping it. "Okay, let's get this over with so we can get some rest." Everyone fell silent as he started the meeting. "How's the building work coming along?"

"Ed's taken charge there," Donald started. "So he'd be best updating you." Ed smiled as Donald nodded across to him; obviously the problems between them had gone during the battle.

"Well. We've managed to rebuild the lower level walls and fortify the entrance. We can work on the upper floors as we go."

"Good," he didn't know what else to say, "Well done."

"Sir," Marcus interrupted. "I've been discussing the pit issue with Donald and I want to take a group inside, see if we can close it." The thought of an entrance so close worried him, and the idea of it being closed certainly made sense. "I'm guessing we killed most of them," Marcus continued, "So it should be empty."

"That's the hope anyway. If our luck holds, we should be able to get inside, scout around and seal it with demo charges. Stop them coming back up that way again." Donald added.

"What do you need from me?" Philip hoped it wasn't strategic advice.

"Just the go ahead I guess," Marcus confirmed to his relief. "As far as I'm concerned, I fall under your jurisdiction, at least until I can contact Head Quarters."

"Wow. I've got an army now then have I," he smiled. "Well, Captain, you certainly have my blessing, and the names Philip, not Sir."

"Okay," he nodded. "Thanks, Philip. I've already got twenty volunteers ready for the mission tomorrow, role call for 06:00."

"Good. Thanks, Marcus."

"Looks like I need to get to bed then," Donald announced as he stood up.

"You're not going tomorrow are you?" Philip stopped him.

"Well yeah, why not?"

"I just…" he didn't know what to say. "Well, I just didn't think it would be your cup of tea that's all." He realised how lame it sounded as soon as he said it.

"I'm getting too old am I?"

"No, that's not what I meant at all." The thought of being alone worried him, Donald had been his support, his rock since the start and it felt natural when he was around.

"Well, maybe I am a little," he smiled. "I just think I'm getting a taste for this danger business again. This place will do fine without me for a day." Donald patted his shoulder as he walked passed. "You've everything in hand here, and Marcus could use some more experienced people."

"Just be careful," Philip called after him. "I don't want to lose anyone else."

"Don't worry. I'll keep an eye on him." Marcus saluted. "Gentlemen, I bid you goodnight." He nodded to the others before he followed Donald down the ramp, leaving the three of them alone with their thoughts. It was Ed that spoke first.

"Time I turned in too I guess," he yawned. "Laura wants me to read Sally a story before she falls asleep, and I don't know how much longer I can stay awake."

"Sounds like fun," Philip smiled. "Thanks for everything today."

"No problems." He smiled back.

"It must be nice having family," Philip mused after he'd gone. "Someone to go back to…" A shadow crossed Ash's face and he realised what he'd said. "I'm sorry… I didn't think."

"It's alright." Ash looked into his cup. "I miss them, that's all. The last thing I did was have an argument with my father, and now I can never apologise for it." Philip watched him as he talked. "He told me that I should make something out of my life, get married and have kids. Nothing he hadn't told me a hundred times before."

"You never know," Philip tried to comfort him. "Your family may be in the tunnels."

"You're right." He looked up from his cup. "I need to go with them."

"No," Philip blurted. "I didn't mean for you to go too."

"No." Ash held his hand up. "You're right. It's the right thing to do. I need to know if they're down there." He placed his cup on the tray and stood up. "I need to get to sleep so I'm up in the morning. Thanks, Philip. Goodnight." He stood and walked away, not looking back.

"Okay then…" he said to himself as he pushed himself to his feet, slipping the crutch under his arm before he limped lonely down to the floor below. He remembered someone saying it was lonely at the top, and right now, Philip knew exactly what that felt like.

Dawn was still some hours off as Marcus approached the group of nervous people. He could see their apprehension as he walked over. Walking into the pit wasn't the best of options on a good day, knowing there could be creatures waiting form them didn't help at all. His men stood to one side, casual but ready, each one experienced and trustworthy; almost all had see serious battles and come through on the other side relatively unscathed, both mentally and physically in most cases.

The civilians on the other hand were a totally different story. They milled nervously together, silently smoking or deeply worried about what was to come. He'd worked with new recruits before, but it had been much easier as they weren't expected to be in a fire fight situation for months; these people might see action within the hour.

Ash walked over with Philip. He could see his leg was still sore and he could see the pain on his face, his eyes red from lack of sleep. To save him further injury, he made his way over to them.

"Are you ready to go?" Philip asked, trying to force a smile and hide his pain.

"Ready as we're going to be, I guess, other than my guys, everyone's untrained. A few of the lads have some experience, but as for the rest..." He shrugged his shoulders.

"You can count me as experienced too." Donald sat at the side, cleaning his pistol.

"Sorry," he nodded. "I'd forgotten you'd seen action." Donald just smiled at him as he continued to clean his gun. "The civvies will be issued pistols, and my guys will take point at all times. Basically, we get in and scout around before we blow the hole."

"Simple," Donald stated. "As long as no one's home".

"We'll have to wait and see for that one. Have you ever fired a weapon before?" Ash jumped as he realised he was being asked a question, obviously not quite awake yet.

"No, not really." He shook his head. "Although I understand you point the end with the hole in it at the enemy, right?" he joked. "And then pull the trigger. I'll be fine once I've seen the basics."

"Good, I want you to lead a group. You've got a good strong head on your shoulders and I don't see you cracking if we run into trouble."

"Wow." He suddenly looked more alive as the pressure was added. "Erm, okay."

"Take this." Philip handed him his pistol. "Keep it safe and make sure you bring it back to me." He liked Ash, there was something about him that made him feel as though they had met before and since meeting, they'd spent a lot of time talking.

"I will do, thanks." He took the pistol from his open hands. "Though if something should happen, I want you to keep an eye on Tommy for me." Philip nodded to him as he slipped the pistol into the back of his pants. "But I do intend to come back."

"Okay then." Marcus's voice cut the silence making the group jump. "Pierce will show everyone how to reload. I hope we don't need to, but it's worth being prepared." Pierce nodded to everyone before he pulled his sidearm from its holster.

"For the next ten minutes," he barked. "I need you all to pay close attention to me. You can't afford to get this wrong in a live fire situation." Marcus watched Philip limp away as Pierce continued his instructions, as he reached the edge of the firelight he stopped and looked back, giving a simple nod to Marcus before he vanished up the ramp.

That simple nod said everything. It said keep them safe and come home, and it said good luck and farewell, at the same time.

As the first rays of sunlight finally hit the city, the group stood looking over the edge of the pit. The soil glistened with morning dew and Marcus stood back to watch the reaction of the civilians as they saw the bodies for the first time. Most looked away heaving, but he was pleased to see Ash and a few others keeping their composure. They might just make it, he thought to himself.

With no way of knowing what they faced down there, or how many of those creatures could be watching them, this wasn't going to be an easy mission. "I don't like this." Kate appeared next to him. "We don't know anything about this place." They'd worked together for so long now it often felt like she was reading his mind.

"You don't want to turn back do you?"

"Hell no, this looks like fun."

"Okay then." He released the safety catch on his rifle. "Can you and Donald find the door?"

Philip watched from the shadows until the group had passed out of sight before he hobbled back to bed. His ankle ached terribly, and he slept fitfully with dreams filled with monsters and fire until a loud bang woke him. He was still rubbing sleep from his eyes when Gimp appeared enthusiastically before him, almost bouncing with excitement as he waited for him to wake up.

He didn't like calling him Gimp, he'd asked him what his real name was yesterday, but he'd only giggled and wandered off. "Philip, Philip…" he squealed, his voice sounding higher than yesterday. "Jolly needs you. Jolly needs you." He rubbed his eyes again and let them slowly focus as Gimp jumped from one foot to the other like an excited parrot.

"Calm down," he shouted, angry at being woken. "Just calm down, I'm coming." he carefully shifted his weight and slid his legs from the bed before pulling himself carefully to his feet. "Was that him banging?" By the excitement on Gimp's face, he could tell Jolly had obviously done something to Gimp's liking, but that could be just about anything from making the prefect roll up, to creating a space ship.

He slowly followed him as he ran off. "Wait up," he shouted. "I can't walk that fast. Gimp!" he called. "Slow down." It took Philip five minutes to reach the top floor, and he spotted Jolly by the furthest wall of the car park as he waved for him to come over.

"I'm coming." He gritted his teeth. "Hold on." The smoke around him was thick and acrid, forcing him to cover his mouth as he got closer. "What the hell is burning?" he asked as he finally reached him. Gimp just laughed, his eyes darting from side to side as though he was chasing a fly.

"Burning?" Jolly sniffed the air. "Oh yeah, that's nothing, ignore the smoke, I was just messing with Molotov cocktails. We've got up to version 1.3 now I think, I've managed to sort out the mixture so it…"

"Jolly!" Philip shouted, cutting him short before he babbled on too far. "I'm cold, and my foot hurts, can we just get this sorted so I can get on with the day please?"

Jolly seemed oblivious to his attempts at getting to the point and ricocheted into a different direction. "I've got something that could help with the pain." He smiled, making Gimp giggle even more. "Or maybe not…" he stopped as he saw Philip's expression.

"Jolly!" He was could feel himself getting angry now. "Please..."

"Sorry. It's not the fire you've come to see anyway, though that is pretty cool. You've come to see this." He held up a cloth bag around six inches in diameter, a small wick of rope poked out from the top. "Isn't she beautiful?" He stroked the bag affectionately. "I've always wanted to have a go at this, but there was never anywhere I could test one without being arrested."

"What is it?" Philip questioned cautiously.

"It's best if I show you, Watch this." He held up his hand before pulling out a lighter from his pocket and lit the wick. "It's got a twenty second fuse on it, I made this out of..."

"Jolly," He nervously stopped him as it started to splutter, "Just throw the damn thing will you." He kept his eyes firmly on the fuse, even though he didn't know what the bag did, he knew he didn't like being this close to it.

"Oh, okay." Jolly turned and threw the bag as far as he could over the edge of the building. "Fire in the hole," he shouted as Philip hobbled forward. The bag landed near a metal waste bin and small tendrils of smoke continued to rise as the fuse got closed to the bag.

"Now, watch this," he smirked as he covered his ears. The bag exploded sending a fireball high into the air, knocking Philip backwards onto the hard concrete floor, his crutch flying off behind him. Gimp chased after it, running in a lopsided manner and he fell over laughing as he reached it.

"What the hell was that?" He accepted Gimp's hand as he helped him to his feet. Looking over he could see the remains of the metal bin as it lay on its side, small fires burnt on the ground around the crater zone. Jolly stood at his side, clapping to himself with satisfaction.

"Well, what do you think of it?" His eyes looked glassy with excitement, and a small blob of spittle rested on his lower lip. "I can make tons of this stuff. The ingredients are easy to get hold of, you just take some bleach and a Pyrex dish and..."

"Thanks, Jolly," he interrupted once again. "But I'll leave the ingredients to you. It's very good though," he acknowledged with a smile. "Is it stable? I don't want to blow the top off the building."

"Oh yeah," he nodded. "Well, stable enough anyway. We found loads of fire works in the back of one of the shops, so I have loads of fuses and stuff to play with, but I need to find more chemicals to mix. Ash said we could use the car." He held up the keys with a twinkle in his eyes as he looked for permission to go.

"Okay. But don't go too far, and don't crash it." He dusted himself off. "Take a guard with you, and if you see anyone alive out there, send them back here."

"Yes, Boss." Jolly tried to salute but failed miserably. "We will do. Gimp!" he shouted. "We can go."

A young woman stepped out of the hastily constructed hut behind them. She was tall, with a pale complexion and her red hair dropped nearly to her thin waist. A black figure hugging dress was held at the waist by a red corset.

"Suzi," Jolly smiled as she got nearer. "This is Philip." Jolly indicated towards him and he felt his throat go dry. "He's the boss so be nice." She turned and smiled seductively as she held her hand out to him, not knowing what he was expected to do, he gently shook it and she smiled at him.

"It's very nice to meet you, Philip," she purred as she looked him up and down. "I do like a man with power."

"Yes. It's, err…" his mouth suddenly feeling dry. "It's very nice to meet you to, er… Suzi," he stammered as she licked her ruby red lips at him, before turning back to Jolly.

"You will get me something special to wear wont you, Sugar?" she stroked her finger down the side of Jolly's cheek.

"Don't worry baby, Jolly will take care of it for you." He smiled patting her backside as she walked away. "You just keep yourself warm for me until I get back." Philip watched her go.

"What can I say?" Jolly smiled as he saw Philip's expression. "I am a god."

"Where's she from?"

"She came in with us on the first day. I met her a few months back at the Fantasy bar in town. She'd been staying at my place with a couple of her mates when everything kicked off." They both watched as she elegantly stepped back into the hut. "She came in late last night with the rest of my mates when they brought the generators in."

"Oh! Right." With nothing more to say he turned and hobbled away, leaving Jolly to get ready for his road trip. He made a mental note to keep the children off the top floor, and not just because of the explosives.

The edge of the pit was even sloppier than it looked; by the time they'd reached the bottom, they were covered in thick stinking mud and Donald tried to flick the worst of it from his hands. The entrance was dark and damp and water dripped from the soil over his head as a foul, putrid stench emanated from deep inside. Holding his breath, Donald stepped under the dripping water and into the tunnel beyond with Kate close behind.

They walked for maybe fifty feet before he started to push glow sticks into the wall at his side; although it was dark, some light at least still filtered in from the outside so there was less terror. The tunnel before them was silent but for the constant dripping of water, and he waved his torch for Marcus and the others to catch up.

"Do you see anything yet?" Marcus whispered as he shuffled up to them.

"No, nothing yet. Maybe we have struck it lucky." He shook his head. "It smells bad down here though. We'll go forward another hundred and signal if it's safe."

"Okay. We'll hold here until then." Marcus waved to the others to join him as Donald vanished once more into the darkness ahead.

"Careful, Kate," Donald warned as the floor started to dip. "I don't want you falling on me if you slip." The ground felt slick under his boots and the water ran from above making it difficult to move.

"Yes, Dad." she joked at his side. "I'll keep my pretty frock clean too should I?" They stopped at a small landing and signalled for the rest to join them again. With no other course to take, they at least knew they'd travelled in the right direction, but he cursed every sound the approaching group made as he crouched in the darkness.

"This isn't exactly stealthy," he hissed when they caught up.

"Elephants..." Kate confirmed as someone swore behind them as they slipped. "Every bleedin' one of them."

Eventually though, everyone had reached the ledge, and the two of them moved forward again alone. The flood water had at least been diverted into a small channel, allowing it to race ahead and the walking finally became easier as the ground started to dry out.

When they reached the floor below he directed Kate to the left and they scouted silently ahead. In less than ten feet he'd discovered the source of the smell, and he retched, spitting bile onto the earth before he pulled his scarf from around his neck to cover his mouth and nose, trying to stop the stench from getting any worse.

The wall of dead was impossible to count but he estimated that maybe a thousand bodies lay stacked before him: men, women and children, old and young though it could easily have been twice that many. By the light of the torches they seemed to move, screaming and clawing for him in the darkness.

Despite the cold he felt himself sweating, the smell of terror almost overwhelmed him and he backed away from the macabre sight until they finally vanished into the darkness again. When he found Kate, she didn't move but just continued to stare at another pile of bodies. He took her by the shoulder and held her to him, feeling her sob against his chest. For a minute they stood together, two living souls surrounded by thousands of the dead.

"Sorry," She smiled as she pushed herself away from him, wiping her eyes.

"Don't you ever apologise for being human, Kate."

"There are just so many..." her voice sounded softer than usual.

"More than that I'm afraid." She looked so small now; her strong, independent demeanour had gone. "There's at least one other pile on my side." He looked into her eyes. "Listen, I want you to go back to Marcus. Tell him quietly what's down here, there's no way the civilians can take this." She looked pale, but he could see she was fighting to regain her control and composure, and he gave her a moment to get herself ready before setting off.

Minutes felt like hours as he knelt alone in the darkness, listening to the gurgling of the stream and the heavy beating of his own heart. He turned as Kate returned with Marcus, pleased to see someone else.

"You're right, Donald, there's no way we can bring civilians down here." Marcus covered his face. "But our guys will have to deal with it."

"I think it's the only way if we want to get this done," Donald agreed.

"Are you okay?" Marcus looked him in the eyes.

"Me? I'm fine," he nodded. "It's not the first time I've seen something like this. I was in Srebrenica in Bosnia, back in '95."

"I read something about that in reports." Kate looked at him with renewed respect, but he guessed she'd seen the media transcriptions rather than the true story.

"It's sort of strange, but once you get past a few hundred it all blurs. The mind can't take in that much death and not be affected." He fell silent as the images came flooding back. "I got out of the Army afterwards." Marcus signalled and the rest of the soldiers came down. Donald was surprised to see Stephen and his friends bringing up the rear.

"We've seen you this far, it would be wrong to let you down now." Stephen explained once the shock had passed.

"You're good lads, and we could certainly use the extra help."

Donald patted him on the shoulders, they were certainly a good bunch of guys. From what he'd gleaned during small conversations he'd had with them, they'd been together when the first attack came and they'd stuck together since.

"Donald." Marcus appeared at his shoulder. "Can you come with me as I check for exits, I could use the backup."

"Anything's better than just staying here." He could sense the time passing above and wondered what sort of day it had turned into, reminding himself that they needed to be back at the base before dark. Leaving the group behind they set off into the darkness.

Crouching low as they moved forward, the pile of dead seemed to go on forever, but suddenly Marcus held his hand up and touched his ear.

`Stop` `I hear` `Enemy Ahead` `Door`.

Donald signalled that he'd understood and readied his weapon, straining to pick up the noise that had alerted Marcus. Slowly it came to him, a rhythmic flapping noise coming from the passageway ahead and he cursed his age; there was a time when he would have heard that before Marcus.

Marcus had vanished by the time the two creatures stepped into the chamber, dragging another human body behind them. They hissed as they spotted the light from the glow sticks and dropped it to the mud. Marcus reared up behind them as they turned to flee, his knife digging deeply into the neck of the first, before he span and threw it into the back of its now running accomplice.

"Let's go," he whispered to Donald as he pulled his knife free.

Philip's ankle ached terribly when he walked on it, so he'd sat down despondently near the canteen and watched as people went by. It was obvious that the elderly weren't really sure what was going on anymore, and just constantly complained about the cold, or the damp. Parents seemed to work with a purpose as they tried to create a home from the chaos for their young, almost like they were nesting.

The single men tried to be useful, trying to look good in front of the women, some of whom still felt they should be treated like princesses, and some people just sat alone crying in the corners, unable to grasp what had happened. The children seemed to manage the best, they played and had fun and didn't seem to be aware of what had transpired, just treating it as one big adventure. With new friends to play with and new places to explore, life was something fun for them. The innocence of children, he thought, not understanding how close they stood to being wiped out.

"Mind if I join you?" Ed wandered over, wiping his hands in a cloth.

"Sure," he nodded, glad of the company. "Pull up a pew." They sat in silence for a moment, just watching the day go by. "You've done a great job today," he finally said.

"Thanks." Ed rested back in the chair. "But to be honest, the others have done most of the heavy work, I just supervised." The conversation dried up again until Ed broached a subject that had obviously been on his mind. "I'd like to start looking at our water supply," he announced. "We have a couple of hundred people now and they're starting to smell."

"I had noticed," Philip smirked, aware that he hadn't changed his clothes in days "What've you got in mind?"

"Just something simple really, something up on the top floor so we can let gravity do the rest."

"Go for it." The idea of a shower sounded like music to his ears. "Did you do this sort of stuff much before?"

"I was a civil engineer," he nodded. "So yeah, sort of, but it's nice to actually build something useful for a change. I was sick and tired of what I did being used to make money for some fat cat somewhere else."

"I guess." Philip could certainly understand Ed's viewpoint, and he thought back to the meeting he had with Mr Rushford and realised he was most probably dead already. "Well, I certainly appreciate what you and the guys have done."

"It's nice to hear." Ed had a good wholesome smile. "Have you heard any news about the others yet?"

"Nothing, fingers crossed they'll manage to slip in and out quietly."

With no way of knowing who or what might turn up next, time was of the essence. Three passages led away from the main chamber, and although he didn't like the idea, splitting them up was the only way to cover them all.

"Kate," Marcus crouched with them by the entrance to the first tunnel, "I want you and Donald to scout the right passage. Pierce, Brian. Take the left. And John and I will take the middle." He turned to Ash and the others. "The rest of you, hold here in reserve. If we find anything, we'll meet back here and regroup. If we can't get back here, we'll engage and the noise should call the reserves in from here to support." Stephen and his guys looked nervous, but there was no time to cover that now

"I want everyone back here in ten minutes. Now move out." The situation wasn't perfect, but he saw little point dwelling on it any further. Everyone knew what they had to do, and the quicker they got on with it the better. He watched his men peel away, hoping he would see them again.

Pierce kept as close to the wall as he possibly could as they advanced. The ground was at least starting to dry out, but a thin film of slime seemed to cover everything. The path they followed meandered all over the place, as though the diggers couldn't make up their mind on the direction.

The problem was that they couldn't see round the corners until the stepped into it and it was starting to stress Brian out. After five minutes he called a halt to listen for any signs of activity. Nothing seemed to be moving ahead of them, thought he guessed the mud would absorb the majority of the noise; it was uncannily quiet.

"There's nothing down here," he concluded. "I'm going to set a claymore to cover this passage, but I think were safe enough from this side.

"Yes, yes..." Brian eagerly agreed. "It doesn't look like it at all. Let's just get out of here, okay." His eyes darted furtively to each side, checking each shadow for anything that could be hidden there. He pressed the mine into the soft mud, directly in the centre of the passage; anything that tripped it would be vaporised, hopefully bringing the roof down on top of them.

"Okay. Let's get back." He patted Brian on the shoulder, trying to re-assure him that he wasn't alone, but he jumped so much he thought it best to leave him to it.

Donald heard the water before he saw it and the rhythmic lapping of waves greeted them as they stepped out of the tunnel. It was impossible to guess how big the cavern actually was, and the light of his torch failed to touch the ceiling high above.

"I don't believe this?" Donald stepped down onto the slick shingle of the beach, dark water lapped gently against the shore. "You are seeing this as well right?" he asked Kate as she broke a light stick and forced it between the rocks by the entrance to the tunnel.

"I guess." She jumped down next to him. "As long as you're seeing a huge lake the same as I am, then yeah." The beach was only ten foot wide, but it seemed to stretch on forever into the darkness. The air felt crisp and fresh compared to the stuffiness of the tunnel behind them, and they stood in silence for a moment, breathing deeply.

"How deep do you think it is?" She cast her torch out across the water.

"No idea," he admitted. "But if you want to wade in and find out, be my guest."

"If only I'd brought my costume," she shrugged. "I guess this is the end of the line then." He had to agree, it certainly seemed pointless to continue any further. With no set direction to go, it seemed pointless to search along it. Donald moaned as he thought of going back into the stuffy tunnel again.

"Come on," he reluctantly called to Kate. "We need to get back. Best set a mine in the tunnel just in case." Kate didn't acknowledge him but stood staring silently out over the water; he walked up behind her, putting his hand on her shoulder.

"Are you okay?" he asked.

"Yeah," she nodded. "I'm fine." She sighed as she turned to leave. "Let's set that mine and get back."

The lower they got, the stench became almost impossible to bear. There was certainly something going on further down the corridor, and Marcus didn't like the feeling of it at all. Pierce was only a few feet ahead of him and he carefully placed each step in an attempt to reduce the squelching sound their boots made in the slick mud. As they neared a turn in the tunnel, he stopped and raised his hand. Marcus approached as quietly as he could, peering round into the chamber beyond.

It was huge. Part of the cave wall appeared to have collapsed, he presumed during one of the recent earthquakes, and what looked like whole trees had been used to hold the ceiling in place; water dripped freely from between the rocks and pooled on the floor at the base of them.

Fires burnt towards the far end of the chamber, and as they watched from their vantage point, someone screamed. It was certainly human, but it didn't last long and the low level rumbling sound flooded back. Pierce was about to move forward when Marcus stopped him. Pointing over towards one of the fires where he could just make out the silhouettes of a group of the creatures as they shuffled around close to its base.

"Okay," Marcus whispered. "Get back up top and get the rest. It looks like we've at least found some of the missing people, and we need to act before there's none left."

"Are you guys okay?" Ash asked. He'd done what he could to lighten the mood already. After the basic introductions, he'd let them have a smoke to steady their nerves. But Billy, one of Stephens's crew kept furtively looking round.

"What?" he jumped. "I'm fine. Sorry. I just don't like it down here." He was a thin sort of man and he certainly lacked self confidence, obviously dragged down here because of his friends.

"Billy's scared," Mike laughed. He looked like the muscle of the team. "He's afraid of Zombies, aren't you?" Mike lightly punched him on his shoulder.

"Don't let your imaginations get the better of you," Nick whispered as he walked over, his machine gun resting against his hip. "I know it's tough, but hang in there." Mike offered his cigarette to him and he took a drag before passing it back. "Thanks," he smiled. "I'm seriously impressed with you all though," he said earnestly. "I'd never have pegged any of you to have stayed here with us. I've seen hardened soldiers buckle under less than this."

"We're good friends is all." Stephen put his arms on his friend's shoulders. "They've been my family for the last eight years." He smiled. "We shouldn't fit together, but it works. I wouldn't do anything without them." They all nodded in agreement.

"Why do you say you shouldn't fit?" Ash asked.

"Well," Stephen explained. "Mike here is a Bouncer, well was a bouncer," he corrected himself. "Billy's unemployable."

"I'm not," Billy protested. "I'm just having a hard time finding a job that fits me." He watched them chat amongst themselves. Their conversation was a good distraction to what was actually going on around them, and their laughter was a welcome change to the silence.

Philip hobbled painfully down the ramp. His ankle ached terribly but there was just so much that needed attending to he wouldn't have a chance to rest it, not yet. He also didn't feel right just sitting round while the others were down in the pit and it was good to see everyone so busy.

People carried supplies, or worked on the defences everywhere he wandered and he slowly realised that people were watching him, not all the time, but he'd seen people stopping their work and they'd point at him. He asked Ed when he found him.

"It's a form of hero worship," he smiled. "I've heard the story of what you did."

"What story?"

"How you single-handedly held your ground at the gate; fought one of the large creatures with nothing but an empty pistol and your foot."

"I didn't do that!" he objected. "I'm not the hero."

"Doesn't matter," Ed smiled. "Look. As long as they believe, then it's not an issue. You're a hero to them, their brave and fearless leader." It sounded wrong, but the more he thought about it, the more it fitted in with what he'd seen. The young girl who'd stopped to offer him a drink, the men who nodded as he passed by. The problem was he hadn't done what they thought and he felt like a fraud.

"You can't dwell on it," Ed explained. "It's for the greater good."

"But they're putting me on a pedestal. That's not right."

"They need a hero to rely on alright." He shrugged. "Just give them that."

"I suppose," he sighed reluctantly.

"Good." Ed smiled. "Let me show you what we've managed to

do so far."

He accepted the use of Ed's shoulder and walked with him into the depths of the car park, the cars that have been scavenged had been pushed out to make space, and utilising space was something that Ed was obviously very good at.

"We've managed to create around twenty cubicles so far," he announced with pride. "Each can sleep around six people comfortably enough." He pushed aside a curtain to one of the cubicles. The inside was sparse, but serviceable. Mattresses had been placed on the floor in the centre of the room for people to sleep on.

"It's not a palace, but it's warm and dry. I've calculated we maybe need another twenty before we've covered everything we need. It's going to be tight, but it's better than nothing."

"That's good news," he nodded, physically impressed with the speed the construction had happened.

"We'll do what we can." He patted him on the shoulder. "Just leave the construction to me and you deal with the people. Just remember they need you to be strong, you're the hero."

Philip forced a smile as he hobbled away; he could understand what Ed meant, but it still felt false.

Marcus watched from the shadows as they dragged someone else into the middle of the room. The man begged to be let go, but they mercilessly stabbed him and tore him open, tearing at his insides before finally throwing his lifeless carcass onto a pile with the others by the fire.

His fingers twitched against his trigger as he watched, but he knew he couldn't act until backup arrived, so he backed up the passage out of the way to wait and it was a tense five minutes before he heard footsteps behind him.

"Listen up," he whispered as they all crouched around him.

"We have civilians in the chamber to the left. I don't know how many or how many guards there are." He scanned everyone to make sure they were listening. "But that doesn't matter; we can't ignore this one, so I want two flanking groups. Flash-bangs first, then we move in. I don't need to tell you what will happen if we get this wrong." He looked at John. "Set two claymores at either side of the tunnel. If all else fails, the last one through can trip the wire. Get back to base and let them know what we've seen. Any questions?"

No one spoke, so he continued, "Good. Let's go!"

The fires emitted just enough light for them to see by, and John set the mines as the rest moved silently into their positions. At a signal from Marcus, three flash grenades arced through the air, landing in the centre of the cavern close to the group of creatures and they exploded in a brilliant white light.

"Go! Go! Go…" he shouted as the bang subsided. Two creatures staggered from the tunnel to their left, and fell in a hail of gunfire. Another received the butt of Marcus's gun as he ran past it, knocking it backwards into the fire. Within a minute it was over, the final shot coming from Ash; with his foot on the back of a wounded creature, he dispatched it with a single shot to the head.

It was then that they saw what they'd been doing to the people. A stone slab sat close to the fire, blood dripping from its sides into large pots. A man lay motionless on the top, his chest torn open where his organs had been removed.

"What the hell is this?" Brian cried, his voice breaking with the stress. He span in a circle, looking from the creatures to the bodies, and back again. "What are we fighting? I can't do this…" He dropped his machine gun to the floor as he backed away from the others. "I just can't do this…" His hands shook uncontrollably as he held his head.

"Brian," Marcus shouted. "Brian, get a grip. Get it together, we need to move."

"No, no." He shook his head as Marcus approached him. "No, I can't do this anymore, Marcus." He pulled his pistol from its holster and waved it in his direction.

"Calm down, Brian. Calm down." Marcus held his hands up, palm open. "Let's get you out of here, okay?"

"To where?" he wailed. "I can't go home." Marcus realised too late what he was going to do as he pressed the pistol against his temple. He moved to stop him; he could see the look in his eyes, a look of desperation and fear, a look that had only one meaning, one way of escape, and a single shot rang out.

Billy was nervous. He'd heard the gunfire from below and now wished he'd been allowed to go with them, but someone needed to wait for Donald and Kate to come back and he'd drawn the short straw. The not knowing what was going on was the worst thing; his imagination started to see shadows moving in the darkness on all sides and his breathing came in gasps as the fear grew.

He stared at the tunnel, trying to see into the darkness, expecting to see the creatures come storming out at him. The silence worried him and he edged a little closer. Step by terrified step he slowly approach the tunnel mouth, when a single shot rang out from below and he jump as something squelching in the mud by his side.

"Easy there!" Donald grabbed his hand to stop him shooting them, and the weapon fired, jumping from his hand.

"Easy," Donald shouted. "It's us. It's us."

"Oh…" he put his shaking hands to his face, "I almost shot you."

"It's okay." Donald reassured him and he pulled his face towards his own as he continued to talk. "It's okay," he repeated calmly as he looked into his eyes. "You're not alone anymore. Okay?"

"Okay." Billy nodded as he repeated.

"Now where is everyone?" Kate bent down and picked up the pistol, clicking the safety on before she passed it back to him.

"John." His eyes watered with happiness at not being alone and he swallowed heavily. "John came back. They've found people, down there." Pointing towards the tunnel.

"That's good news, Billy, good news," Donald reassured him. Looking to Kate she shook her head in silent agreement to his unspoken question. Billy was obviously in no shape to be left on his own, not now.

"Who's up top with the others?" Donald asked.

"Jack went back up to get them ready."

"Okay then, I want you to go get him," he explained slowly. "Bring him down here with you. But first you need to tell him to get the others to spread themselves out along the exit route and get ready to lead the survivors out. Go." He patted Billy on the back and watched as he nodded back. "We'll go down and see what's going on. If we're not back in ten minutes start back."

"You ready?" He turned to Kate after he watched Billy vanished up the slope.

"As ready as I can be." She nodded as she readied her weapon towards the tunnel.

Marcus stared at Brian's body, and he suddenly felt out of his depth, this was way beyond his experience. Normal procedure would be to call base at this point and request support, but here, now, no support existed.

"Marcus!" Pierce shouted, and he snapped out of his self misery as he realised everyone was watching him. If they didn't act now, they wouldn't last long, but he felt like he was losing control again as doubt started to set in.

"Listen up," he shouted. His head felt like it was going to explode and he gritted his teeth as he forced his panic aside. "I want everyone to fan out and check for exits, they must have got in here from somewhere other than the way we came in. Find it." No one moved. God no, he thought, I'm too late; I've led them all down here to die. He clenched his fists as he fought back, with all his strength; he tensed his stomach to stop the fear that rose from his gut.

"NOW, LADIES!" He released the pain as he shouted. If they were going to die here, then he'd at least make sure they died fighting. Everyone snapped out of whatever thoughts controlled them before they vanished into the darkness, leaving him alone with Brian.

"You selfish sod," he cursed as he knelt down next to him, prising the pistol from his cold hand before unclipping his webbing and Bergen. Their resources were so low they couldn't afford to leave anything behind. He pulled the dog tag from around his neck, not knowing why, as there was no one to report it to, but it felt like the right thing to do.

The fire heated his face and he stared into the flames, letting himself be lulled by the moving embers. A movement to his left made him jump. "Don't come in, there's a tripwire at your feet." He could feel the pressure lifting as he watched Donald and Kate stepping over the trap. Donald was a strong character, someone to support him when he needed it and push him along; Kate was a rock he could moor to. They walked over, stopping as they saw the body

"I tried to stop him. I just wasn't fast enough," Marcus tried to explain.

"You couldn't have stopped him." Donald patted him on the shoulder. "You know that. He would have found a way no matter what, if it wasn't now, he would have done it later."

Soon enough the others returned and they were able to help him draw an image of the chamber in mud at their feet. They estimated it was maybe only two hundred feet wide but at least six hundred long. Only two other passages led from it, one to the right and the other at the opposite end.

"Alright, let's break this down into two groups," Marcus announced. "We have another thirty minutes before we have to get out of here. I want you two," he pointed to Pierce and John, "to take some of the reserves and establish cover at the far end of the chamber."

They both nodded that they'd understood.

"Donald, Kate and I will check out the left tunnel. If we aren't back in 5 minutes retreat to the chamber above and blow this chamber before you get out."

"I've got satchel charges with me." Kate opened her pack and passed them over to Pierce. "Best leave them here for you just in case."

Marcus was glad to be active again, even if they could be walking into danger it felt better than waiting for it to come to them and they scrambled up the ramp to the side without looking back at the others.

Pierce stared down the tunnel before them. It was certainly wider than the others they'd passed through, more constructed. The rock here had been shaped by tools and the floor was also rock rather than the mud of the main chamber. Raising his hand he signalled that he was going in for a closer look.

"What are you doing?" John hissed from his position.

"Just cover me," Pierce hissed back as he scurried forward, and John moaned before he followed him. It was an amazing piece of work. The time it must have taken them to carve this out was beyond him. The roof of the tunnel must have been almost ten feet high, with easily enough space to walk four or five abreast. A stale, warm breeze blew up from the darkness below.

They stepped into the tunnel in silence, listening to every sound, too afraid to miss anything that could mean trouble. Maybe twenty foot from the entrance they found an antechamber filled with large barrel like containers. They stood stacked against the furthest wall and he moved to check them out, leaving John.

Each stood over four feet high, and seemed to be made from a smooth shaped stone, sealed with a tight fitting lid. With the tip of his knife, he applied enough pressure to leaver it open and he shone his torch inside. It was filled with a thick dark liquid and it gave of a sweet metallic smell that reminded him of something. He broke the surface gingerly with the tip of his knife and gasped in horror as an eyeball bobbed to the surface.

"Back to the chamber," he shouted as he backed away.

"What is it?" John started to walk over.

"Leave it be, you don't want to know what's in there, trust me," he insisted, holding his hands up to stop him. "I'll tell you when we get back up topside." He broke a light stick and dropping it to the floor, shuddering at the thought of whatever the barrels were being prepared for.

So far so good, thought Marcus as he slowly pulled another survivor from the pit before him. It was slow going, each pit in the chamber seemed to contain at least a hundred people, and they seemed to go on into the distance; the first twenty or so had been empty, the occupants obviously on the pile of dead.

For three days they'd been stored here in the dark, listening as people around them died. Forced to stand in their own filth, crammed so close together it would have been almost impossible to move until, one by one they had been taken out and killed.

Many had been crushed into the walls, or drowned in the muddy waters after they fell and couldn't get up. The stench of fear and urine mixed with the dead was almost overpowering and it was difficult to get them moving. If only they would move faster, he prayed; their luck wouldn't last much longer. "Come on people," he urged. "Let's move it. Come on..."

The route back was at least clear for them to follow, he'd sent Ash back through the tunnels to prepare the way with the others and now at least some of the stronger survivors were helping the others climb out. It was all just to damn slow, maybe two hundred so far had been released, and he just hoped they had time to get them all.

● ● ● ● ● ● ● ●

When Ash finally saw the sunlight above, a smile crossed his face. He felt giddy at the prospect of getting out of the stinking hole and getting back to base. He half ran, half scrambled from the entrance but his boot sank into the soft mud and although he tried to stop himself falling, he failed.

Spitting dirt and filth from his mouth, he quickly scrambled to his feet again and staggered out of the exit back into the real world outside. The sunlight made his eyes water and he rubbed them instinctively with his hands, cursing to himself as he wiped mud further across his face.

Unzipping his jacket, he pulled his shirt up and wiped at his eyes, trying to clear the grit he could feel against his pupil but his eyes continued to water as he scrambled up the slope. He stopped at the top and breathed deeply as he tried to exhale all the dirt and dampness from his lungs, spitting what he could back into the pit below. He found a burst pipe and cupped the water in his hands, splashing it over his face as he tried to wash away the grit and gain his sight back.

After a few minutes he could see enough to travel, though his eyes still watered from time to time, either from the dirt or the brightness of the Sun, but mission in mind he set of. All he had to do now was get back to the base, let them know what had happened and warn them to get ready for the injured, but his stomach rumbled loudly and he realised how hungry he was. With no breakfast or dinner inside him he felt weak and a thought crossed his mind.

I've got time for a little shopping, he thought, and once I've eaten, I'll be able to move quicker, he reasoned. What Marcus didn't know couldn't hurt him, and anyway, it was going to take them a while to get the survivors moving, wasn't it? Everything looked so different in the daylight, so bright and glaring, and he rubbed his eyes again before setting off in search of refreshments.

After ten minutes he spotted a shop in the distance. Just a little detour from the path wouldn't cause any problems, he thought as his stomach rumbled again. Maybe a packet of crisps and a can of coke, or a chocolate bar, or all of them, he grinned. Still rubbing dirt from his eyes he set off towards it.

The security shutters covered the front of the shop and if it wasn't for the car that had smashed into them, he wouldn't have been able to get inside at all. The quickest way in he realised would be through the windscreen but as he opened the door he realised he wasn't alone.

"If only you'd used the seatbelt, buddy," he said to the man as he settled down in the passenger's seat. He landed a kick on the windscreen and smiled as he felt it move a little. How many times had he driven without his seatbelt on? He wondered as he stamped again and again on the window until it finally cracked free.

"Thanks for the ride." he stopped, suddenly realising that he was actually talking to a corpse. He shook his head before clambering through onto the bonnet and under the shutter. The inside of the shop felt warm compared to outside, and thankfully, with the doors still being locked, the food would be untouched from looters.

"See you later," he smirked as he jumped from the bonnet, but his feet shot out from under him as he landed and he crashed down onto the floor, his head slamming into the bumper behind him. Outside the wind started to blow, it howled as it passed the broken shop window and small whirlwinds danced down the street, slowly filling in his footprints as the sunlight started to fade from the day.

Marcus hoped they had enough time left for everyone; he felt they'd pushed the limit of their luck way beyond a reasonable level already, but he didn't know how to stop. There were just too many of them to leave behind. He watched them as they drudged passed, their cold dead eyes just staring ahead as they slowly played follow the leader.

"Keep going!" he urged them on. "Keep moving."

A young woman, obviously too weak to stand tripped and fell before him. Landing hard on the floor she pushed herself to her knees as she looked round for help, unable to pull herself up. He felt the floor shake, thin tendrils of dust dropped from the roof of the chamber but it was only when people started to scream that he realised what it was.

"Quake!" he shouted. "Move, move." People actually started to run. "Keep going. Get to the surface." He motioned them on, to not to stop for anything until they could see sunlight again. The floor bucked below his feet and he staggered back against the wall, this wasn't the place to stop. He could see the girl still trying to stand, a look of exhaustion in her eyes, and he tried to keep his balance as he moved towards her to help.

She looked quite young, her brown hair matted against the side of her face by the thick mud, but her blue eyes smiled at him as he moved towards her and she reached out with her hand. She vanished as a large stone slab dropped free from the ceiling, splashing dust and mud up at him as she disappeared; forever crushed into the earth.

Pierce felt the shaking stop and quickly pushed himself to his knees before picking up his SA80 machine gun and staggered out of the tunnel, back towards the others. His head hurt and he gingerly pressed his forehead, wincing as his fingers caught the exposed flap of skin. Dust tickled his throat and he coughed before spitting on the floor, water dripped in front of his eyes and he wiped it away with his sleeve. His head didn't feel too good, but he'd had worse.

He stopped to look back at the tunnel. The quake must have dislodged his glow stick, so he pulled another one from his webbing and tossed it into the darkness. It landed and flipped over a few times before it finally came to rest near the antechamber entrance.

It moved again as he watched, rising slowly from the ground

and he stood up as it danced in the air before him. Something grabbed his shoulder and pulled him backwards, and he cursed as he hit the floor. Everything seemed to be moving in slow motion, and he watched in confusion as John tossed a flash grenade behind him, before dragging him away.

The explosion illuminated hundreds of eyes, all clawing back over each other to get away from the flare as more creatures behind them pushed them on. His machine gun felt heavy as he raised it and he fired as John continued to pull him to safety. It was like shooting fish in a barrel. The creatures were so closely packed that every shot scored a hit, but still they came. Nick and Steve opened up, blasting into the tunnel as John lifted him to his feet. He couldn't see out of his right eye now; he felt like he was drunk and his feet didn't seem to want to walk anymore.

"You okay?" John shouted to him, but it sounded muffled and far away.

"I'm fine," he slurred. "Just turn me round to face them."

Marcus grabbed for anyone he could. The gunfire sounded heavy and intense, ammo would be running short soon but they needed to save as many as they could. He dragged a man from the pit, sending him running for the exit but he refused to go.

"Get out of here!" he shouted, he didn't have time for stupid people.

"No. My family are still down there somewhere, I'm not going without them." Marcus nodded. It was useless to force him so he pulled another from the pit, this time an old man, so weak he just rolled over and lay in the corner of the chamber.

"Boss," Kate shouted from the passage. "They're down to their last clips, we have to go."

This was the moment he'd dreaded, there were so many people left; he estimated they'd saved only a quarter of the people down here maybe less, and that just wasn't enough.

"Leave us, get out of here." The family man stopped him, it was a simple request, not shouted or forced and he could see that he had made his peace with God and man.

"I can't leave you," he protested.

"You must." The man started to push him towards the exit.

"What's your name?"

"It doesn't matter," he shouted. "Get out of here." He pushed him out of the chamber.

"Marcus!" Kate shouted urgently.

"Give me all the satchel charges you have left," Marcus demanded. "Now." She dropped her pack and removed the charges and handed them over. He stared at them; they looked like such an innocent package.

"Take these." He pressed them into his hand. "Just pull the fuse."

"Okay." He nodded his thanks. "God speed."

"And you," was all he had the strength to say.

"Clip!" John shouted. "Pass me another Clip!" He aimed down the sight and dropped another one as it climbed over the pile of dead and charged from the tunnel. Death was getting tiring; he couldn't feel his fingers properly anymore as each shot jarred his hand. Pierce slapped him on the shoulder and he turned, not stopping firing. Marcus stood in the light of the fires. Finally, he thought, time to get out of here. He pulled Pierce to his feet and dragged him backwards.

"Get to the upper chamber," Marcus shouted. "We'll cover you." He pulled Pierce to his feet and dragged him across the chamber. They stopped half way to give covering fire to the others and by the light of the flames he could see the creatures as they started to retake the room. Grenades exploded amongst them, tossing them aside like leaves, bouncing them off the walls.

"Go!" Marcus shouted as he ran towards them. "Move it." Kate crouched and continued to fire as Marcus primed the satchel charges.

When they reached the upper chamber, John dropped Pierce to the side and waited for the rearguard to reach them. The chamber was still full of escaping survivors. With nowhere else to go, they positioned themselves for a last stand. Dropping their empty rifles they crouched with pistols ready.

A large explosion sent dust and debris flying from the tunnel below and they covered their face as choking smoke swept up towards them. A deep rumbling echoed from below as they anxiously waited for the rest to arrive.

"Marcus!" he shouted between coughs.

"Who's left down there?" Donald shouted.

"Marcus and Kate." His stomach ached; two of his closest friends had remained below to let them escape.

Philip hobbled as quickly as he could down the ramp towards the crowd that had collected there. The news that someone had come back from the pit was spreading like wildfire through the centre and he moved everyone back so Nick could at least catch his breath. He looked like he'd been down a mine, his face was black with mud and he readily accepted the water Philip offered.

"Give him room," he shouted. "Everyone back off. Back away." He walked him to a bench and they sat down, but it was a minute before he was able to speak.

"I ran ahead," he gasped. "To make sure…you were ready."

"Ready for what?" he asked.

"For…" he paused as he spoke. "For the survivors. There's…" he stopped again while he caught his breath. "There's maybe two thousand on their way." Ed walked over with a mug of coffee and Nick accepted it gratefully, sipping greedily at the hot liquid.

Two thousand people, he thought, that's a bloody lot of mouths to feed, a lot more than they had already. "Ed," he shouted. "We're going to need a lot more rooms."

"No kidding," Ed nodded. "But more is better than less, right? I'll get the lads on it."

"Just do what you can," he nodded. "I'll tell Marion to get extra pots on. I bet they're all going to be hungry."

As the day wore on, a steady line of people trudged their way up the ramp into the car park. Most walked, some were carried by others, but all were weary, dirty and hungry. The smell they brought back with them was strong and nasty, forcing Philip and the others to cover their mouths as they passed.

"Everything okay in here?" he asked as he poked his head into the medical area.

Glen held up his hand for him to wait at moment, and he watched as he finished stitching a child's arm. The boy sat on his mother knee sobbing in pain, pushing his head into her chest so he wouldn't have to look as the needle tugged on his skin and he felt himself cringing at the sight. Once finished he wiped his arm with a cloth and bandaged it over as best he could before walking over to where Philip stood.

"It's been a tough afternoon. Eighteen have died from their wounds so far already, at least forty are too weak to walk, and one pregnant woman has so many wounds I can't believe she made it here at all."

"There are still more coming." He pointed outside. "Maybe twice again what we have already taken."

"Okay, just keep sending them, and I'll do what I can. We need more pain killers and bandages though."

"Okay, I'll look into getting some more, just make sure you get a break," Philip insisted. "You're all these people have." Glen nodded. "You let me worry about the supplies." Philip tried to reassure him, "I'll get some more from somewhere."

"Do you need anything for the leg?" Glen pointed as he turned to hobble away.

"No," he shook his head. "I can deal with the pain. Use what you can on the people who need it." He stepped towards the door. "I am going to the kitchen to check on Marion and the food supplies. I'll get something brought over for you. It's going to be a long night."

Donald walked slowly up the ramp, tired and weary from trying to dig the tunnel out as they tried to get to the lower chamber. Philip stood at the top of the ramp waiting for him.

"I'm sorry, Donald."

"You heard then." There wasn't really much to say, his grief still to fresh in his mind to accept.

"Yeah, John told me," Philip nodded. "There was nothing anyone could have done."

Donald nodded. He knew it wasn't their fault, but it didn't take the pain away. They'd dug until their fingers bled, fighting the exhaustion that stalked them until he'd called a halt. They couldn't do anymore.

"I don't know what happened." His voice sounded broken. "They were right behind us as we evacuated the cave, then something exploded and the roof came down. We've lost three good people today." The mental and physical strain of the day made him want to sob, to scream out. He thought he'd finished his grieving but now, after today he realised that it never ended.

"Four," Philip corrected him.

"No," he was sure he counted right, "It was three: Brian, Kate and Marcus." He counted them out on his fingers.

"Ash too..." Philip shook his head. "He didn't make it back either".

"What?" Donald grabbed him by the shoulders. "What do you mean he didn't make it back? We need to get back out there."

"Donald," Philip stopped him as he started to turn around. "You can't, not now."

"I bloody can." He tried to push him away. "If you don't want to help...."

"Stop it..." Philip flared angrily. "That's not fair. I've only just found out myself, Ash is a friend but it's too late to go back out there now." He turned and gestured inside. "We've got hundreds of people in here that need looking after, there's nothing we can do for Ash now until dawn."

"I'm going," Donald announced.

"No. No, you're not." It was Philip's turn now to grab him. "He's been gone for hours. He could be anywhere. If you go now, we'll have to look for both of you in the morning." Donald clenched his fists but he knew Philip was right. "You're shattered," Philip continued. "You need food and rest. Tomorrow, we'll get everyone we can out there looking for him."

"Everyone?"

"Everyone we can spare." Philip looked at him. "This is bigger than Ash now, there are too many people relying on us." Donald rubbed his forehead, smearing the dirt further round his face.

"First thing then?"

"At first light, I promise."

Marcus could remember counting the last of his men through and he was just getting ready to follow them when the blast went off. Flames licked out from the side tunnel as the satchel charges destroyed all the people he'd left inside.

Rubble loosened by the quake fell from above and heavy stone slabs crashed down onto the approaching creatures, forcing those that weren't crushed back into the rear tunnel. Something hit him suddenly in the chest, barrelling him backwards into the corner of the chamber. Whatever it was fell from him, and the room went dark as the last of the fires were put out by the rubble. He screamed as he covered his face with his arms and pulled himself into a foetal position as he waited for the danger to pass or for his end to come.

He didn't know how long he been there, listening to the rumbling sound all around him, but when he finally opened his eyes he couldn't see. Everything was pitch-black, he couldn't see his hands before his eyes; reaching out he tried to feel his surroundings.

He found his rifle and pulled it close to him, feeling calmer now he had his weapon back. It had certainly been a lucky escape, from what he could figure out, the entire roof of the chamber had collapsed and he was lucky not to have been crushed. He reached to the left and his hand rested on something soft and warm. Whatever had hit him before the cave in lay close by, what if it was still alive? Stuck in the small confined space with something that could see in the dark wasn't a nice idea.

"Unless you're going to marry me," a voice calmly said in the darkness. "I would suggest you take your hands of me."

"Kate? Is that you?"

"No," she replied sarcastically. "You're feeling up a monster. You're still squeezing by the way," she reminded him. "Get it off me before I break it."

"Sorry." He quickly removed his hand, thankful she couldn't see his blushing face.

"Hold on while I get us some light."

"You've still got some glow sticks?"

"No," she laughed, as a white light shone against the rubble before him. "Your wind up torches turned out not to be so useless after all."

He'd been right about the cave in, a large portion of the ceiling had fallen free and jammed against the wall, saving them from being crushed, and he patted it gingerly. It was obvious that there was no way they could reach the tunnel back to the higher chamber now and Kate continued to shine the light around, trying to find somewhere that they could climb through.

"There!" Kate pointed the light into the far corner and he could just see where part of the outer wall had collapsed on itself. It would be a tight squeeze, but it was better than doing nothing.

"Think you can get in there?" he asked.

"Oh, I see. First you feel me up in the dark and now you call me fat."

He was about to apologise when she laughed, it was a strange sound to hear in the confined space they were stuck in, alien and weird but he was glad of it. Sometimes, when the world fell away before you, you had to laugh or you'd crack. "Too easy," she said as she carefully crawled towards the exit. "I can feel an air flow," she called. "Come on, let's get out of here."

He crawled quietly behind her for some time, just making out the light as she shone it down the tunnel before her. It was fortunately wide enough in places for them to make good time, but it wasn't long before they came across a problem and she stopped.

"It ends," she called back.

"What'd you mean it ends?" he called. "I can feel the air on my face, and it must be coming from somewhere?"

"No, I don't mean it's a dead end. The tunnel just drops away. I can hear water below but I don't know how far down it is."

"Take this." He pulled his last flare from his webbing and pushed it forward towards her.

"Too far away..." she called back. "I can't bend like that. You're gonna have to come up closer to me." Wriggling forward, he managed to press the stick into a gap between her side and the tunnel wall; the problem seemed to be that her shoulders wouldn't let her twist enough to reach it.

"You're gonna have to push it more." His head now pressed against her as he pushed his hand through the gap. Eventually, she grabbed his flare and fired it before her into the open chamber. The tunnel exploded into light. "It's at least a ten foot drop into fast running water," she called back to him. "You ready for a cold bath?"

"There's nowhere else to go," he called. "Good luck Kate. See you on the other side." There was no need to dwell any longer on their situation and with a grunt, Kate vanished from view, taking the torch with her. The tunnel plunged into darkness again as he heard her splash below, so he shuffled forward and silently followed her.

The water was cold, and he felt his lungs scream as he went under. Surfacing quickly, he raised one arm above his head to fend off any invisible pieces of stone as he allowed himself to be swept along. He knew they didn't have much time before they'd get too cold to survive.

Something smashed into the side of his leg underwater and he shouted out in pain, water instantly filling his mouth and he choked, gasping for air. The eddies turned him and he lost all sense of direction in the darkness, not even sure which way was up at times as he fought to breathe.

Then he spotted something ahead of him. It wasn't bright, but in the darkness it shone like a flare. A small white light waved from dead ahead. Kate had made it, so with all his effort he started to swim towards it, fighting the water until he could finally feel stones below his feet.

"Get your clothes off," she shouted. "Or you'll freeze." Nodding his understanding he crawled from the waters edge, and pulled his top over his head. They had minutes to act and he could feel his fingers going numb as he pulled his boots off his feet and started on his trousers. Kate did the same and quickly they held each other, shaking.

"Don't try any funny business," she warned between chattering teeth.

"You kiddin'?" he replied. "My testicles are so cold they've vanished."

Ash couldn't open his eyes. His head throbbed and his body felt cold and numb as he lay on the floor. His stomach cramped and he could taste the acidic flavour of sick in his mouth. With a grunt he tried to roll over, but pain screamed at him to stop. He winced as he gingerly touched the back of his head, feeling the stickiness of the matted blood in his hair.

Everything was blurred when he eventually opened his eyes.

He could see the car above him and the broken shop window behind him. He tried to drag himself into a sitting position, but stopped as a searing pain shot up his leg. Gritting his teeth he tried again, screaming as the pain intensified.

He forced himself up as much as the pain would let him so he could see the problem better. A piece of metal had embedded itself just below his knee. He tried to move again, but realised the metal was attached to a magazine stand, bent out of shape after the impact.

The pain was unbearable. Clenching his fists, he slowly pulled on his leg. It moved a centimetre before it pulled the unit with it, then another. He took deep breaths, filling his lungs as he gasped air in before pulling quick and hard against the stand.

With a sucking noise the metal released its grip and let go of his leg and he slid backwards into the car. He sobbed to himself as he pulled his wounded leg towards him.

He needed something to stop the bleeding he realised. His body ached all over, and he felt tired; he just wanted to sleep, just for a moment, he thought to himself. A quick nap would do him the world of good. The cold sapped his energy from his body as he closed his eyes and his warm blood continued to drip onto the icy floor.

Their clothes were still cold to the touch but at least Marcus has managed to wring most of the water from them. With no way of making a fire, they needed to get moving again to get their bodies working and build up heat, so he tried to plan their escape. They appeared to be on a small spit of land made up of slimy pebbles. It wasn't very wide, but appeared quite long, widening somewhat at the centre.

"I can see something," Kate whispered after a few minutes. "There's something ahead, by the side of the large boulder." They carefully edged closer, not sure what they faced, and they kept the noise to a minimum until they could finally see what it was.

"There's someone there." She sped up and knelt beside the body. "He looks like he's in a bad way." The man looked like he'd been beaten to within an inch of his life, dried blood covered one side of his face and she pressed her fingers against his neck, nodding that he was still alive.

He jumped involuntarily at her movement, swinging his arm round towards her. She moved to block it, but it stopped when the chains attaching him to the rock went taught. His one good eye opened, staring wildly about around before his body shut down and he collapsed once more into silence.

"Damn!" Kate sat backwards onto the stones. "He scared the crap out of me." She checked his pulse again to make sure he was still alive. "Why the hell is he chained up down here?"

I don't know." Marcus shook his head. "Hang on…" he brushed the mud and dirt from his shoulder. His clothing was stained from what looked like weeks of wear, but the pips he wore gave his rank. "What the hell is an Army Major doing down here?"

"What are you doing?" Kate objected as he pulled his pistol from the holster and aimed at the chain. "Everything will hear you if you fire that thing."

"How else are we going to get him free?"

"Okay," she said after a moment's silence. "You're right, just give me a moment will you?" she begged. "Let me check out the rest of this island first, if he's been put here, there must be a way off, at least then we'll know what we're doing."

He watched the light as it bobbed and weaved in the darkness ahead of him, and the odd curse drifted back to him as he crouched next to the boulder.

"I can see the way out," she smiled as she returned. "I know where we are. We placed light sticks on a beach at the end of the tunnel we searched." She pointed into the darkness in the general direction. "I can see them just across the water. So as long as there aren't any creatures up there we should be able to get out."

"Let's go then!"

Two shots later Marcus grunted as he lifted the Major up onto his shoulders, and followed Kate towards the exit, one way or the other, their journey was going to be over soon enough.

Philip had been dreading this moment, and now, as he stood looking at him, he didn't know what to say. Tommy was busy playing a game with another boy, but jumped up when he saw him and ran over excitedly. "Where's Ash?" he asked, eagerly looking around to see if he could see him. "Has he got lost again?"

"Yes..." Philip nodded. "He got lost coming home."

"He's always getting lost." Tommy shook his head. "He's a Silly Billy."

"We're going to find him tomorrow."

"You promise?"

"Yes," he nodded. "I promise." Tommy stood looking at him. It felt like he was trying to read his mind, almost reading his soul and he felt uncomfortable.

"Okay then," he finally nodded, obviously satisfied with Philip's answer.

He beckoned to the other boy's mother. "Would you mind if he stayed with you tonight?" he asked. "He seems happy here."

"Of course," she nodded before turning to Tommy. "Do you want to sleep with us tonight?" She crouched down to his level. "You can play with Max some more."

"Okay," he nodded. "Just one night though, because Ash will be back tomorrow." He turned and looked up at him. "Philip promised."

He watched them as they walked away. The fact that he'd promised a child something that he might not be able to deliver weighed heavily on his mind. The fear that Ash was dead already caused a pain in his gut that he couldn't shake. As he turned Donald stood behind him, cleaner now than before but a pain still dwelt behind his eyes. "I guess I should get some sleep."

"Donald, wait." He hobbled after him. "I'm sorry.I…"

"No, don't be sorry." Donald stopped, but he didn't turn round to look at him. "You did right, I know you did. It just doesn't feel right, you know, to leave him out there. But don't ever apologise for being in charge." He turned slowly around to face him. "Don't apologise for making the hard decisions. That's what this is all about." He looked at the ground for a moment before he spoke. "You wanted to know why I couldn't be the leader, why I didn't want it."

Philip nodded.

"I didn't want it because I've made enough bad choices in my time. I've made decisions that let people die, and I can't handle that, not anymore." He looked upset as he spoke and he wiped a tear from his eye. "You need to know something though. If Ash is dead, and I pray to God he isn't, but if he is, even if there was nothing you could have done tonight, you're going to regret it for the rest of your life." He lent back against the wall. "That's not a threat," he sighed. "But it's a burden that you won't escape. The guilty feeling in your head will ask you if you could have done something to save him. No matter how hard you try, you're going to have to carry it with you forever." Donald's eyes looked red and tired as he continued, "Being a leader is being able to handle the decisions that get people killed, and still being able to sleep afterwards."

"But someone has to do it." Philip limped over to him. "I watched everyone that entered this afternoon you know." He rested against the wall opposite. "Every man, woman and child that climbed that ramp." He pointed out of the window. "Every one of them would still be in the pit if we hadn't tried. Everyone here would be dead if we hadn't made those choices. Doing that was the right thing to do, I know it was. Losing our friends today wasn't part of the deal though, but I guess it was a trade. We've lost too much already, there are millions dead out there, billions maybe. Civilisation has been brought to its knees, and for all I know we're the only place left standing."

"I never wanted this," he continued. "A few days ago I would have laughed if you'd told me that over two thousand people would look to me to answer their problems for them."

"Don't have doubts now," Donald said.

"I don't." Philip held his hands up. "Not any more. Everyone that came here today passed into my care. Mine, and mine alone, and that's something you made happen." He felt better for getting it off his chest. "I've never had any family, no parents to call when I needed help, or to teach me right from wrong. I just got on with it. Okay, so now the game is bigger, and there's so much more at stake, but the rules are the same." He gestured around. "I didn't want this, but I can see that someone needs to take it."

"You know what, when I first met you I thought you looked like a drip," Donald nodded. "No offence."

"None taken."

"But then the strangest thing happened. You shook my hand and looked directly into my eyes as you did it. You may not have been taught by your parents, but I bet you learnt a lot by trial and error. And because no one tried to change you, you became you. You had no reliance's on anyone else, no need for acknowledgements or rewards, none of the baggage that the others have." He looked proud as he spoke. "Just look at you now, only a few days afterwards and you're stood here with troops at your command and as you said, over two thousand mouths to feed and keep warm. All of which you've done without being asked. You've either done it yourself, or trusted someone else enough to let them do it." He smiled as he looked at him. "A leader isn't about doing all the work yourself, but knowing what to do and what to hand over. I support you fully, more now that I have before."

"That means a lot coming from you," Philip smiled. "Ash is out there somewhere and we're going to find him, because I promised a child we would. Christmas is round the corner and I am not going to let him down."

Kate cringed as the door creaked as she pushed it open; she

crouched listening for any sounds that could mean trouble from the darkness inside, but finally satisfied that the coast was clear, she signalled for Marcus to follow her inside the house. The climb out of the pit had been surprisingly clear of danger. The glow sticks had given enough light to show them the way, but as fatigue set in now, it wasn't wise for them to aim for the base yet, better to find somewhere to hide for the night.

Everything felt cold and damp inside but it was warmer that being out. The roof had collapsed during the last quake, but it was serviceable enough downstairs. Once she'd wedged the door, it should at least offer enough protection from anything that may be on the prowl out side.

The front room looked to be the best option, so she quickly pulled the curtains shut before helping Marcus lower the Major onto the sofa. He was in a bad way; his breathing was heavy and he hadn't regained consciousness since his first outburst a few hours earlier. Marcus didn't look much better as he flopped onto the armchair in the corner, groaning as he stretched his back.

"Hang on here while I check out the rest of the house," she advised and he nodded thankfully, too tired from carrying the Major to object. The house smelt clean enough, even with the dampness that had settled into the carpets upstairs. Unfortunately, the quilts were too wet and damaged to used, but she found some blankets in a wardrobe in the back bedroom that would offer at least some comfort.

As she entered the front room she could hear Marcus snoring from his chair so she carefully covered him with one blanket and covered the Major with the other before she sat down on the floor with her back to the sofa. The Christmas tree that stood in the corner looked wonderful, baubles and tinsel covered every branch and a few presents sat under it so she pulled one free and read the label. '*To, Samantha, Happy Christmas from Grandma and Granddad.*'

She didn't know why she did it, but she opened it, tearing the paper aside to see what had been sent. Inside sat a small teddy bear wearing a scarf and bobble hat. She smiled as she lifted it out;

straightening its hat she held it to her cheek. "I'm going to call you Sam," she whispered to the bear as tears dripped from her eyes.

She cried herself to sleep, cold and frightened in the darkness as she let her emotions out while Marcus slept. She was too tired to fight anymore, too exhausted to care if something attacked now. The thought that Samantha, her parents and her grandparents were probably dead, gone from the world forever, just added more weight to her already heavy heart.

Philip pulled the curtains over his doorway before turning to address his guests. They all looked exhausted and he wanted to keep the meeting as short as possible. "Alright." He hobbled over to his chair and sat down. "What's our situation?"

"I've set a trip wire at the base of the ramp," John began. "It will set off a flare if anything crosses it, and I have two guards on gate duty." Philip could see he wasn't happy sitting in Marcus's place, but he knew the importance of his position. "I didn't set any claymores though in case Ash makes it back."

"Good," Philip nodded. "What's our ammo situation?"

"We've enough for a while, but I'd like to get back to the school tomorrow and salvage what we can."

"I think anything we salvage is going to be needed eventually," he agreed. "Just make sure we get it all." He nodded his thanks before moving on down the table. "Glen, how's the medical area holding up?"

"I'm desperately short on supplies and beds. I've got five wounded that I don't think will make it through the night and a lot more that need antibiotics and such."

"Just let me know what you need." He made a note on his pad. "There are hospitals around here we should be able to get to."

"One good thing, though." Glen yawned as he looked at John. "You rescued a retired nurse; she came in with the others. She's American, called Joanne and she's already offered her help."

"Good, you certainly need the support in there." Glen nodded wearily in agreement. "Hopefully we'll find a few more as we go."

"Ed?" he turned to look further down the table.

"Nothing to complain about." His hair contained so much sawdust that it was impossible to see the real colour anymore. "I've set up a barracks area on the ground floor, living quarters on the second and the hospital and canteen on the third. Jolly wanted to sort the fourth out for himself."

"This is all well and good," Nick interrupted from the rear. "But what about Ash? We can't leave him out there. We should focus all our efforts there, and when we find him we can…"

"If…" Philip slammed his hands onto the table and the room dropped into silence, he didn't look up, he couldn't. "If we find him," he repeated slowly. He didn't want to be the one to say it, but someone had to. "I want him found as much as anyone," he continued as Nick started to object. "But we have to face the facts. We may not find him." He looked around at the faces of the people watching him. "There are too many people depending on us now to throw all our resources to save just one." He sighed.

"We can search tomorrow morning with all the spare hands, but then we've got to pull them back. The facts are we need supplies, both medical and material. We have over two thousand people out there," he pointed beyond the curtain, "that don't have warm clothes. God knows how many children have been orphaned already. So at first light you go out, cover the area, sweep everywhere, find him if you can," he paused to let what he was saying settle in. "But by noon I want everyone back in and working but for a small core group of searchers. Glen, be ready to travel as soon as they get back, grab any supplies you can, make multiple trips if you need to."

"We can't give up," Nick shouted. "We can't leave him out there, it's not right."

"It is right." Donald stood up. "No one likes this, and no one's giving up on him. But Philip's right, there's a bigger picture here. One we can't afford to ignore." They all left and he was finally alone with his thoughts; hobbling over to the mattress in the corner he lay down, pulling the quilt round him to keep warm as he listened to the wind as it howled cruelly outside.

The gull pushed its head from under the scarf. It was desperately hungry and its wings hurt too much to fly but it needed to find food somehow. Step by painful step it waddled towards the bus exit, stopping only to drink the melt water than ran from the floor above as it passed, before hopping out. It landed heavily onto the snow, the scarf that was twisted round its leg made movement difficult but as it fluffed his feathers to keep warm, it smelt carrion in the breeze; at least there was enough food around to keep him going.

Philip watched as the search parties set off. Almost two hundred people had appeared for the search at first light, many of them had been saved from the pit only the day before and although cold and tired, they wanted to get involved, they wanted to help.

Finally he was left alone with the weak, the injured and the old, and he cursed his injury; but for his wound he would have been out there with them looking. He wandered the car park, not that it really resembled one anymore. The floor markings could still be seen in places, but Ed and his teams had built so many walls that a maze had started to develop. Living quarters and store rooms seemed to be appearing at an alarming rate and everywhere smelt of petrol, tobacco and fresh wood shavings.

He pulled aside a curtain of one of the rooms and peered inside, it wasn't a very large room, maybe enough space for three or four families to sleep. There was no space for anything else and he realised that no one really had any personal items left anyway. Other than the odd wedding ring, or weapon they'd carried with them, they had nothing.

He realised he was wearing the same clothes he'd left his flat in at the start, and other than a few items of tat in his pocket, he had walked away from that life; some people had less, most had nothing. The smell of coffee brought him from his reverie and he could see Marion waving to him. She placed a mug of coffee on the counter before indicating for him to come over and get a drink.

"Good morning," she chirped. "Get some coffee while it's hot."

"How are the supplies holding out?" he asked as he sipped his drink.

"Well, we're trying to use up the fresh meats before they spoil, at least its cold enough not to need a fridge." She gestured to a pile of tins in the corner. "We used over two hundred tins of soup yesterday alone. Once we run out, or things go stale, were going to be on tinned meat and vegetables."

"How long can we last then?"

"I've no idea Philip, to be honest." She shrugged. "I suppose it depends on how many people we end up with, maybe a month if we're sensible."

"When Spring comes we can try to plant stuff I suppose."

"That would help," she nodded. "We've got flour and yeast to make bread, and Ed said he'd make an oven for us when he can."

"He's certainly been working hard."

"He's a God send is what he is," She smiled.

"I suppose the more people we have, the more there are that can search for food." He finished his coffee. "Just hold in there as long as you can."

"Don't worry." She took his cup back. "We aren't going anywhere. The ladies and I will keep this going, won't we ladies?" She addressed the group behind her who nodded their agreements back as they continued to work. "See, you have no need to worry, you just keep doing what you do." She looked at him with concern before placed her hand gently over his. "You'll find him you know."

"Who?" he asked.

"Ashfaq," she smiled. "He's out there somewhere." She smiled reassuringly once more before turning back to the other women. "Come on, ladies, let get breakfast ready."

Despite the early hours there were a lot of people around. People sat on any surface that would take them. Ed and the guys had removed all the cars they could and replaced them with an assortment of garden tables; candles or oil lamps burnt on each one and the smoke caught in the steelwork above, where it had started to blacken with soot.

He stopped as a small girl ran towards him, her mother trying to stop her, but she wriggled free and continued towards him, waving a piece of paper at him. "I'm sorry." Her mother said when she finally caught her. "She drew this last night after she saw you when we arrived and she wanted to give it to you. Come away Polly."

"It's okay," he reassured her as he lowered himself down to Polly's level and carefully took the picture she held and turned it over. "Really, it's fine." It was a picture of a castle with turrets, a man stood at the top holding a sword.

"Is that me?" he pointed.

"Yeah," she smiled excitedly. "You're the King, an' I put a crown on your head and everything," she said excitedly. "See there?" She pointed proudly to a yellow line she'd drawn on his head.

"Well, thank you, Polly." He'd never seen a picture quite like it and he could feel his eyes glassing over. "It's wonderful."

She smiled and hugged him, putting her small arms round his neck and squeezed. He didn't know what to do; children had been something he'd always avoided. She stopped as she walked away and turned again. "Thank you for letting us live in your castle," she said with a smile.

Everything had gone quiet and as he looked up he realised that everyone was watching him, smiling at him. Then, someone clapped somewhere, then another. Philip didn't know what to do as more and more people started clapping him; a young woman kissed him on the cheek as he passed, causing him to blush deeply.

He didn't know which way to turn; everyone stood looking at him, trying to shake his hand as he forced his way out. He finally reached the medical room and slipped inside.

"Is that for you?" Glen smiled as he entered, the clapping still continuing outside.

"I don't understand." He carefully folded the picture he'd been given and slid it inside his jacket. "What was all that about?"

"You make me laugh, you don't get it do you?" Glen said as he walked over, wiped his hands on a towel.

"What?"

"Look, as far as they're concerned you're their leader, you're the man who saved them all."

"I didn't want that, I just want people to feel safe."

"Just accept it as a compliment," Glen smiled. "It's better than being shot at. Since you're here let me check the ankle." He gestured for him to sit down and he unwound the bandages. Philip grumbled as he sat down, the idea of people looking up to him felt so wrong, he didn't know where to start, all he'd wanted was a quiet life.

"How bad is it?" He twisted his foot and winced as a pain shot up his leg, his ankle still looked bruised and a purple stain covered the back of his heel.

"I can't be sure to be honest." Glen prodded his ankle, making him wince. "Without an X-ray, there's no way of telling. You might have broken your fibula or just badly sprained it." He tried to twist it a little and nodded to himself. "I'll bandage it as best I can for now, but only time will tell I'm afraid. I guess it's pointless telling you to try to keep it rested."

"Not a chance," he laughed. "Just do whatever you can." Joanne carried over a tray of torn sheets and he gritted his teeth as she pulled the bandage as tightly as she could onto the bruise.

Donald paced up and down the street. They'd searched every

side street for at least a hundred metres, every house and vehicle had been checked, but still nothing. It just felt like he had fallen off the planet and time was drawing on; he'd have to call a halt soon.

Come on Donald you old fool, he thought to himself, think like Ash. What would he have done? He mumbled to himself as he walked. "Talking to yourself is a sure sign of madness," Nick called as he walked over. "We've nothing to report though. We've covered everything from the pit back to here already."

"I know. I know," Donald sighed. "Let's keep at it. We still have at least an hour." They searched on, shouting Ash's name as they searched for any signs of recent activity. Donald was checking the inside of a house when the walls started to shake and it took him a few seconds to realise what was happening.

"Everyone out!" he screamed. "Move, Move." He pulled a young man from the kitchen and pushed him towards the door. A chimney pot crashed down into the road from a house opposite, windows smashed and roof tiles fell in all directions, some hitting the rescuers. The quake passed as quickly as it had come, but the damage had been heavy, many houses already shaken by previous tremors have collapsed in on themselves, sending dust and debris flying in all directions.

Donald was pulling people to their feet when a whistle rang out from a sided street. At first he thought it was a group of searchers caught in the rubble, two of them dragged a third between them, and they waved for him to stop. He gave a shout of joy as he recognised them and he ran over, not believing his eyes, but there they stood, large as life. Kate and Marcus had returned.

The car park was abuzz with conversation as they finally walked triumphantly back up the ramp. For the moment, the failure of the search for Ash was pushed from Donald's mind by the return of Marcus and Kate; he followed behind, pleased with the outcome of the day.

They'd both insisted they were okay, but Glen ordered them in for a check-up all the same. Pierce smirked from across the room at them as they re-told their story; the bandage on his head was stained with blood from his wound but he was otherwise fine and Donald sat at the end of his bed as they spoke.

"So we jumped in," Marcus continued. "Luckily we washed ashore on a small island; it was there we found him." The unknown major lay silently on a bunk nearby, his face had been bandaged as best as Joanne could but he was certainly in a bad way. Donald had seen wounds before, but his man had taken a severe beating.

"He'd been chained there?" Philip confirmed.

"Yeah," Kate joined in from her bed. "To a huge boulder. He had chains all over him."

"Why?" Philip looked between them, trying to make sense of the story.

"We've no idea." Marcus shook his head. "Whatever the reason, those things didn't want him to see the light of day ever again." Donald moved over to where the major lay as Marcus continued, "Maybe he has intel we can use."

"Maybe he was caught during the attacks," Kate suggested.

"I don't think so," he called from the side of the bed. "This badge doesn't belong to any unit I know." He washed the dirt from it with some water. "Whatever he was doing, I guess we need to wait for him to tell us."

"Can we get up, Doc?" Kate begged. "My arse has gone numb already from lying down. We're fine, honest."

Glen nodded his permission. "Just get something to eat and drink before you do anything else." They started to move around but stopped when the major moaned and started to thrash wildly with his arms.

"Grab him," Glen shouted. "Or he'll hurt himself." Donald grabbed his arms and held him down while the others moved in to help. Eventually he gave up his struggle and lay back exhausted on the bed.

"Don't move," Glen advised him as he opened his eyes, staring around wildly "You've been hurt badly, but you're safe now."

He nodded that he understood and Glen told them to let him go. His one good eye was bruised and bloodshot, but he didn't resist as Glen lifted his head to allow him to drink. Philip gave him a few minutes to relax before he stepped into view.

"My name's Philip," he nodded. "Philip Greenwood."

"Hawthorn," the man replied, his voice wavered with the effort of breathing. "Major Frank Hawthorn. New contact division." He winced as he talked.

"It looks like you've got a few broken ribs." Joanne moved towards him, and he groaned as she tenderly applying pressure to his chest, searching for the break.

"I appreciate you're in a great deal of pain," Philip continued once Joanne had finished. "But we need to ask you some questions."

"I will…" he breathed heavily. "Answer all the questions I can." He beckoned to Glen to pass him some more water, sipping it slowly before he continued. "The things that did this to me," he gingerly touched his face, "have been known about since the early 1940s. I was part of a liaison group set up to assist them in their assimilation into the modern world."

"Are they alien?" Philip asked.

"Alien?" he stopped as he thought about the question. "No. Not really, not in the same sense you mean." He licked moisture onto his lips. "They've been on this world as long as we have, maybe longer. We discovered them when we started to dig out deep storage bunkers in preparation for the Second World War; when we accidentally drilled directly into one of their nesting chambers." His chest heaved as he talked, and the pain it caused as he spoke could be seen in his eye. Although weak, his voice carried in the room, almost mesmerising all who listened; an old English accent, deep and rich lay beneath his injuries.

"It took us many years before we could actually maintain any civil form of contact with them though." He shook his head. "We captured a group back in 45 and brought them to the surface. We sent them in secret to every corner of the world. America had some, as did the Russians, anything to assist us in understanding what they were. The Americans lost their's in an accident in the summer of '47, incompetent fools," he sniggered, "they insisted on using a prototype plane they'd taken from the Germans. A high altitude long distance bomber or something it was. They tried to show off, ha." He winced in pain as he moved. When he coughed blood appeared at the corner of his mouth, Glen moved to stop him talking but he waved him away.

"The crash was all over the papers back then, almost blew the whole story to the public. Too big for their boots, the Yanks; not all of them mind." He smiled at Joanne. "But it was only thanks to advances in computers that we made the breakthrough in their language. We were actually able to start serious negotiations with them at the start of the 90's. It was around '92 that everyone else realised the potential and we all agreed to work together."

"So they've been here all along?" Philip pulled up a seat to listen.

"Oh, yes indeed. There have been many reports in…" he coughed again and stopped to compose himself, "Sorry," He apologised. "I keep forgetting what I am saying. Oh, yes, reports in legends about them, if you know where to look."

"Goblins!" Glen exclaimed excitedly. "You mean these things are Goblins?"

"I suppose." The Major yawned as his energy started to subside. "That's a rather crude description of them though." His voice started to slur as he spoke. "They don't use that word to describe themselves, but I guess it fits." He yawned.

"Okay," Philip stopped him, "Let's say that we accept that they are Goblins, why now?"

"It's down to…" his eyes shut and then opened again, "Down to the, Sun…" his eyes closed, for longer this time. "Sun's frequencies…" His head started to rock to the side as he talked and Philip could see he was fighting against it, but the tiredness was taking over.

"He's okay." Joanne smiled as she checked his pulse. "He's just asleep. He's in a lot of pain."

"I need to know as soon as he regains consciousness." Philip looked at everyone "This conversation doesn't leave this room"

"Well, what do you make of that then?" Philip pulled the curtain to his room closed behind him. "I mean, Goblins, really?"

"I guess it's as good an answer as any." Donald shrugged his shoulders as he sat down. The conversation with the Major had certainly given them all lots to think about, and they'd come back to his room to discus it further. "It just doesn't seem logical, monsters don't exist. Do they?"

Philip filled the cups and passed them round before sitting down. "I suppose we've seen enough over the last few days ourselves. I'm just trying to remember the old stories. Wasn't Rumplestiltskin a Goblin?"

"Dwarf wasn't he?" Marcus sipped at his drink. "What were those things in the movies? You know the ones…" Marcus clicked his fingers as he tried to remember "Don't feed them after midnight."

"Don't know them," Donald shook his head. "I suppose the old legends must have been based on something though. I can image that the stories get passed down to each new generation, and they get warped a little each time like Chinese whispers, by the end of it all they're small creatures that live in the bottom of the garden."

"He seems genuine enough." They all listened as Philip spoke. "I don't think he's mad or anything and I guess they must have had him down there for a reason."

"But why not kill him and be done with it," Marcus suggested. "I guess that's what we would have done."

"I just don't know," Philip shrugged, everything seemed impossible, but once you'd fought them, it was hard to not raise the questions. "Why chain someone to a rock on an island? It's just odd. Maybe they wanted him to die slowly; maybe they didn't expect us to attack. Do you believe they're Goblins, Donald?" Philip asked.

"I don't know." Donald wandered to the window and looked out between the boards. "I could go either way I guess." He stopped as an idea dawned on him. "Either way," he repeated. "I could go either way." He slammed his cup down on the table. "Damn it, Ash went the wrong way. Philip we've been looking in the wrong direction."

Ash's body ached all over. Each time he tried to focus, his mind seemed to swim away from him; his thoughts were always just beyond his grasp. He felt like he was on fire and he wanted to take his clothes off to cool down but he didn't have the energy.

It was like he was looking through a thick plastic sheet, everything seemed to shimmer before him, but he was sure someone was speaking nearby. The conversation sounded muffled and distant, as though whispered in a strange language.

Where was he and how had he got here? He tried to focus on the past, on his recent past, but it seemed to dodge aside as he tried to grab it. How had he hurt his head? Where was he? Who was he?

Donald stood looking at the base of the pit, the memories of the previous day still very fresh in their minds. "Remember that he left the tunnels alone," he explained excitedly. "Everyone else went right when they came out." He looked at Nick who nodded.

"Yes, that's right." Nick pointed down at the route he'd taken. "Up the bank by the side of the burst pipe."

"Exactly." Donald felt like laughing it was so simple. "Now, look left." A burst water pipe, obviously the continuation of the one on their side jutted out from the mud across the pit from them. "You see. He just went the wrong way." Donald laughed. "He'd have been disoriented still when he came out, we all were. But we followed the right trail." Donald scrambled across the crater edge to the other side.

"The road looks almost the same." he called to the others as he climbed up and over "Come on."

By the time the others reached the top Donald was already a few hundred feet ahead. He'd hoped to find him straightaway, maybe see him sitting on a bench waiting for them.

"Hold on," Marcus called as he ran up behind. "Which way now? Which way did he go?"

"Well, if he kept at least some of his senses." Donald looked down both roads before him. "He'd have gone right, then left. That's the way to follow on the other side." he started forward. "So let's go that way first. Remember he was hungry, so look for a shop." He led the way, checking down every road and alley he passed. Everyone shouted Ash's name as they started to move faster, feeling positive now that they were on his trail.

"Over there," Kate shouted after ten minutes of searching. "I can see some shops down there". The car stood exposed across the footpath, and the shutters lay open to the elements. Glass cracked under their feet as they walked, their torches scanning the food aisles. Fanning out, they called his name, hoping that he'd hear them.

"I've found something," Nick shouted. "It's his torch. He was definitely here, but there's a lot of fresh blood too."

"So where is he?" Donald felt frustrated now, to be so close only for the trail to vanish was just not fair.

"I guess someone else found him." Nick pointed. "There are footprints in the blood."

"Are they human?" Marcus called from behind the cigarette kiosk.

"Size twelve's by the look of it, so unless those things have started wearing boots, I'd guess so."

Donald walked to the window and looked outside; the snow had started to melt in areas and destroyed any trails they could have used. He climbed through the window and stood on the roof of the car, bellowing Ash's name for as long as he could.

He stopped and listened to the echo; a dog in the distance

started to bark, breaking the silence. Evening was starting to press in and the Sun sat low against the horizon and he watched as it flared again before his eyes. He flew from the car roof as the pulse hit him and he landed hard on the pavement. Static seemed to bounce off his body as it earthed itself to the ground near his feet, and he roared in pain.

He felt hands grab him and drag him to safety just before the car exploded, taking the shop front with it as its fuel ignited.

"You okay, Donald?" Marcus asked as he waving his hand in front of his eyes. "Speak to me."

"What? Yeah, I'm fine." He scrambled to his feet, giggling as the residual charge left him. "Wow, what a rush." He smiled at them before he toppled over.

Philip had followed some of the scavengers that had been sent to search the shopping mall below the car park. Most of the shops stood almost empty now, already looted of anything that might be of use to them, but he was looking for something specific. Finally, he found what he was looking for in a book shop and he thumbed through the pages on mythical creatures before adding it to his basket. He found more on Celtic legends and one on the Fairy Folk, strangely enough stored in the children's sections.

He felt the air pressure change, and his knees buckled under him as the pressure wave passed outside. He waited a few seconds for the nausea to pass before making his way out. His ankle ached with each step but he finally reached the ramp back as Marcus screeched passed him in the car.

Philip cursed his injury as he tried to hobble faster, the books being dropped on the floor to give him better speed. By the time he reached the medical bay his heart was in his mouth. Had they found him? Had they found Ash? Pushing aside the curtain he staggered in panting.

"I didn't have time to stop and pick you up," Marcus stopped him as he entered "Everyone's okay," he reassured him. "Glen's just completed his checks but he'll be fine."

"You found him?" He tried to look passed him.

"No," Marcus shook his head. "It's Donald."

"What happened?"

"It was the damn stupid flare," Donald shouted from the bed. "I'm okay. Tell him I'm okay, Glen."

"He'll be fine," Glen nodded. "His blood pressure's a little high, and I bet he hasn't been eating or sleeping properly, but that's no surprise".

"I'm okay," he objected, though his eyes told a different story and Philip looked at him. He just didn't seem to be able to accept defeat, the thought of failure forced him to keep on fighting and he wondered what he was running from.

"He should be fine after a day or two's bed rest," Glen concluded.

"I don't need bed rest," Donald moaned. "Philip, we almost found him, we need to get back."

"We found his torch," Marcus nodded is agreement. "Donald's hunch was right. Ash must have taken the wrong way when he came out of the pit. It looks like he was hurt, there were boot marks from others but the trail went cold."

"I guess we can take it that he's alive at least. They wouldn't have carried him off if he was dead."

"I guess," Marcus nodded. "If the creatures had found him, he'd certainly be dead."

"But we're no closer to finding him?"

"No," Marcus conceded. "We're not. He could be miles away by now."

"Then we stop looking." He didn't like the thought but there seemed to be no other option. "If he's alive, he'll find his away back to us. He knows where we are."

Ash felt soft fingers force his eyes open and something bright shone into them. "Well he's a lucky one," a voice said close by, obviously female. "If you hadn't found him when you did, he'd have died for sure."

"How is he?" a well spoken man asked.

"I won't know for a while if there's any brain damage," the woman replied. "I've bandaged his leg and head as best I can; all we can do now is wait and see." He flexed his hand, feeling his fingers tighten as the muscles moved. His body ached all over and there seemed to be a fire in his leg that burnt deep into his consciousness when he tried to move.

"Water," he mumbled. "Can I have water?"

The Major woke just after dark. He looked much better for his rest but Glen warned them not to keep him talking for too long. Philip watched him as he tried to speak, but the effort caused him to wince as his ribs pushed back. Blood still soaked into the bandage over his eye and Joanne kept on wiping blood from the side of his mouth as he finally overcame the pain and spoke.

"I overheard one of them talking..." his eyes closed slowly before he snapped himself awake again, obviously fighting the urge to sleep. "I learnt their language." He smiled despite his pain. "We kept it a secret from them. I always used a translator when we met you see, to keep them in the dark," he explained, obviously proud of the subterfuge, "and I guess it paid off. They felt safe to talk in front of me when the translator wasn't around." Then he slowly shook his head. "I must have given something away though when I learnt about their plan to attack, because they came for me. I tried to escape, but they hunted me down in the tunnels. They wanted to know what I knew, what I'd told my superiors. They beat me, fed me enough to keep me alive and gave me foul medicine if they thought I was going to die. That was over a month ago."

"You survived for a month down there?" Marcus nodded respectfully. "That can't have been easy."

"If I'd told them the truth, they would have killed me for sure, so I had to hang on, to hope for a rescue or for a chance to escape..." He rested back on his pillow, and Joanne gave him a sip of water.

"Anyway," he finally continued. "I found out they'd waited thousands of years for this to happen. You see, a long time ago, they used to live above ground, the Sun was much younger then and its light hit the earth at different frequency. But as with all cycles, that one came to an end." He closed his eye again, Philip thought he'd fallen asleep and was about to leave when he suddenly continued, "Once everything settled down again, the frequency of the sunlight had changed and it started to hurt them. Their skin couldn't absorb the x-rays properly you see, and it burnt them, cooked them alive. So they went underground."

"I still find this hard to believe," Marcus said not unkindly as he stood at the foot of the bed. "For all this time they have been beneath our feet?"

"Not all the time, no. It turns out that they could still surface at night; they prefer a new moon more than a full one, even the full moon can be so bright it hurts them." He looked at Marcus with his good eye. "Each time they came to the surface they caused stories. Myths were created, stories of creatures that stole babies from their cots, creatures that hide under your bed and got you when you slept. But over the millennia they've dwindled down, producing less and less offspring each year; each new birth being more accustomed to the darkness until they stopped altogether."

"So why now?" Philip pressed.

"Why?" the Major laughed, dribbling blood down his chin. "The Sun's changing, maybe even changing back to the way it was. They started to re-populate many years ago as the time got near, growing in numbers, breeding better and stronger children as they started to feed again. But they can't come back if we're here, so their plan was to attack and increase their food store at the same time. The more they feed, the more they'll produce."

"That explains the bodies we found, they must have been gorging themselves."

"And not just in Manchester." The Major shook his head. "Almost every city in the world will have been hit and we let them do it. They gave minerals to us, diamonds and gold. They gave us the food of the earth and for our sins, we fed them."

"What? We gave them people to eat?"

"There was nothing I could do," the Major replied defensively. "The world leaders started off by sending convicted criminals to them. People without families, no questions asked. Then in return for lining their own pockets, our governments slowly sold everyone out. People where taken from the streets at night, vanished without a trace. The more they turned a blind eye, the more money they got. Parliament hasn't been working for the people for years. They just filled our lives with false promises and deceit, never delivering on anything, but promising the earth." They all stood in silence, listening to the story unfold before them.

"So the Prime Minister was in on it."

"Oh yes. Don't get me wrong, the old ones tried. They kept a proper system, but the newer ones..." He nodded. "America, France, Russia, even the Chinese fell in line."

"So what's next? We destroyed their pit," Philip said. "We won."

"Won?" the Major barked before resting back on the pillow. "I wouldn't say you've won. Not by a long shot. You destroyed only a small part of the problem. You took out maybe a hive, there are millions more, and you can bet that the other hives are aware of what you've done. No, Philip you've not won just delayed the real fight."

The gull felt content; its stomach was full of the carrion it had found and now that it had found a safe spot deep in the rubble of a house to hide in, it started to feel warm again. The scarf that was still stuck round its leg now blocked the hole it had crawled through, stopping the wind and snow from following it inside.

It laid its head on the folds of the material and could smell the human on it. It remembered them, the small one and the bigger one and it would certainly try not to eat them if it found them again. Closing its eyes it fell asleep as the sky outside was afire with the lights of the borealis.

"Good morning." The voice belonged to a middle aged woman, her blonde hair and blue eyes made her look younger than she was, and she wore a pleasant and honest expression on her face. He smiled as he opened his eyes. "How do you feel today?"

"Thirsty." His mouth felt like it had been filled with wool, and a glass of water was pressed gently against his lips. "Where am I?" he asked after the water had revived his tongue. It still felt like it had a film of dust over it and he tried to rub it against his teeth.

"You were found by one of our food parties yesterday," a man said from the doorway. "Do you remember anything?" He tried to focus on the voice but his head hurt as he turned it.

"Careful." The woman stopped him moving. "You took a nasty knock."

"How, how bad am I?" He felt sick to talk and his eyes watered as he tried to see. He could make out a blurred blob that he presumed was the man who had asked the question.

"You suffered a concussion," the woman told him. "I don't know how badly though." It was difficult to hold onto what she was saying as his mind swam before him and colours flashed behind his eyes when he closed them.

"What do you remember?"

He understood her question, but he found forming the answer difficult. He could almost see the words he wanted to say swimming round behind his eyes, but they fell away as he tried to stop them.

"Nothing," he eventually answered. "Where am I?"

"You just need to rest for now." He felt something prick against his arm and a warming sensation pass over his body and the world slowly started to fall away from under him.

"I've given him a sedative for now," the woman said. "Let him sleep."

Who am I? He screamed as he fell into the dark void of his mind. Who am I?

"Is the pit still open?" It was morning and Philip was pleased to see the Major sat up in bed. He still looked pale, but he certainly looked more alive than before.

"Yes," he confirmed. "We haven't done anything with it yet, though Marcus did mention blowing it closed. Why do you ask?"

"I was thinking last night. They don't like being above ground anymore than they need to, so they'll keep underground where possible. We can presume they have passages that connect them to all of the other hives."

"So we should close it then." It seemed obvious to Philip. "That would stop them coming out."

"No." The Major shook his head. "Don't be a fool man, think about it. If we know where they're coming from, we can prepare better. If the pit is closed they'll make another exit somewhere else. Think of them like an ants nest, if you fill on one hole they make a new one."

"Okay," he nodded. "I'm with you so far." He sat on the side of the bed by the Major's feet. "What you're suggesting is that if we leave the entrance open and a trail for them to follow, so we can ambush them along the way."

"Exactly," he smiled, nodding weakly. "The more of them you take out before they get here, the better chance more of the people will survive. Divide and conquer. Oldest military strategy there is."

He stopped talking and waved over to Joanne. "Is it time for breakfast dear? My stomach is growling something terrible at the moment."

"I'll get something sorted shortly for you, Major." Joanne replied as she tidied the room.

"A cup of tea would go down a treat." He smiled at Joanne before turning back to Philip. "I'll leave you to it. Marcus seems like a good man, he'll know how to set the traps."

"I can get that organised," he nodded. "You just rest and get your strength back."

He slowly opened his eyes. The world has stopped spinning at last and as the room came into focus, a man stepped into view.

"So you're awake then." The man smiled. "Let me introduce myself. My name's Ken. Welcome to the last outpost of civilisation. Take it easy now." He nodded reassuringly as he moved to stop him from sitting up. "How do you feel?"

"Terrible. I feel like something ran me over."

"It's the bang on the head. Doc said I should give you these when you came to." He handed him a cup of pills. "Just general headache tablets and antibiotics for the leg." he reassured him. "Nothing to worry about."

"Why am I not in a hospital?" he looked round the dirty room, concrete walls and candles didn't constitute the healthcare he expected.

"What's the last thing you remember?" Ken moved a chair closer to the side of the bed and sat down by the side of his bed. He tried to piece together his memory but they felt blurred and distant, moving aside as he tried to recollect them.

"I remember… watching TV, and then the power went out." He desperately tried to focus on the memories that evaded him. "That's about the last thing I can recall." He shook his head. "Sorry. My name is Ashfaq, by the way." At least he could remember something.

"That was a week ago," Ken informed him. "You must have been somewhere safe to have survived this long." He placed something hard and cold into his hands. "You had this when we found you."

"I had a gun?" The weapon felt heavy and solid in his hand, too real to be a fake, and a cold sweat flushed across his body. "Why would I have a gun?" Had he killed someone? Was this the police trying to trick him into a confession?

"The gun isn't a surprise. A lot has happened in the last week, a lot has changed, and nothing for the better. The power went out when the Sun flared, and then later we were attacked."

"You were attacked?" Although it was tattered and dirty, he could see he was a soldier by his uniform and the thought of someone attacking sounded wrong.

"No," he shook his head. "Not just me. The entire country, maybe even the world; I don't know for sure. All I do know is that we've managed to survive this far by keeping out of sight. We hide down here at night, only coming out at mid-day for a few hours to collect food."

"How many are here?"

"We have almost a hundred so far."

"A hundred, is that all?" He shook his head. "A hundred, are you sure?" He could feel himself starting to panic, there was too much to take in, too much to process.

"Do you think you can walk?" Ken offered his hand in support. "There's something I think you need to see?"

"Where are we?" he asked as he limped along behind Ken. The natural gloom of the concrete walls mixed with thick smoke, and the light danced in odd shapes against the walls from the barrels of burning wood, giving the underground a dark, eldritch, medieval feel. He liked Ken; he was a solid sort of a character in a world of mystery and confusion.

"It's just the underground car park of an office block," Ken explained. "I stumbled across it just after the dawn of the first attack, and it seemed like a good enough place to hide out."

"I still don't get it." Ash stopped. "What actually attacked?"

"I can show you. I think that might be the best way to get you to understand." He gestured towards the rear of the area. "We caught one a few days ago."

As he hobbled towards the rear of the room, Ash started to make out something small chained to a post. It pulled against its bonds; its thin gangly body glistened in the firelight, and it hissed venomously as they approached. Ash froze as it turned and looked at him; its large black eyes seemed to probe deep into his very soul. It opened its mouth to reveal a row of sharp pointed teeth and it hissed at him.

"Ya'jooj!" he exclaimed. "Ya'allah, protect me!" He staggered away from it; tripping on some rubble he almost fell, but Ken grabbed his arm.

"It can't get you," he reassured him. "I've been trying to talk to it; find out what it knows and what it wants, but I can't get anything out of it."

"Just get me away from it please," he begged. He felt a deep shiver run up his spine and he felt his head going dizzy.

"Sorry," Ken apologised. "Maybe it was a little too early to show you that, but you had to understand what we face. Are you okay?"

"Yeah, thanks." He waved him away. "It just caught me off guard." He started to feel the tablets kick in, and the pain in his head and legs subsided a little, bringing some relief. Was that thing real? It felt easier to deny what he had seen, to pretend it was someone in a mask, but there had been something about the way it looked at him that said it was real, deadly real. He shivered again. "Okay. How can I help?"

"Good," Ken nodded. "I didn't think you were one of life's victims, we have enough of those already. But, if you're up to it, we need help shoring up the outer wall, or you can help Jim with the bus."

"I know more about engines than I do DIY."

"Over to Jim you go then." He helped him back to his feet. "I'll get Stu to show you the way. There's something I should have done a while ago."

He called to a man stood by an oil drum warming his hands, who looked up and waved before he ran over.

"Stu!" he patted him on the shoulder. "Can you take Ashfaq here over to see Jim? He should be able to lend him a hand."

"Sure, Boss." Stu smiled as he stood up, his impressive build was in total contrast to his open and honest face. His blonde hair had been cut close to the bone, making him look almost bald. "How's your head?"

"I've had better days," Ash nodded.

"You looked really bad when you came in. To be honest I didn't think you'd make it but Kirsty is a bit of a magician when it comes to bumps and bruises." They started to walk slowly along. "Anyway, welcome to the underground." He gestured around him. "It's not much, but we call it home. Jimmy's just over here." He pointed to a recess in the wall. "Jimmy!" he called. "Jimmy you have a visitor." A single shot rang out behind them, making him jump as it echoed off the concrete and they both ducked instinctively.

"Crap," Stu cursed as they turned towards the sound.

Ken stood over the body of the creature, pistol in his hand.

"About bloody time he got rid of that." Stu spat. "That thing gave everyone the creeps I can tell you; dirty things." Ken dragged the corpse away behind them and Stu called again, "Jimmy, are you here?"

"Yeah, yeah, hold your horses," A voice shouted from behind one of the vehicles. "I went for a wee alright. Is that okay with you or what?"

Ash almost let out a snigger as Jimmy stepped into view. A dog eared role up hung from his mouth as he approached them, still pulling his pants up.

"No, it isn't alright," Stu shouted. "I expect you to be hard at it twenty-four seven, hell I don't expect you to eat, sleep or be merry," he laughed.

"Bugger off," he smirked. "I'm not being paid anymore. Anyway, I don't see you helping out." He flicked the role up away and pulled another from behind his ear. "Who's this fella then?" He pointed towards Ash, eyeing him critically.

"This is our new guest, Ashfaq. Ken sent him over to help you out on the bus."

"Did he now?" He scratched his face, leaving a grease trail on his cheek. "Come on then." He handed him a spanner. "If you're gonna help, you might as well get started."

● ● ● ● ● ● ● ●

"Gentlemen," Philip addressed the room, "Thank you for coming." I hate meetings, he mused, always have and always will. Attending them had been bad enough, but now I have to run them. He cleared his throat before continuing. "You're here as the leaders of your respective groups. Marcus for the army, Ed the builders, Jolly the Scientists and Donald, well the people." Each nodded as their name was mentioned, though Jolly's enthusiastic waving made him smile.

"As you know," he continued. "I've been talking to the Major, and from what he's told me..." he paused as he tried to word it properly. "We've got a storm coming. The battle we've fought already was with only a small part of the main force." There was a collective moan from the group. "It looks like we've only managed to stir up the nest, certainly not remove it."

"If we close the entrance won't that stop them?" Ed asked.

"No," Philip shook his head. "No. We need to leave the pit open for now, not blow it shut."

"But if we close it they can't get out that way, can they?" Ed continued.

"Agreed, but the best option we have is if they do come out that way. If we close it," he explained, "they could come up anywhere. This way we know where they're coming from."

"Ah," Marcus nodded. "You want to lead them into a trap."

"Exactly." Philip pointed at him, pleased that the conversation was going in the right direction. "If we can funnel them into a..." he tried to remember the words the Major had used, "a kill zone. We should be able to drastically reduce their numbers before they get here."

"There's something else you need to know about," Jolly nervously interrupted. As he stood up, small pieces of food dropped from his shirt onto the table, and he quickly brushed them away before wiping his hands on his stomach. "Hi everyone." He smiled nervously. "er..." he stammered. "Well, it's like this. I used to read a lot on the internet, conspiracy stuff and the like. Anyway there's this theory." He gesticulated as he talked. "Imagine that we have er... been here before. Not here in this room," he shook his head, "but here on the earth, thousands of years ago sort of thing." He wiped his brow with his arm.

"Anyways, the theory is that we've been here at least four times since this place got built, but each time we got wiped out by Mother Nature and had to start all over again." Philip quickly realised that compared to Jolly, he wasn't that bad at public speaking after all.

"The Sun's blasted the earth with magnetic wave's okay, that's what's killing the internet systems and power." He absent mindedly adjusted himself in his shorts; sweat had started to develop under his armpits and he was obviously very nervous. "The Earth's a temperamental thing as it is, so, a strong enough hit from the Sun could de-stabilise the tilt of the planet." He brought a football up from below the table; he'd written North on the top and South on the bottom.

"See this ball." He held it in front of him. "Just try to imagine this is the Earth." Small beads of spittle started to appear in the corner of his mouth. "We have True North here, and like Magnetic North here. Well, if the electromagnetic pulse hits here for example." He pointed to a spot half way down the ball "Then it could create a new Magnetic –."

"A new North Pole?" Ed sat forward in his chair. "Are you serious?"

"Yeah," Jolly nodded. "Think about it." He tilted the ball round so the point he had used as an example was at the top. "The Earth would slip. The outer crust would slide over the lava below until North is... er... well, North again."

"That can't happen..." Ed interrupted. "Can it?"

"At the moment I'd say anything is possible." Donald turned to Jolly. "Let's say you're right, how fast would it turn?"

"I don't know," he shook his head. "I've been watching the North Star at night and it's moved." Jolly slowly shook his head. "Plus the compass isn't pointing right anymore, I've been checking since we got here." The room was eerily quiet for a moment as everyone tried to digest what they have been told before it erupted with questions, everyone started talking at once, asking questions and demanding answers. Jolly just stood shaking and Philip could see that it'd take a lot of his courage to stand up and tell them.

"Everyone needs to sit down and shut up." He'd never liked raising his voice but this was one of those moments. "NOW!" Everyone stopped. "That's enough. Let's just focus on the main plan rather than anything else at the moment." He stood up, resting his hands on the table as he spoke. "Marcus I want you to focus on laying out the trap and general defences. Ed, you shore up any gaps in our walls, store provisions, make us a bunker of some kind. Do whatever you need to do, but we don't have time to sit here whingeing about it."

"Jolly, I'm assigning you to work with Marcus. I want you to develop some more weapons for us, anything that will explode." Jolly simply nodded, eager to be the one not talking anymore. "After you've shown Ed all you know about this possible polar shift thing." He slowly looked round the group. "Put your fears behind you for now, if the worst happens, we won't have to worry about the shift, but I'm damn sure I'm not going to let us go out without a fight. Get everyone working that can, I don't want to hear any complaints. Not today." The meeting over, everyone stood and the room cleared, Donald remained behind closing the curtain as the others left.

"Why are you still here?"

"Just checking you're alright." He poured two drinks and placed one before him "There's been a lot going on."

"I'm fine. The stress isn't a problem now." He took a sip from his glass, letting the liquid burn his throat a little.

"It's hard to believe everything though," Donald continued

"I don't know, I guess we've always believed in monsters." Philip turned and looked out of the window. "I remember my grandmother warning me to be careful of the fairies at the bottom of the garden, and the bogyman in the wardrobe." He smiled to himself at the thought. "Can we do it, Donald?" He turned back to his friend. "Can we expect everyone to fight again?"

"If we have to," he nodded. "And maybe the Major's wrong. Maybe nothing will happen."

"No. He's right." He put his glass down. "When you think about it, if that was all of them, then the Army should be here, but they're not. No, this danger's real enough; the problem isn't where they will come from but when."

Ash liked working with Jim. Before all this, Jim had been a mechanic, so as long as he had a vehicle to tinker with every day was the same for him. The death and devastation outside he was able to ignore, as long as he slept with his family at night he was able to block everything else off. Ashfaq stood by the side of the bus as Jim stretched into the engine.

"The batteries got a charge now," he announced triumphantly. "I just can't figure out why she won't start." He hit something in the engine violently with a spanner before pulling himself free. He rubbed his hands on his top, pulled a role up from behind his ear and lit it before offering it to Ash.

"No thanks," he declined. "I'm good." Jimmy shrugged and put it back between his lips.

"That's not just tobacco is it?" Ash asked, the smoke smelt

sweeter than normal and made him cough.

"No. Sorry man," Jimmy said, "does it affect you?"

"Asthma," he explained. "That's all. No, don't worry about it."

"You're all right, Ash," he smiled. "I understand you don't remember much since." He touched his head as he spoke.

"No, I lost the lot."

"Funny isn't it." He put the tool down and took a swill from a beer can. Ash was amazed Jimmy could work; at any one time he was either stoned, drunk, or both. "All you had to do last week was grab your mobile and call someone if you was in trouble. Distance wasn't an issue; I've mates in Canada I called every month. Not any more though, not now the old spark has gone." He slapped his head before clicking his fingers. "Spark plugs, damn it, why didn't you remind me to check them?" he smiled. "Too much weed in my fag." He climbed back under the bonnet. "The good thing is," he continued from under the hood of the bus. "That if the vehicle is old enough, they didn't rely on modern computer circuits." He lifted his right leg so he could reach in further, grunting as he twisted into the engine. "Give that a try, will ya," he shouted. "The keys are in already."

Ashfaq climbed into the bus and sat down in the cabin before turning the key. Nothing happened so he tried again.

"Nothing happening," he shouted "I take it you have changed the water in the battery?"

"Yes I have," Jimmy called "Don't go preaching mechanics to me buddy. Cheeky bugger." His cigarette smoke curled its way over the bonnet. "Alright, leave it to me. I'll get the old girl working."

Ashfaq climbed back out.

"Tell you what though, see that Honda over there? Why not have a bash at that, see if you can't get that one started."

The Honda was parked close to the exit and apart from it needing a paint job on the rear panel; it looked in pretty good condition. He hobbled over to it to have a closer look. He looked up at the exit sign as he neared the car and he felt like he'd seen it somewhere before but his head hurt as he tried to think. He could visualise the height sign hanging the other way round and he tenderly touched the back of his head, wincing as the pain flashed across his eyes.

"Keep you hands off it or it won't get any better."

Ash turned, snapping out of the déjà vu.

"I just got a feeling I'd seen something I recognised," he told Kirsty as she walked over. "The exit looks so familiar for some reason." He frowned as he tried to recall more.

"That can happen," she nodded, brushing her unwashed blonde hair from her face. "Your memory should come back as the swelling goes down, hopefully." She checked the bandage on his head to make sure it hadn't slipped. "Let me check your eyes again, I want to make sure that I didn't miss anything; head wounds can be nasty."

He stood still as she shone the light towards him. Kirsty was nice, she was a bit older than he was, but she had a very relaxing smile and a caring touch. It reminded him of his mother, how she used to tend to him when he fell, cleaning the cut and putting the plaster on.

"I just wish I knew what happened to my family," he said as she continued to check him over. "It's the not knowing."

"Maybe you don't really want to know." She slipped the small torch back into her pocket. "I was working when they came; I hid in a utility room and stayed there all night." A guilty look crossed her face. "I could hear the others as they screamed outside, but I didn't open the door, I couldn't." The pain showed in her eyes. "The next morning I managed to make it home, but my family had gone." Her eyes started to well up and she bit down on her lip and stopped herself crying. "I hope your family is safe, Ash." She forced a smile. "Maybe you've just become lost from where they're hiding. I really hope you find them again."

"Thanks. I hope you find yours too," he nodded at her. "They took lots of people prisoner you know, they didn't kill them all. There were loads underground in pens."

"How do you know that?" she stared at him. "What do you know?"

"I don't know." He looked down at the floor as the memory

faded again. "It's like…It's like…" he growled as the words evaded him. It was hard to explain, like a dream fading in the morning.

"You mean people could be alive? My husband and child could still be alive?"

"Yes. No. I can't be sure." He slapped the roof of the car in frustration. "I just know people survived. I just don't know how."

"You both okay?" Ken asked as he walked over, obviously attracted by Ash shouting.

"Ash believes they didn't kill everyone; they've taken prisoners. People are still alive." Ken turned to look at him. Staring at him as he thought things over, it made him feel very uncomfortable.

"So then," He finally spoke making Ash jump. "Does that mean you've been down there? Maybe escaped even? Do you know from where? Do you know anything at all?" Ken was eager for information, but that was exactly what Ash didn't have.

"I'm sorry." He shook his head, feeling like a failure. "If I remember anything, I'll come and tell you."

"You do that." Ken nodded to them both before turning and walking away.

"He is a good man." Kirsty smiled as they watched him go. "None of us would've survived if it wasn't for him. He doesn't talk much, but his heart is in the right place. We all owe him a lot."

"I'd better have a look at this car." He nodded towards it, trying to change the topic. "It's not quite a BMW, but it'll have to do." He felt bad as she walked away and he hoped he hadn't given her hope that he couldn't substantiate? This memory loss was a nightmare for him; he needed to get home, to check on his family.

He popped the bonnet of the car. That's what I'll do, he thought to himself, I'll get this thing working and go home. I'll come back once I've had found them, bring them back here. He locked the bonnet open, the support bar only just making contact with the housing, but it would hold for now.

Philip was amazed how everyone seemed to be just getting on with things. Each time the stakes were raised, the more people stood up to be counted. All he could hear now was the banging of hammer against metal and the sawing of wooden beams. Corrugated iron sheet were being nailed to the outer boards on the first floor and Ed shouted instructions to the workers, cursing when they got it wrong before showing them how to do it himself.

"If we can lock this floor and the one above down, we'll stand a better chance if they get past the gate," he explained when Philip managed to stop him for a moment. "At least they won't be able to burn us out. We've installed shutters on the outer walls so we can open them when we need to."

Philip just nodded, Ed seemed excited, and as long as it worked, everything would be okay.

"And if they do try anything, we've got some bulk timbers to lock them closed. Oh! Come and see this!" Ed put his hand on his shoulder and led him towards the exit ramp. Philip watched as a group of men added the finishing touches to a metal frame with what looked like an oxyacetylene torch and once satisfied that whatever they were doing was finished they waved up to them.

"Give it a test run?" he called.

"Okay, guys," the foreman shouted. "Move out of the way."

"One of the lads gave me this idea," Ed explained as the men cleaned up and moved away. "He was out scavenging when he spotted a set of large railings on the front of a house. He told me about how, when he was a child, he'd impaled his leg on one when he tried to climb over it. So we cut it free and attached it to this." He gestured towards the construction.

"Clear the ramp!" he shouted before pulling on a piece of rope that had been led just inside the doorway. The stopping blocks sprang free of the construction and the railings that had been welded to a bracket swung down in a vicious arc.

"Wow!" Philip was impressed. "So if they come up this way, we can stop them?"

"That's the idea," Edward nodded. "We're going to place another two of them at points on the way up. Marcus will set some explosives under the last part, so if we need to we can blow it and cut ourselves free from the rest of the ramp."

"Let's hope we don't need to." He smiled as he limped back inside. "Good work though, very good work."

The contrast made him squint into the gloom inside; the snow outside made everything bright and crisp but inside it was dirty and smoke stained. He spotted Tommy at the same time that Tommy spotted him and he jumped up excitely and ran over.

"Philip. Philip," he called. "Has he come back yet?" his eyes wide with hope. "Have you found him?"

"Not yet. But we're still out there looking," he lied. "I think he's hiding from us."

"He is a dodo head," he stated matter-of-factly "I like being with Mrs Parkinson, but I want to go home." His face looked sad. "I miss Ashfaq."

"I know you do, Tommy." He ruffled his hair with his hand. "We all do."

"Take it another twenty paces." John didn't look away from the field glasses as he spoke, but he knew Pierce would signal the information to Kate. "That's about as close as we can have them going off without taking us with it." He watched Kate mark the snow. "Anything closer than that and we might bring the building down on us."

"That's not good," Pierce smirked. The bandage on his forehead was matted with dried blood and his eye was still red but he'd refused to stay in the infirmary.

"No..." John replied. "Not good, actually very bad."

"Yes," he agreed with a grin. "Very bad indeed." They left the house and walked down the road to join the others.

"Okay, Chuckle Brothers," Marcus smiled. "Just set the charges. Remember to leave at least fifty feet between each one. Stagger them on either side of the road as you go out."

"You sure they're going to come this way, Boss?" he asked as he started working on the first satchel charge. "This is a lot of ordinance to waste if they don't come this way."

"Don't worry," Marcus nodded. "We've blocked all the other exits with vehicles and debris. This is the straightest route to us, so they should come straight out of the pit and straight down this road."

"And if they don't?"

"If they try to go another way, we've set flash bangs against the barricades. When they go off, it should cause a stampede in your direction."

"That's such a nice thought," Pierce interrupted. "Anything but letting us have the night off."

"Anyway," Marcus smiled. John could see he was getting slightly angry at Pierce, it wasn't protocol to talk like this to your commander, but these were special circumstances. "You let me worry about the plan, after this, we need to rig your safe house to blow."

"You know that sounds so reassuring," John said. "There's nothing we like more that sitting on a bomb."

The house they'd chosen sat directly facing the road they expected the attack to come down. The upstairs bedroom gave them a perfect sniper point, and there was a clear escape route to the rear.

The house itself was in relatively good condition. Other than the dining table that had been forced up against the front window for security and warmth, you would have been forgiven for thinking anything was wrong in the world at all. Pictures of the owners hung on the walls, the television sat dormant in one corner and a fish tank sat to one side. Pierce tapped at it with his pistol.

"It looks like there's still something alive in there, I can see it swimming around at the back."

"Come away and leave it be. If it sees your ugly face looking in at it, you might kill it," Kate smirked.

Pierce didn't turn around but just gave her two fingers.

"Talk me through your exit strategy again." Marcus pulled John aside. "How are you getting out, upstairs or downstairs window?"

"Upstairs," he confirmed. "I don't want to be coming down the stairs with that lot coming in the front door. As long as the car starts first time we should be half way back by the time they spring the trap."

"Make sure you draw as many of them into the kill zone before you trip the explosives though," Marcus suggested. "I want to knock the wind out of them before they start. Just do what you can to take out as many of the big ones that you can, the less of those around, the better."

"Yes, sir," John saluted jovially. "Anything else I can do for you while we're at it? Foot rub? A manicure maybe?" He new it wasn't going to be an easy job. Being on the front line held a lot of responsibility, and in all likelihood, he knew they wouldn't make it back at all, so a little humour helped him cope.

"Yeah." Marcus punched his helmet lightly "I want a Sunday Dinner; roast beef, Yorkshire puddings and all the trimmings. I also want you two to make sure you get out. Don't risk yourselves over nothing; am I clear gentlemen?"

"Today is not a good day to die," Pierce nodded. "We understand Boss, don't worry. No heroics."

"Well, some heroics," John added. "We want to have a few future schools named after us"

"But not posthumously," Pierce cut in. "I want to be adored by scantily clad women all over the world when this is over."

"We'll do one final check on the barricades while you two settle down and lock yourself in." Marcus shook their hands. "Remember to put the ladder to the back window before you close up. Here," Marcus tossed the car keys to Pierce, "I don't want it scratching, and I know how much petrol is in the tank."

"Yes, Dad," they chorused together as Marcus left by the front gate.

"Oh! Before I forget, there's a twelve volt battery in the front bedroom," he advised them. "I set the wires into it already, just trip the circuit when they're in range."

"See you back at the base boys," Kate smiled wickedly.

Ashfaq dropped himself down onto his sleeping cot. His back ached almost as much as his leg did, and that wasn't half as bad as his head. Every muscle in his body had been worked. If he hadn't been moving batteries, he'd been bent over tightening bolts or cleaning plugs. He lay still, hoping the pain would subside as his thoughts turned once more to his family.

The gap in his memory was almost killing him and he didn't like the feeling of not knowing. As the eldest, he had certain responsibilities; he needed to watch out for his younger brother, and his cousins who constantly asked him for support or advice. But now he was alone and he missed the stress his family had put on him.

With no one else to turn to, he turned to his faith. Though the room wasn't perfect and his clothes weren't clean, he knew it was time to pray. He'd missed most of the prayer times but as the Sun had set he would at least be able to do Maghrib.

"Ken, do you have a compass," he called.

"Sure." He removed it from his belt and passed it over and Ashfaq found his directions before passing it back.

"Thanks," he smiled before carefully closing the door.

Philip watched as the Sun set on the horizon, casting the last of its heat over the ruins of civilisation below. Most of the skyline that he had grown up seeing had gone; the fires had destroyed those buildings that the quake had missed. He turned away from it, not wanting to think about what he was now starting to refer to as the past; he couldn't allow himself to dwell on anything beyond what was important. That's why he'd come to the roof; Jolly was his last call and he wanted to see how far he'd got before he finally turned in.

A group of singers sang Christmas carols in one corner. The sound wasn't perfect, but it was beautiful to hear all the same, and he stopped to listen to them for a moment, mouthing along as he tired to remember the words. Even though it was cold, no one seemed to mind, and with the smell of Barbequed chicken and sausages rising from the kitchen below, it was easy to relax and pretend nothing bad had happened.

He couldn't see Jolly though. It wasn't really surprising considering the amount of people around. He had almost given up when he spotted a door opening in the distance and a man stepping out of one of the larger huts Jolly had created, so he made his way over. As he got closer he started to make out the sounds of laughter coming from inside; no children seemed to want to play here, and the lack of lights kept everyone else away.

He carefully pushed the door open and stepped inside, after all he was allowed, wasn't he in charge? Fairly lights twinkled gaily from the ceiling and some awful music played from Jolly`s laptop in the corner. The brightness was a huge contrast to the dullness outside, and it took his eyes a few seconds to adjust.

The room looked spacious and well laid out; bunks had been put against one wall, and in the centre of the room sat a large chimney, burning hot, its funnel leading out of a hole in the roof above. As he looked round at the occupants he felt very over dressed. Black leather, metal piercing, bare flesh, or a mixture of all three seemed to sum up almost everyone he saw, it was like a Christmas scene from hell.

He recognised a few of the people as those that had returned from the pit and without exception they were all in their early to mid twenties. Everyone in the room had stopped talking as he entered and they all watched him suspiciously, pale faces stared at him. Someone waved at him from the rear, she wore a long and low cut white dress with a black corset fastened tightly round her waist.

"Listen up you lot," she stood up and shouted as he approached. "This is Philip. Jolly says he's okay, so relax." There was a murmur around the room before they turned back to their conversations. "Sorry about that." She smiled sweetly as she sat back down next to her friend. "They get quite defensive when new people show up, especially people in power. Are you looking for Jolly?"

"Yes!" he suddenly blurted out as he realised he was staring at her chest. "Have you seen him?"

"He said he'd be back shortly, do you want a drink?" she smiled, beckoning him to sit next to her. "He had something to finish off with Suzi, tying up some loose ends here and there I think he said. He thought you'd have come up earlier though."

"I would've been," he replied loudly, almost shouting as the music got louder. "But something came up."

"I bet it did." She smiled cheekily as she slid her hand under the table and touched his leg making his knee jump and almost knocking the bottles over.

"Careful sugar," her friend smiled. "If you spill them, you're gonna have to pay." She was a little plumper, her breasts threatening to burst out from her top as she talked. He was acutely aware he was starring at her and he just wanted the world to open up and swallow him.

"Are you okay?" the first girl asked smiling. "You've gone a really funny colour. Do you want me to take you back to your room?"

"No!" he squeaked in a slightly higher pitch than he had hoped he would. "No, that's okay, thanks. I need to be going anyway. Er... When you see, er, Jolly, tell him I dropped by." He stood to leave and realised she was looking at his crotch.

"Just come and find me if you want?" She licked her lips. "My name's Gina."

He finally reached the door and pushed it open, gasping as the cold air hit him and he carefully re-adjusted himself before limping back towards the ramp and the safety of the lower levels.

"Philip, hang on!" He stopped and waited for Jolly to catch him up. His jowls seemed to wobble as much as his stomach, and as he reached him he bent down to catch his breath. Gimp ran up behind and Jolly passed him a weirdly constructed set of tins and tubes he'd been carrying.

"Sorry," he coughed. "I didn't think...you would... come up this late. Suzi and I." Philip tried to stop him. He didn't want to know the sordid details, but Jolly continued regardless. "We were... just working on...the ignition of one of the vans."

"Oh!" He felt the relief washing over him. "Sorry, I thought you and Suzi were..."

"Avin' it off?" Jolly smiled. "Na. Maybe later if I'm lucky. Gina told me she was winding you up back there. She is a very naughty girl that one. She likes you though." He winked.

"Oh, good," he nodded. "She seemed...nice." Visions of her cleavage appeared in his mind as he thought about her.

"You don't know her well enough to call her nice. She's clever mind you. She's training to be a teacher. Sorry, was training," he corrected himself.

"A teacher?" That shocked him.

"Yeah," he continued. "Junior school kids, eight to nine year olds. Her friend Deborah's a traffic warden."

"Oh!" The thought of her attacking drivers came all too easily to his mind.

"Not that she isn't flexible mind you. Gina, I mean, not her friend. Gina keeps in shape."

"So, anyway." He swallowed, desperately trying to re-rail the conversation. "You were working on the ignition switch?"

"Oh no." Jolly shook his head, smiling. "Not the ignition switch, basically how to ignite them."

Jolly went on to explain the plan despite all his protests. Everything seemed to end in something that went boom. Philip noticed how he got very excited when he talked about blowing things up; he made sounds and waved his arms as he exploded things in his head.

Philip tried to understand what he was saying. It wasn't that he wasn't clever enough to understand, but more because Jolly got so excited when he talked that he spat from the corner of his mouth and mumbled.

Suzi walked seductively over. She was wearing leather boots that ended just below her knees, black fishnet stocking, a short leather skirt and he presumed by the look of it, a rubber top. She smiled at Philip as she approached before whispering something into Jolly`s ear, making him stop and look at her.

"Really! Now?" He smiled like a little boy. Philip could see that the shopping spree Jolly had taken hadn't been just for explosive materials. Well, not in the sense of exploding materials he'd expected, but the world was collapsing around them, and he saw no point in ruining anything for him.

"You guys get off and enjoy the evening. I'll come up in the morning and you can show me what you have." But Jolly had already turned away, following closely behind Suzi like a little dog.

"Good night, Philip," Suzi called. "Sleep well." He watched them go before turning to wander down the ramp

"A teacher eh?" he smiled.

Pierce watched the Sun set from the upstairs window. What little heat it had provided quickly vanished, and he pulled the Thomas the Tank engine quilt round his shoulders in an attempt to keep him warmer. John stamped up the stairs and he turned as he entered.

"Bovril?" he sniffed as he entered with a tray of goodies he'd scrounged from the kitchen. "You lovely man you." He took the cup and sipped at the beefy liquid as John sat at the end of the bed.

"You can't beat it can you," John smiled. "Oh! That reminds me, I thought we had a problem before, did you realise Kate issued our rations again?"

"She's a right cow at times is that woman. Curry again was it?"

"Vegetable," he nodded. "But do not fear, my fine friend." He put one hand behind his back. "Being the very resourceful person that I am, I took the liberty of checking out the kitchen downstairs, and, voila!"

"What the hell is that, a pot noodle?" His face dropped. "There has to be more than just that."

"You're not a noodle fan then?" John looked dejected. "It's Chicken and Mushroom?" He showed him the flavour as though this made a huge difference.

"No. I'm not." Steam rose from the mug, warming his face. "Why do people think that just because I'm bloody Welsh that I like Pot Noodles?"

"Well, don't you? There's other stuff as well." John indicated the tray behind him "The kitchen looks pretty well stocked. Go take a look."

"You keep watch then while I go and see what I can have for dinner." He stood with the quilt still wrapped round his shoulders and shuffled towards the door, leaving John to keep watch. With all the curtains closed downstairs he was at least able to use his torch while still maintaining light discipline. He quickly checked the front and back rooms as he passed them to make sure everything was secure before walking into the kitchen.

He found the basics as he searched: tea, coffee, bread, an assortment of crisps and snacks, and he stored some in his pockets for later. He smiled as he found the jackpot: tinned Spam, tuna, corned beef and an assortment of soups stood stacked in one cupboard. He grabbed what he could and shoved them into his webbing before returning to the room.

"Did you see the Christmas tree?" he asked as he dropped the food onto the bed.

"Yeah, looks nice doesn't it." John didn't turn around, the field glasses pressed to his eyes as he tried to gain some more night vision. "My Ma used to take ages setting ours up, she had some right old decorations, she did," he chuckled to himself. "I remember one year, I stood on a glass one in my bare feet. I was hopping round trying to keep the blood of the rug while trying to avoid her slap at the same time." He chortled to himself at the memory. "Did you find anything down there?"

"Oh, yeah." Pierce moved the tins around. "Some Bully Beef and some ham, what I wouldn't give for a plate of chips to go with them." He looked wistfully out of the window. "Oh, some large pickled onions too."

"No fried egg?" John turned his back to the window.

"A fried egg!" Pierce licked his lips at the thought. "Yeah, runny though."

"Now you've gone and made me hungry as well" John rubbed his stomach. "Thank you very much."

"Eat your Pot Noodle if you're hungry"

"Not yet." He cradled the plastic pot in his hands.

"This is proper survival food this is. It keeps the longest, and depending on the flavour, you'd rather eat your own foot first." He tossed it onto his pack as he turned to look out of the window again. "I tell you what though; if the Moon goes in we're going to have a real problem seeing anything out there. Visibility is tight as it is."

"You want me to go and rig a wiz pop up?" Pierce suggested. "That way if anything passes it will trip the line and the flare will at least give us something to see by."

"I knew there was a reason we kept you around," John winked.

"Well, I'm not just a pretty face you know." He blew a kiss back at John. "Keep a watch, if you see anything, signal me." He grabbed the flare from his pack. "And keep your dirty hands off my ham."

Once downstairs he carefully opened the front door and slipped outside. Everything was so still and the air smelt fresh and crisp; he looked up into the night sky, taking in the panoramic vista above him before stepping out of the garden and into the street beyond.

The snow crunched loudly as he walked and he felt like every house was looking at him. He shook his head, trying to dislodge the idea that in every window, a creature watched, waiting to pounce. "Stop it," he hissed to himself as he moved behind a car. Trying to stay in the shadows as much as possible, he made his way slowly to the end of the street and started to set the flare.

Ash was cold and he shivered uncontrollably. With nothing else to do he'd turned in for the night, but he couldn't sleep. No matter how he positioned himself, the cold seemed to get him somewhere. He pulled the blanket over his head and closed his eyes. He tried to clear his mind, to bring back the memories that dwelt just beyond his vision.

What have I got myself into, he asked himself. Where is my family, is any of this real or is it just a dream? His head seemed to bang in time with his heartbeat. If only I could wake up.

John watched Pierce through his scope; it was just possible to make out his silhouette as he moved across the frosty path. He scanned the area ahead, trying to probe into every nook and cranny and he realised how much easier life was when the night scopes worked. Now he strained to pick out any difference in the shadows.

Something moved in the corner of his vision and he focused quickly on it; he could have sworn there was something there, by the house just behind Pierce. He stopped breathing as he waited for it to move again, straining his eyes to see.

"Hurry up man.," he hissed, panic building inside him. Pierce seemed to be taking ages to set the flare and he tried to will him to finish quickly when the shadow moved again.

He didn't know what to do, Pierce was facing the wrong way so he couldn't flash him. He looked through his scope again trying to confirm that something was there. He swore as he scanned the area, his heart pounded in his chest. Pierce still hadn't moved. Time seemed to slow down and every sense was on over time as the adrenaline pumped through his body, excitement and terror at the same time.

The shadow moved from the garden, but now there was no way to fire, the round would pass through the creature's body and hit Pierce, killing them both instantly.

"Turn round," he groaned loudly. "For God sake turn round!"

Philip didn't feel like sleeping, there was so much going on that his mind didn't seem able to stop itself. The thought that they may have less than two days left to live kept jumping into his mind, and he went over the points in his head one more time to check everything had been covered.

It wasn't that things weren't going well. On the contrary, everything had moved along at a fast pace with very little problems. Edward had managed to exceed all expectations on the structural side of the building.

Donald had pitched in wherever it was needed, cooling hot heads and just motivating people when they grew tired or depressed. Marcus had put a plan in place to recruit as many able bodied people as he could to bolster his ranks of defenders and Jolly...well, he'd figure out what he'd done in the morning.

He rolled over, pulling the duvet around himself some more, but he just couldn't get comfy; it was then that he realised he wasn't alone. A shadow stepped out from the corner of the room. He didn't know how long they had been stood there for as the curtain wasn't exactly a strong deterrent.

His hand groped for the pistol he kept at the side of his bed but stopped as the shadow stepped into the moonlight. She wore high heeled black leather boots that reached half way up her calf, a black low cut dress with a white leather belt and her dark hair hung loosely down to her shoulders.

I must be dreaming, he thought as she walked silently over to him; her hips swayed hypnotically and he felt his heart beat increasing.

"Gina?"

"You were expecting someone else?" she smiled as she climbed onto the bed and kissed him deeply on the lips. "You didn't really want to sleep tonight did you?"

He stopped as soon as he heard the noise behind him, his brain screamed that something was wrong and he grabbed his knife from his belt and lunged. The young girl screamed in surprise, and it took all his strength to stop the blade hitting her and plunge into the wooden gatepost behind her. Moving quickly he covered her mouth, fearful of what her scream would bring down on them. He pulled the blade free and realised how close he had been to gutting her where she stood.

"Quiet," he commanded. "I'm not going to hurt you," he whispered harshly. "But if you keep on making noises other things might." He held his hand in place until he felt her relax a little. "I'm going to move my hand away, please don't scream, okay?"

She nodded that she understood.

"Who are you?" he whispered at her. She looked almost feral, her hair was dirty and matted to the side of her head.

"My name is Clare," she sobbed.

"Listen, Clare." He had to act fast before the shock took over. "Are you alone?"

"No." She pointed to the house. "My mum and brother are inside."

"Do you live here?"

"No," she shook her head. "We came here this afternoon. We hide at night, but I couldn't sleep and was watching from the window when I saw you pass."

"Well, tonight you all stay with us; go and wake them, tell them to grab their stuff but be quiet about it." As she entered the house he waved his torch to John, signalling everything was okay before returned to fix the flare in place. Sweat stood out on his brow despite the coldness of the night as the remains of the adrenaline pumped through him. He couldn't believe how close he had he been to killing her?

Fortunately they all moved quietly along until they reached the house and John urged them quickly inside, closing and locking the door behind them. No one had spoken as they entered, though a look from John reminded Pierce how dangerous it was for them to be here. Five minutes later they were standing in the kitchen together listening to the noise from upstairs.

"You know what we're doing here right?" John whispered in his ear. "What if they attack now? What the hell are we expected to do?"

"You think I don't know that?" Pierce retorted angrily. "What was I suppose to do? Leave them there to be blown up?"

"Well, no but..."

"Well nothing. They need help, and they might as well stay here until morning, we can get them back to base then." He could see John didn't like the situation, but there hadn't been any better option. "Plus she was all alone and needed my help."

John stopped and looked at him, "She needed your help? Oh, I see. You want to be the hero?"

Pierce couldn't stop the smirk crossing his face.

"I don't believe you, even out here on the edge of a disaster zone you manage to score."

"It's not like that," he whispered. "Well, maybe it's a little like that."

"Okay," John conceded. "But in the morning, they go back to base."

"Thanks," Pierce smiled. "I owe you one."

"You owe me more than bloody one." John turned as the woman entered the room. "Boss." He saluted sharply at him. "I'd best be getting back on watch if it's all right with you." He turned to the woman and nodded as he left. "Madam."

Pierce knew this was going to cost him later, but it was a price he was happy to pay. "Thank you, John," he nodded. "Call me, if anything changes."

"Sir," he replied sharply before he pulled the door closed behind him. The woman brushed her blonde hair from her face as she remained standing nervously in the doorway. Her blue dress looked worn and tattered, but Pierce thought she was the most wonderful thing he'd ever seen. There was something naturally beautiful about the image before him, and they stood silently looking at each other for a moment before he remembered what he was doing.

"Please, sit down," he smiled, moving round to pull a chair from under the table. "Would you like something to drink?"

"Anything would be fine," she smiled; her voice was soft and mellow. "I can't remember the last warm drink I've had." She continued to talk as he made the drink, "Thank you, I didn't realise the Army was still around."

"To be honest, we're not." He put her drink on the table before her and sat down "There aren't many of us left."

"Oh!" She looked down at her cup. "I'm sorry, I just thought…" She started o cry. "I just thought it was over." He moved closer to her to offer some support; as he knelt beside her he could see tears running down her cheeks as she fought to control herself.

"Come on." He put his arm gently around her. "You're safe here," he lied as she rested her head against his shoulder.

"I'm being daft," she sighed as he stroked her hair.

"No," he smiled. "Not at all, you've been through a lot." She sat up and wiped at her eyes with a piece of cloth, forcing a smile before sipping at her drink.

"I'm sorry." Pierce stood. "Where are my manners? My name is Pierce and that was John."

"Sarah," Sarah replied. "My children are James and Clare."

"What about their father?"

"Not around." She shook her head. "He never was really."

"So I take it you've been on your own since this all started?"

"Yes. Well apart from the few others we've met."

He wasn't surprised to hear there were others out there. She looked slightly uncomfortable as she sipped her drink.

"You need to get some rest, you look tired."

"It's just been so hard." Sarah reached out and held his hand. "We have lost everything." Tears ran down her face again.

"It's okay." He moved and sat down next to her. "Listen, you've done everything you could.".

"I was so scared." She forced a smile as he leaned forward and brushed a tear aside with his thumb and she lent forward, putting her head against his chest.

"It's okay now," he whispered as he ran his hand over her hair again. He'd go to hell for what he was thinking, but something stopped him acting on it; either it was the lack of beer, or the realisation that this wasn't just a girl he met in town, but it didn't feel right.

Sarah cried for a long time as he sat held her. Everyone was in the same position, everyone was scared, and he realised he was exactly like her. He had nothing to go home to, no worldly possessions other than those he had in his pockets. When he'd been on manoeuvres it was easy to separate the job from his life. But now, the fact that he may never see any of his family or friends again weighed heavily on him.

Treat it like a mission, he reminded himself as he felt himself slipping. Sarah's sobbing slowed as she finally dropped into a deep protected sleep. He knew he should try to lower her down, but when he tried she held on, not wanting to let go. Only three hours until I need to swap with John he thought, I guess I could be in a worse position.

The sunlight didn't care what it shone upon. It shone on the rivers and fields as equally as on the corpses and the ruins of civilisation. A light steam rose as the snow and frost gave up its fight, causing small streams to mix with blood before running between the bricks and onto the roads beyond.

The gull had slept well, and it could feel its strength coming back as it flexed its wings. It limped out from his hiding place and raised its head to the Sun before screeching loudly, waiting to hear a reply from the other gulls that might be near but none came. It was confused, despite the warmth of the Sun and the clear air, something seemed wrong; nothing seemed out of place, no creatures hunted nearby and there was no threat to be seen, but something flashed danger into its mind.

It didn't understanding what was wrong and it turned its head quickly to each side in case something crept closer. It'd never felt this feeling before; even when it had fought something there had not been this intensity, this pressure.

Its beak sliced a chuck of flesh free from the nearest body and it dragged it back into its nest. It didn't want to be outside; it was time to lie low.

Philip yawned and stretched, he felt more alive than he ever had before. Rolling over he rested his arm on Gina's shoulder and she mumbled under her breath. He carefully lifted the quilt and looked underneath. Very beautiful, he grinned, and she'd certainly taught him something last night.

With a new sense of hope growing in him, he rolled out of bed and quietly dressed before walking to the window and pulling back the curtain. The sunlight shone brightly on the road and he breathed in deeply, letting the air circulate round his body before he exhaled.

"Morning," Gina called from the pillow. "Do you have to go to work today?" Her arm reached out towards him, grabbing at the air, beckoning him back to the warmth of the covers. He was very tempted to just climb back in next to her, to share maybe his last day with her, and why not, hadn't he given enough already?

"Yeah, I do," he replied glumly as he walked over and kissed her. She put her arm around his neck and pulled him close.

"But you certainly want to come back to bed with me," she stated with a coy smile. "I can tell these things."

He kissed her again and his stomach grumbled loudly as a hunger grew inside him.

"Happy Christmas," she smiled as he pulled away. "I gift myself to you."

"Isn't that slavery?" he laughed.

"No." She shook her head as she climbed out of bed. "Slavery is when it's against someone's wishes, this is just fun. I'll show you later." She stood naked before him and he found himself staring at her body wistfully.

"Later my sweet." She licked his lip, and winked as she left his room. He let the memories of the previous night wash over him for a moment, then with a sigh, he decided it was time to face the world. If today was going to be his last, then he was ready to see it through to the bitter end.

"You look happy this morning," Donald shouted as he walked up the ramp. He was sat eating his breakfast, a large mug of coffee before him.

"I feel great thanks. How are you?"

"Considering what's been happening, I'm not too bad. If I had the morning paper I'd be happy. Though I guess I know what the front page would read." Donald pointed at his ankle. "Nice to see you properly back on your feet, I thought you'd decided to permanently put your feet up."

"Yeah, yeah," he smiled. "Very funny. It still hurts, but not as much as it has been. Anyway, Joanne said it looked more like a strain that a break." He sat down next to him. "What you got planned for today then?"

"I thought I'd give Ed a hand again. There's a nasty looking crack on the third floor. I really don't want it falling in on us." He rubbed the bristles on his chin. "After that, I fancied a nice wander in the gardens before a boat ride on the water." He held his mug up to his mouth, his little finger pointing out. "Why? You need anything doing?"

"There's nothing more important than the crack," he conceded. "No. I was…well. Just checking up on you, I mean, well you know, we haven't really had time to stop since we first met."

"Yeah," he nodded. "There are good days and bad days. We just keep on moving I guess. It seems like years ago now that this all started." He stared into his cup, all humour gone from his face. He looked up at Philip, a tear rolled down his face before he angrily wiped it away, almost ashamed to be upset. "Sorry."

"You don't ever need to apologise to me, Donald, you know that. Without you a lot of us wouldn't be here. Hell, none of us would be. I know losing the building must have hurt but…"

"The building?" he shouted "You think losing the stupid place upsets me?" He quickly stood up; the anger behind his eyes caused Philip to step away and Donald took a number of deep breaths before he spoke again. Philip didn't know what he'd said but he'd obviously touched a nerve.

"I'm sorry." Donald shook his head as he composed himself. "It's not your fault." His face had flushed red. "Just promise me something."

"Anything," Philip said.

"Promise me you won't leave anyone behind, be the best you can be for everyone. Everyone is important."

"I promise," he nodded. "Donald, what's wrong?"

"Nothing." He looked away, rubbing his hands over his round face before he turned back round. "Nothing at all. Forget about it. It's not your problem." He picked up his mug and walked back to the counter before wandering silently away.

Philip watched him until he was out of sight. He'd seemed like his old self again before he left but something was obviously wrong. This was the second time he'd see this happen, the outburst and the anger. There must be something, Philip thought, something about Donald I've missed.

●　●　●　●　●　●　●　●　●

Marcus arrived at the safe house just after dawn and was surprised to find it full. He stood in the doorway watching everyone eat their breakfast for a moment before he coughed. Pierce and John jumped guiltily to their feet and saluted.

"As you were, gentlemen." He waved his hand, and they lowered their salutes. "How long have I been gone?" Pierce looked confused for a moment, and Marcus felt sure he was about to announce the hours and minutes, before it dawned on him what Marcus was referring to.

"Oh! No, no it's not like that. Sorry, Boss. Allow me to introduce our guests. This is Sarah and her two children, Clare and James."

Sarah started to stand but Marcus stopper her.

"No need to stand." He nodded politely. "It's nice to meet you." He felt a smile was in order so gave one. "Gentlemen, a moment." He nodded for them to follow him outside, and they left the family to their breakfast.

"We found them last night," Pierce explained as they stood in the front room. "It looks like they've been moving round. I'd gone to set a flare and I almost killed her daughter. We didn't know what else to do so we brought them back with us. Sorry."

"You did the right thing," he smiled. "It just caught me off guard that's all. Anything else to report apart from developing a family?"

"No, sir," they both answered in unison.

"Tell you what," he smiled. "Why don't you both take them back to base? You're not needed here again until tonight, so you might as well get some proper food in you."

"Yes, sir. Thank you, sir," they smiled.

"Morning," Philip called as he spotted Jolly climbing out of the back of a white van that stood near the ramp on the top floor. "What do you have for me today then?"

"What's that?" he indicated the thing Gimp carried. "I saw you with it last night. Does it blow up or something?"

"That?" He shook his head smiling. "Nope. It doesn't blow up." Gimp sniggered as he took it back. "This is…" he paused as he thought of an answer. "Well, it's medicinal." Philip couldn't imagine what medical use it might have and why it was up here instead of in the infirmary. Gimp seemed to find his lack of understanding very comical and continued to snigger.

"Okay." Jolly held it up. "It's a bong alright, it relaxes me. Helps me remember how to make stuff." He looked embarrassed, like a school child caught by the headmaster smoking behind the bike sheds. It wasn't as though there was anything Philip could do about it, even if he really wanted to.

"Does it help?" he inquired.

"Does it ever?" He gestured for him to follow. "Let me show you."

He led the way to a corner of the roof, hidden away by boards and sheets. A group of men stood together, leather pants, large boots and greasy looking hair. He guessed they were all stoned in some way or another. "Rick!" Jolly shouted to one of them. "Rick, give it another test fire will you!"

Rick put his thumbs up and plodded over to a pickup truck. Brackets and pieces of metal seemed to protrude from odd angles all over it, one piece longer than the others.

"Watch this." Jolly nudged him. "We need to give it another test run anyway. It's powered by one of the generators." Philip watched as Rick loaded a tin onto a platform at the end of the longest pole. "Ready when you are, Rick." With a roar the generator kicked in and the longest piece arced upwards and collided heavily into a cross beam above the drivers cab. The entire pickup seemed to jump at the force of the impact, and the metal container catapulted high into the air and out over the edge of the car park.

"The paint weighs the same as one of the large grenades Gimp makes," Jolly informed him as they moved to the edge. "But with the added bonus we can see where it lands. Rick, what colour paint was it?"

"Red. Can you see it?"

"No," Jolly shook his head. "It must have gone over the houses. Damn it. I need to figure out a range finder on it. It's useless! Unless we want to completely miss the target each time."

Despite the lack of visible results, Philip was impressed; the can had easily cleared 400 metres. Rick appeared behind them, he was tall and broad, with a mop of brown hair on his head, two rings in his bottom lip and what Philip believed was an Xbox button in his earlobe.

"That was awesome!" He looked over the edge trying to spot the landing site.

"Go and see where it landed, will you?" Jolly looked as excited as Rick did.

"Yeah." He half-bounced and half-ran towards the ramp. "Sure."

"What else do you want to see?"

Philip looked round, small groups of people seemed to be industriously working on one thing or another. "That's fine for now," he smiled reassuringly. "I know you have more up your sleeve." He wanted to find Gina, even though he knew he really needed to stay focused on his duties. "I guess we can rely on you later if they attack."

Jolly was jotting notes down on a pad, until finally he realised he was being talked something. "What?" he looked up. "Oh yeah. We should be okay, I guess."

"What do you mean, should?" the way he said it worried him.

"Well," he slowly said. "Most of these guys are pacifists, they might look rough, but they don't really do violence."

"Well the violence is going to get them if we don't succeed, talk to them, Jolly. We need everyone to be ready."

"I'll try," Jolly replied reluctantly before walking away,

doodling in his pad, and Philip watched him go. Marcus had already told him about the extra bombs and cocktails Jolly had provided. The catapult would certainly help if he could aim it better and the hundred or so people he'd managed to collect looked mean enough, but would be useless if they didn't join in.

It was obviously now a bad idea to have let him choose his own workforce. They certainly seemed to enjoy mixing and building things, but when push came to shove would they fight? It was a question that worried him.

John wasn't happy at all. Certainly, the idea of spending the day back at base was a welcome one, but sitting in the back seat of the car with two kids wasn't his idea of a good time at all. He turned and smiled at James who sat next to him.

"You alright?" he asked. James looked nervously at him before turning away.

"He doesn't talk much," Clare told him. "It's nothing personal; he doesn't really talk that much to us either."

"Oh, right, oh."

"What's this place we're going to like?" James poked him.

"Well..." he tried to think of a way of sugar coating it and failed. "It's a big car park, but there are lots of people there." He thought for a moment. "And lots of food. I bet we can find you something good to eat."

"Do you have a tin of sausages and beans?" James asked.

"For you I'm sure we can find some," he smiled. "If we get there in one piece anyway." He shouted the last part to Pierce who swerved to avoid a burnt out car. "Can't you drive any better? This isn't a tank."

"You are driving quite fast," Sarah commented. "Are you all okay back there?"

"I think James might be sick, but I'm alright," Clare replied.

"Alright... I'll slow it down," Pierce called.

"Oh I see, when a lady asks you to slow down, you do, but when I ask…" John smirked.

"I just don't want to have to clean the back seats. I know what you get like."

"Once." John shook his head. "One time was all, and you know I was ill."

As Philip reached the ramp another tin of paint arced into the distance, followed by a chorus of whoops and cheers from the spectators; he just hoped Jolly didn't break the thing before they needed it. As he walked down the ramp he started to hear what sounded like raised voices and pretty soon he realised that someone was arguing, and it sounded heated.

"What's going on?" he demanded as he reached the lower level. A plump man detached himself from the group and raced over to him, obviously distraught at something. His tie flapped over his shoulder as he ran.

"I say, Philip!" he spluttered. "Philip! You are the man in charge around here are you not?" His voice was squeaky, with a quite prominent lisp.

"I am," Philip nodded.

"I need to report something to you." The man tried to pull himself up to his full height, but his stomach stopped him. "Am I really expected to work with my hands? I don't do that, I won't do that."

"Really?" He spoke calmly; he'd expected something like this to happen sooner or later as the social levels started to leak through. "And what do you do Mr…?"

"My name is Theak." The man almost spat the K at the end. "Reginald Theak."

"Well Reg." He purposefully reduced his name down to its base level before putting his arm casually over his shoulder. "What did you do before all this happened exactly?" Philip looked him over, his pinstripe suit was worn and dirty, but he'd still managed to maintain a handkerchief in his top pocket. His balding head and round chubby face made him look like a monk.

"I am a banker," Reg stated as he straightened his tie. "I work with money not with paint." He stood defiantly before him. "This sort of business is not right for me. Common people paint so you have to find me something better to do, something more at my level. I need to be in charge of something."

There was something about Reg that instantly annoyed Philip. It wasn't his clothing, though it was obvious he'd avoided getting it dirty so far, nor was it his voice, though that was unpleasant. It was his attitude.

Philip smiled at him but it wasn't a pleasant, happy smile, it was the smile of a man who was close to the edge, someone who didn't care anymore. He'd seen enough people like Reg in his life to know it wasn't worth the effort to try to reason with him.

"Well, Reg. Let me explain something to you." Philip started to lead him away from the others. "I bet you drove a nice car before this and had nice holidays didn't you?"

"What...What's that got to do with anything?" he spluttered as Philip dragged him along. He tried to resist but Philip was having none of it. He led him through the canteen before pushing him into the Medical centre, shutting the curtain behind him.

"Mr Theak." He forced him up against the wall. "Let me explain something to you, I'll keep it plane and simple so your upper class brain can take it all in." Philip's face was inches from his face as he spoke. "All the money has gone. All we have left now are us, and we work together." He could see Glen start to come over but Philip raised his hand to stop him without breaking his stare on Reg.

"We need to work together in order to survive, and I do so want to survive, Mr Theak, I really do." Reginald squirmed under Philip's hands but he held him against the wall. "Do you know what the alternative looks like? Do you know what it looks like if we don't support each other? When you re-possessed houses on people so you could line your pockets, did you ever see the results?" Reg looked very uncomfortable now, his face red with panic he tried to push away but Philip was having none of it.

"Well, Mr Theak. You wanted to be in charge, and you are going to be. For once you are going to see what these people have gone through already. This is what you and your kind caused to happen because you were too greedy, too self centred to actually help." Philip pushed him back towards a curtained off area at the rear of the room and forced him through it. He felt angry, he really wanted to hurt Reg, but he knew that wouldn't do any good. He needed to make a point.

Behind the curtain lay the men, women and children who had perished so far. With no time to bury them as yet, they had been stored here until a place could be found for them to finally rest.

"This is what your kind has done to the world, the politicians and the money men. The fat cats who looked after themselves, the men who sold the world for a handful of diamonds." He pushed him further in and Reginald fell to his knees, sobbing at the macabre site before him. "Was it worth it?" he shouted.

"Glen," he called. "I've found someone to deal with the dead. Reginald here is in charge of burying them all, make sure he works hard."

"I won't do it," Reg shouted a last act of defiance. "You can't make me."

"Really?" Philip reached over and pulled Glen's pistol from his holster and levelled it at him, pressing the barrel against his forehead. "You have been given an order." He cocked the weapon. "I am more than willing to do what I have to do, Reg, because I believe in the greater good. I believe in tomorrow, we don't have time for petty problems brought on by too much good living. Not as others suffer, not at the expense of others." Reg backed away, starting to mutter an apology. "You are a leech, Reg," he continued. "You have grown fat from the misery of others. With your interest rates and your offer of loans that cannot ever be repaid. I remember the recession, everyone suffered but the men at the top, well now it's your turn."

Philip stared at Reginald, the gun steady in his hand, no doubt behind his eyes. "You have options Reg, of course you do. You can be part of this." He gestured around him. "Or you can go on you way, leave this place and go on your own. What's it going to be?" He had never felt so calm before, it was the best therapy session he could have asked for. He almost laughed, the situation was absurd, but enough was enough, a line had been drawn in the sand and he wasn't going to back down.

Reginald's bottom lip quivered and his eyes glassed over before he lowered his head in defeat. "What do you want me to do?" he sobbed and Philip lowered the gun, switching the safety on before handing it back to Glen.

"John and Mike have found a place for the bodies," he explained to Glen. "Mr Theak here has agreed to take charge of the transportation and burial of them."

Glen nodded, allowing himself to breath again for the first time since the gun had been drawn.

"I want the bodies to be wrapped in cloth before we move them out, some last dignity for them at least. I'm going to call a general meeting for everyone in about two hours, so almost everyone should be on the roof with me. I figure they need to know what we know." He looked at the Major as he lay on the cot nearby.

"Well done," he mouthed.

When Philip reached his room he punched the wall. He'd so wanted to pull the trigger and splatter his brains all over the room. That pompous fool had felt he was better than everyone. How had civilisation come down to this, how have we fallen so far, he asked himself? The government was corrupt, that had come to light with the expense scandals, but compared to what had happened since that had been just like taking a small sweet from a baby.

In the past, politicians had done their job because they felt a need to help the people, but then it had changed. It was all about the power and the money; they'd sat in their ivory towers and ignored the world, well now their towers had tumbled down.

"You okay?" Donald knocked on the door frame. "I've just seen Glen," he smirked. "I think you actually made that twerp wet his pants. Wish I'd been there to see it."

"It's not funny." Philip shook his head, though a smile appeared on his face. "I wanted to shoot the prick."

"He wasn't worth wasting the bullet on." Donald patted him on the back. "Well, my jobs done. Do you need any help elsewhere?"

"Yes," he nodded. "I've decided to tell everyone what's actually going on. If we're facing death, then the people should know about it. We've seen enough cloak and dagger from our leaders in the past. If I'm going to lead, then it's going to be with a clean start."

"Are you sure about that? Sometimes ignorance is bliss, we don't want a panic."

"I'm positive," Philip smiled. "It's the right thing to do, get everyone together in two hours on the top floor."

"What the hell? Do you think you're now then?" Jim laughed as he stood behind Ash looking at the car. "I like it though. It says I commute with attitude."

Ash didn't turn round but he smiled behind the welding mask; the flame from the torch licked over the sides of the bonnet as he continued to weld sharp pieces of metal onto the car.

"It's funny," he shouted above the roar of the fire. "Last night, I remembered something I'd read." He switched off the torch and put the mask on the bonnet. "People choose the paths of their own lives, be it victor or victim, and that you claim your role by the choices you make along the way. I've been a victim for too long." He drank from a can of coke at his side. "It's time for me to choose a new path and I'm sick of hiding. I don't want to die like a scared animal."

"Cool man, I can dig it." Jim scratched his head. "What you thinking of doing?"

"Getting out of here for a start, I want to make a difference. I can't sit around not knowing what's happened to my family. Tomorrow morning I am going out to find them."

"I'm coming too then," he smiled. "If you find them, there's no way your can bring them all back in that."

"I thought the bus didn't work."

"It doesn't, well not at the moment." He waggled his finger. "But if we work on it together, we should be able to figure it out."

"The world is three days," Ash quoted. "As for yesterday, it has vanished, along with all that was in it. As for tomorrow, you may never see it. As for today, it is yours, so work in it."

"Nice, I like it."

"Let's do it." They shook hands

"As long as we can put blades on it like yours."

Philip climbed onto the roof of the truck. Almost two thousand pairs of eyes had been crammed into every little space they could to hear him, and as they looked at him, he could feel his nerves going.

"Today," he began, but Donald quickly stopped him.

"No chance they can hear you at the back."

He sighed to himself. When this sort of thing happened at the cinema it was loud and dramatic, now it was his turn. Philip Greenwood, leader of possibly the last remaining people in England, and he couldn't even get everyone to hear him. Jolly passed him a traffic cone with the end cut off it.

"Best thing we have," he explained.

"Okay then." He looked at Donald. "It's time to tell them the truth."

"You sure about this?" he relied. "It's you last chance to change your mind."

"Yes, I'm sure, they need to know." Philip swallowed heavily as he looked around. Everyone stood expectantly waiting for him to speak, waiting for him to lead. Nodding to himself he raised the makeshift megaphone to his lips.

"Today we stand at a crossroads. The battles we've won have just been a small part of the war and there is more to come." Groans rose from the crowd. "I won't lie to you. It's not going to be easy and it will be a hard fight, and we know what to expect from them. But... we do not have to fear them. We have options. We can give in, sit down and do nothing or... we can fight. Fight for our future, fight for the children of tomorrow, fight for our right to be here." He raised his fist to the sky.

"This is our town, our world, and I will not let them take it from us." He could feel them watching him. "I won't give in, I will not lie down. I choose to fight, but I cannot fight alone. Who will fight with me?" The crowd remained silent and he started to sweat. It looked so easy in the movies, so easy to instil the pride of the people, to give them strength and hope. He felt like crying, like running away as the silence engulfed him.

"I choose to fight," a woman called from the back.

"And me," a man called somewhere from his right.

"I'll fight for my child." A man lifted his daughter. Then another joined in, one by one, ten turned into a hundred, then a hundred into a thousand, their voices joined together until a thunder of stamping feet and cheering voices filled the air.

"This world is ours," he shouted exultantly. "And we will not give it up. When they come, they will face a force to be reckoned with."

As Philip made his was back to his room he was touched by the crowd, or his hand was shaken as he passed people, and when he finally reached his room he staggered inside.

"That was very impressive," Gina said as she sat at the table.

"Thanks." He closed the curtain behind him. "That was a close call though." Donald knocked against the frame and entered behind him, he nodded to Philip before sitting down next to Gina and lent back in his chair with look of satisfaction on his face.

"Come in, Donald," he said. "Make yourself at home why don't you".

"Thanks, Philip," Donald smiled. "I will. How are you doing Gina?"

"I'm doing very well, thanks for asking," Gina chirped. "Very well indeed, thank you. How do you feel?"

"Very motivated," he smirked. "Have you seen them all working out there?" He stuck his thumb over his shoulder in the direction of the door. "It's like an ants nest." Donald stopped as another knock thumped against the door frame and Ed walked in.

"I don't know about you," he said as he pulled the curtain closed behind him, "but... I choose to fight." He raised his fist as he said it, punching towards the sky causing Gina and Donald to burst out laughing. Philip stared at them as they laughed, then reality dawned on him.

"You staged it! You staged it all." He felt deflated.

"Don't look at me." Donald held his hands up. "That was all Gina's idea." Donald pointed his thumb at her. "I was telling Jolly your plan to tell everyone and that I needed the space, and she overheard."

"It was only as a backup plan," Ed continued. "Your speech was excellent, really got me motivated." They laughed again.

"But it was a lie," he moaned. "The crowd. The cheering. Everything."

"No it wasn't," Donald stopped him. "But reality isn't like the movies; life just doesn't work that way. There are no scripts to follow, you told them what you wanted them to hear, we just got them excited about it."

Gina stood up and kissed him on the cheek. "I'm sorry," she said. "I only wanted to help." Leaning closer she whispered in his ear, "If I've been bad, you should punish me." She pouted at him.

He looked from her to the others. He should be angry. "I guess it worked out in the end," he conceded.

"I'll tell you something though," Edward smiled. "I think equal rights are back in fashion. I heard one woman say that if today was going to be her last, then she wasn't going to die owing anything to any man."

Pierce gave Sarah a hug before he climbed into the car. He could see the tears running down her face and he forced a smile.

"No kiss?" John asked as he slowly pulled away from the kerb, his tires slipping on the snow.

"No, it's not like that."

"Sure," John smirked. "You're just setting her up."

"No it's not," he stopped him before the conversation deteriorated as it usually did. "She's not that sort of woman and I don't want to rush anything. I've been out with enough hippocrocapigs in my past; it's time for something different."

"Are you serious? You do remember where we're going, and what's going to happen don't you?" John lent over and looked in his eyes, causing the car to swerve to the side.

"Get off me." He pushed him back in his seat. "Just watch the road will you. I know what we're facing alright. I just want something real to come back to."

"You're serious?" John looked shocked. "Does she feel the same way?"

"I think so," he smiled. "I hope so, but I don't know for sure."

"You dog." He punched his leg. "Okay then," he smiled as he accelerated towards the house. "Let's get this done and go home."

Philip watched until the car vanished round the corner before he closed the new wooden hatch on his window. Gina sat at the table smiling at him.

"Your eyes still twinkle," he observed. "How can you be so calm?" He was amazed at how good she looked, how alive. "How have you kept your faith?" He sat down, taking her hand in his.

"Faith has nothing to do with it," she smiled. "You just have to believe everything has a path, a reason, and everything has a start and a finish." She shrugged. "I guess I just don't get panicked like everyone else. I don't see the point. If I live, then I live. If I die then there is nothing I can do about it, so I might as well enjoy the ride."

"Is life that empty?"

"Empty?" She looked shocked. "Life's far from empty. It's full of wonder and magic. How can you appreciate the light unless you stand in the dark sometimes? There can be as much beauty in a dead rose as a live one." She stood up before him, hands on hips. "Life's about living, experience each day to its maximum, don't you see that?"

"I guess," he shrugged, not really understanding it at all.

"Not the right answer." She stood and walked round behind him and quickly cuffed his wrists together.

"Hey!" he objected. "I thought you said I was in charge."

Outside this room you can be," she smiled. "But being in charge is a heavy weight on your shoulders. So, before you need to face the chaos outside, I'm going to teach you something." She kissed his cheek.

"What's that?" he asked nervously.

"I'm going to teach you how to accept the inevitable."

"It's starting to get dark," Ash announced as he walked back in from outside. The smoke from the fires inside made his asthma play up, so it felt good to get outside and the fresh air felt good in his chest. "It sure is quiet out there."

"What do you expect? There's no one out there." Ken looked at him, smiling.

"I know that." He shook his head. "What I meant was there are no birds. You can usually hear at least one or two before the Sun goes down, but it's deathly quiet out there."

"I can't say that I've ever really noticed." Ken shut the bonnet on the Capri he was working on. "Has Jim got his bus working?"

Ash watched him as he rubbed a cloth caringly over the bonnet, wiping away his greasy hand marks from the metal.

"Yes he has," he nodded. "We got it going, but I don't think it'll last long. It looks like the suspension has gone, and the rear axle's almost had it. He'll be lucky if he gets twenty miles out of it."

"It will have to do," Ken nodded. "We can always hide again while we get more cars working." He rubbed an invisible fleck from the windscreen affectionately. "I always wanted one of these."

"Get something to eat," Ken called to him as he grabbed the shutter and pulling it down, closing the underground to the outside. "If you're going for your family in the morning, you'll need your strength."

Pierce stared out from below his quilt; midnight was quickly approaching and he was bored. His legs ached as cramp set in but it was his turn to keep watch, not that he was doing it alone. John sat next to him under his quilt, occasionally moving to keep the blood flowing.

"It's eleven thirty two," he whispered. "Do you want a brew?"

"Okay," John replied. "I'll make it." He pushed himself to his feet, stamping blood back into his frozen toes. "Tea?"

"Don't ask stupid questions." He shuffled closer to the window. "If it's warm and wet, and not your piss I'll drink it."

"Once," John laughed. "Once and you never forget."

"Dirty get you are." He pushed him towards the door. "If it hadn't been dark, you wouldn't have got away with it. I still owe you for tha…" His words froze in his mouth as the room swam with light. John dropped into a crouch and scrambled back to the window quickly pushing it open.

Pierce did likewise, grabbing his Minimi machine gun and bracing it against the window sill as he pressed it into his shoulder, finger on the trigger. "You see anything?" He watched the shadows as the flare floated down.

"No… Nothing yet." John looked through his scope. "Wait for your eyes to adjust."

His stomach knotted and his heart beat heavily in his chest; it didn't matter how much training you had, you never lost that feeling when the world was about to go to pot.

"There!" John pointed. "To the right, near Sarah's house."

He watched as the shadows moved. A number of the larger creatures stood shielding their faces from the light, a group of smaller once clambering around them, pushing them on. John breathed in and pulled the trigger.

A shot rang out in the darkness and one of the creature's heads turned into a fine mist, Pierce heard the howling of the creatures nearby as they realised what was happening and he opened up with the machine gun, cutting them down as they surged towards them.

John was on fine form, and before he stopped to reload he'd managed to drop four of the larger creatures; countless more of the small ones had fallen under the barrage of bullets and the barrel of his machine gun started to glow red in the darkness.

John stood, dropping the quilt from his shoulders. "They're almost at the line," he screamed above the sound of the gunfire. "Do it, do it now."

Pierce grabbed the cables, and offered a prayer to God as he clicked the wires across the battery. Everything ceased to exist for a hundred metres in front of them as the earth buckled as the charges exploded. Hot shrapnel sliced into the mass of the creatures, tossing them into the air like rag dolls.

The blast wave roared towards them, throwing anything that got in its way aside before slamming against the house. Pierce ducked as the windows exploded inwards, but John was picked up and thrown heavily against the back wall and glass showered into the room above his head, forcing him to cover his face with his arms.

The explosion continued to rumble on as fire billowed into the cold dark sky, the flames tumbling over themselves as they rose higher and higher; pieces of brickwork and bodies fell back to earth like meteorites, causing more damage to what few survivors were left on the road.

"John!" Pierce shouted as he pushed himself to his feet, despite the thick smoke that filled the room he quickly found him. "Come on," he screamed. "We've got to move." He grabbing his arm and tried to pull him up, but he didn't respond. "John!" he called again as he pulled his head up.

Blood and glass covered his face but he was still at least breathing. "Wake up! Damn you, wake up!" he screamed. "We have to go!" He pulled on him again, dragging him sideways onto the landing when John's eyes suddenly shot open and he gasped for breath. "We have to go," he repeated. He pulled him up to his feet and lent him against the wall as he turned to grab their weapons. The street was on fire, most of the houses had gone and thick smoke slowly crept down the street, glowing red as it passed over the fire.

Had that been it? Had they stopped them? Nothing seemed to move as the wind blew the smoke across the ground. The curtains flapped slowly as stillness settled outside. Then something moved, parting the smoke as it came forward, then another. A deep primordial scream filled the night as a thousand demons cried out for vengeance.

"Move!" he pushed John onto the landing before dragging him to the back bedroom and over to the window. John staggered with him, he looked dazed, and multiple wounds on his face and chest ran with blood. Timing was important now and he was conscious of the creatures approaching outside. Once they opened the door this house would cease to exist, and they had to be well away before then.

"No ladder," John mumbled as he looked outside. "The blast has blown it over". He could almost hear his life ticking away as each second brought them closer to the door. "Out of the window you go then soft lad," he muttered as he pushed John out. "Sorry," he called as he watched his feet vanish into the darkness below, before he climbed over the window frame and followed him.

"I really hate you," John managed to hiss through clenched

teeth as he grabbed his arm and pulled him to his feet.

"You can hate me later. Now move it." They reached the car and he pushed John into the backseat before jumping behind the wheel.

"The keys!" He slapped his hand into the wheel. "You halfwit John, No one was going to steal the bloody car," he screamed as he reached over, pulling John onto his side as he searched for them. "Give me the bloody keys."

Philip was filled with apprehension and dread as he watched the horizon. The first explosion had woken everyone from their sleep, and now they all stood expectantly on the roof watching the fires burn before them. Tense minutes passed and he found himself almost bouncing on the spot.

The next explosion made everyone jump. Only because they had expected it to happen but didn't know when; the mushroom cloud rose into the clear night sky, small pockets of fire periodically appearing though it.

"I hope they got out," he whispered. He couldn't take his eyes off the column of smoke that rose before him.

"We can only hope." Marcus put his hand on his shoulder. "We have maybe thirty minutes."

Philip nodded.

"Alright people!" he shouted. "Battle stations!"

Ash couldn't sleep; no matter how he lay or how much he tried, strange images of his past started to flash behind his eyes, so after a while he got up and he tinkered with his car instead, at least it kept him busy and stopped his mind wandering.

He pushed the cleaned spark plug back into place and pulled

the next one out when the world shook, dust and plaster fell from the roof. Ken was first to his feet and ran into the main area shouting out orders for people to grab their weapons.

"That was a Satchel charge," he announced. "I've got to see where that came from." He ran to the door and quickly pushed the shutter up before disappearing into the darkness beyond. Minutes later he reappeared, running excitedly back down the ramp. "They're to the south." He waved in the direction. "They must be to the south. Let's get going."

"Two seconds," Ashfaq shouted. "I just need to finish the plugs." He reached back under the bonnet and started to slide them home when a second explosion rocked the room. People screamed and staggered where they stood, holding themselves up against the walls as the ground shook. The car bonnet wobbled slightly on its loose support before crashing down onto Ash, smashing him into the engine block.

Everyone stood waiting expectantly now for the attack to happen; the perimeter fires had be lit, and they would burn brightly and hopefully give them some warning if anything moved below. Young children cried as their parents ushered them onto the relative safety of the top floor before returning to their positions with what weapons they had.

"How long would it take them to run here if the car didn't start?" Philip felt sick with nerves. It had been twenty minutes now since the explosion and there had been no sign of Pierce or John.

"I don't know." Marcus shook his head. "In daylight, maybe twenty minutes, but in the dark?" He shrugged his shoulders. The main entrance door had been closed and barricaded from the inside, and the lookouts stood expectantly at every corner of the roof ready to call out as soon as they saw anything. There was nothing left for him to do now but wait. He held the SA80 Marcus had given him close to his chest, the butt resting under his arm.

"Remember," Marcus reminded him. "When you need to reload, don't ram the magazine in, a steady push is all it needs. Breathe in and hold it when you fire, it should give you a better aim. Not that I think there won't be enough to shoot at."

"It's been a pleasure getting to know you, Marcus." He held out his hand.

"It's not over yet," he smiled. He looked at his hand. "But yeah, you're not bad for a pencil pusher. It's been an honour."

They shook.

"Well, like I've always said," Philip smiled, "I wasn't really any good at it anyway." Marcus patted him on the back before turning to the expectant crowd.

"Remember," he shouted, "single shots only. Don't waste ammo. One shot should be enough to take one down, maybe two if you're lucky. I don't want to see magazines being wasted on dead bodies."

Kate and Nick shouted out instructions to the other newly armed people they'd been assigned, drilling them on what to expect. Each had their own team of people to control now, and everyone was scared.

With so many people standing silently waiting for death to come it made the silence overpowering. He needed to find a way to take their minds of what was coming. They needed a beat and he knew just were to find one.

"Mather chot!" Ashfaq cursed as he opened his eyes, pushing the smell salts away from him. "Did Jolly blow something up?"

"Who the hell is Jolly?" Kirsty put the lid back on the bottle.

"My memory!" he shouted excitedly. "It's back, I remember everything". He sat up, a large smile on his face. Despite the red, sore looking bruise he felt so much more alive. "My memory," he repeated.

"It's back. Where's Ken? I need to speak to Ken. We don't have much time."

The music they played wasn't perfect, but they played with an energy that was contagious and more importantly they played it loud and pretty soon, the beat took over. Philip tried to speak to everyone he saw, smiling and patting their backs, giving encouragement to everyone.

Anywhere he saw fear, he would dig up all the jokes and humour he could, and he didn't stop until the buzz of conversation almost drowned out the music. A young man appeared behind him, calling his name.

"Philip, Philip…Marcus sent me," he panted. "He said… they've come."

When Philip arrived back, Marcus just handed him the field glasses and pointed into the darkness, the perimeter fires flickering in the wind.

"I don't see anything." Philip scanned the fires for movement.

"Jolly." Marcus waved and a flaming sack arced out above his head, sailing majestically in the air it trailed white smoke behind it before it landed just beyond the perimeter, exploding in a sticky fireball. Maybe twenty creatures died as the hot jelly splashed over them, but that was enough to illuminate the hordes behind them.

"Holy Mary mother of God!" Philip shouted. "There must be thousands out there."

Stu stood with Ken on the street; the smell of fire was strong and fresh in the air and they stood in the middle of the road watching the flames in the distance. The snow clouds overhead reflected the light of the flames back down on to the remains of the city.

"Come on, Ken, let's get back inside. It could have been anything going off, might even have been a house fire that's smouldered for a while, it could have been..." He stopped as the roar of an engine echoed off the buildings around them, followed by the screeching of tyres.

A car skidded round the corner almost on two wheels, flames billowing from its rear. The driver slammed on his brakes as he saw them, managed to skid to avoid Ken, but ended up mounting the curb before stopping suddenly as he collided with the corner of a building, throwing himself hard against the windscreen.

Stuart ran over and pulled the door open whilst Ken pulled the driver out and dragged him free. He could see a man trapped in the back seat and he tried to pull the seat forward, but the impact had damaged the lever it and it wouldn't move.

"Easy now," he called to the man as he tried to move. "I'll get you out just hold on a moment."

"They're behind us!" the man shouted from the seat and Stuart stepped away from the car to look back the way they'd come. Everything looked silent, and he was about to ignore the warning when one of the creatures ran into view. It slipped on the snow as it tried to make the turn but stopped as it saw them.

"Ken," he shouted. "We've got company." Smoke started to rise from the cars engine as Ken fired, killing it with a single shot; it span as the bullet hit it, lifting it from its feet before its lifeless carcass landed flatly on the snow, but no sooner had it stopped twitching when more ran screaming round the corner.

They both fired indiscriminately into the mass before them, the clatter of gunfire echoed off the buildings as their muzzle flashes illuminated their determined faces. It was like shooting fish in a barrel; each time the creatures turned the corner they ran into a volley of lead.

Stuart stopped to reload as more men appeared from the bunker to join in the defence. The creatures died in their hundreds and things seemed to be going well until the first of the giants reached the intersection.

Stuart had seen these things before from a distance, but they'd never fought one, usually preferring to stay hidden and safe rather than draw attention to themselves, but now it was impossible to hide. Great globs of spittle flew from its jaws as it roared and another appeared behind it, kicking the bodies of the dead with its feet as it started to move towards them.

Stuart jumped as the bonnet of the car flew open as the engine caught fire; he realised his position wasn't safe anymore as the flames rose higher behind him, and it was then that he remembered the man in the back seat. He continued to shoot as he moved backwards, quickly looking into the back seat.

Smoke swirled around inside, obscuring his view and making it almost impossible to see anything. He managed to look closer, peering in as he tried to see if he was still alive, when a hand suddenly slapped against the glass a few times, leaving a bloody smear on the glass before slowly slipping from view again. He had little time to act, swinging the machine gun round he smashed it against the window, showering glass inwards.

Reaching through he searched with his hands, glass shards from the broken window dug deeply into the soft flesh of his underarm and he screamed with pain as he finally grabbed what he hoped was the man and pulled. He screamed again as he lifted him upwards, feeling the glass slide back out of his arm before he finally pulled him free. He could see his feet dragging the weapons with him, but they dropped back onto the seat as he finally kicked himself free.

Flames appeared on the front seats as he carried the wounded man across the road; the others continued their rate of fire and bullets splashed into the closest creature's thick chest, but it continued forward, seemingly oblivious in its anger and rage to the fact that one of its arms hung lifeless at its side. He dropped the man onto the pavement and ran back to the car, they needed the weapons if they were to survive and he was the only one who could get them.

● ● ● ● ● ● ● ●

"So we're surrounded." Philip stared into the darkness beyond while the others stood waiting with him.

"It looks that way," Marcus replied. "The lookouts have reported them at every side."

"So that's it then, there's no escape." He'd planned for this moment in his mind over the last few days, but now it was here it terrified him. "Are we ready?"

"As ready as we can be," Donald confirmed. "I've got my team by the main entrance." A blood curdling roar stopped them and they turned to look into the darkness. Only the one at first, but more joined it until a blast of sound rose all around them.

"We'd all best get to our positions," Marcus suggested as the sound of the enemy grew louder.

"Good luck, everyone." Philip shook their hands as they turned to leave but he stopped Jolly from going. "Not you, I need you to promise me something." He held his shoulder firmly as he looked at him; this was something that had kept him awake. "If we fail, and they manage to get to this floor, I want you to spare the children the horror of what is to come." Jolly looked confused. "We can't let them get to the children."

The colour drained from Jolly's face as he realised what was being asked of him, and it took him a moment to get his emotions under control. "I understand," he answered carefully. "But it won't get to that"

"But if it does."

"If it does." He nodded despondently. "I'll make sure it's quick and painless." The roaring stopped and silence fell as the creatures charged, covering the ground like black treacle. "Philip, do you remember the other day when we talked about the ignition for the van?" Philip turned and looked out at the approaching creatures. "Well, when they pass that one." He pointed down to the road. "Count to three". At two hundred metres they passed the van Jolly had indicated, skirting round it like water around a boulder.

"What's in there?" Philip asked.

"Four oxyacetylene tanks, a block of C4 and some nails."

The rear doors of the van blew open as the canisters exploded, and a white fireball expanded outwards as the van ceased to exist.

"Bloody hell!" he shouted as he tried to cover his face with his hands, but the light was so bright he could still see it even with his eyes closed.

Ken shouted at Stuart to stop as he turned and ran towards the burning car, but he moved to quickly for him and all he could do was watch as Stuart slid round the side and out of sight before he had to resume firing.

Spent shell casings jumped past his vision as he fired bullet after bullet into the creature before him. It was less than twenty feet away when it finally stopped, falling lifeless to the floor. The second creature howled with anger at the sight of its dead comrade and threw great lumps of masonry towards them. He ducked as one bounced off the wall to his side, and he continued to fire at the thing as it climbed over the prone and bleeding body of its partner. As it continued towards them, it was then that the car's fuel tank exploded. The blast wave picked it up and threw the creature hard against the wall as the heat of the explosion licked out, showering the road with metal and glass.

Philip staggered back as the shockwave passed over them. Pieces of burning flesh fell from the sky, hitting the ground with a sickening thud. Further explosions were heard around the perimeters as the other vans exploded with the same ferocity as the first.

"Yeeehaww!" Jolly screamed exuberantly. "Take that you evil little buggers." He danced around, punching the air with great satisfaction. Even Marcus laughed, though more out of shock that joy.

"Damn, Jolly," Philip laughed. "All I can see are spots in front of my eyes. What are they doing? Someone tell me what they are doing?" Marcus stopped and looked out over the edge; the burning wreckage gave of a lot of light, making visibility much clearer.

"They're backing away," he laughed. "You scared the hell out of them." Marcus hugged Jolly before dancing round with him.

"First blood to us then." Philip nodded as he wiped the tears from his eyes. He could feel the morale growing around him. They had not only survived the first attack, but killed thousands of them, and they hadn't even got close enough to be a worry.

"How many more of them do you have?" Marcus asked.

"None." He shook his head. "That's it I'm afraid."

Ken was momentarily blinded in his left eye, so he closed it as he maintained his firing. When he managed to glance over to the wreckage of the car, all he could see was black smoke and flames billowing high into the air.

As the second one fell, two more appeared at the corner. He kept firing as the creature charged towards him. Don't panic, he reminded himself, take your time. He levelled his weapon and fired three shots cleanly into its face, blowing chunks of flesh free; it screamed in pain before toppling backwards into the snow.

There was no time to rejoice though as more appeared at the end of the street. He shouted for the others to retreat, to pull back to the underground. He dropped his empty rifle to the ground and drew his pistol. He tried to make each shot count, each bullet needed to cause the maximum damage if they were to make it out of this now. They reached the entrance but he realised the shutter would not hold them back for long. With the other two now safely inside he fired once more as he prepared to join them, but his foot slipped on the snow and he fell sideways on the pavement, his pistol spinning free from his hands.

They were close now, charging uninterrupted towards him. With nothing else to do, he drew his knife; at least he might damage one before they got him, he thought. He turned as someone shouted. The burning metal of the car moved as something pushed itself free before dropping a door to the ground. Steam rose from Stuart's body as he stepped free of the wreckage, his clothing still burning as he raised the machine guns he held in both hands.

He screamed as he fired, the 'Minimi' did its job and at such close range its bullets ripped through the bodies before them. As the magazine finally clicked empty the last of the creatures slowly toppled backwards; Stuart continued screaming as his finger pulled on the now useless trigger, blood running down his right arm and dripping from his burnt and crisped fingers. Ken scrambled over to help him, he was hot to the touch and pieces of Stuart's skin had stuck to the weapon in the heat but he carefully prised his finger free.

"Are you alright?" he asked when he eventually stopped screaming.

Stuart stood looking at the devastation before him. His eyes moving quickly over the scene as his adrenaline continued to race through him. "Great, man," he smiled. "Just great!

An hour had passed since the last attack and nothing moved outside. People started to relax, to laugh and joke, some even started to think Philip had exaggerated the enemy's strength, and that he was just trying to scare them to keep in power.

"Don't let it get to you," Gina said. "You know different."

"It doesn't get to me." He shook his head. "If that was all they had, I can live with being wrong."

"Maybe the bright lights have put them off."

"I don't know. I don't think it's like them to just retreat, not now, not after everything that's gone on. I just don't trust them."

"You're right, Philip. Don't trust the little buggers." Major Hawthorn limped towards them. "They might be a lot of things, but they're not stupid."

"Shouldn't you be in bed?" Philip was surprised to see him up. He was still a mass of bandages and fresh blood was still visible from his eye.

"Bed is for the dead," he stated. "I'm not lying down while the rest of you fight. I can still be useful." He staggered and Gina moved in to help him. "Maybe something light though." He forced a smile.

Marion appeared behind them pushing a serving trolley, offering a drink from her tray to anyone who wanted one. She waved as she saw Philip and pushed her way over to see them. "I thought you might need a drink," she offered.

"Thanks," he nodded as he took two, passing one to Gina. "That's very thoughtful." Marion smiled and wandered off to a group of men stood against a wall. It amazed him how people dealt with panic; no one seemed to have cracked under the pressure tonight and he felt proud of that. If this was the last place on earth for mankind to survive, it would survive with dignity and coffee.

"You alright love?" Andrew asked, as he opened the door to the kitchen as Marion returned with her empty tea trolley.

"I'm fine dear," she smiled in reply. "Just getting some more drinks." He wheeled the trolley over to the stoves for her, where William, their son, stood watching the pots of boiling water. He felt he was too old to go with the children and had promised his dad that he'd keep out of the way should anything happen, if he could stay down here helping his mum.

"You eating again," Andrew scolded; he could see his mouth was full of something. "Just make sure you help down here okay." He ruffled his hair with his hands before turning to kiss Marion and retrieve his shotgun from where he'd put it on the trolley. His knees ached as he walked and he wished he was young again.

He'd been very active as a lad, no sport had been outside his skill, but now he was the first to admit those times had gone. Now his once stocky frame had sagged in the middle, his knees had gone and he lost his breathe walking to the shops.

"I'd best get back." He tried to smile reassuringly at them. "I don't like leaving Mike out there on his own."

"You just be careful, dear." Marion tried to look confident in front of her son, but Andrew could see she was nervous.

"I will, love." He smiled as he let the door swing shut behind him before turning to return to his position. The corridor was quiet with only a faint sliver of moonlight illuminating the floor. "Mike," he called. "You want a brew before Marion goes out again? Mike?" The door opened behind him as Marion started to come out again, but he quickly stopped her.

"Stay inside for a moment will you love." He held his hand up behind him.

"Be careful," she whispered as the door closed again.

"Mike?" he called again as he raised the old shotgun he'd been given and cocked both barrels. "Mike, stop messing around!"

Something hit him flat in the chest and he screamed in pain as claws racked downwards, tearing his shirt and skin alike. It was too close to fire at, so he tried to grab its head with his left hand, and as he staggered backwards he knocked the kitchen door.

The light flashed out through the gap, pushing the darkness away and he could see three of the creatures crawling towards him. Just before the terror took over he managed to grip the one on his chest and he slammed it hard into the doorframe cracking its skull, just as the others grabbed his legs.

He fell backwards into the kitchen, his arms grabbing out for anything that would stop his fall, but he just ended up throwing the shotgun behind him before landing hard on his back and he heard Marion scream.

"Get back!" he shouted to her as they climbed over him, clawing at his face and neck. He managed to push them back enough to let him punch outwards at them, but they continued to slash into him, tearing into his thigh. He grabbed a pan from a shelf but a creature pinned his arm to the ground.

They seemed to laugh as they came in for the kill, a shrill sound like a pack of hyenas as they approached him. Despite his struggling he couldn't get up and they got closer and closer to him; he could taste their hot breathe in his mouth. William screamed behind him.

"Nothing attacks my family," he shouted. "Nothing." He gritted his teeth as he pulled both triggers of the shotgun and Andrew watched as the creatures exploded above him as the pellets ripped through them. At such close range it tore their limbs free from their thin bodies. The unexpected recoil lifted William up and slammed him hard into a table, and he fell limp to the floor.

The gunshot had made everyone jump back into a state of alertness and it was moments later that Philip skidded round the corner, almost tripping over Andrews's prone feet. Hands pulled him to his feet but he stopped as he saw Marion. She sat at the rear of the kitchen, holding her son's body in her arms, tears running down her face.

"He saved us both," she said as she held his limp body to her. "He saved us…"

Marcus counted to three with his fingers and stepped round the corner his pistol ready as Kate shone her torch into the darkness, highlighting the body of a man, his throat sliced so deeply his head had almost been removed.

A few feet beyond him stood the creatures that had killed him and Marcus smiled as he opened fire, his bullets making them dance as they hit home, spinning limbs off at odd angles as they tore though muscles and bones. He stopped firing, letting the muzzle cool down as they moved on further down the corridor hunting anything that shouldn't be there.

"They should both be okay," Joanne smiled as she finished wrapping the bandages around Andrews's stomach. "It's a good thing you never went on a diet."

"And to think the doctor told me to lay off those kebabs." Andrew tried to laugh, but the pain in his stomach stopped him. William lay on the next bed, unconscious but breathing deeply.

"We found another six groups," Kate reported to Philip who stood in the doorway. "They must have crept up over roof of the shopping centre."

"It would have worked too," Andrew said proudly. "If my boy hadn't got the shot off." He held Marion's hand as he looked across to him.

"Why don't you stay here for now?" Philip suggested. "That wound isn't deep, but it'll bleed a lot."

"No." He winced as he slowly pulled himself up from the bed. "I'm fine. Anyway, you need every hand you can get out there." He could see that there was no use in arguing with him, he certainly wouldn't want to be the one lying down at the moment.

Jolly stood patiently watching the next wave attack. He'd ordered no one to fire, and he watched them getting closer with a smirk on his face. They passed an outer marker that he's set and he nodded for Gimp to trip the wires across the battery.

Ten feet in front of the oncoming mass, a line of flash bangs ignited. The creatures stopping dead in their tracks as the wall of light and noise appeared before them. The closest creatures pushed backwards, clawing at the ones behind as they tried to escape the burning light.

Dancing a little jig he turned and pointed once more to Gimp, and the bins that stood so silently on the car park exploded, sending small mushroom clouds curling up into the night as their flammable contents sprayed out over the bulk of creatures trapped by the light.

He hopped around with excitement as he watched them fall burning to the floor. He was having fun now; for all his life he'd wanted to blow things up and now his dream was coming true. The defenders cheered as the assault seemed to stop once more, the charge faltering as they collided with the creatures behind them.

"Oh yes!" he shouted. "They are running away." But a roar of command called out from the darkness, forcing them forward. The creatures threw themselves against the flames until a bridge of dead bodies made the advance possible again.

"Oh, no." He hadn't expected them to come on so quickly. "Philip," he shouted. "Here they come."

The catapult fired again as Philip finally reached the roof.

"Here they come again," Marcus shouted as he saw him. "Cover the rear." He pointed. "I'll cover the front." The catapult fired again as he ran, sending another barrel out into the darkness.

"Let them get closer," he ordered. "Make every shot count." It was the most desperate few seconds he'd even experienced, watching as they got closer and closer. Thousands of them swarmed towards them; the sound of their footsteps was like thunder.

"Fire!" he shouted.

The wall erupted with muzzle flashes; tracer rounds arced into the front lines and the creatures fell as bullets slammed through them before tearing into the ones behind. Discarded shell cases clattered to the floor but still they came. "Grenades." he ordered as they drew into range.

One bang after another rocked the ground, echoing up the walls before fading into the night. The screams of the dying even managed to reach them at their lofty heights.

"Keep firing," he shouted. "Don't let them get to the walls."

Donald liked the entrance, the way it had been designed forced them into a bottleneck and they crushed each other under foot as they charged, screaming and bellowing with rage and hatred at the putrid humans that defied them.

He pulled on a rope and the first barricade swung down in a vicious arc, its spikes ramming deep into the chests of the first to arrive, pinning four or five on each railing.

"Petrol Bombs!" he shouted and fire fell from above. The creatures at the front were unable to retreat due to the force of those behind and they burnt in their hundreds.

The stench of petrol and cooked flesh filled the air with a choking stench, but the attack finally faltered before breaking into full retreat. Donald patted the defenders on their shoulders as they watched them go, bullets from above continuing to drop the ones at the back. So far, so good, he thought.

Philip stopped as the sound of a thousand birds flapping their wings filled the air. He thought it was something Jolly had invented until someone in the darkness screamed. Burning arrows rained down onto the roof, cutting deeply into anyone unlucky enough to be caught out in the open.

He watched as the men operating the catapult danced as the cruel barbs thudded down into them, setting the wooden frame on fire and the catapult started to burn. One man tried to crawl away, but more arrows landed in him and he lay still.

"Stay where you are," the major shouted. "Everyone stay in cover." People lay screaming or crying everywhere. It was impossible to guess how many have been injured. Jolly started to stand, to try to help his fallen friends but Philip grabbed his arm, pulling him back against the sides.

"But people are hurt!" he protested. Jolly was still trying to break free and help his friends when the next wave came. This time arrows as black as night fell onto the dead and wounded, like pins into a pin cushion they fell. Jolly gave up his attempt to help and fell backwards against the ledge, screaming as they bounced off the wall behind him.

"Get everyone off the roof," he shouted as the next wave came to an end. He dragged Jolly to his feet and pushing him towards the ramp and the safety of the lower levels. They had precious few moments before more arrows could fall and the people moved too slowly. But as soon as Philip turned his attention to the others, Jolly made a dash for the hut on the far side of the roof.

"Jolly!" he shouted, but he couldn't go after him, there were too many still to move. "Get to cover," he shouted as more people ran for the ramp. "Get below."

He and the Major worked their way through everyone, pulling them to their feet, dragging them from the false protection of the edges and pushing them towards the lower levels. Marcus appeared at his side, shouting and dragging people with him. Less than a minute later the roof was almost empty as the third wave dropped silently from the night sky.

Jolly ran like he'd never run before, his feet thumping flatly on the concrete floor as arrows bounced around him; by sheer luck they missed, and he reached the safety of his hut, forcing open the door with his shoulder before he threw himself inside, sliding across the floor as he kicked the door closed behind him. Despite the cold, sweat ran down his back and armpits.

He didn't like death. The sight of his friends lying there seemed to do something to him, to churn up emotions he thought he'd long since destroyed. Although he'd enjoyed creating things that would kill or maim, it had always been from a distance; this was the first time he'd seen death up close and personal and he didn't like it, he felt angry.

Small hands grabbed him and helped him to his feet. The children sat huddled together in corners and as he looked into their sad scared faces he remembered the promise he'd given to Philip and his mind started to plan.

"Oh, my God!" Kirsty exclaimed at the wounded warriors returning down the ramp, and without exception they were all bleeding from somewhere. Stuart staggered after them like some half dead zombie, the hair on one side of his head had been singed almost completely off and the skin on his hands looked blistered and burnt.

Between them they supported the two newcomers towards the medical area. Ken winced as he lowered the first man down before turning to support Stuart.

"I'm okay," he insisted as Kirsty moved towards him. "It's just a few minor burns, maybe a broken rib," he explained, as the blood continued to drip from his fingers. Ash moved over to help but stopped as he recognised the wounded men.

"That's Pierce and John." He looked with concern at Kirsty. "What are they doing here? What's happened?" He tried to speak to them. "Where's Marcus?"

Kirsty pushed him away as she started to work on them.

"I thought I recognised them." Ken grabbed Ash by his shoulders. "You remember again don't you?"

"Yes," he nodded "I remember everything."

"Is it over?" Margaret called as Philip reached the lower levels, she was sat chatting with a group of older women. "Did we win?"

"No." He wiped his face with his hand. "Not yet."

"Oh!" she replied. "Well good luck young man." She smiled before turning back to the conversation. "He says it's not over yet," she explained to anyone who would listen.

It was sad to watch; it was as though their minds were unable to comprehend what was going on and he wished he could be like that, to put away his worries and concerns, his fear and dread, and he jumped as Marcus grabbed his arm.

"How many did we lose?" he asked. Philip shook his head. The numbers were impossible to guess, his mind was filled with the images of the people reaching out for him, begging for help. Until this moment he had still felt like it could be a dream, a weird, strange nightmare. But after seeing the amount of blood he understood which reality he was in.

"You did everything you could." Marcus pulled him close, pressing his head into his shoulder as he sobbed. "It was a tough call, but the right one to make." He pushed him back, staring into his eyes. "Are you okay?"

Philip didn't have time to answer as another roar from outside indicated the next charge and it snapped him back to his senses. As he ran to the main gate he wiped the tears away; no time, he thought, no time.

Kirsty wiped her hands as she stepped out into the main room. "Although there's a lot of blood," she explained, "the majority of the wounds appear superficial. They both should make it."

"Good." Ken smiled at the news. It had been a tense few minutes while they waited for her report, but now it was in Ash waited for Ken to start asking questions and it wasn't long before he led him towards the back of the car park, away from the others.

"So," he asked as he rested back against a car. "What can you tell me?"

"I remember it all now. They're hiding out at the shopping centre." He held Philip's pistol in his hand. "We managed to enter the pit," he explained. "We saved so many people before they attacked us. That's where I'd been when you found me."

"Okay." Ken looked tired as he spoke, more worn and battle weary than before. "You thought we should change the game plan, stop hiding. What do you propose now?"

Within five minutes every available driver sat in their respective cars, revving their engines as they waited for the off. Pieces of metal had been hastily attached to their outsides and an armed guard had been added for extra security.

Ash helped Jim loaded up the bus with every last piece of ammo and spare weaponry they had, and they struggled to lift the last few petrol canisters on board.

"I thought you said the bus wouldn't make it very far," Ken shouted from his Capri, the noise of the engines almost deafening now. "Better leave her behind."

"No way, man," Jim protested. "This old girl can make it, and if she can't, she might as well go out trying." He patted the side of the bus lovingly. "You can make it, can't ya love?"

Donald looked pleased to see them when they finally arrived at the entrance, though his smile faded as Philip explained what had happened.

"Well, so far the ramps held," he reported. "Though now I guess it's going to get harder."

"Well. I can set the last of the claymores here." Marcus indicated to the front of the gate. "If we have to withdraw they should at least give us enough time to get away to the next level." Philip noticed the way he said '*If*', as though it was the lesser of the options they faced rather than the more likely, 'When.'

"What's the ammo situation like then?" Stephen enquired. "What do we have to throw at them in the next wave?"

"We're down to our last magazines now," Marcus frowned. "Not many grenades left, and were out of flash bangs. And now with the catapult out of action, we've lost its ammo too."

"How many are left do you think?" Stephen asked as his friends crowded round him to hear the answer, the prospect of close quarter fighting not being on the top of their lists. Philip didn't know what to say. For all their efforts, for all the bullets they'd fired the last thing he'd seen as he left the roof made it look as though they'd hardly touched them. He couldn't tell them they'd destroyed maybe a quarter if they'd been lucky.

"About a dozen," he lied with a smile. "Maybe twenty tops."

"Oh," one of Stephen's friends smiled, "easy then." They laughed even though it was an obvious lie, and Philip felt glad he hadn't told them the truth. "What's that smell?" He covered his nose as a strong repugnant odour filled his nostrils as thick smoke billowed under the barricade.

"Go on Mike," Stephen smiled. "You tell him." Mike stood looking out of the barrier to the outside.

"It's KFG," he shouted without turning round, his focus directly on the approaching enemy.

"KFG?" Philip had to ask.

"Kentucky Fried Goblin." Mike smirked as he turned round to face them for a moment. "You'll get used to it eventually."

Laughter was a good sound to hear. It lifted the mood of them all and for a moment the battle was forgotten. But not for long as arrows thudded loudly into the gate, reminding them of the enemy outside and cutting their laughter short as the roar of battle once more reached them, forcing Mike back to his vigil.

Ash wound down his window as he pulling up next to the other cars. It felt good to be behind a wheel again, and even better to have his memory back. He just hoped everyone was still okay back at the base.

"Everyone ready?" he shouted. "Follow me then… Charge!" he shouted, pointing his arm forward as he pressed the accelerator down and sped from the car park. He skidded onto the road as he cleared the ramp and the others fell in line behind him. Jim honked his horn excitedly as he slowly followed, his gears groaning dangerously at each change.

Ash hadn't realised how much of a mess the streets had become, but after so many earthquakes and resulting fires, pieces of rubble lay everywhere and burnt out cars littered the roads, and it took a lot of skilful driving to avoid them.

"Hold tight!" he shouted to his guard as he slammed into the side of an old campervan, sending it spinning of the road, his passenger looked pale. "What's your name?" he shouted as he swerved to avoid the remains of a bus.

"Lionel," the petrified man screamed back, his fingers gripped the dashboard.

"Well, Lionel." He pressed his foot down hard as he bounced over the remains of a chimney stack, his hubcap spinning off into a shop window as he landed. "You're in for the ride of your life." He felt alive. He was driving at high speed through the streets of Manchester; the wind whipped in the window and made his hair dance. If only his old friends could be here now. This was the sort of thing they always dreamed of doing. Nothing would stop them now.

"Mike! What's going on out there?" Philip called. "How far away are they?" Mike didn't move but continued to stare silently outside as the roar of the enemy got nearer; more arrows hit the door as they started to move towards him.

"Mike?" Stephen called. "What's going on buddy, stop messing around?" He ran over and put his hand on his shoulder. Mike moved slowly, dropping his arm to his side and the pistol he'd held clattered loudly as it hit the floor.

"Mike?" Stephen whispered as he pulled him backwards, grabbing him as he fell. The shaft of an arrow protruded from what was left of his face.

"Oh, no!" Stephen screamed as his friend dropped. Jack and Billy ran over to help, but it was obvious it was too late. They'd done so much together as friends, stuck together through thick and thin.

Philip recalled how they'd been the first one's to lead the group on that first day, how they'd.... Donald barged past, breaking the spell that had befallen them all at the death of their friend.

"They are almost at the gates." He started to fire through the spy hole. "Fire back damn it. Fire back or we loose the gate."

Philip jumped to action, running forward he added his bullets to the defence. The creatures charged with their weapons held high. Their bare feet slapped on the frozen ground as they came, passing the mangled remains of the fallen, they slipped on frozen blood before climbing over the cold dead bodies to get at them.

Up the ramp they charged, but the enemy were too many for them and their bullets too few. With a loud groan one of the bigger creatures smashed into the barricade, bending it over before snapping the beams like twigs.

Each trap was triggered, but at each one less and less of the enemy died. As the giants broke each in turn they finally arrived at the last barrier. The gate they hid behind.

"Get back!" Marcus ordered. "Back to the ramp." Dropping their useless weapons they withdrew, Stephen reluctantly leaving his friend where he lay as heavy fists slammed into the wood, showering the insides with splinters. The last of the petrol bombs fell from above, setting the beast alight and as the door finally fell, Philip watched it start to crawl inside, flames licking the ceiling from its burning back. Tense moments passed as it continued to crawl towards them like a demon from hell before Marcus detonated the last of the claymores and blew it apart.

Lumps of burning flesh exploded from the entrance, showering the creatures behind that had urged it on with blood soaked steel balls. Many fell, but it wasn't enough to stop them.

They cautiously approached the entrance now, expecting burning death to rain down on them at any moment, or hot fast death to flash towards them. But nothing came and one by one they gained entrance and started to build their ranks. They yammered and clawed at the defenders, eager to feast on the enemy that defied them for so long.

All Philip could do was watch and wait for it to come. As he drew his machete he spoke softly. "Make them pay dearly for each step they take. Kill as many as you can." There was no need to shout now.

"We need to be here." Ash pointed at the map he'd found in the glove box. "I guess we're here." They crouched in front of his car trying to see by the light of its single remaining headlight. "If we take the left back there." He pressed his finger onto the map leaving a dirty smear. "We end up back on the main road. Shouldn't that get us there?"

The problem wasn't the route, but the road conditions. There had been so much surface damage caused by the quakes that large sections of the road had either fallen away into nothing, or jutted out above the ground at an impossible angle.

"It's so close, but we can't get there." He felt impotent, unable to help his friends when they needed him. They'd meandered across the east side of Manchester a number of times now, always having to back track when they once again found their path blocked.

"If we can't use the roads," Stuart shouted excitedly as he

looked over his shoulder, "then let's not."

"How else can we get there?" He was starting to feel angry and didn't want to play games.

"Look, here!" Stuart grabbed the map and drew a path with his finger across the golf course to the motorway. "I bet once we get there, we can find a way across, and once we hit the motorway we should be fine. There's no way all the lanes can be blocked."

"Sounds like a plan," Ken shouted from his car. "Let's move!"

The frost lay undisturbed on the ground and the grass glistened as the Moon shone above. A fine mist moved slowly from the trees and settled serenely around the sand traps. A rabbit nervously poked its head from its warren at the side of the fairway. It could hear thunder coming, but the air didn't smell like a storm. It raised its head and looked out over the grounds but quickly ducked back underground as the tree line exploded.

"Watch out for the green!" Lionel screamed.

"Watch out for the green?" Ashfaq screamed with joy as he repeated Lionel. "I'm aiming for the flag." His tyres cut into the frozen earth tossing grass and soil in all directions. He skidded along the side of the golf course, not even attempting to slow down as it ploughed through a fence. They travelled this way for about a mile, before finally smashing through another fence and landing hard on the road on the other side.

He skidded to a halt, the motorway stood before them, a dark silhouette against the night sky. "Is this junction six or seven do you think?" he shouted, but Lionel didn't answer, he just sat with his eyes closed as he continued to hold on to the seat belt for dear life. "Wimp," was all he could think to call him as he accelerated away.

"Charge!" Philip shouted as he waved his machete before him. With screams of rage they ran, their boots thumping hard on the floor and an assortment of weapons in hand. Marcus threw a grenade before them, deep into the mass of waiting bodies, and the explosion ripped into the rear ranks at the same time that they slammed hard into the front rows; the creatures fell in confusion as Philip tried to kill enough of them to force them back out of the entrance.

He swung wildly as he cut deeply into the enemies' flesh. The advantage was with them, and they used their size to its full effect, crashing into the well pack ranks of the enemy before they could counter attack.

He kicked forward, feeling the satisfaction as his boot connect with the head of a creature, sending it spinning backwards out of the car park. But these tactics wouldn't last long. Fatigue started to set in and they started to lose ground, slowly being pushed back over the bodies of the slain one step at a time, as more and more of them entered from below.

Relief came as Kate rushed in with more defenders behind her and they pushed tables in front of them, forcing the smaller creatures back before they managed to shore up the entrance again as best they could. Philip finally sank to the floor. Every muscle in his body ached but they had managed to regain the gate without losing anyone else. Marcus slumped next to him, blood soaking from a gash in his forehead.

"I need a beer," Philip sighed.

"I need ammo," Marcus countered. "How long till dawn?"

"Hours yet." He stood up, his machete blunt and chipped after hitting so much bone. "I don't know how much more I can take"

Ash pulled off the motorway, skidded to a halt at the bottom of the ramp and climbed out through the window. He felt giddy as the adrenaline continued to pump through him, whereas Lionel opened his door and fell out onto the road before throwing up onto the footpath.

293

"We made it," he pointed, though there was no real need. Flames licked into the sky and the horizon looked like it was on fire.

"What's your plan now?" Ken called as his Capri pulled up alongside, his breathing sounded laboured as he talked, as though each word hurt.

"It's a case of hit and run I reckon," Ashfaq stated. "I go straight up the road as fast as I can. That should draw their attention."

"Stop a moment, Ash." Ken called to the group. "I want everyone that's not behind the wheel of a car to set up a blockade here," he indicated. "If we can lead them back, then we can hit them with all we have."

"We?" Ash had planned to go it alone.

"Yes, We." Ken didn't look like he was in the mood for an argument. "We've come this far, and you'll need backup, so we're coming too." Smoke billowed from its exhaust and lumps of grass fell from its fenders as the bus finally arrived. With a hiss the doors opened and he climbed out. "Told you I'd get the old girl here." He smiled, a dog eared roll up hung loosely from his mouth. "What've I missed?"

Six cars in total revved their engines as they prepared to set off, each one sat in silent prayer as they made their peace with the world.

"Good luck guys," Stuart shouted as they started to pull away.

Ash accelerated as fast as he could down the road, the others doing their best to keep up with him in the icy conditions. As the scene came into view he swore to himself as he realised how many they faced. The entire area was packed with them as far as he could see, so at a little over eighty, he pressed his foot to the floor and ploughed into their rear ranks, sending bodies flying.

His windscreen cracked as a head bounced off it; bows and arrows snapped under his tyres but he continued to accelerate, feeling his axel jump as it crushed their small bodies under its wheels. He sounded his horn as he neared the junction, the car starting to groan as it dragged the carcases under the chassis.

"Come on!" he screamed as the car started to shudder as it mowed them down. The momentum was with him, and he shouted with joy as he cleared the other side. He looked in the mirror and watched as more headlights smashed through the lines behind him. Half a mile down the road they pulled in, skidding round to face the right way again, but one car was missing, lost somewhere in the mass of bodies.

He could only just see out of the windscreen now but it didn't really matter, he was going straight again anyway, and with a nod to Ken he set off once more. This time they fought back, a dozen arrows landed in their bonnets or smashed into the broken glass of the windscreen. He reached sideways and touched the shaft of an arrow that had embedded itself in Lionel's seat, and he thanked the heavens it hadn't been closer. Ken pulled along side, matching his speed as they ploughed once more into the mass.

Everything was going well, and he felt sure they should be close to the other side when Ken slammed into the missing car, flipping him over onto its nose from the impact before tumbling into the creatures beyond, coming to a stop upside down on the road.

Ash cursed as he watched Ken vanish in his rear mirror before he broke out the other side. He yanked on his handbrake and twisted the wheel as hard he as he could. His wheels smoked before they gained traction, plunging him once more into the fray, back to his friend.

He sounded his horn as he skidded to a halt besides Ken's upturned car. Kicking the passenger door open with his foot he shouted for him, and frantic seconds passed before something moved inside. Flames erupted on the road as the fuel tank ruptured, spilling its contents behind them, but the flames fortunately made the creatures back away and gave Ken a chance to crawl out.

It was painfully slow to watch, and the flames had started to jump back towards the car, and so with no other option he climbed onto the road himself and pulled him free from the wreck, before dragging him back and forcing him into the seat.

He pulled the pistol from his belt and ran round to the driver's side, shooting a creature at almost point blank range as it moved towards him; swinging the door open he dropped into the seat and shifted into reverse.

The door tore from its hinges as it slammed into a post at the side of the road, and as he slammed on the handbrake he quickly grabbed Ken to stop him falling as the car span once more, before he slipped it back into gear and sped away.

Jolly slowly pushed the door open and peaked out, no arrows had fallen for at least half an hour now, and the sound of the cars was such a temptation he just had to see what was going on. He tiptoed over the bodies of the dead before finally reaching the edge and looking over.

A car exploded below and something hit him in the forehead as the shrapnel spiralled into the air, knocking him onto his back, and he realised how close he had been to being decapitated. Blood trickled from the wound as he lay staring up at the sky, and the stars slowly started to move before his eyes.

"I need help," Ash screamed as he pulled up next to the bus. "Help me." Gunfire ripped out as the rear guard halted anything that had tried to follow them back, and over the noise of battle no one could hear him shouting.

"Ash," Ken coughed. "Come here." Blood ran from the side of his mouth as he spoke and he beckoned him closer and Ash knelt by his side.

"I'll go and get help," he reassured him, and he stood to leave, but Ken grabbed his arm; his hands were covered in bright red blood. Ash pulled his shirt carefully open, and moaned as he saw a sharp piece of blue metal protruding from his side and thick red blood seeping around the wound.

"Sorry." Ken forced a smiled. "I couldn't have you taking all the glory now could I."

"Ken!" Ashfaq sobbed, tears running freely down his face. "Let me get the first aid box, we can stitch it?" He could feel his hands shaking as he looked at the wound, it didn't seem real.

"No, Ash. I'm sorry." Ken gasped as pain shot through his side. "It's in too deep. I've seen enough wounds to know what the bad ones look like. There's nothing you can do for me." Ash felt like he would burst, he wanted to scream, to shout and stamp at the world. It wasn't fair. "I just wanted to thank you for giving me a chance to die fighting." He smiled. "If I'd told Kirsty I was injured, she'd have stopped me coming. This way is better."

"We've finished them off." Stuart smiled as he ran towards them, but stopped as he saw Ash's expression; he realised that something was very wrong, and he turned and ran to get help from the others. Alone again, Ash knelt beside him, tears welling up in his eyes.

"It's been an honour and a pleasure to have known you, Ken." His stomach knotted as he spoke and he couldn't contain his anguish any longer. Over the last few days Ken had become more than just a leader and it didn't seem fair to lose him now.

Only two other cars had made it, and it wasn't long before everyone solemnly approached them.

"Don't be like this." Ken smiled at them. "It's been fun." He coughed and a trickle of blood ran down his chin. "I do have one request though." He wiped the blood away with his hand. "I always wanted to go out with a bang. Jim, would you mind if I took the old girl out on one last ride?"

They helped him out of his seat and slowly carried him to the bus. Blood ran from the wound now, soaking Ken's top and trousers. Jim tried to salute before putting the keys gently into Ken's hands.

"She sticks a little in third." He tried to smile. "Drive her well, Boss." Tears welled up behind his eyes and he was unable to watch as he slowly climbed in.

"Ash," Ken called as he sat painfully in the seat. "You make sure you get home."

The door closed with a hiss before the bus spluttered to life. The gears crunched painfully as he engage them, but eventually it slowly started to pull away, picking up speed as it approached the intersection. They watched it go in silence, and it was a moment before Ash spoke.

"What's did we leave on board?"

"All the C4 we had and the spare petrol canisters." The horn sounded in the distance.

"Good luck, Ken," he shouted, tears running down his face. "God speed my friend, God speed."

Ken spat the blood from his mouth onto the dashboard. He knew he didn't have long left now as the internal bleeding slowly sapped his strength. He patted the grenade he'd shoved between his legs, his insurance policy against being eaten when he'd gone.

He honked the horn loudly as he passed the burning remains of his Capri, before turning the old girl round towards the front of the car park, almost flipping the bus over as he bounced of the kerb at the junction, but he scattered creatures to the wind.

Thanks to the higher vantage point the bus gave him, he could see a group of the bigger creatures as they stood waiting to attack; so with his targets set, he dropped into a lower gear and with grim determination, accelerated towards them, humming the Battle of Britain theme as he smashed anything that got in his way aside.

"What's he doing?" Philip watched through the slit between the tables as the bus careered into the creatures, cutting a path through the enemy's ranks as it rolled by. "He doesn't have enough speed to keep that up." The horn sounded loudly once more as it collided with the monsters, knocking one over and it stopped in a mass of steam and smoke. All he could do was watch as they swarmed over it, screaming with glee as they tried to climb inside; the remaining larger ones smashing down viciously onto the roof of the bus, tearing sheets of metal free.

The fireball that followed knocked Philip physically backwards, flaming debris sliced violently into anything less than a hundred feet from the blast, and anything within thirty feet just ceased to exist.

"Damn!" Philip exclaimed as he covered his eyes, the blast leaving an impression on his retina as every crack in the defensive wall shone white as the flames continued to burn brightly outside.

Ash angrily wiped the tears from his eyes as he drove, they'd seen the flash of the explosion, but the certain knowledge that Ken had actually gone only added to the pain in his heart. The flaming bodies of the dead looked like shooting stars as they turned in the air, finally dropping back to earth.

He mounted the kerb at high speed, casting aside all before him as he drove deeper into the enemy. Hundreds fell under their wheels as they pressed on with their assault. The three cars caused what damage they could, the guards inside ready to kill anything that got too close.

He turned in a wide sweeping arc and quickly skidding to a stop at the base of the ramp, effectively blocking it with their cars. He pushed the doors open and ran towards the entrance, shooting and killing anything in his path. Stuart turned and fired behind them, acting as a rearguard as the creatures swarmed over the vehicles, their blood lust rising as their hatred for mankind grew.

Arrows chased their movement up the ramp, and Ash stopped as Stuart shouted as an arrow thudded into his shoulder, knocking him to the ground. He tried to stand but his feet couldn't find any traction on the blood soaked ground, and as he slowly started to slide down towards the enemy but he continued to fire his machine gun, his screams rising above the clatter of the weapon.

299

● ● ● ● ● ● ● ●

Stuart could see them getting closer. He couldn't fire enough bullets to stop them all and he expected to feel the blades of the enemy against him. He was almost out of ammo when Ash suddenly appeared by his side, his pistol firing at the closest ones. At least I won't die alone, he thought.

Suddenly something grabbed his collar and dragged him backwards before men charged past him, screaming at the creatures, slashing and chopping at anything that moved. As he finally made the entrance, someone shouted orders in the darkness and they pulled back. They retreated slowly up the ramp, slashing at anything that dared approach until the barricade was hastily re-created at the entrance, just before the arrows thudded into them again.

"We made it Stu." Ash smiled as he appeared by his side. "We made it."

"I'm back," he grinned as he moved to shake Philip's hand, but Philip hugged him instead.

"You lucky sod." Philip couldn't stop grinning. "We thought we'd lost you. We searched for days."

"Na," he smiled. "It would take more than a few thousand monsters to keep me away." He swung his backpack from his shoulders. "I brought you presents from my trip." The bag hit the floor, and ammo spilled out. "I figured you could do with some."

"You're a real sight for sore eyes." Marcus smiled as he slipped the magazine into place, grinning as the weapon became useful once more.

"You rascal." Donald came stomping towards him roaring.

"I love it when I get a reception like this." Ashfaq beamed.

"Welcome back, lad." Donald crushed him with a bear hug

before Philip told him to put him down.

"We have maybe another hundred people waiting on the other side of town," he gasped. "We couldn't get any more in the cars," he quickly explained.

"You need to get back to them now!" Jolly appeared at the base of the ramp behind them. Staggering forward, half blinded by the blood that ran into his eye he grabbed Philip's shoulder. "It's starting."

"What is? That bang on your head has addled you; the fighting's been going on for hours."

"No, not the fighting...The Poles," he shouted. "The poles are moving, we're going to flip."

Philip knew it was a desperate idea but there seemed to be no other way around it. If Jolly said they needed to move, then they needed to move. Ash would have to get back to the others to warn them, which meant they had to get Ash back to his car. But this time, as the barricade was removed, they came out armed and ready to fight.

A hundred men surged forward and bullets flew in every direction as they cut a path before them; the dead lay in piles many feet deep around them, but still the enemy attacked with a blind lust for death, an unquestionable devotion to the annihilation of mankind.

Finally, on reaching the cars, Ash climbed in as the rest of the men slowly fanned out around him, keeping the creatures away. The engine revved and he accelerated quickly into the space they had cleared for him; frozen entrails jumped from the wheels as he rammed his way out.

"Back inside," Philip ordered. "Everyone back inside." He turned to retreat but their path was blocked. In their urgency to clear a path ahead they'd completely missed the creatures to the side that now cut them off from the safety of the car park.

They backed up to each other making a tight circle of men

surrounded by a sea of approaching death. As the bullets once more began to run out they started to fall. One by one they screamed as cruel blades made it close enough to slice into them. Philip dropped the rifle as his ammo ran out and drew his machete from his belt. "We didn't think this through did we," he yelled to Marcus.

"No," he replied. "But I guess we did better than we ever thought we would."

"It's not over yet," Donald yelled beside them. "Look."

A battle cry rose from the car park as the Major lead a fresh wave of defenders down the ramp towards the creatures. With frying pan or cleaver, the women started to cut, slash or just beat a path through towards them. He could see Marion as she swung wildly at anything that dared approach her, splitting skulls as easily as she would eggs.

"Push," he shouted. "Push towards the women." He could feel a soft breeze starting to blow against his face, making it harder to shout. Smoke from the many fires moved strangely, hugging the ground as the wind blew onto them.

A creature lunged at him but he managed to side step its attack before grabbing its arm. He sliced down, cutting cleanly through the bone before pushing it away, throwing the amputated limb at the closest creature. As the two groups almost joined the enemy became restless and threw themselves at them with such ferocity they almost lost the line. Donald stood next to him, kicking out and slashing at anything he could.

"We can't keep this up for much longer," he shouted, as another man fell screaming to the floor, a blade thrust deeply into his back; it was then he spotted Gina amongst the women. She brought her arm round in a swing, cracking the skull of a creature with a rolling pin and Philip panicked, she shouldn't be out here, not her.

Distracted, he allowed a creature to get close to him and it lunged at his stomach; seeing it too late he could do nothing but wait for the pain to come, but Donald barged into his side, pushing him clear of the weapon and moving himself into his place.

He heard him scream as the blade sliced into his stomach, the creature twisting the blade as it pressed forward. Donald grabbed at its arm, trying to stop it pushing any further before he punched it hard in its face. Philip grabbed him, putting Donald's arm round his own shoulder to support him as they moved step by step towards the ramp. With their path finally clear they started to retreat inside.

Philip passed under the entrance and moved back into the space beyond before collapsing to the floor with Donald still in his arms. Marcus kept the other moving in, channelling them to the floor above to stop any blockage before the rear guard started up the slope.

From his position, he could see Stephen and his friends fighting off the enemy as they backed their way slowly up the ramp, before they finally turned and ran for safety. He stopped at the top to urge his friends on, but with less than twenty feet to go, more arrows fell, piercing them in the backs. They staggered a few more paces before they dropped lifeless on the ramp. Marcus pulled Stephen away from the entrance, as they slid the barricade back into place more arrows fell outside.

"So tired…" Donald whispered, his breathing coming in harsh, broken gasps, pain showing on his face with each breath he took. "I'm so very tired."

Jolly dropped onto his knees to avoid the gale that was building as he crawled towards his hut. Pieces of debris passed him at speed now as the wind increased its power. His chin wobbled as he made his way carefully amongst the dead. Finally reaching the door he pulled himself inside.

"Come on," he shouted, but the children sat huddled together, too afraid to move. "We need to get you out of here. We need to go." Something banged into the hut, making them jump. He knew he needed to do something. He had to get them up and moving. A small boy sat crying in the corner and he stumbled over to him, trying to grab him but the boy pushed him away.

"No, I'm scared," he cried.

"Me too," Jolly shouted above the wind. "But we need to go. Take my hand, we need to go now." The wind slammed the door shut behind him, shaking the walls and he felt the building start to move; with no time to waste he grabbed for the child again.

"Give me your hand!" he screamed above the noise as his hand closed around the boys arm and he pulled him up. Staggering to the door he made him crawl out, made him lead the way for the others to follow, and one by one they moved.

The wind was turning into a gale as eventually he carried the last one out. A large board slapped into the side of the hut, spinning out of control before it continued on its way and narrowly missing them both, but he finally reached the ramp, rolling down it into the darkness below.

All Philip could do was hold on to Donald as the ground shook beneath them. He felt like he was on a freight train; everything rattled around him and people shouted as they held on for dear life. He wanted to find Gina, to make sure she'd made it back it and was safe, but it would have been impossible to even stand.

The pressure forced them to the walls and all he could do was hold his friend close and hope everyone else would be okay, terrified that Gina hadn't made it back.

A car smashed into the walls outside, thumping heavily into the outer metal beams in front of him and he covered his face as debris embedded itself into the wall above. The entrance barricade vanished as the wind sucked if free, and he watched as a tree cart-wheeled in the air, roots and all, before vanishing beyond his vision; creatures crawled against the concrete walls to get inside before they where pulled away, howling as they vanished from sight. But as the pressure continued, he found it harder to breath, his chest fighting each breath he took until darkness engulfed him.

"Are you alright?" Marcus asked as he shook him awake, and he sat up with a start. The world had finally stopped moving and now everything was quiet and still.

"I'm fine. What happened?" he spluttered but Marcus had already moved on. Sunlight shone in through the entrance, he'd never been so happy to see the dawn and he wanted to feel the sunlight on his face. Donald moaned at his side, blood soaked through his shirt from the deep wound below and his breathing was laboured and erratic so with gentle hands, he lifted his head and his eyes slowly opened.

"Donald." Philip held him. "Glen's on his way."

"There's nothing Glen can do for me now lad." Donald looked old and frail, the weight of the last few days looked like they had finally caught up with him. "Help me up will you. I want to see the Sun for one last time." Taking his friend's weight once more, they made their way slowly to the roof. Glen ran towards them with his kit, but stopped as he saw the wound, confirming Donald's prognosis and he stood silently as the walked on.

The roof was mercifully empty but for a few broken branches; the bodies of the dead had been blown away in the winds, and only the blood stains showed where they had died. "Rest me down here will you." He pointed towards the ledge.

"Donald. You can't die, not now," Philip pleaded.

"Of course I can. Philip, listen to me." He pulled him close as his voice became quieter. "Don't worry about me." He spoke slowly, each sentence being drawn from deep inside him. "It's time for me to go, to see Mavis again." He smiled as he said her name. "I should never have left her you know." He closed his eyes as he continued. "She'll understand why though, wives do that," he nodded.

Philip sat cradling his head against his shoulder. Mavis? He remembered her from the first day they met, she was the woman trapped under the rubble. The woman Donald had walked away from to save the others. "We still need you here, Donald."

"No you don't. You haven't needed me for a while now." He patted Philip on the hand. "Listen to me, I've had to live with my decision to leave her every day since then, and I'm tired now." His head started to sag against him.

"Thank you," Philip whispered.

"For what?" his voice was just a whisper, his eyes had closed.

"For believing in me." Tears ran down his face and he felt his friend struggling for each breath, slower and slower.

"You, just make sure... You believe in yourself... from now on." He suddenly opened his eyes as he stared at the Sun, and he breathed in deeply one last time; as the air left his body his soul went with it, leaving Philip alone to weep.

The rubble moved and small stones rolled free. Bit by bit they fell away as something dug its way free. Finally the hole grew large enough, and the gull poked its head out. The air smelt fresh and new, full of promise and hope as he flopped unceremoniously onto the ground.

It felt young again, lighter than before, and he unfolded its wings, flapping the dust and dirt from them. With its wounds almost healed, it was time to fly and it lifted gracefully into the air, each beat taking it higher into the crisp blue sky.

The world stretched out before it as it dived low over the ruins, the scarf trailing gracefully behind it. Below it could see people moving, and people meant food so with a screech of joy it banked hard and flew towards them.

THE END....for now...

Lightning Source UK Ltd.
Milton Keynes UK
UKOW04f2354051214

242713UK00002B/48/P